Praise f␣␣ ␣␣␣

"In *Oliver's Travels*, Clifford Garstang deftly explores the fragility of memory. Ollie, an aspiring writer, must navigate the mundane while, at the same time, imagining a life of fulfillment for his alter ego, Oliver. Garstang displays his gift for contemplation and characterization as Ollie moves undauntedly in search of answers to life's questions and discovers, in this journey marked with wanderlust, how the past and the present will forever share porous boundaries."

- Jon Pineda, author of *Let's No One Get Hurt*

"One man's search for the truth about himself—a tour of his own head that winds up taking him on a tour of the world. A witty, humane meditation on the slippery slope of childhood memory."

- Jonathan Dee, finalist for the Pulitzer Prize, author of *The Locals* and *The Privileges*

"This is a novel with an edge and a heart, constantly riveting and always smart, not to mention funny! Its humor, in part, derives from the keen intelligence and the pitch-perfect nature of the sterling prose. A must read."

- Fred Leebron, author of *Six Figures* and *Welcome to Christiania*

"A twisty metafictional and metaphysical tour of the world—and the author's mind—that examines not only how humans make stories, but how they make us. Fascinating and endlessly surprising."

- Liam Callanan, author of *Paris by the Book* and *Listen & Other Stories*

OLIVER'S TRAVELS

Clifford Garstang

Regal House Publishing

Published by
Regal House Publishing, LLC
Raleigh, NC 27612
All rights reserved

ISBN -13 (paperback): 9781646030064
ISBN -13 (epub): 9781646030330
Library of Congress Control Number: 2020941114

Interior and cover design by Lafayette & Greene
lafayetteandgreene.com
Cover images © by 89338183/Shutterstock

Regal House Publishing, LLC
https://regalhousepublishing.com

The following is a work of fiction created by the author. All names, individuals, characters, places, items, brands, events, etc. were either the product of the author or were used fictitiously. Any name, place, event, person, brand, or item, current or past, is entirely coincidental.

Printed in the United States of America

For Kathy and Becky

Precognition

It's not raining, but there's a fine mist in the air. As I walk, a stray dog trots into view on the right, crosses in front of me, then drops back. A bird calls, an owl or a magpie.

I take small steps, as if I'm in no hurry. This is why I've come.

It's not raining, but the air is filled with water. I am drowning. The dog crosses my path. An owl hoots.

I stop before a door and enter. The dog is gone, the owl, the mist.

I sit across from another man. It's as if I'm looking in a mirror.

I say, "They told me you were dead."

The man says, "I was."

Part I

1

I should have gone west, like the man said. After graduation, I should have thrown my shit into the back of my ancient Impala—my sister's castoff when she had twins and upgraded to a kid-friendly Subaru—and headed west. And by west I don't mean Terre Haute, or any of the other small cities within spitting distance of Cambridge, Indiana, my tiny college town. I mean California. I mean getting on I-74, hooking up with I-80, and coasting for a couple thousand miles until I hit the Pacific. Once I got there, I'd have found work in San Francisco or LA, or maybe I'd have kept going, explored Micronesia, Japan, Southeast Asia, India.

"Travel," my favorite teacher, Professor Russell, said to me more than once, "is the key to the locked door of consciousness." Travel. That's what I *should* have done. Especially after what happened between me and Russell, which I don't even want to think about.

Instead, I've come home to the single-story brick ranch in Indianapolis where I grew up, where my divorced father lives with my wounded-warrior older brother.

Dad starts in on me before I've had a chance to unload the car.

"Ollie, is that a tattoo?" he asks from the front stoop, pointing at the tribal design on my bicep, a recent acquisition meant to demonstrate my independence. (No, the irony wasn't lost on me.) He shakes his head. "You kids with your tattoos and pierced whatevers."

For the record, I do *not* have any pierced whatevers.

He leaves me alone while I move into my old room, then lets me have it, not for the first time: "Why didn't you major in engineering or some useful subject that would get you a real job."

Dad, who never went to college, is a salesman—widgets or automotive parts or something.

"Philosophy is useful," I say, probably without much conviction. I'd started out in premed, but that didn't last long. "I learned how to think. There's no skill more valuable than thinking."

My father snorts and shakes his head again. But that's not the end of his complaints: my hair (too long); my grades (dismal); my job prospects (nil); my mother (a bitch).

I've been home five minutes and already I want to leave. What am I doing here?

I notice how shabby the house has become. When she still lived here, my mother subscribed to *Architectural Digest* and *House & Garden*. On a shoestring she made the living room look like a photograph from one of those magazines: vases filled with fresh flowers, colorful sofas and chairs with contrasting pillows, Impressionist reproductions on the walls. She worked her magic outside, too, and we had the nicest yard in the neighborhood. A graceful maple tree dominated, hedges surrounded the lawn, and wide flowerbeds lined the drive.

Now, it looks as if the lawn hasn't been mowed yet this year, or the hedges trimmed, or the flowerbeds weeded. Inside is no better: dust-covered furniture; a pile of newspapers next to the sofa; tracks of mud from the front door; and there's a pungent, unidentifiable odor emanating from the kitchen. Rotten cabbage? Sour milk? I can't tell which.

While my dad is at work, I'm left to my own devices. Watching daytime TV grows old fast, so I look around for something else to occupy my time. On the shelf below the coffee table I come across one of Grandma Tucker's photo albums that's been sitting there for years, unopened since she died, I'd wager. I've forgotten about this album. I lift the cover, inciting a brief duststorm, and there's fat Grandpa Tucker, in black and white, waving for the camera. On the next page is a fading Polaroid of Mom and Dad, standing in a driveway somewhere. I have no idea where. They're squinting in bright sunlight and look like they might actually be happy. There's one of my sister Sally-Ann in a cowboy hat sitting on a pony. My brother Q holding a string of tiny fish he caught. Me in a bassinet.

Then there are snapshots of people I'm less certain of. When Dad comes home I point to a picture of him and a much younger man who looks a lot like him.

"Who's this?" I ask.

"Me and Scotty," he says.

"Scotty?"

"My brother."

Uncle Scotty. I'd nearly forgotten about him, but I remember that face. What was it Mom used to call him? The "World Traveler"?

"No one has mentioned him in eons," I say. "Where is he? Still exploring the world?"

"Dead as a door nail," my father says. "D-E-A-D dead."

"But I thought—"

Dad disappears into the bathroom, where, I know from experience, he might be enthroned for hours.

After my father's gone to bed, I pull out the album again and look at the picture of Scotty.

Dead? I don't believe it. How could I not remember Scotty's death? They would have told us. Scotty the adventurer died while climbing Everest or surfing in Bali. Gored by a rhino in Tanzania. There would have been a funeral, right? An obituary? I guess I was young, but surely I'd remember that. There would have been anguish and mourning, and then there would have been stories told about him at subsequent family gatherings. "Remember the time when Scotty…?" and "Scotty always loved this song," and "What a shame Scotty isn't here to enjoy this."

Thinking of him now, an image comes to me: Uncle Scotty playing basketball in the driveway with Q. I'm too little, barely able to hold the ball in my pudgy arms, but I watch. When he jumps for a rebound, arms outstretched, he soars. Like

Superman, I thought then. Like a gazelle, I think now. And then another image: At the lake where we took summer vacations, my father's idea of travel being the long drive to a rented cabin in Minnesota. I'm wearing an orange life vest, a mere puppy waddling on the dock, crying for the greater adventure of water. Q wades in the reedy shallows hunting minnows and crawdads, but Scotty swims out into deeper, darker water and back with bold strokes, powering through the chilly lake, then emerging, leaping onto the shore like a mythological being.

That's Scotty. A superhero who went off to conquer the world, leaving us all behind. Could I have been mistaken all this time? Did they tell me he was dead and I somehow got it wrong? Did I forget?

Spending time with my brother Q, short for Quentin, which is also our father's name, might make being home tolerable. But he has, essentially, barricaded himself inside his room since getting out of the army after his last Afghanistan deployment.

When I've been here for two days and he still hasn't emerged, I knock on his door.

"It's open," he says, his voice low and gruff, unwelcoming. I turn the knob and push, stirring the haze of cigarette smoke.

"Hey, Q," I say.

"Little brother," Q says.

He's sitting in the dark, not reading, not watching television, not doing anything as far as I can tell. He twists in his chair, opens the mini-fridge next to the bed, and pulls out a couple of Budweisers. He hands me one. It's still morning, but I pop it open and drink.

He nods toward his desk chair, so I sit. The desktop is bare except for an overflowing ashtray and a black box with the army insignia.

"I'm glad you're home," I say. "Safe."

He nods, laughs, and I don't know what to make of that.

"Was it awful?" I can't imagine, of course. And of course it was awful. A stupid question. But what are we supposed to talk about, if not that?

He lights a new cigarette.

"How can you stand living with Dad?" I ask. "It would drive me nuts." Another mistake, apparently, judging by the dark, vacant stare.

I pick up the box on the desk. "Is this a medal?" I ask. "Did you do something heroic?"

He takes the box from me and tosses it into the closet.

"Okay, then," I say. "You're right. Enough about the past. Moving on. Look to the future, as Mom always says." I wait for him to speak, and then I say, "I'm thinking of taking a road trip. You know, see the world, and all that. Like Uncle Scotty."

At that he raises an eyebrow.

"Or maybe I should get a job," I say, second-guessing myself already. "Grow up, you know? Get on with my life. What do you think, Q? What should I do?"

He shrugs and smokes. It occurs to me, too late, that he's asking himself these same questions. It kills me to see him this way, shutting me out, shutting all of us out, but I get up and leave him to his solitude. What else can I do?

I drive up to my sister's place, an imposing modern house on the city's north side. I ring the bell, then knock, but there's no response. I hear crying, in stereo, and let myself in.

"Silly?" I call, using the nickname I gave her when I was two, or so the family lore goes. "Sally-Ann?"

She rushes to the door, kisses my cheek, and hurries off again to tend to the babies, who aren't really babies anymore. She returns with a plump child on each hip, hands one off to me—is it Jeffy? Or is this one Jerry?—and then dashes away to put the kid down for his nap. The one I've got is a bundle of bulges, like a balloon animal. He looks into my eyes, full of wonder at what he sees. Then Silly comes back to get him, and he twists in her arms to watch me as she carries him away.

The boys down, she returns, breathless, and I ask, "Do you remember Scotty?"

"Who?"

"Dad's brother Scotty. Our uncle. Remember?"

"Oh, sure. Joined the navy when we were kids, right?"

The navy? Was that it? I don't remember anything about the navy, but it sounds right. Was his big adventure on a ship, sailing the globe?

The boys howl from the nursery, and Silly zips off. She reappears, fleetingly, they howl, she runs to them, and I don't think she notices when I leave.

I've given this a lot of thought. If Uncle Scotty found a way out, I can too. The navy's not right for me—I'm not a big fan of the U.S. military just now—but something will turn up.

One thing I know for sure: I can't stay in Indianapolis.

2

The Impala survives the trip to Virginia. I steer the lumbering beast to the curb in front of Mom's rented split-level in a compact subdivision just outside Winchester. Wherever that is. I know I'm in the right place because the GPS on my phone tells me so. Plus, there's my mother's Audi sitting in the driveway, still with Indiana plates three years after the divorce.

Why didn't I go west when I realized I couldn't stay in Indy? Money, for one thing. I don't have any. And for another thing, my mother begged, in that passive-aggressive whine all mothers seem to have: "You've been out there in Indiana with your father all this time, and I never get to see my Ollie." No mention of the fact that she was the one who left us, not the other way around.

And there was one more reason I didn't go. I imagine it took serious guts for Uncle Scotty to leave on his adventure—if that's what he did—but I confess that I'm deficient in the courage department.

It looks like Dad isn't the only one to ignore the yard. I know it's only a rental, but in the time she's been here Mom has apparently done nothing with the outside. Half the grass is brown, the rest thick with weeds. There are no trees or flowers. And the bushes underneath the front windows are shaggy and overgrown.

I step out of the car and Mom appears on the porch, arms stretched wide. We hug. She didn't make it to my graduation—no one in the family came, even though I was the first to finish college—so the last time I saw her was Christmas at Silly's house. She looks thin, a little unsteady, and pale, but good, professional in a navy blue suit. Her hair is permed in tight curls, and for the first time, I notice she's beginning to go gray.

At least Mom has made her mark on the interior: red accent walls in the living room, yellow in the dining room. Calla lilies adorn the coffee table. For my benefit? There's carpet, which I know she doesn't like, but she's covered the gray expanse with colorful rugs.

"It's so good to see you, Ollie." She hugs me again. She smells of peppermint. The whole house smells of peppermint. "I know you're going to love it here."

"Sure, Mom," I say.

I already know I can't stay.

The bedroom my mother has set up for me is upstairs, the former guest room, down the hall from her own. It's pretty basic, like a dorm room, with a bed, a desk, and a chair, which is fine with me. It's only temporary, after all. She's hung nothing on the walls, but I plan to remedy that with posters I brought with me. I ferry boxes from the car—all the stuff I had at school, plus crap I collected over the years in my room in the Indy house. I don't even know what's in most of them, but I stack the boxes along the wall to get them out of the way.

I unfurl a print I've always liked, Blind Justice holding her scales, but in the image a pile of stones on one side is out-weighed by a feather on the other. I'm not sure what it means, exactly, but I suppose it's an indictment of our justice system, how sometimes perceptions trump hard evidence. Or some-thing like that. I stick tape to the corners and pick a spot for it above the desk.

Mom is watching from the hallway. "How's Q?" she asks.

"Okay, I guess. He doesn't talk much."

She sighs. I'm sure she knows this already. "And Sally-Ann and the twins?"

"They're all fine, Mom. Silly sends her love."

Over the bed I hang my all-time favorite poster, one that has migrated from the bedroom of my childhood, to college, and now here: an antelope, my self-selected totem animal, be-ginning its leap, as graceful and bold a creature as ever existed.

❧

It's Monday morning, and Mom has left for work in the insurance office where she's a secretary. But she's made a pot of coffee and laid out an assortment of bagels and pastries and also the local newspaper.

The front page is all about politics. Will Obama be reelected? The locals interviewed for the article disagree as to whether that would be a good thing.

The back section is open to the help-wanted ads.

Nice, Mom. Subtle.

I peruse the ads. Truck drivers and nurses seem to be in great demand, as are fast-food workers. That's maybe all a philosophy degree is good for, and I'm beginning to think my father was right. But then another ad catches my eye. A community college needs adjunct teachers of English.

Teaching? I can do that. This wouldn't be permanent, of course. A stopover. While I figure out what's next.

For a long time I've harbored a fantasy—that's all it's been, despite a couple of creative writing classes in college—of being a writer. I'm thinking of the greats, like Sartre, Camus, the existentialists I studied in school. And don't lots of writers, especially when they're first starting out, teach? Their days are spent in the classroom, but at night they're exploring new worlds on the page. I sense a possibility. I'll be a writer who also teaches. I tear the ad out of the paper and set to work on my application.

The college calls me in for an interview. Useless major? Impractical degree? Apparently not. I'm tempted to call my father.

On the appointed day, my mother wishes me good luck and offers to make a big breakfast. But my stomach is already churning; eating anything would be fatal. This is all new to me, having bypassed interview season with my fellow graduates who knew what they wanted to do.

As I swing the Impala into the college's parking lot, I see a pile of black-and-white roadkill, and the smell of skunk is overwhelming. It doesn't help that it's crazy hot for May, which makes the stink worse.

It's a good thing I don't believe in omens.

I get out of the car and, holding my nose, size up the place. Traffic roars on the nearby interstate, the tops of speeding tractor trailers visible from where I stand. Beyond that loom the hazy slopes of the Blue Ridge Mountains. The afternoon sun broils the hayfield campus, comprising nothing more than a quadrangle of squat brick boxes connected by cracked walkways. I am both deflated and oddly encouraged by this decrepitude. It's the perfect place to prove my father wrong.

I hunt for the office of the dean, which, as it turns out, is situated in the one building graced with landscaping: a pair of dogwood trees, their young leaves already insect-chewed and pocked, stand sentry beside the glassy entrance. Each tree is ringed by a puddle of tulips long past their prime—drooping, singed, competing with clumps of dandelions and knotweed. I consider returning to the parking lot, climbing back into the car. But I picture my father's smirk and my mother's wringing hands and push through the doors.

Outside the dean's office, wobbling fans thrum, deployed— or so the gum-chewing receptionist tells me—because the AC is out, reason unknown, repair pending. I sit. I wait.

A willowy African American woman with short, tight curls emerges from the office and asks, "Oliver Tucker?" Her ID badge identifies her as dean of Humanities. "I'm Helen Venable."

"Call me Ollie," I say, a not-unintentional allusion to my favorite nineteenth-century novel.

Dean Venable raises an eyebrow at that but extends her hand, which somehow is cool and dry despite the heat and humidity. She shows me into her hot, cramped office and takes a seat behind the overflowing desk. I sit opposite and sweat in my wool sport coat, the only professional attire I own, while the dean studies my résumé. Skunk, though fainter inside, is still in the air.

There's another fan here, but it gives no relief from the heat. Its breeze flutters two stacks of paper held in place on the dean's desk with shimmering rocks the size of hockey pucks. Are they geologically significant? Spelunking souvenirs from one of the area's many caverns? Or maybe Civil War relics from a nearby battlefield? Before I can ask about the rocks, she speaks again.

"Teaching experience?" asks the dean while running a knuckle down the sparse page. The tip of her index finger appears to be missing. Given that I'm short a couple of toes myself, I'm sensitive to such digital deficiencies. So what happened to her finger? Was she born that way, like me? Was it truncated while collecting the mysterious rocks?

"Tutoring in undergrad," I say, prepared for the question about experience. The newspaper ad specifically asked for teaching experience, but mine is, viewed without the embellishments I've rehearsed, negligible. "And I taught English as a second language for a service project junior year."

I wait for the dean to look up, to confirm her acceptance of this puffery, but the woman now seems to be memorizing my transcripts, and I pray she won't notice the D in Spanish. It was the subjunctive mode that sank me.

While I'm waiting to hear about the job, I go through the boxes I've piled in the bedroom that I haven't looked at since I was a kid.

When I'd packed up in Indianapolis, I was in too much of a hurry to get out of there to be selective and dumped the contents of my desk into a big box. Now, though, I pull everything out, piece by piece, and make the call: keep or toss? High school report cards? Toss. A picture of me in a tuxedo with my high school girlfriend, Mimi, who dropped out of college, got married, and is living in Mississippi or Missouri, or someplace like that? Toss. A key chain with an Indycar racer, sporting tiny rubber wheels that actually spin? Keep.

Dried-up pens, misshapen paper clips, a cheap solar calculator, ticket stubs to a Colts game, a smushed pack of Trident, aviator sunglasses with both lenses cracked. Toss.

Here's something. A folded piece of yellow paper with writing, blue ink, block letters: *Ollie, I'm so, so sorry. Love, Scotty.*

Whoa. Scotty again. What was he sorry for? Why the hell don't I know what became of Scotty?

Keep.

❧

I bungled the interview at the college, I'm sure of it. The dean saw right through me, knew from the start what an impostor I am. But that's all right. It's fine, in fact. I don't think teaching is really for me.

Action is called for. Time to get busy. Seize the day, and so on. I should check online job listings, post my résumé on Monster.com, join Linkedin or some other networking site.

But in those places, to find what you're looking for, you have to *know* what you're looking for; I'm not there yet.

I go to the kitchen, pour myself a cup of coffee, and open the local paper again to see if there are any new help-wanted ads since the last time I looked. Factory worker, graveyard shift. Auto mechanic, experienced. Dental hygienist.

My throat feels scratchy. Is that a cold coming on? I cough, tentatively. Do I feel better? Or worse? I take a sip of coffee, but, no, coffee's not good for a cold, is it? I pour a glass of orange juice and drink. It tastes bitter. Has it gone bad? Does orange juice go bad? Or is it that my cold has affected my senses, making everything sour? My throat is worse, I'm sure of it. I'm definitely coming down with something.

Maybe I'm thinking about this all wrong. It isn't a job I need. An adventure is called for. I should be looking at maps, not want ads.

Where should I go?

❧

When Dean Venable calls to offer me a job, I hardly know what to say. She rattles off numbers—my salary, the date classes start, the time and date of orientation for adjunct faculty—but none of them stick, and I'm too nervous to ask her to repeat everything so I can write it all down.

Thanks to my somewhat exaggerated claim of experience and my lack of a master's degree, I've been assigned two non-credit sections of English as a Second Language for the fall semester. Fortunately, classes don't start for a couple of months, time enough to bone up on how it's really done. *Repeat after me: Hello, my name is Ollie. What's yours?* How hard can it be?

The job is not quite worthy of a champagne celebration, or even updating my Facebook status, but it's way better than being unemployed and completely dependent on my mother. I'll have time to write. I'll save up for that adventure, do it right. It's a start. A journey of a thousand miles, etc.

3

So. I'm on my way. A job. A plan, of sorts: I'll teach. *And* write.

In the meantime, to fill the summer and keep my mother off my back while I'm waiting for classes to start, I mow lawns for pocket money and, between lawn-care gigs and other odd jobs, muse in coffee shops. Winchester isn't the Paris of the existentialists I admire, but it's not without places to hang out.

There's one café downtown I particularly like. They've got all the specialty coffee drinks anyone could ask for and a decent sandwich menu. Paintings by local artists line the walls, a nice small-town touch. A cabinet near the cash register holds an assortment of games and puzzles, including a chessboard that's always in demand. Plus, the tables and chairs are a wobbly mismatch of dark wood, and the Pandora station they play is just as eclectic—anything from Frank Sinatra to Aimee Mann, with a little reggae and hip-hop thrown in.

One morning when I'm not working, I stake out a table at the coffee shop, order a medium dark roast—it's cheap and comes with a free refill—and open a spiral notebook leftover from college. If I'm going to be a writer, it's time to get started. I've never written poetry before, not even in my creative writing classes, but the idea of being a poet appeals to me. I'm picturing myself as Ginsberg, or maybe Bukowski, a revolutionary poet to unsettle the masses. I stare at the blank page. I doodle: a stick figure, a smiley face, a star. One of my scribbles looks like ocean waves, so I draw a sailing ship and daydream about a voyage, visiting distant lands, meeting the locals.

Poetry may not be my thing, and now I'm thinking I should give fiction a shot. A character begins to take shape in my head, an amorphous cloud at first—torso, limbs, a face gradually coming into focus.

Where to start?

My mind wanders and I look around the shop. A woman at the next table is reading Gertrude Stein, stealing glances at me from time to time. I'm wearing a favorite T-shirt, one with a leaping antelope, just like the poster in my room. Is that what she's looking at? I consider speaking to her, maybe quoting from Stein—a rose is a rose is a rose—but, the bold antelope notwithstanding, I hesitate. The woman is cute, in a perky, plain sort of way, wearing preppy pastels and a delicate cross on a gold chain around her neck. A streak of red drips through her honey hair like a mistake, and I'm staring at it the next time she looks up.

She smiles a crooked smile. I smile back.

The second time I see the woman in the coffee shop we exchange nods of recognition, and then, after an awkward pause, I summon the courage to speak.

"I'm Ollie," I say. I don't offer to shake. I'm in the antelope T-shirt again, grass-stained, surely reeking of my morning labors, and my hands are a grimy mess.

"I'm Mary," she says. Her voice is crisp, pleasant, her smile broad. The white shorts she's wearing almost disappear against her pale thighs. Virginia is looking way better, suddenly.

I move to her table before I can talk myself out of it. We exchange the basics: family, hobbies, jobs. As it turns out, Mary's also a teacher at the college, on summer break, although in June and July she's teaching one section of remedial English for kids who aren't quite ready for higher education.

"What's it like working there?" I ask.

"I love it," she says. "It's been my dream to be a teacher since I was a little girl. I suppose it sounds ridiculous, but I can't wait to meet the students every semester, can't wait to get into the classroom and be a part of their lives. You know?"

"Yeah, I do," I say. But I don't, not really. I don't have that kind of passion for teaching, at least not yet. I can't see myself like Professor Russell, spouting the same concepts, asking the same questions, year after year. For me, it's only a means to an end.

"I was born to be a teacher," Mary says.

Oh, god. To have such certainty! I haven't even started yet, and already I know this isn't for me, not long-term. And I'm even having doubts about the writing. But I'm impressed that she's so passionate.

"You were reading Gertrude Stein the first time I saw you," I say. "*The Autobiography of Alice B. Toklas*. Wasn't that a great book?"

"I hated it," she says. "I don't get them, Alice and Gertrude. A couple of weirdos. And I don't mean their sexuality. It seemed like something I ought to have read, but I couldn't finish."

"Oh," I say. I'd hoped we could discuss Stein's genius, her relationship with Alice, what their lives in Paris must have been like. How their expatriate status gave them a new outlook on society, both in France and at home. How they weren't afraid to be themselves over there. How Stein basically reinvented literature. I try not to sound disappointed when I ask, "What are you reading now?"

"It's by Margaret Atwood." She holds up a library copy of *The Handmaid's Tale*.

"I read that in high school," I say. "Great stuff." If we can't talk about Stein's alienation and innovation, maybe we can talk about Atwood's allegory of repression. We spent close to a week on it in my AP English class back in Indianapolis, and I've got lots to say. I scoot my chair closer to Mary's. This will be fun.

But then Mary says, "It's stupid."

"Oh," I say.

"It doesn't even make sense. How did these women let themselves get into that situation? Women are smarter and stronger than that. It could never happen."

Another dead end. So, if we can't find common ground in the books we like, maybe there's something else?

"How about a movie sometime?" I ask.

She blushes and nods.

❦

When I arrive to pick Mary up for our date, first I meet Barney, Mary's chocolate lab, who limps to the door, tail spinning, sniffing my feet, my jeans, my hands. His eyes are cloudy, and a liberal sprinkling of white covers his snout. I always wanted a dog, and on this one thing my father backed me up, but Sally-Ann has allergies, so pets were out of the question. I kneel down to Barney's level, scratch behind his ears, and stroke his rich brown coat. He trots after me as I enter the house, so hopefully I've won him over.

Next I meet Mary's parents, Bill and Lydia Berger, to whose two-story brick house in a quiet neighborhood Mary returned after graduation from her all-women's college on the other side of the Blue Ridge Mountains. It's been three years, though, three years teaching at the community college, and she hasn't moved out on her own. That's fine for her, I guess, but if I'm still living with my mother three years from now, I'll shoot myself.

The house is nice enough, in a faux-rustic sort of way. There's a woven rug in the entry, a gilt-framed mirror over a weather-beaten console table. I glimpse the darkened dining room on one side, living room on the other, lit by the glow of a television.

Bill is an engineer, Mary has told me, Lydia a librarian. Bill—heavyset, dark, almost olive complexion, a widow's peak—shakes my hand indifferently, raises his thick brows when Mary says my name, as if he's detected something about me from the label my parents stuck me with, maybe associating me with that old comic from way before my time, or the snaggle-toothed puppet. I get that a lot from his generation. Lydia stands behind him, grinning and nodding at everything we say. She gestures invitingly toward the living room, where I detect the scent of air-freshening cinnamon, and Bill glares at her, as keen to be rid of the intruder, I'm guessing, as I am to be gone.

"Show's in a few minutes," I say, holding up my wrist without looking at my watch. "Next time, maybe."

There are footsteps on the stairs. A boy—a young man,

really, lanky with broad shoulders and a mop of dark hair—descends heavily. We all look in his direction, Barney included. I'm struck by his resemblance to Mary.

"That's my brother, Mike," Mary says, with a dismissive flick of her fingers as she pulls me toward the door.

I manage a wave to the family and a last, lingering glance at the brother.

On the way to the theater we make nervous small talk: the weather, the class she's teaching, the lame music on the radio.

"It was nice to meet your family," I say.

"I could tell they liked you," she says.

"I didn't realize your brother was—"

"A dork?" She laughs, and so I laugh.

How was I going to complete that sentence? So handsome? And why has my mind been on him since we got in the car? So…what?

Here's what I know about Mary so far.

Through most of college, she dated a guy, Brian, who went to an all-boys school. They recently broke up. I dig further, but she squirms under questioning and shuts down. So that's all I've learned about this Brian character, except I don't think she's really over him.

She likes coffee shops as much as I do, but she doctors her coffee in ways that I find abominable. Even when she's not drinking a flavored latte, she adds lots of milk and a ton of sweetener. I don't say it, but I'm thinking: what's the point? I love real, unadulterated coffee. Black, no sugar. It's the one trait I've inherited from my parents that I actually appreciate.

She's had Barney, the chocolate lab, since she was twelve, which means they've grown up together. When she starts to talk about him tears well in her eyes. The old boy's in decent shape, but he's…old. I can't know exactly what she's feeling, never having had a dog myself, but even I get sad at the prospect of what's coming for Barney.

Mary had her tonsils out when she was seven. This comes

up when we are getting ice cream after a movie, because doesn't everyone eat a lot of ice cream when they have their tonsils removed? She likes ice cream. Her favorite is mint chocolate chip, which makes me gag. I'm a butter pecan man, myself.

Mary's father went to Virginia Tech, but is originally from Cincinnati, so he's a Reds fan, and so is Mary, although they've followed the Nationals since the franchise moved to DC. My dad is a Reds fan, too, oddly enough, and we went to a few games at Riverfront when I as a kid. A lot of my friends at school were from Chicago, so now I like the Cubs.

Mary struggles with her weight. She's not fat or anything, but she could stand to lose a few. Those are her words, not mine. To me she looks great, curves in all the right places, plush, not bony. She's been talking about taking a Pilates class, but so far it's only been talk.

Mary and her brother don't get along. She calls him a ne'er-do-well, because he's had a couple of run-ins with the law, minor stuff like underage drinking and a public brawl (and because, I gather, she's never been in trouble in her life). Also, she doesn't like to be told that they look alike—she spluttered, coughed, and turned red when I said that—even though they totally do. It's the eyes.

She's got excellent teeth. I almost asked if her father was a dentist until I remembered he's an engineer. And more important than the teeth? She's got the sweetest breath ever, like honey.

"Let's do something different," Mary says one evening.

I'm all for that, although our small-town options are limited. We've seen all the movies showing within a fifty-mile radius. On previous occasions I've nixed the gospel concert in the park—too religious for me—and she turned up her nose when I suggested miniature golf.

"Lead the way," I say, willing to accept whatever she has in mind for the sake of our budding relationship.

I drive, and she navigates us to a strip mall I've never seen.

The only lights in the place belong to a bar called The Blue Note. I look at Mary with surprise and newfound admiration. A bar?

But it's not just any bar. It's a karaoke lounge that is, thankfully, nearly deserted. I like music as much as the next guy, but I'm no singer. After I had to sing a solo in a grade school recital, my father offered to get me singing lessons, which I understood later was his uncharacteristically diplomatic way of telling me that I was terrible. The lessons never happened, and I rarely sing unless I'm alone in the car or the shower.

Mary, though, has a lovely singing voice. She does amazing imitations of Celine Dion, Whitney Houston, plus some older divas I remember my parents listening to—Barbra Streisand and Ethel Merman. It's uncanny. She picks a song for me to sing, too, but I refuse unless we do a duet, so we perform one that Natalie Cole did, digitally, with her dead father, Nat King Cole. Mary is so wrapped up in the song that she doesn't notice when I stop, letting her go solo.

The singing done, we order a last round of beers.

"That was fun," I say. "You have a beautiful voice."

She blushes, which is perfect. There's nothing false about her modesty, which I love. I kiss her cheek, delighted to see this side of her.

We sip our beers and listen to another customer sing. The woman is awful, a screecher, but I can totally relate, so I don't mock her (which I might otherwise be inclined to do).

When the music ends, Mary asks, "What do you want, Ollie?"

Right now I want you, Mary Berger, is what I almost say, but I'm not sure what she means, so what I actually say is, "Want?"

"I mean, what's your goal? We're all here for a purpose, I believe. What's yours?"

No one's ever asked me that before, so I don't have a ready answer. I pick up my beer, look into Mary's eyes to gauge how serious a question this is, and I see that we've moved way past small talk.

"Okay," I say. "I think we all have the same purpose, whether we realize it or not, and that's to explore the world around us. To learn, to understand, to take it all in."

She thinks about that for a minute and shakes her head, clearly unsatisfied.

"Let me ask it a different way," Mary says. "Who are you, Ollie Tucker? Who are you going to be?"

Good question, Mary. I'm afraid to say, *I'm going to be a writer*, in part because I don't yet believe it myself.

"What about you?" I ask, by way of deflection. "Who are you going to be?"

"Teacher," she says with confidence. "Wife," she adds, with less certainty, looking down at her beer. "Mother."

"You've got it all figured out," I say.

"Yes," she says, "I do."

4

I finish a yard job—we've had a lot of rain lately and this client's grass is out of control—and head to the coffee shop, thinking Mary might be there. She's not, but it's dark and cool in the shop and the iced coffee is perfect. So is the music, an instrumental mash-up of Beatles tunes, and I open my notebook to get some writing done.

But I start humming to the music and gazing at the new artwork on the walls, manipulated photographs of dilapidated barns and farmhouses, and I'm doing no writing. I'm not even thinking about writing. I'm thinking about Mary, about how lovely she is, how smart and talented.

The coffee is gone, ice rattling in the plastic cup as I try for one last sip. I close my notebook. There's nothing waiting for me at home, so I figure I'll drop by the Bergers' to say hi. An unannounced visit is risky, I know, having once in college walked in on a girl I was dating making out with a guy who was supposed to be her ex, but it seems like the right thing to do at this stage of our relationship.

I park in front of the house and as I approach the door I hear music. It's something classical, I know that much, but whether it's Beethoven or Bach or some other composer, I couldn't say. The music stops and starts again, at which point I realize it isn't a recording. Someone is playing the piano. I know Mary is musical, and has a voice like a Siren, heavenly and enchanting, but this is astonishing. I stand on the stoop and listen, not wanting to interrupt such beauty.

I'm startled when the door opens. Mike looks at me through the screen like he's never seen me before, but then recognition dawns and he beckons me in, pointing toward the living room and the source of the music. When I hesitate, he puts his hands on my back—his touch is electrifying—and nudges me forward.

If Mary hears me enter the room she doesn't let on. She keeps playing, her fingers running up and down the keyboard effortlessly. Occasionally she stops, goes back a measure or more, and starts again, correcting some mistake I haven't noticed. I dabbled with a guitar in college, never progressing beyond basic chords, but the piano is far beyond me. In a class called The Philosophy of Art, Professor Russell talked about the uniqueness of music as an art form because how one hears it depends on the interpretation of the performer. Its meaning is a collaboration of composer, musician, and listener, unlike visual art forms or literature. And at this moment, hearing this composition, this listener is completely enraptured by this musician.

Eventually, she gets to the end of the piece, pauses, and only then turns to look at me. I applaud.

"Ollie!"

"Surprise!" I say. "I hope I didn't startle you."

"No," she says. "But you did make me a little self-conscious playing."

"You knew I was here?"

She points to the shiny surface of the piano above the keys. "I saw your reflection when you came in." She blushes when she says this and looks at her feet, apparently embarrassed by her confession.

"I didn't know you played," I say. "It was beautiful."

"You like classical music, Ollie?"

"Sure," I say. "I love Beethoven." I look toward the sheet music on the piano, the cover of which reveals my mistake. "And Mozart," I add.

"You're sweet, Ollie. Did you know that?"

The Fourth of July has never been my favorite holiday. I never know quite what to do and it seems as though the day drags on. First there's some sort of outdoor activity like a hike or a swim, then a cookout, and everyone is still partying late at night when the fireworks happen.

This year, being new in town, I've got nothing planned, but Mary invites me to a picnic. Her parents are joining their friends for a big neighborhood barbecue, and Mike is off somewhere with his buddies. Even my mom is going to a party with some people from work—she dressed up in a ridiculous red, white, and blue outfit for the occasion. So Mary and I are on our own, which suits me fine. I spend most of the day reading at home— the coffee shop is closed, as I learned when I nearly broke my arm trying to open the door—but early in the evening she picks me up and takes me to a park in the center of town. We leave the car at the foot of a hill and walk up a path to an overlook that must be the prettiest spot in the area.

We settle ourselves on a blanket in a wide clearing that has views in three directions. There's Winchester down below us, looking quaint and peaceful, but off in the distance are the hazy blue mountains. While I was reading this afternoon, Mary must have spent all day cooking, and I feel guilty as she pulls fried chicken, biscuits, potato salad, and even a small cake out of the basket I lugged up the hill from her car.

"What a feast!" I say. "You've outdone yourself." Which is a ridiculous thing to say, because this is the first time Mary has cooked for me, so I have nothing to compare it to. Maybe she does this every day. The compliment, though, is received with her standard blush and lowered eyes, which is so cute and en- dearing I can barely stand it. I move on the blanket to be closer to her and kiss her cheek—I considered planting a kiss on her mouth, but we're not alone in this park—which elicits a giggle and a playful slap at my hand.

In fact, the park is growing crowded as dusk gives way to dark. There is a loud boom and someone nearby shouts, "It's starting." Suddenly the sky is filled with a brilliant red shower of sparks, and then one in white, followed by blue. On and on the display goes, and with each explosion I feel Mary move closer to me. It's partly because a cool breeze has sprung up, but by the time the fireworks reach their climax, my arm is around her and she's leaning her head on my shoulder. I want to stay here forever.

But Mary is teaching a class the next morning. She's worried about Barney, who is afraid of fireworks, and about the breeze, which is apparently a portent of a coming storm. Everyone around us is packing up to go. We do the same, trudge down the hill, exhilarated by the evening but sad that it's over, and head home.

We pull up in front of my mom's house, which is dark. I don't know if that means she's not home or is home and has already gone to bed, and as much as I would like to invite Mary in, I'm not sure what to do.

"Wasn't that wonderful," Mary says. "A perfect night."

"It really was," I say, and I mean it. "I think I'll write about it."

"What do you mean?"

"I mean, maybe I'll write a short story about a couple—" I stop myself, because did I just call us a couple? "—a couple of people who have a picnic in the park on the Fourth of July." I realize that the story needs some kind of conflict, and I'm imagining the appearance of an ax-murderer or some such, but I don't say that to Mary.

"I didn't know you were a writer, Ollie."

"I'm not. I mean, not yet." I can't believe I just told her this, something I haven't yet told anyone. "But I'd like to be. Sort of. I know it's foolish."

"No it's not! I think it's wonderful. I wish I were creative like that. Will you show me your work?"

"My work?" The light over the front door has just come on, an indication that my mother is inside and probably watching us. "Sure," I say. "Someday." I lean over and kiss her, wondering if my mother can see. I let my lips linger on hers before I back away.

"Goodnight, Mary," I say. "I had a wonderful time." Because I did.

&

Mary and I take an August day trip to DC. We've been dating since June, and this trip is our getaway from the Valley, one last day of freedom, a tiny expedition, before the grind begins at the college: fielding excuses from students, grading solipsistic essays, keeping classrooms animated, killing time, if not actually teaching. Or so I've been warned by other adjuncts. Not by Mary, of course. She's totally into it.

We're gawking tourists in the big city, kissing under a searing sky in front of the Capitol Reflecting Pool; eating ice cream on a shady bench outside the Hirshhorn; sipping cold beers at a riverside bar in Georgetown. High wispy clouds and a soothing, hot wind remind us that summer is still in full swing. I take her hand as we stroll down Pennsylvania Ave.

I can't stop smiling. Is this what it's like to be in love?

At the close of the day, worn out by our explorations, we find a table at a busy coffee shop near the White House. While Mary writes postcards to family and friends, I pull a pristine composition notebook from my book bag, purchased for this occasion. No more leftovers from college. This is too important. It occurs to me that in the future I'll look back at this moment: the day I embarked on my voyage. Weighed anchor. Hoisted the sails. Etc.

On the notebook's first line, I write my given name, *his* name, the name for this character I've invented in my head and will now bring to life on the page, my alter ego: Oliver. Not Ollie, the child's name I've been saddled with since birth. I underline it. Oliver. I underline it three times. Oliver. Oliver. Oliver.

If travel is the key to consciousness—Professor Russell again—and if I'm settled here in Virginia for the foreseeable future, with Mary and my job, I'll have to let Oliver do my traveling. *Oliver's Travels*, I write. I underline that, too.

Who is he, this Oliver? What does he look like? Does he have my blond hair, my pale skin? Is he too thin, like me? Gangly? Are his features also angular, his nose and jaw sharp? Or does he look like Scotty, with the broad shoulders, straight nose, and strong chin? Or maybe the tattooed barista in this coffee shop? The shirtless jogger I saw on the mall? The muscular Georgetown bartender?

This is what writers do, isn't it? They borrow from life to

create a composite, a truth that is in some ways greater than the truth. They bend the facts; they shape reality. This is Oliver, who shares my past but invents his own future. Scotty, but not Scotty. Me, but not me.

And what about his career? Not a teacher, certainly. Something more ambitious. Maybe he's a globe-trotting lawyer. Or an investment banker. He lives in Washington, maybe. Or New York. His brownstone—no, his Tribeca loft—brims with original artwork, modern masterpieces. Definitely not my father's ranch in Indianapolis. Or my mother's Shenandoah Valley split-level. Or he's posted overseas. Paris, maybe. Singapore.

Oliver would be single, I think. Once married, maybe. Divorced, because shit happens, even with the best of intentions.

He's a man with great appetites, who hungers and is desired. A man who *does* things, travels, takes action. Who overcomes obstacles.

He's intellectual. Charitable. Extroverted. A son of privilege. A world traveler.

Me. But not me. Or is he Scotty? How does his story start? *This is how it begins,* I write.

Amidst the whirr of the grinder and the hiss of the steamer, with the notebook open before me, pages now filled with my incoherent jottings, I lift my coffee and gaze for inspiration at its dark, placid surface. I picture Oliver and make another note on the page.

"What are you writing, Ollie?" Mary asks.

Mary: looking crisp and tidy, despite our grueling day of touring, pretty in navy shorts and a pink blouse, the ever-present cross around her neck, the funky red streak in her hair nearly, but not quite, rinsed away, her postcards of Washington scenes scattered on the table: the phallic Monument, the gaudy cherry trees of the Tidal Basin, the ornate Smithsonian Castle, a pair of pandas at the zoo.

"It's nothing," I say. "A sketch."

I've told her I plan to be a writer, and she's encouraged me in a don't-get-your-hopes-up kind of way, but I haven't yet shown her anything I've written.

She snatches the notebook from the table. "This is how it begins," she reads aloud.

"Give it to me," I say and snatch it back. "It's a story."

"Which is it, Ollie? A sketch? Or a story?"

A sketch of a story. Beginnings. Possibilities. About Oliver, who travels, who has the life I don't have, not yet anyway.

"It's a story," I say again. "Maybe a book."

She laughs, as if I can't possibly be writing a book. Or maybe that's not what she means by her laugh, but that's what I hear: I'm twenty-two; I've never been anywhere or done anything; what could I have to write about? But that's the point, isn't it? I don't have anything to say, but Oliver does.

"Is there a girl in the story?" Mary asks. "Is she beautiful?"

"Sure there's a girl," I say. I make another note: Young Oliver has a girlfriend, too, with silky blonde locks, black curly tresses, frizzy red hair. She's sleek and exotic, European, or maybe Asian, wears designer clothes. "She looks just like you."

During this period before classes start, Mary and I are enjoying each other's company. We go to movies, eat ice cream, swing on her parents' front porch and, modestly, chastely, make out. I begin to imagine a future with her. Is that crazy?

Granted, she's not interested in conversation about the serious topics that engage me—literature, politics, philosophy, art—but we still find plenty to discuss. Having studied piano since she was ten, she knows way more about classical music than I do, and I'm learning from her about her favorite composers—Debussy, Chopin, Rachmaninoff. There's baseball, even though we root for different teams, so we talk about that. She got into horseback riding in college at Sweet Briar, which I find interesting, even though I don't know the difference between English or Western saddles, Arabians or Appaloosas.

It's nice. I'm happy. I resolve not to blow it. I resolve not to flee when she shows signs of wanting a commitment. College, by definition a time for short-term relationships, is in the past. This time, a commitment is not out of the question.

And then, while we're sitting on the porch, talking or kissing or whatever, her brother comes into the picture, either bounding up the steps after a run or waving as he shoots out the door on his way to the mall or the basketball courts or wherever. Although Mike is tall and wiry, an athletic build nothing like Mary's, his face is exactly like hers, the plump lips and dark round eyes. When Mary and I are alone again, when I lean in to kiss her, I see Mike.

What the hell? What is Mike doing in my head at this critical moment? I close my eyes and banish him from my thoughts.

At Mom's house, I look once again at the note from Uncle Scotty I found in my box of stuff. I suppose the reason I'm thinking about Scotty so much is the disruption of moving to a new place, building a new life, longing for adventure that seems out of reach. That and the picture of him I saw in the photo album at Dad's. And writing about Oliver's travels. In any case, he's been on my mind.

Despite what my father says, I don't believe he's dead. Not only am I sure I would have heard about his death long ago, I no longer believe anything my father says. He claimed, after she walked out on him, that my mother was having an affair. Preposterous. Unsubstantiated. He insists that Michael Jordon was the best basketball player ever, when it's obvious that LeBron James deserves that title. Plus, he voted for John McCain.

I figure my sister must know something. Talking to her on the phone can be chaotic because of the twins, so I send a text: Wot rly happd 2 Unc Scotty?

While I wait for her reply, I go through the rest of the boxes I brought from Indy and find only a few family photos: Mom and Dad, Q and Sally-Ann, but no pictures of Scotty. I wish I'd taken that one from Dad's album.

The text answer arrives: HIIK.

I puzzle over that for a minute before I get it. Hell if I know.

Q isn't much for texting, so I give him a call, although I don't expect that to yield much either.

"Hello?" he says.

It sounds as if I've woken him, but I'm glad I had a reason to call. I haven't spoken to him for a while.

"Q, it's me. Say, you remember Uncle Scotty?"

"Sure."

"Do you know what became of him?"

"Why?"

"No reason. He popped into my head is all. What happened to him?"

"Dead."

"Yes, that's what Dad says, but I don't believe him. If he's dead, how? When?"

"Hell if I know."

"Silly said he joined the Navy."

"Doubtful," Q says.

"Why?"

"Pacifist," he says.

I do no better with my parents. Mom looks at me with frustration, hesitating, then tells me to ask Dad. Dad won't say anything other than repeating, "He's dead," which convinces me that: (a) there's more to the story; (b) Scotty's almost certainly not dead.

If he's not dead, where is he?

5

As I consider the prospect of teaching, I realize how much I miss college, being a student. There was always a schedule. A map to follow, a plan and a goal. Rules. Places to be. A community. Not to mention the excitement of learning, the constant exploration and discovery.

It wasn't always easy. Every day was a challenge. Classes, papers, complicated texts, the concepts we were expected to master. Professor Russell, my philosophy teacher and mentor, made me think critically, made me question everything I thought I knew. What the textbooks said. What my parents told me. What everyone accepted as fact.

Russell was tall and lean, not in an obviously athletic way, but sturdy and erect, like a tree, and he sometimes pulled his longish brown hair into a ponytail. He almost always wore a corduroy sport coat and a skinny tie, as if he was mocking the dress code for faculty at our pretentious little college with these thrift-store finds.

One day in my Intro to Philosophy class he asked us: "If I say I know something, does that mean the thing I say I know is true?"

Blank faces were the norm in that class. If the other kids were like me, they'd never been asked to really think before. I wanted to shake my head, but because no one else was moving, I held still.

"If the thing is demonstrably false," Russell persisted, "then it isn't true, and how can it then be said to be known?" He paused, greeted with more silence. "Aren't all statements subject to doubt on some level? If a statement might not be true, how can I say I know it? In essence, then, nothing can be known. Put another way, my certainty that a statement is true does not, logically, make it so."

A prankster in the back row called out, "Will this be on the final?" Laughter erupted, and Professor Russell smiled.

"You can bet on it," he said.

I may believe something to be true because it's what I have been taught. But if I am not certain that the thing is true, this is an acknowledgment that the thing may be false. And if I acknowledge that the thing may be false—a story my father has told me, for example, or my Sunday school teacher, or a memory—I cannot be said to know it.

Bottom line: Belief is not knowledge; truth lies somewhere beyond belief.

One of the neighborhood kids when I was growing up was convinced he was adopted. Jimmy's worry could have been the result of seeds planted by an older sister, which is a bit of torture siblings have always employed, but as a casual observer, a ten-year-old at that, I thought there was good reason to believe it. He had blond hair, the parents were both dark; his eyes were blue, theirs were brown; they both had prominent noses, but Jimmy's was petite, or at least unobtrusive; they both loved music, but Jimmy was tone deaf. He didn't fit. It made sense that he was adopted.

No such doubts for me. Although as a boy I had little in common with my father in the way of hobbies or interests (I didn't enjoy golf or bowling, and those were pretty much the only things that got my father out of the house besides work), my brother Q and I both looked like him. Q, especially, had the same square jaw and ears that were small and high on his head. My features, though still angular, were slightly watered-down versions, as if the gene pool had been diluted some by the time I came around, but the resemblance was plain enough in my eyes and hair, the sharp nose.

Those familial likenesses aside, however, there's one physical trait that's all my own: I have only four toes on each foot. I possess my full complement of fingers and, as far as I know, the requisite number of bones, muscles, organs, and brain cells, but the little toe on each side is nothing more than a nub, a useless protuberance, perpetually red, like an enormous, angry zit. One of the clearest memories I have of my childhood is my father's insistence that I wear something on my feet while in his presence—socks, shoes, slippers. I didn't understand why, when Q and Sally-Ann were both allowed to run barefoot inside and out, but to mollify my father I would comply, or avoid him altogether.

When I was three or four, I realized what the problem was. I had learned to count, and at the swimming club we belonged to I noticed Q's feet.

"One, two, three, four, five," I said, pointing at each toe, probably the upper limit for me at the time. And then I looked at my own foot. "One, two, three, four." I looked back at Q's foot and then at my own, counting again. I looked at Sally-Ann's feet and counted. I counted my mother's toes. Uncle Scotty's toes. And then I began to cry.

"Crybaby," Q said. "It's just a stupid toe."

But it wasn't the missing toes I was crying about. I had finally understood why my father hated me.

Professor Russell asked our class, "What is consciousness?"

As usual, he was met with puzzled looks, even from those of us who had read the assigned material for the day.

"Is it separate from the body, an energy that exists apart from the corporeal self?" he asked. He'd started the class behind a podium, but now moved toward us, pacing the length of the front row while he posed his questions. "Or is consciousness merely cognitive awareness, the recognition that a thing exists? How, in that case, does consciousness relate to the thing of which it is aware? Are their existences separate? Or does one depend on the other?"

I raised my hand and Russell nodded. "I like the sense of belonging that unified consciousness implies," I said. "If consciousness exists at all, it makes us almost immortal, doesn't it? As long as *it* exists, we exist."

The entire class laughed, but Russell nodded vigorously. "Absolutely," he said. "In fact, in some religions, that's where the idea of heaven comes from, the notion that when we die we merely move to a different realm within the universal consciousness."

"So how do we find this consciousness?" asked a guy in the back of the room. "How do we see what's inside it?" He was laughing as he asked the question, which encouraged more laughter from the class.

"All you have to do is travel and keep your eyes open," Russell said. "That's the key to the locked door of consciousness."

The dream has come to me from time to time over the years, and now it's back. The face I see in the dream is indistinct, more shadow than snapshot, and I don't know who it is. Sometimes I think it must be my grandmother, who, when she lived with us, occasionally came into my bedroom at night to check on me, to convince herself that I was still breathing. The face could be hers. But now, because of the note I found, because of that picture I saw at Dad's, I have an idea that the face belongs to Uncle Scotty. The nose, the chin. The soft eyes. Is it Scotty's face in the dream? Or maybe it isn't a dream at all. A memory?

Uncle Scotty owned a tiny car. A Corvair? Karmann Ghia? I was too young to distinguish. Whatever it was, it had been my grandfather's, passed to Scotty when the old man's stroke confined him to bed. Or Uncle Scotty had saved for it, working summers at the country club, as a caddie, or a lifeguard, or…I have all those memories, stories I was told, different versions of the same story. They can't all be true.

He comes back to me in bursts, like film clips. We went for rides in that car, radio blasting rock and roll, coasting down steep Southern Indiana hills, long straightaways where Uncle Scotty's hands flew free, raised in surrender to gravity, laughter howling behind us like exhaust. Is this my memory? Or my imagination? It seems so vivid, more than a movie playing in my head. I can feel the wind in my eyes, hear the laughter, smell the newmown hay.

He was athletic, I think. Musical. I remember a thin voice, singing along with the radio. I remember a guitar he played for us sometimes. And I remember delicate fingers that spread like a spider's legs, as light to the touch.

Touch? I remember his touch. On my leg. My arm. My back. Is it Scotty's touch I remember? Is that the dream?

Then he went away. He was gone. The car, the music, the laughter. Gone.

Waiting, waiting, for the semester to start. We're almost there. In the meantime, I scribble in the notebook. Oliver this and Oliver that.

Who is this Oliver who's crept into my head and won't leave, this fiction who seems more and more real?

The picture of him now in my head resembles Scotty, my adventurous uncle.

But who was he as a boy?

I watch his life unfold. The family vacations at their beach house, Oliver and his brother, Declan, who was into all things military. And his sister. Patty. No, Pamela, the eldest. Self-absorbed, she's writing in her diary. Declan broods, poring over a book about World War II he's found in the house's library, part of his wealthy grandfather's collection. Oliver, bored with the book he's found, eavesdrops on his parents and learns that his uncle is in trouble. He's going away. For years, his father says. What did he do? Where is he going?

After our classroom discussion of consciousness, I visited Professor Russell in his office, wanting to know more. He pointed to the chair across from his desk. I sat and my gaze took in the towering bookshelf behind him. Hegel, Schopenhauer, Ayer, all the philosophers we were reading in our classes. Kant, Hume, Husserl.

"Did you have a question, Ollie?"

I laughed, because for a moment I'd forgotten why I'd come, and I was startled to hear him speak my name. But now I looked at him.

"Right. I was wondering, is it possible to alter consciousness?" I asked.

"That depends on what you mean." He fiddled with the knot of his skinny tie, and I thought my question had made him nervous.

"I guess what I want to know is, does consciousness include awareness of the past?" There was that dream I'd had all my life, the memory that didn't make sense. Had something happened to me? Who belonged to that face? "Like, is there a way to recover lost memories?"

"Maybe," he said. We'd wandered far from the point he'd made in class and he was clearly hesitant to continue.

"How?" It wasn't like me to be pushy, but I needed to know.

He twisted in his chair, slowly—reluctantly, I thought—and pulled a book from the shelf behind him, sliding it across the desk to me: *Zen Mind, Beginner's Mind* by Shunryu Suzuki. I knew something about Buddhism, of course. I'd read *Siddartha* in high school, like everyone else, and my comparative religions class had covered the basics of the different branches, Hinayana, Mahayana, and various schools within them, like Zen, and... That's about all I remembered.

"Meditation?" I asked, doubtful. "Isn't that just sitting and thinking?"

He laughed. "Not exactly, Ollie. More like not thinking."

Puzzled, I nudged the book back toward him.

"There isn't another way?"

His eyes were burning through me, and I wondered what nerve I'd struck. Had I broken some rule of student-teacher etiquette?

Just then, commotion broke out in the hall outside his office, a couple of boisterous students, what sounded like an argument, playful shouting, but it showed no signs of abating. He got up, closed the door, and returned to his seat.

"There might be other ways," he said.

Was I supposed to understand what he was talking about without him saying the words? Because I didn't. My face must have given me away.

"There are," he began, looking over his shoulder as if to be sure we were still alone, "pharmaceutical options."

"You mean drugs?" I asked.

Keep your voice down, his expression begged. "Drugs?" I repeated, almost whispering.

He shrugged, as if giving in to the inevitable, now that the topic had been broached. Still, I could see that he weighed how much to tell me.

"Psilocybin, LSD, peyote," he said. He turned back to his bookshelf and pulled down another volume, this one worn and dog-eared: *The Teachings of Don Juan* by Carlos Castaneda.

I'd heard of Castaneda but hadn't seen his books. I opened it, flipped through the dog-eared pages, and began reading about a drug-induced trance. Now I understood his hesitancy. I looked at Professor Russell, probably with a mix of shock and admiration.

"Does it work?" I asked.

He reached across the desk, took back both the books, and shelved them. He returned his burning gaze to me and said, "Yes."

I sit on the floor of my bedroom in Mom's house and I close my eyes, recalling what Professor Russell taught me about meditation. I want to summon the face from the dream, but all I can see is young Scotty from the photograph. Tall and handsome, grinning.

Was it Scotty in the dream? Was it Scotty who came to me in the night?

6

After class one day, Professor Russell asked me to stop by his office. When I got there, he was putting on his coat to leave.

"About our earlier conversation," he said, leaning over his desk and writing on a notepad, "come to my house tonight around eight." He ripped off the sheet of paper and handed it to me—his address.

This was a puzzle. I liked Professor Russell and was at ease talking to him in class or his office. But I'd never seen him off campus. I didn't know anything about him. Was he married? Did he live alone? I assumed he wanted to tell me more about how to alter consciousness and expand the mind, something he wasn't comfortable discussing at school, but maybe it was something else.

I wondered if I should even go. I wanted to go.

Professor Russell lived in a quiet neighborhood not far from campus: tree-lined street, kids on bicycles, manicured lawns, wide front porches. A yellow light glowed next to the door. I hesitated a minute—still time to back out, to tell him I'd forgotten the appointment or had a conflict—but then, convincing myself there was nothing to be afraid of, I marched up to the door, took a breath, and rang the bell. A dog barked, but only once, half-heartedly, as if he'd done his job and beyond that wasn't terribly concerned.

The door swung open and there, a cocker spaniel at his heels, was Russell, barefoot, wearing jeans and a Princeton T-shirt. It felt wrong somehow to see him out of his sport coat and tie, as if a deep secret had been inadvertently revealed. He was fitter than I'd realized, a runner I guessed, like me. With a sweep of his arm he invited me in. I looked around for signs of a wife, family, a housemate, but saw nothing. Just the dog, who looked up at me, head cocked.

"Kick off your shoes, if you don't mind," Russell said.

"My shoes?"

"Yeah. Kind of a rule of the house, you know? An Asian thing."

"Right. Sure." I looked down at my sneakers, glad I'd worn socks, even socks with holes. At least my vestigial toes would be covered.

Professor Russell led the way to a dark room at the side of the house. As my eyes adjusted I saw a masculine space, his study. The walls were lined with bookshelves, like his office at school, but punctuating the rows of books were exotic artifacts—masks, wood carvings, clay figurines, bronze statues. Dozens of them.

"Wow," I said, "what a cool place." I stepped closer to the shelves and leaned in to examine one of the statues, an intricate bronze piece with a forest of arms and an enigmatic smile. I reached out but thought better of touching it.

"That's Kwan Yin, in the Tibetan style," he said. "She's a bodhisattva of compassion and mercy."

"Wow," I said again, spinning to take it all in.

"Take a seat," he said.

But there were no seats, just pillows scattered on the rug, some kind of Persian carpet. When I didn't move, Russell sat cross-legged on one of the cushions and waved toward another. I copied his movement and sat.

"Where did all this stuff come from?" I asked.

"Travels," he said. "Asia. Africa. South America. Research is the great thing about my job. Philosophy is everywhere. I'm really just indulging my innate curiosity, exploring the world of ideas, my own consciousness, you might say. And, as I said in class, for me, travel is the key."

"About that."

"You have questions?"

My legs were already stiff in that bent position, and I squirmed, resetting myself. "For starters," I said, assuming he didn't want to jump right into a discussion of the drugs, "how does meditation work?"

He nodded, but not like a professor answering questions in the classroom. More like a friend sharing his experience, an older brother. As he spoke, I couldn't help but think of my brother in Afghanistan, what he was going through there. I hadn't heard from Q in weeks, and that had me worried.

"Meditation is a way to sublimate the self," Russell said. "To let consciousness emerge. It takes years of practice, but the idea is to think about nothing, or, rather, to not think about anything, which is different. If you can do that, you can see it more clearly."

"See what?"

"The goal. Truth. Calm. Peace. You clear away the fog of confusion, and reveal what's real. What's important. It's like the ultimate destination, you know? It's where anyone would want to go if they knew how to get there, if they knew it existed."

"Heaven?" I asked. I wasn't sure what he meant, but it sounded like something from a long-ago Sunday-school lesson. Or were we talking about an actual place on a map? Had we come back to travel?

He nodded again. "I get why you might think that," he said. "But, no, the Christian heaven is a bit of sugar candy concocted to placate the masses, to give meaning to our otherwise meaningless existence. What I'm talking about is *nirvana*, a plateau we can reach right here on earth."

"Years of practice, you said?" I glanced up at the statue he'd told me about before. Tibetan? Compassion and mercy?

As he had in his office, Russell hesitated. "It's worth making the effort, Ollie. Anything worth having is."

"But you mentioned another way. A short cut? The drugs?"

"Well, yes. Some people say that the drugs—peyote, psilocybin, LSD, one or two others—do alter consciousness. It's not quite the same as the feeling you can achieve through meditation, the elevated state of awareness, but it's…faster. More unpredictable, but faster."

"You've done it?"

"I meditate daily."

"But the drugs?"

Russell leaned back on the cushion and reached into his jeans pocket, pulling out a folded piece of paper. He opened it to reveal two tiny, colorful postage stamps. "Do you want to try it, Ollie? Do you want to grow your mind? Find the truth?"

෨

Four years ago, Q was back from his first deployment to the Middle East, at home in Indianapolis. My parents were still together then, barely. I was a sophomore, floundering.

Q handed me a beer. I looked over my shoulder to see if Mom had seen. Drinking wasn't new. Drinking *at home* was.

Q shrugged. "Fuck it," he said, lighting a cigarette. Q didn't smoke until he went to Afghanistan. What else had changed?

I popped the top on the beer, drank, throbbed with the petty rebellion.

"Professor Russell says—"

"Who's this guy again?" Q asked.

"He's my adviser. My philosophy teacher. He says—"

"A professor. Philosophy, no less. I bet he's been in school his whole life. Never had a real job, am I right? Never been in the real world."

"That's what I'm trying to tell you, Q. Maybe there *is* no real world. What if it's all in our imaginations? Everything. This cold beer—" I looked over my shoulder again "—pleasure, pain, all of it. Illusion."

"Bullshit," he said.

"Just think about it for a minute."

"You want real? Go to fucking Afghanistan. Better yet, don't."

"But what if it's *not* real?"

"It's real, all right. Believe me. It's fucking real."

"But how do you know?" It sounded like a game, the kind of mental masturbation we did in school all the time. But it wasn't a game for Q. I saw it in his eyes: they grabbed on to me and wouldn't let go.

Q drank his beer. I drank mine.

"I'll tell you how you know. You know because you feel it," he said. "You feel fear when the bullets fly and the bombs go off. You feel disgust when somebody else's blood soaks your sleeve and their guts land on your feet. You feel anger when your buddy gets killed right in front of you. You feel pain when you get hit."

"Wait. You got hit? You mean shot? Jesus, Q."

"No biggie."

"Q, that's huge. Do Mom and Dad know?"

"I thought it was all an illusion, little brother. A big lie. So what difference does it make one way or another?"

"*Maybe* it's an illusion," I said. "I don't know." I saw it in those relentless eyes. Q had changed.

"Well, I know. It's fucking real as hell."

"Yeah?"

"This is how I know." He pulled the T-shirt over his head, revealing a scar, red, indignant, that stretched from his shoulder to his armpit. "Because I've been to hell and back. It's real."

Oliver's semester abroad is a relief from the tedium of Harvard, the pressures of family. New mountains to climb, literally and figuratively. Auf wiedersehen, Cambridge.

I write this late at night. My mother is in bed and I'm sitting with my notebook at the kitchen table. Earlier, I'd been at the mall with Mary, sipping Cokes in the food court. We were playing that game, the one where you look at the people around you and make up stories about who they are. It passed the time pleasantly enough.

A silver-haired gentleman in a suit and tie, a briefcase dangling from one hand, marched by us, obviously in a hurry to get somewhere.

"He's a banker," Mary said. "The briefcase is stuffed with money he's delivering to the department store."

I shook my head. "Not a banker," I said. "A bank *robber*. He's in a hurry because the cops are on his tail. Any minute now the boys in blue are going to run through here and nab him."

"Maybe you should tackle him now, Ollie. I bet there's a reward. You could be rich!"

We laughed at that, of course. And on it went. A blonde woman in sunglasses who was obviously a movie star scouting locations for her next film. A middle-aged guy with a crew cut who was a football coach killing time at the mall until the season began.

"See that guy?" Mary asked, nodding toward a dark young man, maybe Middle Eastern, no more than a boy really, in a hoodie. "He's a purse snatcher. Or a terrorist. One of the two."

"Because he's dark?" I asked. It's one thing to label a well-dressed white guy as a bank robber, but I was uncomfortable with the stereotype she'd chosen for this man.

"It's just a game, Ollie. All in good fun."

But was it? We watched as the man entered the food court and joined a young woman at a table, kissing her before lifting a child out of a stroller and cuddling her.

Which is why I'm writing now about Oliver's semester abroad in Zurich, where he meets the exotic and dark Maria, a woman, let's say a Mexican woman, in the *rathskeller*. To impress her, he takes a seat at the piano and plays ragtime, one of his many talents. They drink wine together, or brandy. Later, they're strolling on the Bahnhofstrasse, window-shopping, and a light snow is falling, when out of nowhere a dark-skinned man grabs Maria's purse. She shrieks, as if in pain, and Oliver gives chase. The sidewalks are slick but Oliver is fast, angry, and as they skid around a corner he tackles the thief.

My heart is racing as I write the scene, feeling the exhilaration that Oliver feels from the confrontation. He is afraid, but determined and angry. He is alive and he knows he is alive. Q understands this. Maybe I'm beginning to see his point. What would Professor Russell say?

Maria would want to reward Oliver, and so they move on to her flat. They sip more wine, watch the snow caressing the window, and undress. They make love, of course. But in the glow of their lovemaking—my heart is racing again—they speak again of the thief, a Turk, Oliver has concluded.

"Immigrants," Maria says. "I hate them."

Oliver bristles. "What are we if not immigrants?"

They argue. It's different, she says. We're all seeking opportunity, he says. But he steals, she says. To feed his family, perhaps, Oliver says. And Oliver is thinking of the young man, handsome and solid, wondering where he is now.

"I would like to kill him," Maria says.

7

I'm thinking of Oliver's Travels, his European adventures with Maria and the purse snatcher, which makes me think of Uncle Scotty, wherever he might be, and this memory surfaces: Mom and Dad have gone out to a party somewhere and left me at home with Scotty. Are Sally-Ann and Q there too? No, I can't hear them, can't hear the steady thump of the boom box from Q's room, or Sally-Ann's shrieks and laughter as she gossips on the phone.

I'm five or six, in the living room watching TV. Nickelodeon is on, a show I've seen a hundred times, but the sound is low. I'm bored and my Gameboy—Q's Gameboy—is broken. When I peek into the kitchen, Scotty is at the dining table, books spread in front of him. Fingers of one hand trace words in an open book; with his other he writes on lined paper. He doesn't notice me.

I push the front door open and go out into the yard. The grass feels cool on my bare feet, my toes, the nubs of my missing toes. The sky is dark, but the porch light is on, and long shadows cross the driveway. I follow the shadows into the bushes at the edge of the yard, an adventure, the edge of my world. Inside the bushes, the light from the porch filters through the leaves like stars. I curl up and gaze skyward. I count the stars: one, two, three, four…

I open my eyes when I hear my name. I don't remember where I am. It's dark. I'm cold. The stars are gone. I hear my name again.

"Daddy?" I say. I curl my feet beneath me so he won't see my toes.

"Ollie!"

It's not Daddy's voice, though. I feel hands on my arms and

I'm being pulled from the bushes, the leaves scraping my arms. It hurts.

"Jesus, Ollie, you scared me to death. I've been looking everywhere for you!" It's Uncle Scotty, and he's holding me tight, squeezing me, too tight. I'm crying. I can't breathe.

Uncle Scotty carries me inside, his hands brushing my head and back. When he puts me to bed, he lingers beside me, pressing his body against mine, arms pulling me close, and says, "Whatever you do, don't tell your mom and dad, okay? It's our little secret?"

He puts his hand on my chest. "Okay?" he asks.

It's our secret. Scotty touching me. A secret. Did this happen? What else happened?

I'm sitting at the kitchen table, writing in my notebook again. Oliver has just defended Maria from the swarthy purse snatcher, but he is the kind of man who will help his attacker, the immigrant who needs to feed his family, and maybe that's how he changes the world. Is he naive to think it matters? Could I do the same? Or would I turn my back, let nature take its course?

My mother is craning her neck to see what I'm writing.

"Mom," I say. "Stop."

"What?" she asks, pursing her lips. "I only wanted to know what my brilliant, college-educated son is scribbling all the time in that notebook of his."

Scribbling, a toddler incapable of staying within the prescribed shapes of my coloring book. Is that what she thinks?

She does this sometimes, especially when she's offended. She speaks of me in the third person, as if I weren't sitting across the table or standing right next to her. As if I were a character in *her* novel.

"After four years of writing dull papers in school," I say, "I thought I'd try my hand at some fiction. Short stories, maybe a novella. This is just a rough draft."

"May I read it?"

"No." God, no.

"My son, the famous author, won't even let his mother read his work."

"Mom."

"What?"

"It's rough still. Maybe you can see it when it's more polished."

"At least tell me what it's about. Is it about us? Your dysfunctional family?"

"We're not dysfunctional." Not compared to that family on *Arrested Development* anyway, but I don't add a qualification. "To answer your question, though, no, it's not autobiographical."

That's the point, isn't it? My reality is unbearable, or at least unknowable. This is a new reality, a new world.

"That's what all writers say, I bet."

"Very funny, Mom."

"So, is it about something that happened in college? That girl you dated? What was her name? Rhonda?"

"Her name was Rachel, Mom, but no." Rachel, whom I caught making out with her ex. That *would* make a good story.

"Who, then? I bet it's that professor you always talked about. He seemed like an interesting man. So intelligent. Is it about him?"

Professor Russell. Expanded consciousness. World traveler. Maybe it *is* about Russell. That hadn't occurred to me. If not about him, exactly, he at least made it possible. Without Professor Russell, there would be no Oliver.

"Is experience real?" Professor Russell asked in one of our classes. "Or does it exist only in our imaginations? Only in the consciousness? Does it have flesh? Blood? Is memory real? Is memory knowledge? Can we be said to know what we remember? Or has the passage of time altered reality in some way?"

That day at Professor Russell's house, I reached for the tab he offered, not a pill, as I'd expected, but a wafer. The body of Christ. I pulled my hand back, as if sensing heat that would burn.

"What is it?" I asked.

"LSD," he said. "Drop it on your tongue and let it dissolve."

My hand floated in the air between us.

"You're hesitant," he said. "Perfectly normal. But let me tell you about this drug. LSD: Lysergic Acid Diethylamide. It's illegal, although perfectly safe for most people, despite what the government will tell you. It's not addictive. Like other psyche-delics, it alters perceptions, opening doors that have remained closed, allowing us to see, really *see*, the world around us. And, more importantly, to understand our own minds, to navigate consciousness."

"Just consciousness?" I asked. "What about memories?"

"What do you mean?"

"Can it help you remember something? Something you think happened, but you're not sure?"

"Yes, I've seen that in the literature. In one case I read, a young woman, experimenting with LSD, saw visions of her father abusing her. The visions were graphic and specific, and they convinced her that she had repressed the memory of the abuse. Her father denied it, but the mother—the parents were divorced—was a credible ally. There was no evidence, though, and nothing could be proved. Still, the girl was convinced that what she'd seen while tripping was real and not a hallucination. I'm afraid it drove her mad."

"Mad?"

"She killed herself."

"Shit."

"Right. I don't blame the drug, though."

"But she saw something in her consciousness, with the aid of the LSD, that maybe didn't really happen?"

Russell nodded.

"So what caused the memory, or the hallucination, or what-ever it was, if it wasn't the drug?"

"I don't know. I believe *something* happened, but it may be that she wasn't able to see it clearly, even with the LSD."

I watched his eyes, dark and serious, waiting for me to act, to decide, one way or the other. I cleared my throat.

"I think I'm not ready to try the drug," I said.

"I figured." His voice was neutral, not judging. There was even a trace of a smile on his lips. He folded the paper with the tabs of LSD and returned it to his pocket.

I had so much to learn from him, and I was hungry to start.

"So, not the drug," I said. "But can you teach me how to meditate?"

"It's not as simple as it sounds. It's not hypnosis. Are you ready to open your mind?"

He crossed his legs on the cushion, sat up straight, and pointed at my feet. At first I thought he was pointing out the hole in my sock, or my missing toes, but then I realized he meant I should imitate his position. I folded my legs, straightened my back. He nodded.

"I'm ready," I said.

"Open your mind, Ollie," he said. "Open your mind."

?

Oliver would not have been afraid to take the drug.

I write about his post-college trip to Asia, now in Bali, the perfect place for him, the end of the road, as far away from his family as he can get. Just the waves on the beach, constant, tempting. The bars in Kuta, art in Ubud, temples, music, beer, beautiful Balinese, beautiful Australians, women and men both.

He's backpacking with Barry, a guy he met in Bangkok, who takes him to a cafe. It looks like all the other cafes, and bottles of Anker beer arrive, along with a menu.

"A very special menu," Barry says with a grin.

Special, indeed: blue meanie mushroom omelets, blue meanie soup (with carrots), blue meanies sautéed with onions and garlic (over rice).

They order an omelet to share. It's greasy and gritty, barely edible, but that's hardly the point. It takes a while, but as the mushrooms begin to grip him, Oliver sees his environment with rare clarity. Everything—the narrow shadow on the sand that seems to come alive, like a snake, the courtyard rooster that flees at his approach, the bottle of beer that spews its contents,

like vomit, when Barry knocks it from his hand—is uproarious-
ly funny and tragic at the same time.

He sees his future with Maria, stormy and passionate, ultimately unfulfilling, and with his father, cold and distant. Barry,
craven and self-absorbed, disappears. Oliver settles on the
beach, nowhere to hide from the midday sun, and watches the
relentless waves, coming, coming, coming, unstoppable.

What should I say to Mary about my feet? My missing toes?
What would Oliver say? There will come a time, soon, I hope,
when she will see them. Or rather, not see them.

When I was about ten, having done my best until then to
hide my deformity from other kids, I developed the urge to find
out what had happened to me. Why were the toes missing? I'd
always been afraid to ask. After all, if my father was so ashamed
of me, there had to be some reason. But if I knew what that
reason was, I figured, even if it was really horrible, then I could
explain it to other people, like my classmates who were sure
to tease me when they saw those nubs. It was only a matter of
time, I knew, and I wanted to be prepared.

I dared not ask my father, of course, who wouldn't tolerate
being reminded of my inadequacy, his less-than-perfect child,
but my mother was a different story. One Sunday afternoon I
approached her in the kitchen while she was making dinner.
Dad was playing golf, I think, and Q and Sally-Ann were off
somewhere with friends. I edged along the counter and leaned
against the sink, sighing heavily to let her know I was there.

"Finished with your homework, Ollie?"

"Yes, ma'am."

"And your chores?"

"Yes, ma'am." My chores were a joke. I was still a kid. It
was my job to keep my room tidy, which I was inclined to
do without being told. I dusted. I even vacuumed. The hard
work—taking care of the yard and doing the laundry—fell to
Q and Sally-Ann.

My mother shook some kind of spices into a pot on the

stove and stirred, sending steam and the tang of chili into the air.

"Can I ask you something?" I asked.

"May I," she corrected.

"May I?" I asked.

"No," she said, and then laughed. "Yes, of course you may ask."

"You know my toes," I said, "the little tiny ones?"

The trace of her humor vanished and she stopped stirring. She turned to me.

"What about your toes?"

"What happened to them? Why are they so little? Everyone else has regular toes."

"Oh, my," she said. She wiped her hands on a dishtowel and reached up to retrieve the cookie jar from a high cabinet. She opened the refrigerator and took out a carton of milk. I could see she was thinking about what to tell me while she poured our glasses. She put a few cookies on a plate—homemade chocolate chip, Dad always insisted on homemade—and led the way to our dinette table.

She sat at the head of the table, my father's usual place, and waited for me to get settled next to her and take a bite out of one of the cookies.

"What brought this on?" she asked.

"Nothing," I said, with a shrug. "I just wanted to know."

"So," she said. "Ollie, you know that God works in mysterious ways. I guess he decided you didn't need those toes. They don't really do anything, anyway. Maybe in the future no one will have little toes and God's just trying it out on you."

I took a sip of my milk while I thought about that. I shook my head.

"Not buying it, huh?" she said. "Okay. Well, the truth is, I honestly don't know. When you were born, the doctor noticed right away. But he couldn't come up with an explanation for your toes. It could have been a million things."

"Like what?"

"Like a virus, or an accident, or anything. Or it might have been nothing. There's just no way to know."

"Yeah, but what might it have been?"

"That's enough, Ollie. I've told you everything I know. Truly. Some questions just don't have answers. Okay? Sometimes we just don't know."

A question without an answer? How is that possible?

The face recurs. The dream, the memory, whatever. What is it I'm trying to remember when I see that face? Is it like that girl Professor Russell told me about who took drugs and recalled that she'd been abused by her father. Is that what my mind has repressed?

The face. Is it Scotty? He touched me. Is that what I can't remember?

Or is this one of those questions without answers?

When Q came back from Afghanistan for the second time, he took me out to a smoky pub. I was still in college, still underage, but Q was some kind of war hero, wounded twice, written up in the local papers, so no one asked questions.

"Well, little brother, here's to reality." He raised his mug, and I clinked mine against it.

"You still think your life is an illusion?"

"Maybe," I said. I never really believed that. I was just repeating Professor Russell's argument, but it was too late to confess this to Q.

"Bullshit," Q said.

"Look at it this way," I said. "If our experiences were real and not an illusion, we would have control over our fates. We could change our reality."

"And we can. I can change your reality in a heartbeat. And mine. All it takes is a bullet in the brain."

"Still an illusion."

"Death is real, Ollie. Believe me."

❧

Here's my question, something Professor Russell was never able to answer, at least not in a way that made sense to me: What is memory? Is it energy? Does it have an existence apart from the body? Apart from consciousness? When we forget something, where does that memory go? And how can memory be fallible? If we remember it, how can it be false unless it is deliberately fabricated?

And a related question: On the one hand, I cannot observe a past event, and therefore I have no valid reason to believe it occurred, even if I think I remember it. I cannot be certain that it happened. The past, it seems to me, like the future, isn't real. And yet, our senses retain impressions of past events—images, sounds, tastes—that cannot consciously be altered. Are not these impressions evidence of the past event?

If consciousness survives us, does memory persist in the void? Do our memories live on?

If I remember it, didn't it happen? And if I don't remember, could it have happened anyway?

What did Uncle Scotty do? Why can't I remember?

8

Each week at my mother's is the same, like the CD you listen to over and over again, not because you love the band or the album but because that's what's in the machine, and it just plays when you turn it on. During the week I cobble together odd jobs—lawnmowing is regular, but I've powerwashed, painted, fenced, exterminated, babysat, dog-walked, even house-cleaned—and on the weekends I take Mary to a show, always one of her choosing.

One night toward the end of the summer we see an oldie, *Sleepless in Seattle*, which I find silly and predictable, cloying and superficial, but which brings Mary to tears, even though she's probably seen it a dozen times.

"I can't believe you didn't like that," Mary says as we stroll down Main Street through the syrupy heat toward our usual post-movie sundaes at the Ice Dream. This isn't Zurich or Mexico City or Bali, or wherever Oliver finds himself in my story. Mary isn't Maria.

"I didn't say I didn't like it," I say, although I *didn't* like it and don't even want to talk about it because there's obviously nothing to talk *about*. "I thought it was…pointless. Like a novel that maybe has an okay story but doesn't really mean anything. No depth. No subtext. There's got to be subtext to make it interesting. Don't you think?"

"Pooh on subtext," she says. "I thought it was brilliant."

I nod, conceding for the sake of harmony. Is this how it will go with us? We can't talk about books, and apparently movies are out too. At least her father raised her to be a baseball fan.

We share a sundae. I do my best to eat only from one end of the dish, so as not to encroach on Mary's half, and also avoiding any of the ice cream that Mary's spoon has touched. I try not to think the word *contaminated*, but it stays in my mind like a neon sign, the glow still visible when it's been switched off. I hope Mary hasn't noticed, tonight or any of the previous nights I've done this.

"Delicious," I say, and put my spoon down, leaving the remainder for her.

When I take her home, Bill and Lydia are asleep, but brother Mike is in the living room watching television with the dog. Barney leaps off Mike's lap to greet Mary, but then resumes his place. It's a war movie, the one about the young private being rescued during the Normandy invasion. Talk about depth. The room is dark, except for the flashing screen. While Mary goes to the bathroom, I sit with Mike. I look at the screen. I do not look at Mike.

During a commercial for razor blades, I search for something to say. I know nothing about Mike, his interests, his hobbies, and I don't know where to start, so I say, "Good movie?"

"Blood," he says. "Guns."

Apparently, he's not drawn to the subtext either. I don't tell him war's nothing like that, not anymore. My brother won't talk about it—they sent him to Afghanistan twice—but I can tell from what he *doesn't* say. There's no glamour. It's not a movie. It's hell.

"I'm thinking of enlisting," Mike says. He's headed to college this fall, Mary has told me, not the Army. So is this enlistment thing new? The family doesn't know?

Now I look at him. I see the light from the television dance on his bare arm, as if the war is projected onto his body, and I can see the boy as a soldier, rugged and deadly, brave, battling the enemy for a convenient lie. I can't tell him about Q, what it's done to him. He doesn't want to hear.

What is meaning? Why do some entertainments move us and others leave no impression at all? Some stay with us and others are quickly forgotten. Is it solely a matter of the questions they ask? Or are there other triggers, different for each of us?

When the handsome private is mortally wounded on the beach, what affects us? Is it the prospect of the loss of his beauty that evokes our tears, the loss of possibility he represents? Our lost innocence? Or is it simply the senselessness of war that toys with our emotions? Forces us to confront our fear of conflict and our longing for peace? Would we feel the same if he were deformed? Misshapen in some way? Missing toes, for example?

But why should it mean anything at all? Is there something inferior about art that on its surface stimulates emotion? Is Jackson Pollock more important, whatever that means, than Andy Warhol?

Professor Russell would argue, I think, that Pollock through abstract expressionism is seeking a truth, making a statement about the nature of art itself, and therefore about life. Whereas Warhol, with pop art's representationalism, is merely ironic. It captures reality without actually saying anything about it, and is therefore built on a lie.

When I explain Professor Russell's theory to Mary as we're driving to the mall to see yet another romantic comedy, she's gazing out the window.

"You weren't listening," I say.

"No, I was listening," she says. "You just weren't saying anything."

"I beg your pardon?"

"You think I'm stupid because I believe in romance. Because it makes me cry. And, by the way, I happen to like Andy Warhol. That soup can is soothing."

"But it doesn't mean anything. Pollock changed everything. What's so important about a giant cartoon of Marilyn Monroe or Chairman Mao?"

"You think that didn't change things? Take the soup can, for example. Art hasn't been the same since. It killed the Pollocks and the Rothkos and all the other pretentious men, almost all of them men, by the way, who tried to force us to see the world through their cracked lenses. Pop art gave us a new lens, a fresh way of looking at things. Can you honestly say that you don't think about Warhol's painting when you see a can of soup now? An ordinary can of soup, but now you see it in a completely different light."

"But—"

"But what, Ollie? Are you going to tell me I don't know what I'm talking about? That I'm wrong?"

"But what does it mean?"

"Why does it have to mean something? It doesn't mean anything, Ollie. It just is."

"No meaning," I say.

"No meaning."

"It just is?"

"It just is."

ॐ

"Charity Begins at Home." That's the title of a talk some visiting professor from Harvard is giving at the college tonight. It's a hot night, muggy, and although the topic does nothing for me, I agree to go with Mary if only to familiarize myself with the college campus. The lecture hall is air-conditioned, which is another plus.

We're there early, so we sit near the front, and I'm instantly transported back to my own college experience, still fresh in my memory. I miss it. Despite the subject matter of tonight's talk, which sounds deadly dull, I'm actually looking forward to hearing what this professor—any professor—has to say. A few minutes before the talk is scheduled to start—there are only half a dozen or so people in the audience besides Mary and me—Dean Venable escorts a stout woman with tight white curls into the lecture hall, gets our attention by clearing her throat, and introduces the woman as Professor Eileen Connor of Harvard University's Institute of Philanthropy.

Connor is wearing a navy blue suit, all business, very professional. She's in her fifties, I guess, with a confident demeanor, like she's accustomed to public speaking. In fact, although there is a podium at the front of the room, she steps in front of it—I remember Professor Russell doing this too, a trick to get and hold the attention of the class—and begins talking without notes. Her voice is strong, projecting as if there might be people in the back of the room who can't hear, although we're all sitting in the first three rows.

It's not quite what I was expecting. From the title, I thought we'd get a philosophical discourse on charitable giving, but Connor, who has come out to Winchester from DC where she was attending a conference, is all facts and figures. Americans give this much annually, people in other countries give that much, tax policy is a factor, nonprofits couldn't survive without these donations, and so on. She's sharp, but I'm sorry to say that her speech is a snooze. There's a question-and-answer period at the end, but no one raises a hand. We're all anxious to get out of there.

Afterward, Mary and I go out for ice cream. No surprise there. We're not sharing tonight. She gets the mint chocolate chip, as usual; I get the butter pecan, and we sit at a table outside the shop. The night is still hot, but there's a breeze, and it's reasonably pleasant. I'm thinking about what I *thought* was going to be discussed in the lecture.

"So what do you think, Mary," I say. "Is charity a myth?"

"Yes," she says without hesitation. "That's something my father taught me long ago. Altruism is dead and probably always has been. No one does anything without the expectation of a reward—whether it's a tax break or a free pass into heaven, we practice charity because we expect to get something in return."

I'm more surprised by the fact Mary has any opinion at all on this subject than the position she's taken, which does sound like something her father would say, an excuse for a lack of generosity.

"Do you really believe that?" I ask. "I mean, isn't it really a question of logic, not quid pro quo? Society functions better when the haves share with the have-nots. Philanthropy is a means of achieving harmony in the tribe or society or whatever."

"But that proves my point," she says.

"So we shouldn't give of ourselves? No money, no volunteering?"

"That's not what I'm saying, Ollie. We need to be clear about what our expectations are. People do things for a reason. It's what keeps the world moving."

She has a point. People do things for a reason. They don't suddenly remember things that didn't happen. And they don't just disappear.

∽

We're sitting on the porch at the Bergers', sipping lemonade, reading, when Mike comes home from a run. I watch him jog up the porch steps. It's a particularly humid day and he's drenched in sweat, his T-shirt glued to his solid torso. He ignores us as he enters the house and we resume reading. In a few minutes, cleaned up and dressed, he's out the door again, car keys in hand. Did he even see us? He hops into his Jeep and drives off.

When he's gone, I look at Mary, who's engrossed in her book. And now I wonder if she saw *him*. Are they invisible to each other?

"He doesn't want to go to college, you know."

"Who?" she asks without looking up.

"Mike. Your brother."

Now she looks up. "He told you that?"

"He wants to join the Army."

She snorts. "The same Army that's wreaking havoc around the world? Sowing unrest in Central America and the Middle East in order to leave the common people weak and dependent? That Army?"

"Whoa. Where did that come from?"

"It's the truth, Ollie."

"You know my brother's a vet, right? And wasn't your dad in the Marines?"

"That was different," she says.

"How so?"

"He was defending democracy. We were in a real war. And

anyway, he'll never let Mike join. He expects more from his only son."

"Ah. Parental expectations. I understand that."

Did my father try to stop Q from enlisting? And is he disappointed in us both?

Mary dog-ears the page in her book and closes it. I have to resist the urge to grab the book and at least attempt to fix the damage she's done. But it's Mary's book, it's a cheap paperback, and if she doesn't care, I shouldn't.

"Can I ask you something?" she says.

"Shoot." I grin, but I don't think she caught my sly military pun.

"What's with you and Mike?"

I open my mouth to answer, but I'm not sure what she's asking. "He's your brother. So I'm interested."

She shakes her head. "I've seen the way you look at him, Ollie. That's not brotherly."

"I don't know what you're talking about, Mary." But I know exactly what she's talking about. "You're imagining things."

"Remember that movie we saw?" Mary asks. We're in the coffee shop. Again. We come here so often I worry the kids who work here—because that's what they are, kids barely out of high school, with pierced eyebrows and illiterate tattoos—will talk about the boring couple who can't find anywhere else to go. Which is true. But still.

"Which one?" I ask. "We've been to a bunch." One of those rom-coms, no doubt, that she loves and I despise. What do I see in this woman?

"You know, the one where the girl owns a little bookstore in New York and the guy runs the big, bad book chain that's going to put her out of business?" Mary is drinking a latte. I have my usual—dark roast, regular.

"I have no idea what you're talking about."

"How can you say that? We loved that movie. And afterward we went out for ice cream."

"We always go for ice cream after a movie."

"But we talked about the movie."

"We always—"

"This was different, though. Because the movie was about books."

"A movie about books? I think I would have remembered that."

"Exactly. How can you be so dense? People don't just forget things."

"I'm sorry, but I really don't remember the movie. Could you have seen it with someone else?" We're not exclusive, at least I'm not, not technically, although I don't even *know* anyone else. Maybe she went out with another guy who actually likes those sappy comedies.

"Ollie, I swear, sometimes you make me crazy."

"I'm sorry. I don't mean to."

"I know."

"Help me remember, then."

"I don't understand how you could forget."

"You've never forgotten something? Never?"

"Well, sure, but I remember when I'm reminded."

"So the memory goes away and then comes back?"

"Something like that, I guess."

"What if it never comes back? Can't that happen?"

"You mean like amnesia?"

"Sure. Like amnesia. That happens all the time, right?"

"When people get conked on the head or something. Were you conked on the head?"

"Not that I remember."

An exasperated look. "You're saying you can't remember the movie because you have amnesia?"

"Not exactly. But how could I forget so thoroughly? How could it be simply wiped from my mind?"

"You're hopeless, Ollie. You sat right there across the table from me and ate a chocolate—" She stopped. Her face turned dark, as if a shadow had passed over.

"What? What's wrong?"

"It wasn't you. I mean, I thought it was you, but when I pictured you eating the sundae, I realized it wasn't."

"Who was it?"

"It wasn't you, Ollie."

So there *is* another guy. I knew it.

9

With both of us living at home, intimacy is a challenge for me and Mary. Somehow, when I was a teenager, and everybody lived with family, I found a way to be with whomever I was seeing at the time, as far as it went—second base, third if I was lucky. Backseats. The bed of a pickup. On a blanket under the stars. Stolen moments. In college, when I finally did manage to do the deed, we still depended on either cooperative roommates (the dorm) or cover of darkness (the campus meadow). But we're grown-ups now, more or less, and furtiveness no longer seems appropriate or conducive.

I discover one day that my mother will be working late, so I call Mary and invite her over for dinner.

"We'll be alone," I say, and I can tell from her silence that the import of our aloneness has not registered. "All by ourselves," I add. More silence. "My mother won't be home for hours."

"*Oh*," she says, the truth finally dawning. She giggles, which I take as a good sign.

I straighten the living room, put clean sheets on my bed. I'm not much of a cook, but I get the spaghetti sauce going, garlic bread, a salad. The house smells great. My mom has a thing for Josh Groban and I put one of his CDs on the stereo because it's the kind of romantic music I bet Mary loves—pretty, but soulless.

I open a bottle of wine, Chianti. I don't know anything about wine, but when I saw it on the shelf at Kroger it sounded romantic. Plus, it was cheap. I greet her at the door with a glass. She giggles, just as she had on the phone. Is that the way it's going to be?

I don't say anything, but lead her upstairs to my room. At least it's not the bedroom of my childhood, with sports trophies and model Indy cars, but she does linger, briefly, before my antelope poster. Is she as inspired as I am? She doesn't say anything, but we sit on the edge of my bed and sip our wine. She's grinning, nervous or eager, I'm not sure which, and giggles again.

I take the glass from her and put both our glasses on the side table. I move closer, lean in to kiss her, and before I know what's hit me I'm on my back with Mary straddling my chest.

This was my plan, of course, to take this next step in our relationship, but I can't help but worry that my mother will return early. With Mary rubbing her crotch against mine, though, it doesn't take long for that worry to recede, replaced by other, more pressing matters. My shoes come off, her sweater, my pants, her skirt, my shirt, and now we roll so I'm on top, off comes her bra, my shorts, her panties, we roll again, we pause for protection—just enough time for a vision of Mike to sneak into my brain—we couple, we writhe, we thrust, we grind, we roll again, and I'm no longer worried about my mother walking in on us, or anything else, with the possible exception of the disturbing presence in my mind of Mary's brother.

We lie next to each other. I feel the sweat on my chest, my back, the lingering tumescence of my penis, our commingled fluids seeping into the sheets.

I wonder if she's noticed that my socks are still on. I force myself to shift my focus away from my toes and think instead about Mary and what has just happened.

Mary and I are just sitting down to dinner—the spaghetti is overcooked, spongy and bland, but it hardly matters and neither of us mentions it, still in the aura of our frantic lovemaking— when I hear my mother's key in the front door. I'd forgotten about her. Now I wonder if maybe she'd come in earlier, heard what was going on upstairs, and retreated until it seemed safe. It's what I would have done, so why not? Better to avoid the embarrassment, the messy reality?

Mary is slightly disheveled, her normally tidy hair an

uncombed jumble, and I suspect I'm no tidier. I tuck in the half of my shirt that dangles over my jeans. And my mother is no idiot, so surely she'll know with a glance what we've been up to.

"Hi, kids," she calls, before finding us in the kitchen.

"Hi, Mrs. Tucker," Mary says. "Join us? There's plenty."

I glare at Mary, but she's focused on my mom and the effort is wasted.

Mom laughs, shakes her head, which is a relief because who would want his mother hanging around when he's just had amazing sex with his girlfriend, but instead of heading up to her room as I fervently wish, she takes a wine glass from the cupboard and sits at the kitchen table with us. Resigned to this intrusion—my sigh isn't meant to be audible, but it probably is—I pour for her, noticing that her hand is anything but steady, and I wonder if she's really been at work all this time.

"So," Mom says.

"So," I say.

Mary blushes. I feel the heat in my face.

"So," I say again.

I feel a certain amount of relief. The sex with Mary was rushed but successful. Very successful. Obviously, from the way she took charge, she has more experience than I do, which comes as a surprise, but I'm okay with that. I don't think I embarrassed myself, is what I'm saying. It was good. Really good. For both of us.

There was that moment, near the end, when I closed my eyes and caught a glimpse of Mike, Mary's brother, but it's not like I said his name, at least not out loud. It was fleeting. And when Mary quickened our rhythm as we reached the end, and my eyes opened in amazement at what I felt, it was only her I saw.

Still, the fact that he entered my consciousness at all is disconcerting. After Mary questioned me about my interest in Mike, I've made an effort to avoid talking about him in her company, and if he happens to be present I make sure I'm looking only at her.

༄

Mary has choir practice tonight, so I'm on my own. I think about going to a movie, something Mary wouldn't want to see, but the only film at the mall I might be interested in is another war story, and I'm not sure I can handle that. And anyway, I persuade myself, I should spend the time writing, not hiding in a dark theater.

I don't want to stay home, though, with my mother hovering, and the coffee shop is closed, so I head to the library. Our public library is a great resource for the community, and I'm always pleased to see kids of all ages there, doing homework, or diving into books for pleasure, or whatever. There's a reading room on the second floor, and I find an empty table and open my notebook.

I've been thinking about Oliver and Maria. They aren't really suited for each other, despite their physical attraction, their blazing sex, and yet there they are, an attractive couple. He can't stay away from her, despite her flaws, and so when he returns from Bali, he goes to visit her in Mexico before he starts graduate school—a joint law and business program that will lead, ultimately, to a place in the family firm, a global investment bank.

They tour Mexico City and then Maria takes him to a village in the shadow of the volcano where he meets her family. Her father, a retired banker with time on his hands, proudly shows Oliver his workshop, while Maria and her mother supervise the preparation of lunch. Over quesadillas and squash flower soup, he meets Miguel, Maria's handsome brother. His resemblance to his sister is uncanny, the same lips and piercing dark eyes. And that night in the cantina, Miguel's gaze meets Oliver's. Miguel challenges him to a round of tequila shots, and then another. Oliver has no choice, and no chance.

༄

Miguel. Mike. What is it about him? Why can't I shake him? Is it because of what Uncle Scotty did to me? And what *did* Uncle Scotty do to me?

I write about Oliver as a boy, taking lessons from the tennis pro at his father's club. Sam is tall and blond, with a deep tan, demonstrates form and technique, grip and footwork. He places his hands on the boy's shoulder and elbow to correct and mold his swing. Later, they're alone in the locker room.

Or: Oliver's math tutor, Carlos, a handsome dark graduate student who visits each week and sits with Oliver in his bedroom.

Or: Oliver's piano teacher. His scoutmaster. The camp counselor. His Uncle.

How did their attentions affect him? Is that why he's attracted to Maria's brother, Miguel?

Repeat a lie often enough and it becomes the truth. Repeat a memory, whether or not the memory is flawed, and the same thing happens.

Is memory unreliable? Why is eyewitness testimony in criminal cases so often wrong? Do people misinterpret what they see? The man running from the scene—was he tall or short, white or black, wearing a sweatshirt or a jacket? Or does the memory fade over time? I thought the man was tall, but maybe, now that you mention it, he wasn't all that tall. And maybe he wasn't black. I might be mistaken.

Memory isn't a tape recorder. It's not a camera. Or it is, in a way, but the tape, the negatives, can be altered by time and subsequent events, distorted. Research has shown that memory is fragile, subject to forces that, like a fun-house mirror, will twist remembered images into the unrecognizable. The problem is that we don't realize that this transformation has occurred.

I remember it, but did it happen?

10

The summer is passing, passing.

At night, if I've had yard work, I come home with barely enough energy to remove my dusty, sweat-soaked T-shirt and jeans. If I haven't had work, I've spent the day in the darkened living room, avoiding the heat that unnecessary movement and light would surely exacerbate.

One afternoon I'm lying on the couch, meditating, trying to practice what Professor Russell taught me, albeit in an unorthodox position, when my mother calls. She's leaving work early and plans to stop at the grocery on the way. Do I want anything?

I rouse myself, shower, and flee.

Blinded. A blue haze floods the mountains, but overhead the sky is bright and hot. The Impala is painful to touch, inside—a coffin.

I roll all the windows down and let the thick air envelop me, the streaming current a relief until I hit a red light, and now, by contrast, the indolent heat is suffocating. I fumble for the sunglasses that I think are in the glove compartment, hoping they will relieve the burning sensation, at least in some deep-rooted psychological way, but my hand comes up empty. I edge forward, anticipating green, anxious to move.

But there's nowhere to go, no destination that draws me. Mary is in class, her summer misfits attempting to master the basics of the shitstorm that awaits them when the fall term begins. I've joined a gym, but I never show up; the bulk-mad behemoths with their greasy ponytails and bulging biceps intimidate me. I pass the mall, going nowhere, then circle back and park near the Cineplex. I gaze at the offerings listed on the marquee: a comedy I've seen with Mary; a highly touted sequel to a classic sci-fi thriller; the latest in that series about the boy wizard, which I saw without Mary, having waited in line for two hours on opening day with a throng of middle schoolers; a war movie, this one about Korea.

The last makes me think of my brother, Q, and then of Mary's brother, Mike, and I picture him in uniform, mud splashed across his cheeks and bare arms, bravely defending the city, or seizing the city, or whatever.

Now, I'm keen to see the war movie, but in my panic to avoid my mother I've left home without my wallet. A cluster of quarters congregate in the Impala's cupholder, but not enough. If not a movie, there will be some form of distraction inside the mall and, at the very least, cool air. Halfway to the entrance, I turn to confirm the realization that I've left the windows down. I consider going back, rolling them up, but with the quarters in my pocket there's nothing to steal except my tattered Cubs cap and a bent-spoke umbrella. I glance at the searing, clear sky. I shrug again. Better to leave them down than to come back to a microwave later.

The dim mall swallows me, cold air spilling around me like rushing water. Through glass walls I see bored clerks behind gleaming display cases, listless shoppers floating from rack to rack, touching, stroking, keeping cool, forgetting, drifting, not buying. We're all fish, treading water in this giant aquarium. What would Professor Russell say about that?

The flow carries me on an undulating path, past cosmetics and lingerie and vitamins and gadgets. In the distance, at the confluence of mall halls, a coffee shop beckons. It isn't Starbucks, it isn't even the quaint locally owned shop I favor downtown, but it will help pass the time. I have quarters enough for coffee, I think. As I approach, fingering the coins in my pocket, mentally counting my limits—can I afford a large, an Americano?—I see Mike. Mike and another boy, slouching over iced soft drinks.

I stop, dead in the water.

We are not puppets. I have no patience for fate. But why else, other than the whim of the gods who place us in the arms of temptation, or conflict, or danger, have I been drawn to this mausoleum, this mallsoleum, except to run into Mike, whom I've been doing my damnedest to avoid.

He nods when he recognizes me, and I nod back on my way to the counter. Over the grinding of the beans—I have just enough money, with a nickel to spare, for an espresso—I strain to eavesdrop on Mike's conversation. But the interference in my head is too much. The coins, fate, the gods, all jangle deafeningly. And now I'm sure, because I refuse to check, that Mike and his friend have left.

Overpriced coffee in hand, I turn slowly, feeling the heat of the cup, and see that the other boy is now gone—what have the gods done with him?—and Mike sits by himself. Is he watching me? Or is he pretending not to watch? Is he waiting for me?

It's not that I'm attracted to Mike. Of course not. Why would I be? He merely represents possibility. A vehicle through which I might imagine a different, uninhibited life. He's like Oliver. In fact, I conclude, Mike isn't even real. He's a figment of my imagination presented by the gods as a test. "If you were Mike, Ollie," the gods are asking, "who would you be?" If you had balls, who would you become?

I stand beside Mike's table, awkwardly, aware of the choice I've been given.

"How've you been?" I ask. But, no, it's the gods quickening my heart.

"All right," says Mike. He leans back in his chair, his broad shoulders stretched wide, like wings. Is that some kind of signal? A message I'm meant to understand? The gods again.

He doesn't ask me to sit, so I remain standing, shift my weight from foot to foot, shift the scorching cup from hand to hand.

Now he nods toward the empty chair. He has sent his friend away, I surmise, in hopes that I will come to him, and I, ever obedient, have done exactly as I was meant to do. The strings pulled, I sit.

"Mary tells me you're off to college in the fall," I say, although I remember he's thinking about enlisting. That's about all she's told me about Mike, nothing about hobbies or girlfriends. When I ask, trying not to sound too interested, she changes the subject. He's Bill and Lydia's favorite, I suspect, the privileged boy child, and she'd rather talk about Meg Ryan and Tom Hanks than her brother.

"That's the plan," he says.

"Sounds like you're not too thrilled with the plan."

Mike shrugs. I've always thought a shrug was all about the shoulders, but Mike's is a whole-body shrug. Even his handsome face contorts with indifference.

"Plans change," he says, mysteriously.

We speak of nothing. He mentions Mary's old boyfriend, hints that Brian might still be in the picture. Mary has talked of Brian more than once, in a way that is meant to sound reassuring, but isn't. It has the opposite effect, in fact, and Mike's use of the guy's name raises doubts. Who is this Brian? Is she with him when she's not with me? Is that who she saw that movie with, the one I couldn't remember? Mike's measuring me now, eyes questioning, wondering if I care about the rivalry. Is he asking for Mary? For Brian? Or himself?

What will be, will be, I think. I'd like to meet this Brian character. What am I dealing with here?

I have to leave. Not because I have anywhere to go, but because I cannot stay with Mike, the shoulders, the chest, the face that is a copy of Mary's. Because I am reminded of what Uncle Scotty did to me, what he is still doing. I stand, I back away, I tip my nonexistent cap, I retrace my steps through the deathly corridor of zombified shopping, toward the parking lot. But long before I step outside, before I leave the delicious chill of conditioned air, I see the rain pouring into the open windows of my car. A downpour. A flood.

🙠

I'm invited to join Mary and her parents—but not Mike, apparently—at church. Mary has pointed the building out to me as we drove through town. It's Episcopal, a stone edifice right out of the middle ages, more fortress than house of worship, with elaborate stained glass windows that even I can appreciate.

She says there's an organ in there that creates the most heavenly music, and the windows are even more beautiful from the inside.

I have to admit that sounds appealing, in theory. But I'm not going to church with her.

When I was a kid, my parents made me go to services and Sunday school. My father never went. Sometimes, rarely, my mother would join me, but most often I would be accompanied by Sally-Ann, who was into it big time, and Q, who was as bored as I was by the whole affair. But that's about all I remember of the experience.

That's not quite true. I don't remember the services, but I do remember sitting in a dank, windowless classroom in the church's basement, with cartoon-like drawings of Jesus on the wall. We're sitting in tiny chairs around a low table, all these little kids drawing scenes from a Bible story, including one boy who had created an astonishingly vivid picture of Jesus on the cross, complete with bright red blood dripping from his hands and feet into a pool on the ground. There's an older woman in the memory—blue hair, she smells sweet, like my grandmother. She might *be* my grandmother, come to think of it, who claims to have taught Sunday school when my father was a boy. A pretty harmless memory, all in all, but also kind of creepy.

One Sunday morning when I was about nine, Q announced between mouthfuls of pancake that he wasn't going to church that day. "I'm old enough to make my own decisions," he said, "and I've decided I've got better things to do than sit in a stuffy old shoebox listening to a bald-headed hypocrite go on and on about some hippie who may or may not have lived two thousand years ago."

My mother didn't start sobbing immediately. It was more like a leaky faucet. A drip at first, then another, and then the floodgates opened. Why she cared about Q's announcement, given her own sorry attendance record, is anyone's guess. Maybe she hoped her children would make up for her transgressions and still earn her a spot in heaven. My father barely looked up from his newspaper. Given that he had opted out long ago, I imagine he didn't think he had to pick a side in this argument. Sally-Ann, though, was horrified by Q's blasphemy and ran to her room to avoid the fallout.

As far as I know, Q never went to church again, although I can't say for certain he didn't do some praying while he was in Afghanistan. His teenage rebellion, however, opened the door for me.

A few months after that scene, after weeks of summoning my courage, I said at breakfast one Sunday, not quite as defiant as he had been but bold for me, "I don't think I'll go to church today." Again there was barely a ripple in my father's newspaper. My mother, though, looked as if I'd just told her there was a spider on her nose. I was prepared with my reasoning, rehearsed the night before with Q, but this time she didn't argue. She didn't cry. She took a sip of her coffee, a bite of her scrambled eggs.

"Fine," she said.

From then on, Sally-Ann went alone.

To Mary's invitation now, I say, "Gee, Mare, I wish I could, but I promised my mother I'd do something for her."

"Like what?"

"Chores. Errands. Something."

"You can't do it later?"

It seems wrong to lie my way out of going to church, although where I think retribution might come from is uncertain. I shift tactics.

"I'm not a churchgoer, Mary."

"That's okay, Ollie, I know people worship in their own way, but you can come with me, can't you? Just this once?"

"When I say I'm not a churchgoer, I mean I'm not a believer."

"I don't understand."

What's not to understand? Some people believe and others don't. Professor Russell helped me see that. It's a matter of faith versus reason. I choose reason.

"No offense, Mary, but religion is—" I stop. Of course whatever I was going to say next—Bullshit? Hogwash? The opiate of the masses?—would offend her. And I don't mean to offend. Maybe lying to her was better after all, but I've already gone too far down the road of truth. "What I mean is, for me, it doesn't make sense. I've reached some different conclusions based on the evidence, or lack of evidence, is all."

"Sense? It doesn't have to make sense, you know. That's the point of belief."

"But that's—" Again, there is no way to complete my thought without hurting her, or entering into an endless theological debate. Logic and faith don't belong in the same conversation, much less sentence. Maybe someday I'll try to convince her of that, introduce her to the work of some of the great atheist philosophers. But not yet. Not today.

"I can't go, Mary," I say. "It's not me."

Faith. There's something to be said for faith. Faith requires no thought. No analysis. No logic. No effort. It's the opposite of knowing, of truth. It is the disregarding of evidence. And yet, faith, like knowing, admits no doubt. Faith assumes the truth of its object, and in that way, in the certitude of the holder of faith, it is the same as knowing.

Philosophy is faith, of a sort. It is the belief that the world is supported on a foundation of logic. It is a rejection of the supernatural, the unexplained.

Professor Russell, in a seminar called "Faith and Reason," challenged one of my classmates, a black kid from Gary, Indiana, named Alex, whom I knew only from pickup basketball games at the campus gym. He was way better than me, with the sweetest jump shot ever, and I enjoyed his on-court banter.

On the first day of class, with twelve of us scattered around a table in a seminar room, Alex said, unbidden, "I believe in God." His pronouncement silenced the chatter of students settling in, opening notebooks, closing backpacks. We all stared at him, but his gaze was fixed on Russell, as if demanding a reaction.

"Well," said Russell, "that's as good a place as any to begin." He stood up, walked to the white board, and wrote in red dry-marker, *I believe in God.*

"Now," he said, facing Alex, "tell us why."

We would eventually read Hume and Kant, Kierkegaard and Hegel, even Nietzsche and Darwin, but at that point we'd read nothing. Alex was on his own with his faith.

"How can you not?" he asked. "When you see the grandeur of a sunset, a mountain's majesty, the awesome power of the ocean, can there be any question that there is a God who created them and put us here to enjoy them?" Powerful stuff for a kid from the mean streets of Gary.

There was snickering from the end of the table, but Russell silenced it by raising his hand.

"This is essentially the watchmaker argument put forth by Paley in the eighteenth century," Russell said. "And theologians and philosophers have been making variations of the same case since the early Greeks. It is not easily refuted, and certainly deserves our respectful consideration." He looked from face to face around the table as if he might be preparing to identify and rebuke the guilty snickerer. Alex looked pleased that he'd been defended in this way.

But in the very next class, Russell demolished the watchmaker argument as being based solely on faith, devoid of logic and evidence. By midterms, Alex had stopped attending class and playing ball. I ran into him once near the end of the semester. He was smoking a cigarette outside the drugstore where he worked part-time, sitting on a bench, watching the sunset.

Instead of joining Mary and her family for church, I settle into the living room at home and write about Oliver and Maria. He's discovered she has strong opinions that don't match his own. He's known that from the beginning, hasn't he? Since Zurich and their run-in with the thief?

He doesn't expect her to submit to his will, of course, to like the same books and movies, to share his politics and philosophy. His beliefs.

But what do they have in common? Do they have a future together?

11

I'm sitting on Mary's front porch, waiting for her to emerge. We're going to see the new Harry Potter movie at the mall, over my objections. It's not that I don't like the franchise—those books have been a secret passion of mine since *The Sorcerer's Stone* came out and I've seen each of the previous movies on their opening days—but it's Halloween and the little theater downtown is showing *Reefer Madness*. Not sure how I made it through college without seeing that classic and I don't want to miss out again.

The swaying porch swing induces sleepiness, my thoughts wandering to Oliver's travels, so I'm startled when Mary sits down next to me and buries her head in my chest. She's crying. Sobbing.

"What's wrong, sweetie?" I ask. "Is it Barney?" I've been dreading the day when we have to say farewell to her old dog. I'm not totally insensitive, but I'm not usually a crier myself. I'm sure I don't do a good job of comforting other people who are.

She mumbles something into my jacket that I can't understand.

"What?" I ask.

She lifts her head. "Sylvia," she says, looking up into my eyes.

"Is that someone I know?"

Now she sits up, wipes the tears from her eyes, and sniffles. "You know, Sylvia, my student from last semester. I talk about her all the time."

"Ah," I say.

I don't remember the name, but it's true that Mary talks incessantly about one particular student, a dark-haired beauty with, according to Mary, an exquisite tattoo on her shoulder, a copy of Edvard Munch's *The Scream*. Supposedly, she's a talented writer with, Mary admits, an over-dramatic style that both enlivens and blurs her essays. As I recall, she's prone to embellishment and hazy with source citations.

"What's wrong with Sylvia?"

"Rape," Mary says, whispering.

My whisper matches hers. "Rape?"

"She left just before you came."

"When did this happen? She came here?"

"Last night. Her date."

"So she called the cops? Went to the hospital?"

"No."

"No? Why the hell not?"

"Lots of women don't, Ollie. It's not an easy thing to do. They blame themselves. They're ashamed. Or pressured by the guy, or their families—their fathers, usually, who think it disgraces *them*."

"I get that, but Jesus. Tell me what happened, because this really makes me angry."

"Not much to tell. It was really hard for her to talk about it. She was at this guy's place. She didn't want to have sex, but he forced her."

"She went to his place. Willingly. Then he forced her."

"That's what she said, yes."

"Are you sure?"

"Yes, Ollie. She said he invited her to his place last night for a drink and then he raped her."

"This is the girl who embellishes her essays, am I right? That was your word. Embellish." I know I sound like a jerk when I say this. I'm just trying to understand what happened.

"She has a flair for the dramatic, yes."

"So do you believe her? About being forced?"

"Why do men always take the side of the rapist?"

"Whoa, Mary. I'm not taking anyone's side. I'm just asking if there really was a rape. I mean, if she didn't call the police, and she didn't have an exam done, and she's got a history of *embellishing*, what does that tell you? Where's the evidence?"

"Ollie, you don't know what you're talking about. You can't know what it's like. We live in a rape culture. It happens all the time. And I can't believe you're sticking up for a rapist." She pulls away from me now. Her tears have been replaced by fury.

"I'm not doing anything of the sort. Any guy who would do this is a scumbag. An animal." It's an emotional subject. I get that. I'm doing my best to keep my voice steady, hoping it will calm Mary down.

"Worse," she says quietly, less angry now.

"Okay, worse. I'm just trying to figure out the facts here. Why is that a bad thing? Look, I grant you it's a horrible crime that's all too common, and I don't understand what makes some men think they're entitled to do it. It's disgusting and horrible and a rapist deserves the harshest penalty we can dish out. But let me ask you another question. Why you? Why did she come here? You're not a doctor or a trained counselor. You're not her mother or even a friend, really. You're not a cop. You're not a lawyer. Why you?"

"For advice, I guess? Because I'm a woman? Because she couldn't talk to her family? I don't know. She just did. Why does that matter?"

"Here's what I think. A possibility, anyway, just a theory, so don't get mad. Maybe she needs some attention. She wanted an audience, and you're the one person she can lie to without consequences. If she tries it with her family, they'll either blame her for what she says happened or they'll demand action. If she goes to the police and it turns out her story isn't true, there are consequences. But you—good, kindhearted Mary—you'll give her exactly what she needs, which is comfort. Attention. A shoulder to cry on."

Mary stands. Her sudden movement sets the swing reeling.

"Bastard," she says. She turns her back to me, goes inside, and slams the door.

What? What did I say?

Mary won't take my calls. I want to apologize, although I don't think I have anything to apologize for. Still, she must be really pissed at me, and I want to make things better. I had allowed

myself to imagine a future with her. That I would share with
her my doubts, my dreams, and she would help me in my search
for the truth. About Uncle Scotty, about everything.

But after our argument about Sylvia, I wonder what my future holds. Does it include Mary?

I do some reading on the subject of rape, trying to understand Sylvia and what she has told Mary. I'm shocked by what
I learn. A surprisingly high percentage of women in the United
States experience sexual assault at some point in their lives, but
in other countries it's even worse. And that's just counting the
rapes that are reported to the police. I read on, but it's too horrible. Do you know how many children are victims of sexual
assault? And of course the number that goes unreported is far,
far higher.

I spend an afternoon writing about Oliver in graduate
school. Maria has left for Mexico, making it clear that she
and Oliver are finished, so he devotes himself to his studies.
Although most of his classes are in the business school and
law school, he enrolls in one course at the government school
on the administration of public health programs in which he
is assigned to a project team with four other students. After
they introduce themselves—one woman from Nigeria tells a
story about being raped by bandits, a woman from Bangladesh
tells a similar story about her sister—Oliver proposes a topic
for their team's project. The prevention of sexual assault is
a public health crisis, he suggests, just like AIDS or malaria.
Why shouldn't they design and plan the implementation of a
program to address the problem? Thank you, says the Nigerian.
Yes, says the Bangladeshi in a near whisper. Yes, thank you,
that's perfect, says the only other American in the group, Sylvie.

꙰

Mary finally calls. She wants to meet for coffee, to talk things
over, she says. So I head to the coffee shop, and as I approach
I can see through the window that she's not alone. She's with
a young woman, and I guess it's the student, Sylvia. I have a
very bad feeling about this. What could possibly be gained?

What difference does it make if I believe her story? Either it happened or it didn't. Either she reports it or she doesn't. Leave me out of it.

As I sit, Sylvia won't look at me, and I'm sure Mary has told her that I think she's lying. Which of course is not what I said. But what I actually said has passed into irrelevance as Mary's distorted memory of our conversation, rooted in her own bias, has ascended. Her version is all that matters.

Sylvia may not be able to look at me, but I can't take my eyes off the tattoo, which is even more intricate and exact a replica of *The Scream* than I'd imagined.

"Sylvia, honey," Mary says, "tell Ollie what you told me."

She shakes her head, but begins to speak, in fragments, just words: Date. Jell-O shots. His place. More booze. The couch. His hands. Clothes. No. Force. Push. No. Dick. Stop. Inside. Stop. Her tattoo screams.

Now she looks at me. "Professor Berger says you don't believe me."

I look at Mary, attempt a scowl to let her know I feel betrayed, and then back at Sylvia.

"I never said that. I didn't. What I said was I think you should go to the police. But the longer you wait, the harder it's going to be to make a case against the guy."

"They won't believe me either."

"I did *not* say I don't believe you. I don't even know you. But the police would investigate. Talk to the guy. Get his version of events, spot the inconsistencies in his story. Make him pay for what he did. Isn't that what you want?"

"I'm not lying."

"Then do the right thing and help protect other women from this jerk. If he's a predator, stop him now before he does it again."

"You still don't believe me."

"It doesn't matter what I believe, Sylvia."

The frustration rises in my voice because my point is not getting across. It's not helping matters and I dial that back, breathe, start again.

"The only thing that matters is the truth. Rape is a horrible crime. You were powerless against this guy, but you're not powerless now. You can do something about it. And if you don't, you will live your whole life thinking no one believed you, that you had to suffer this violation alone. Eventually, even you will begin to doubt that it happened. It will fade from reality and become just a bad dream."

And I realize I'm not talking about Sylvia anymore, but whatever happened to me as a child. Did it happen? Or was it just a bad dream? Have I only imagined it? It was so long ago.

Sylvia's eyes fill with tears. "Why would I lie about this?" she asks.

When Sylvia leaves the coffee shop, Mary cries again.

"You were so mean to her," she says between sobs.

"I didn't mean to be," I say, but I know that's how it sounded. "Here's the thing. She needs to be more convincing than she is now. I wasn't there, so I don't know what happened. But I do know it's easy—"

"Easy? Nothing about what she went through is easy."

"It's easy, as I was saying, to make allegations, especially to a friend or confidant. And you and I don't know anything about what happened. We don't know, for example, if there really was a guy. She didn't give a name or a description or an address or anything at all to convince me he really exists. Those kinds of details matter. You said she's dramatic—maybe she sat home Saturday night with nothing better to do and made it all up. Everything. The guy. The date. The rape."

"Ollie, that's a terrible thing to say."

"Yeah, it is. And if it really happened, it must have been beyond awful for her. I understand that."

"You can't."

Can't I?

"No, you're right about that," I say. "I can't, not really. But I do understand that an allegation is not a fact."

"You and your facts," she says. "You make me tired."

"Let me ask you something, Mary."

She looks up expectantly.

"Were you with Sylvia the night she was raped?"

"No. You know I wasn't." A suspicious look. She doesn't see where I'm going with this.

"So you didn't see it happen, right?"

"No, of course not."

"You weren't there when she had all those Jell-O shots? You weren't in the room when they started making out on the couch? You didn't hear her tell the guy to stop when he climbed on top of her? You didn't see him force her legs open?"

"Ollie, stop! I said I wasn't there. I was with you."

"And so how can you be so sure of what happened?"

"Because she said it happened."

"And you have no doubt whatsoever? Even though you weren't there to see it."

"Well—"

"Given Sylvia's track record, there's no doubt in your mind that she's telling the truth?"

"What's your point, Ollie? What's your goddamn point?"

What can be done? I write: Oliver's project team pulls together an impressive report filled with statistics, case studies, and a specific proposal for action that draws on each team member's expertise. They design a program that is part education, part legal and medical policy reform, and part public relations to draw attention to both the problem and the solution. Their professor is effusive with praise and suggests that they apply for a grant to implement their program on a trial basis. Will it really help stop sexual predators?

Do I doubt Sylvia's story because I'm uncertain about what happened to me? Am I a victim? Or have I imagined it? If it happened, why didn't I tell someone? When I was a kid, maybe four, five, six, Uncle Scotty did something to me. Was I raped? Did he do that to me? How could anyone, *anyone*, do that to a child? Why didn't I tell someone? Why didn't I go to my father and tell him that Uncle Scotty had touched me, or worse? Or my mother? Or Q? Because it was our secret. Because Uncle Scotty told me they would be angry if they found out. Because I was ashamed. Because I loved him. Because…I don't know why. But I didn't tell them.

And then it stopped. Uncle Scotty was gone.

Is that the reason he disappeared? Is that why I am the way I am? Why Mary isn't enough. Why no woman is enough? Why I am attracted to Mike, to that boy in high school I refuse to think about, to the boy—no, let's be honest here, there was more than one—in college? Why I find intimacy with *anyone* so difficult. Is it because of Uncle Scotty?

I want to scream. I want the world to see. But I need to know the truth. My memory isn't enough. I need proof.

No one will help me. No one will believe me. I have to find out on my own. I will find Uncle Scotty. I'll kill him if I have to, but first I'm going to find out what he did.

12

I had just started my sophomore year of college when my mother packed her car and left town one day while my father was at work. He came home, I've imagined, wondering why there were no cooking smells, no gurgling pots in the kitchen, no clinking of ice in the highball glass. He would have looked in the garage and found it empty, my mother's Audi missing. He would have checked the bedroom, the bathroom, the basement, despite having already reached the obvious conclusion that she was gone. He would have phoned her office and had no one pick up. He would have suspected, then, that something was amiss. A tiny voice in his head would have told him that this was not her ordinary tardiness. She hadn't gone out for drinks with friends after work. She hadn't stopped at the grocery store to pick up something for dinner.

He would not have called the police, not yet, because surely there was a simple explanation, a matter he could handle on his own. He might have called her friends, but none of them would have news for him, because my mother would have been selective in whom she confided.

He would have searched for a note in the kitchen or the bedroom. He might have found one.

Go to hell, it might have said.

On the phone the next day, my mother said to me, as if reporting on an interesting book she'd read, something she sometimes did, "I've left your father."

Not that I was surprised, not after years of shouting matches, allegations, name-calling, threats, accusations, and ultimatums, but I said, "You what?" On second thought, I *was* surprised. I didn't think she had it in her, not to mention the planning that must have gone into it—the new job she'd lined up in Virginia, the house she'd rented, packing her clothes and possessions and hitting the road without his catching on. Impressive.

I didn't have to ask why, but she offered an explanation anyway. A partial one.

"I've always hated Indiana," she said.

"Hey. I live here, you know."

"Of course you do, dear. But so does your father."

"But why Virginia of all places?"

There was no family connection that I was aware of—she'd been born in Illinois and raised in a suburb of St. Louis—and as far as I knew she'd never even been to the state. An old boyfriend? A current lover? She wouldn't say.

"Why not?" was all she said. It was the job, I learned later, a position in the same company she worked for in Indianapolis.

I waited to call my father, thinking I shouldn't let him know that I knew, lest he assume there was some kind of conspiracy. He should be the one to call me with this bombshell, I thought. But he didn't call, and he didn't call. Q was a million miles away in Kabul, Sally-Ann was distracted by her babies and refused to talk to me about it, although I tried a couple of times.

So finally I called him.

"Everything okay up there, Dad?" I heard music on in the background, not some depressing crooner, either, as I might have expected, but an upbeat Broadway show. *The Music Man?*

"Sure, Ollie, why wouldn't it be?"

"I don't know, I just haven't heard from you in a while. I wondered."

"Everything here is just fine and dandy. Hunky-dory. Peachy keen."

❧

That was then, three years ago. This is now.

"And another thing," my mother says, after she's already asked where I've been, with whom, and how I've been spending my time, "Mary left a message."

I guess Mary has forgiven me, because she's texted and left messages on my cell phone every day this past week and now on my mother's voice mail. Next I'm expecting to find her sitting in her car, parked across the street with a pair of binoculars. That's fine, but I'm not sure I've forgiven *her*.

"Let me guess," I say.

"She wanted to know if you were sick. Are you sick?"

"In a manner of speaking."

"She left her number. I wrote it down—"

"I've got it, Mom. Anything else? No more complaints, criticism, wise counsel?"

"Don't be a smart-ass."

"A product of my environment."

"She seems like a nice girl, Ollie."

Here's the thing. My mother has never met a girl I've dated, not since high school, anyway. I did date a fair amount in college, usually a different girl each year because multi-year relationships seemed too permanent, but they were nothing to write home about, literally, and so I didn't. There was Sandy during my freshman year, a redhead from Cincinnati who transferred someplace in Ohio because, she said, our school was too small, like living in a fishbowl; I dated Brenda for most of sophomore year, but in the spring she hooked up with a townie who drove a convertible, and I couldn't compete; junior year, the year I lost my virginity, I dated Nancy, a petite classics major from Indy, until I couldn't stand to hear her recitations in Latin and Greek one more time; and then senior year I thought I was getting serious about Rachel, a dark-haired New Yorker who, at some point right before graduation, made it clear that she enjoyed having sex with me but had no intention of marrying a gentile. So, there was really nothing to report to my parents on the girlfriend front. I'm pretty sure Mom—Dad, too, no doubt—was getting the idea that maybe I didn't like girls. So imagine her relief when she came home recently to find me with Mary, our respective states of undress and dishevelment suggesting, if not exactly proving, that we had just engaged in premarital sex. In her opinion, that makes Mary a nice girl, or if not nice, at least marriageable. Or, if not marriageable, proof that I'm not gay, which is almost as good.

In the mail, which my mother has asked me to retrieve each day so that I might discard before she has to deal with it any correspondence that looks like it might be from my father, I find a postcard from Mary stuck to the back of this week's issue of the *New Yorker*, to which my mother subscribes but which neither of us reads. There's a stack of them on the coffee table, leaning menacingly like a certain Italian tourist attraction.

The postcard is a photograph of the Tidal Basin in DC, one of the souvenirs Mary picked up on our recent day trip. It reminds me of Oliver, whom I conjured that day, and I can imagine him sending postcards from his travels—a photograph of Angkor Wat, maybe. The Taj Mahal. The Sphinx. Borobudur.

Professor Russell invited me to his house for meditation instruction. The plan was for me to show up on Tuesday and Thursday nights at around nine p.m. The first night, when I was early and actually strolled around the block once so I wouldn't seem too eager, he was laughing as he opened the door.

"Ollie," he said, "you need to lighten up."

I must have looked puzzled because he said, "What I mean is, this isn't a class you have to be on time for." He ushered me into his study and pointed me toward a cushion on the floor. He settled onto another cushion a few feet away. "Look. I saw you pass the house earlier. You could have come in then. I appreciate your punctuality in that other world"—he waved a hand toward campus—"but for our purposes here, being rigid like that is going to work against us. On this voyage, there is no scheduled departure time."

And so it began. Clark—he asked me to use his first name during these visits—explained the concepts to me. He'd light incense and we'd start with short periods of guided meditation, just five minutes to begin with, where we'd focus on the breath.

"It might seem foolish at first," he said, "but it's all part of the process of letting go, letting your consciousness emerge."

Each night he explained a little more, and gradually the meditations grew longer. I felt as though I was really making progress. Afterward, we would talk quietly about the experience, but we'd move on to other things too: life, music, books, art. His travels. Except for school, nothing was off-limits.

For our first session after my mother left my father, I arrived ten minutes early. I had to wait a minute after I rang the bell, and when Professor Russell—Clark—answered the door I rushed straight to the study and took my seat on the cushion. I probably didn't even say hello.

"Is something bothering you, Ollie?" he asked.

It all came out. My parents' separation, Q in Afghanistan, Sally-Ann's babies—which I realized were in a different category of problems, but they somehow added to the weight I was feeling. How could anyone bring babies into a world that was so fucked up?

"You're not the only one, Ollie," he said. "Think about it. My parents divorced when I was in high school. Half of all marriages end in divorce. It's common. And, unfortunately, a huge number of families have a member who has served in Iraq or Afghanistan. You're not alone."

I felt foolish then for letting those things get to me. I guess that's exactly what I'd been thinking, that this was my mess, the worst situation ever, unique to me, and of course Clark was right.

"Meditation is just the thing for you right now. Let's push it to thirty minutes. Don't think about your brother or your parents. Don't think about anything. Concentrate on the breath. Breathe in, breathe out. If you start to think about something, don't blame yourself. Just begin again."

He leaned forward and tapped the little brass gong he used to get us started. I closed my eyes, and we were off.

Mary and I are taking a break. That's how I explain it to Mom, who asks me daily about her. As yet, there's no one to take her place, so I spend the evenings at the movies by myself, or reading, sometimes writing, in the coffee shop. It's not a stimulating lifestyle, and I'm once again questioning my decision to follow my mother to Virginia.

One night I come home from the movies to find my mother on the couch in the living room. She's sprawled there unnaturally, her head on a pillow, arm twisted beneath her, one foot on the floor. If it weren't for the glass and the empty bottle of wine on the coffee table, I'd be worried that someone has hurt her. But the scene is too familiar, one I've seen replayed over and over this summer.

Silly complains that I'm no help with Dad and Q, but what am I supposed to do about Mom? She's alone, and I feel terrible about it, but what am I supposed to do?

I'm writing in the coffee shop. On the page, Oliver is struggling with direction, nearing the end of graduate school. He's with Sylvie, the woman from that public health class, or no, that would never work out, he's now seeing another woman, Marja, a Dutch student, but he's facing major career decisions. He has job offers from three large corporate law firms with international practices. He'd like to learn the ropes in New York and one day move to a foreign office to live as an expat. But which to choose?

As much as it would pain him to do so, Oliver considers calling his father to get an opinion about the three firms. His investment bank has done work with most of the important firms in the city, so he's sure to have views. But he knows his father expects him to come and work with him at the bank, so it is likely to be an awkward conversation. Instead, Oliver reasons, he'll make his own choice, then call his father to announce he's accepted an offer, a *fait accompli*.

But before he can decide, his father calls *him*, a rare occurrence.

"To what do I owe the pleasure?" he asks.

"I'm afraid I have some bad news, Oliver. It's your mother."

After the funeral, attended by hundreds, Oliver's family

gathers at home. The mood is somber, of course, but his brother and sister tell stories about their mother, her quirky sense of
humor, her foibles and idiosyncrasies, and that helps to lighten
the air. She leaves a void, but her children are buoyed by their
warm memories.

Is that what it would take to free Oliver to begin his travels?

Is this what it would be like if something happened to my
mother? Would the family come together, to reminisce, to heal?
Would Scotty be there?

13

It's time to begin my search.

I open my laptop, summon the Great God Google, and type *Scott Tucker* in the search box. Results: 58,700,000 hits.

I'll never find him.

Adding *Indiana* to the search narrows it down to fewer than a million hits. But still.

I try every combination. I search various other family members' names, estimate when Scotty would have been born and narrow the search that way. I add the high school he probably went to, something we share, but I get nothing. Too much to be helpful.

If he's dead, as my father claims, where's the obituary? If he's not, there must be a trace of him. I need specifics—date and place of birth, full name, all that. Why won't my parents talk about him?

I'm in the park, stretching, using a bench for support, trying to convince myself that taking up running again is a good idea, when a woman approaches on the jogging path. She looks at me, assessing the threat level, I suppose, and keeps going. Her stride is uniform, her posture erect, her pace modest, so I fall in behind her. After a long layoff, my own gait is more of a trudge and feels as unnatural to me as dancing. Her brown ponytail bounces, and I watch her, keeping up, more or less. After a while she slows and I have no choice but to close the gap until we're even. She smiles and resumes her previous pace, and we run together. I soon exceed my limits, however, while she looks as if she's just begun—fresh, unwilted, dry.

Am I going to kill myself to prove my manhood to this woman I don't know? Or will I make some lame excuse—a pulled muscle, a pressing appointment?

"I'm beat," I say, my breathing labored. "You're too good for me. Thanks for the run." And I slow to a stop, bent over, hands on my knees. She waves and keeps going, but then turns around and comes back.

"That was so refreshing," she says.

"The run?"

"No. Your honesty about why you were stopping. No macho games. I like that."

"The best policy," I say, trying not to wheeze.

"My name is Katrina."

"Ollie." We shake hands.

"Nice to meet you, Ollie," she says. "See you tomorrow?" And she takes off running back the way we came.

In my notebook, Oliver has begun his travels in earnest after reluctantly accepting a job with his father's bank. He starts in New York, acclimatizing himself to the bank's culture, and then relocates to London. No, Singapore, financial capital of the emerging markets, shouting distance from Asia's other banking centers.

On one of his frequent trips to Hong Kong, Oliver is at his favorite Hong pub, a place in the Lan Kwai Fong entertainment district that's usually crowded with a cosmopolitan set, a mix of expats, business travelers, and Anglicized locals. A woman draws his attention. She's tall and loud and easy to spot over the shouting drinkers who jostle for position at the bar. Her streaky blond hair flows behind her, as if she were facing into a gale. He watches her carry two stouts to a bistro table in the corner, joining a Chinese couple, the man in a sharp business suit, the woman in a dress that Oliver recognizes is expensive—either that or a designer knockoff from one of the mainland sweatshops that his charity is trying to get shut down. The standing crowd surges and the blonde woman disappears from view, so Oliver focuses on his drink and the spicy cashews the bartender has set before him.

It's late, and Oliver is thinking of calling it a night, returning to his hotel, just down the hill from the bar, maybe ringing Maria in Singapore—that's the expression he thinks, ringing, because British English still reigns here even though the Union Jack no longer does—but he's finally landed a seat and he savors it while he sips his last beer.

He senses the woman's sudden presence next to him, catches a whiff of coconut, before he sees her. He turns; she leans on the bar, flicks her hair back, and smiles a broad, white smile. Her eyes shine and her tan is dark, as if she's just come from the beach.

"I'm Kat," she says.

"Nice to meet you, Kat," he says. "I'm Oliver."

"You were staring at me, Oliver."

"I apologize if I made you uncomfortable," he says, sensing that she would prefer honesty to dissembling. "But you're a striking woman and I couldn't help myself."

"No excuses," she says. "I like that." She smiles again and sits.

They have one drink, talk about everything from the National Book Awards to the NBA playoffs. Oliver's imagination is racing back to his hotel with Kat at his side, pushing Maria from his thoughts, but when Kat takes the last sip from her Guinness she stands and presses her hand on his shoulder so he'll stay put.

"That was fun, Oliver," she says, and reaches to shake his hand.

"It certainly was," he says. He's on the brink of saying something like, "the night is still young," but this, too, he senses, would be the wrong approach with this woman.

"And now I'll say goodnight and go home, leaving you curious and perhaps a little frustrated. We'll both get up in the morning, alone, and go to work, and tomorrow night I'll probably be here again. If you're here, too, we can get to know each other better."

"That sounds delightful."

She says, "Ciao," and slips out the door.

He walks down the hill to his hotel. She was right about

both the curiosity and the frustration. She'd been coming on to him, no question, and doing an outstanding job of stirring his interest. He saw her check his hands for signs of a ring, and he noticed she had none. They were on a bullet train bound for a certain destination—her place or his, no question about that, either—when she put on the brakes. Was it fear? He didn't think so. A tactic? Most likely. Leave the fans wanting more? It had worked.

Mary has stopped calling. My mother has stopped asking about her. Life goes on. More and more I think about Oliver, how he and I are manifestations of a single consciousness, each a figment of the other's imagination. Am I real? Or is he?

My sister calls on a Wednesday night and announces that she'll be arriving on Friday evening for a visit, and wouldn't it be nice if we could all go out to dinner, her treat. My mother is frantic, enlisting me in the assault on household dust and cobwebs, clutter and general inattention. All day while she's at work I'm supposed to be cleaning, preparing the guest room for Sally-Ann—I'll be moving to the couch in the living room for the duration—scrubbing floors of their grime, relieving the appliances of accumulated spills, stains, and moldy leftovers.

On Friday, my efforts having passed inspection, we're waiting for the arrival. My mother fixes herself a drink, bourbon and soda, her second of the night, assuming she didn't hit a happy hour on the way home from work, and the ice chimes as she lifts the glass and sips. It's a sound I associate with my mother and father, together, the ritual unwinding after long days, preparing to cope with the trials of parenthood, easing the stress of marriage. But now it's just my mother.

"What time did Silly say she'd get here?" my mother asks.

"You talked to her, Mom. You said six." It's close to seven now.

"She's late."

"Maybe she meant Indiana time," I say, aware that Indiana time is the same as Virginia time, but my mother nods and accepts the bogus explanation. I imagine Oliver dealing with the unfathomable time changes as he circles the globe, spinning his watch first one way, then the other, as if it were the time on the watch face that determined his location and not the other way around. I close my eyes and see the hands of Oliver's watch, a gold Rolex, twirling like a propeller.

"I think I hear a car," my mother says. She rises, drink in hand, and peers out the window.

I haven't seen my mother this excited since one of her co-workers back in Indiana appeared on *Jeopardy*, losing in Final Jeopardy on a zoology question about wombats. ("This burrowing marsupial feeds mainly on grass, leaves, and roots.")

A car door slams. Footsteps approach. My mother puts down her drink, brushes her hands over her skirt, and checks her appearance in the hallway mirror. She pulls the door open just as the bell rings.

"Silly!" she shouts, as if Sally-Ann's visit is a surprise.

I haven't seen my sister for a few months. Her hair is short now, streaked, trying to look younger. Is that a tattoo on her ankle? We can compare.

"I'm exhausted," she says, thrusting her belly forward in an excruciating backstretch. "And my name is Sally-Ann."

"Silly dear, you're pregnant."

"Yes, Mother, I know."

"Again?" I ask.

Sally-Ann glares, then settles heavily onto the couch.

"How's Jacob?" my mother asks.

"Business is dead," Silly says, then bursts out laughing. Jacob is a mortician. It's the same joke she's told a million times since she married him. I don't laugh. My mother makes herself another drink.

Instead of going out, which I know my mother has been looking forward to, we order a pizza from Papa John's that shows up in twenty minutes. Despite her long drive, Silly is full of talk at the table.

"The twins are a marvel, as always," she says between

mouthfuls of pepperoni and green pepper, her favorite. "They're excited about having a little brother or sister."

I pick the peppers off my slice, building a mound at the side of my plate. My mother does the same with the pepperoni.

Silly wipes her greasy fingers on a napkin and takes a long slurp of Coke. "So. The reason I wanted to visit is we all need to talk." Now she's rubbing her belly, as if making a wish on the laughing Buddha. "About Q, I mean. And Dad."

At the mention of my father, Mom goes limp. The excitement over Silly's pregnancy goes out of her like air from a balloon, like stink from a skunk, and she slumps in her chair.

"I thought Q was doing better," I say.

"He was. Ups and downs, you know?"

Q hasn't been the same since his last deployment to Afghanistan. He won't talk about it. No one but me knows he was wounded, or if they do they haven't mentioned it. I'm sure he saw some serious shit over there, or *did* some serious shit, and it's hit him hard.

"Is he getting help?" I ask.

At this, Mom perks up. The suggestion that there might be someone who can help Q, someone other than her, someone competent, a professional, seems to lift her spirits.

And then Silly pokes her with another hatpin. "No. He was seeing a VA shrink for a while, but he stopped. Says it's a waste of time."

We've lost Mom again.

"What about Dad?" I ask.

"He's useless, of course. The two of them. I swear. They're more than I can handle. With the twins and now the baby on the way. And Jacob." As if Jacob is just another child she has to take care of.

And now I see where this is headed.

"The thing is," she says, "it would help a lot if you'd come see them, Ollie. Relieve me for a while? Pull your weight now that you're out of college."

"No way."

"Why not?"

"I tried. I was there, remember?"

"For about a minute."

"I've got stuff here. Work. Life. Mary."

"Mary—that's the girl who keeps calling and you don't call her back? Doesn't seem like much of an obligation." She takes a bite of pizza and keeps talking with her mouth full: "Don't look at me that way, like I don't know what's what. Mom told me."

"Mom doesn't know everything."

"No? She knows more than you give her credit for."

"Like what?"

Our mother's head is cradled in her arms on the table, and she appears to be asleep.

"Like lots of things."

Katrina, for example? Oliver? Mike? Professor Russell?

And now I'm thinking that whatever happened with Uncle Scotty is a secret everyone knows but me.

What is illusion? Is it not possible that Katrina is an illusion? That I am an illusion? That all of this—the coffee shop where I write, the Sinatra ballad on the Pandora station, the laptop itself—is an illusion?

If nothing is real, or if the only plane of reality is an existence I cannot truly experience, then what can I be said to know? What is truth? The chair beneath me feels real. I know that it is a chair. But if it is an illusion, what do I know?

"When you wake in the morning you experience certain sensations," Professor Russell said. "You feel pressure on the bladder and need to relieve yourself. You feel hunger and need to feed yourself. You may feel cold and need to cover yourself. But do these sensations exist apart from your experience of them? There is no thing such as 'hunger' or 'cold,' except inasmuch as other beings may also experience them. Your 'hunger' is not separate from my 'hunger' and your 'cold' is not separate from my 'cold.' And what are beings, what is consciousness, but a collection of these shared sensations? But if the sensations themselves are not distinct, isn't it also possible that the consciousness that experiences those sensations is not distinct? That is, rather than individual selves, we might be, all of us, merely manifestations of a single consciousness."

To which our class on "The Origins of Identity" greeted him with stunned silence. We looked at one another, absorbing the impact of what we had just heard, uncertain of our own existence, much less that of the person sitting next to us.

Manifestations of a single consciousness? What the hell does that even mean?

If nothing else, seeing Katrina is going to get me fit. For one thing, she runs all the time. We meet in the park, we head out on the trail, and when she notices that I'm struggling she urges me on.

"Just a little more, Ollie. You can do it!"

So I keep going, and every day it gets a bit easier.

And another thing, she's a wildcat in bed. It's not just sex, it's a workout. Which, I have to confess, is a nice change of pace from my previous girlfriends, including, especially, Mary. Of course it helps that she has her own place, seeing as how I do not, but her lack of inhibitions is the primary factor, and makes up for my chronic reticence. She likes to be in charge, which is fine with me. And she says my bicep tattoo is a turn-on, which in my view makes it totally worth it. When I was with Mary, I sometimes also thought about Mike because their resemblance is so strong. But when I'm with Katrina, she makes sure my attention is focused on her. No room for anyone else in the bed.

We don't, however, go out on dates. I invited her to dinner once, thinking it was the natural thing to do, maybe a movie, too, and she said no.

"Why not?" I asked. "I thought we were having fun together."

"We are," she said. "So why mess it up with formalities?"

"Formalities? Going to dinner in public is a formality? Everyone has to eat."

"You know what I mean. Dating. Getting dressed up. Holding hands. All that."

"I promise I won't hold your hand."

"Ollie," she said. End of conversation.

After one of our park runs, Katrina and I cool down, stretch and then head to our cars, which are next to each other in the parking lot. As I'm climbing behind the wheel of the Impala, thinking of Oliver's mystery woman in Hong Kong, I say, "See you tomorrow, Kat."

She stops, the door to her BMW open, and says, "It's Katrina."

At this point we've been doing our, um, workouts for a couple of weeks, and I thought I'd earned the right to use a nickname.

"All righty then," I say. "See you tomorrow. *Katrina.*"

When I show up in the park the next day, and the day after that, there's no sign of her. I call her apartment several times and get her voicemail. I imagine her checking the caller ID while the phone rings and rings. Pretty soon I take the hint.

In my notebook, I write *Katrina* and underline it three times.

And then I write about Oliver's return to Singapore when his fling with Kat is over.

It's been long enough of a break, I think, and I dial Mary's number.

Bill picks up. "Well, hello, stranger," he says. Then he's silent, but I picture him mouthing my name to Lydia, who is no doubt at his side, and perhaps to Mary, sitting across the kitchen table from him.

"Is Mary there?" I ask.

"I don't know, fella, let me check."

I hear muffled whispers as Bill receives instructions as to how he should respond.

"I guess she's not here. Good to talk to you, though. I'll tell her you called."

He hangs up on me. It's no worse than I expect or deserve. I've been ignoring Mary. I haven't returned her calls. I haven't responded to the postcards or notes I've received in the mail or found tucked under the windshield wiper of the Impala. I'm sure she doesn't understand what happened; I barely understand it myself. I only know I didn't have the strength to see her then. To give her what she wanted. Or to file Mike away somewhere deep in my psyche to be safely ignored. Maybe I do now. And besides, Katrina has disappeared.

I try again the next day, and the next, and always Bill gives me the same story. On the fourth day when I call, it's Lydia who answers.

"She doesn't want to talk to you, Ollie," Lydia says. Lydia has this thing about honesty that Bill does not, apparently. "You hurt her feelings, you know."

"Yes, ma'am," I say. "That's why I want to apologize."

I hear whispering, questions, doubts. I understand doubts. I have doubts myself.

"Hello?" Mary sniffles into the phone.

14

The long wait is over, and school has at last begun. My official title at the college is Adjunct Instructor of English, which isn't as grand as it sounds, although it satisfies my mother for the moment, especially because I'm sure she hears Assistant Professor instead of Adjunct Instructor. In any event, it means that I am a semi-regular member of the faculty and can cut back on the lawnmowing and odd jobs, which hadn't paid much anyway and managed to sap both my energy and creativity. It means that my "office" is in a gray building, in a gray cubicle that I share with other adjuncts, some of them pretty gray themselves. It also means I am poorly paid and overworked.

I sit at my workstation, squinting for lack of light, and hope that students don't appear for the conferences that I have so generously, but somewhat disingenuously, offered on the course syllabus. Between classes, when I've prepared for the lesson (or struck upon the exercise or time-eating word game that I will substitute for a lesson), I pull my notebook out of my book bag—my mother has given me a lame briefcase that I dutifully carry as I exit the house each morning but leave behind in the Impala because I am not a big enough dork to pull it off—and let my pen hover over the page.

Oliver in Vietnam, I write. *Oliver in Indonesia*. Ink flows from pen to paper, like a winding river twisting between the blue lines. I sail along, navigate the turns and rapids, the confluence with the great river, the emptying of mind and matter into the majestic ocean as I follow my peripatetic hero around the globe, from his semester abroad in Zurich, to his tryst in Mexico, backpacking in Asia, his romantic conquests in Europe, his business conquests in China and Singapore, his volunteerism on behalf of the world's poor and unfortunate. I lose track of where he's been and what he's done, who he's slept with, his trials and tribulations, his good deeds. I even find the line between Oliver's life and my own blurring.

Did I sleep with Katrina, or was that Oliver? Is it Oliver who's attracted to Mike, or is that me?

I glance at my watch—why? Coming up for air? A buzzing fly?—and see that my first class will begin in seven minutes. With my book bag slung over my shoulder I rush along an endless, sterile corridor toward the classroom. I see Mary drifting toward me. We both bob and weave in the current of students and teachers. Our eyes connect. She smiles. I smile. That wasn't so hard, was it?

The class is oversubscribed, like most in this department. Too many students in need of basic English skills or remedial reading and writing, or generally unprepared to meet the demands of college, even *this* college: older students long removed from the schools; learning-disabled teens who need to acclimate to a new routine; and, in my classes, immigrants, students of English as a second language. I try not to think of them as misfits.

A cluster of Latino students has captured one corner, but the rest of the classroom appears ethnically and linguistically diverse, generally bearing out the impression given by the names on the roster I've received from the department secretary: a dozen or so Russians and other East Europeans; five or six Chinese; two Africans; and one Korean. I call the roll, making a first attempt to match names to faces. There's a boy in the back, tall, leaning his head against the pale blue cinder block wall, who looks like Mike. It's been a few weeks, almost two months, since I've seen Mike, and I wonder if it's possible, and also wonder why Mike might be enrolled in my class. But the boy answers to a Slavic name. "Call me Sasha," he says, his voice deep, accent guttural, and I make a note: Sasha. I think of Oliver and the characters he meets in his travels. Women. Men. Young men like Sasha.

While on assignment in…Kazakhstan, say…Oliver teaches

a class at the local law school, helping students to understand private companies, securities, and corporate governance. While his interpreter repeats in Russian his introductory remarks, he gazes at the faces in the class, his eyes drawn to a handsome boy in the last row...

"Mr. Ollie?" asks one of my Chinese students, bringing me back to my own classroom.

"Yes," I say, studying my syllabus to reorient myself. Repeat after me, etc. The hour passes.

As I approach my cubicle after class, a tiny flap of white paper grabs my attention. Even from a distance I can see Mary's handwriting, the elongated hoops, the wide humps of the *M* in her name, the smiley face she imposes onto the *O* of mine: *Ollie, Call me, Mary.*

To launch our reconciliation, Mary invites me to join her and Bill and Lydia for a meal at their home. I don't tell my mother because I know she'll be hurt. I rarely eat with her, because her drinking makes it too painful, and I've never invited anyone to our house for a family dinner. So I tell her that Mary and I are going to a movie and will probably grab something quick at the mall. I feel guilty about lying to my mother. I do it anyway because the alternative is too horrible to contemplate. It's not the first time. She's happy that Mary and I are back together.

Mary meets me at the door and shows me to the living room, whispering a warning. "Don't mention Mike, whatever you do. Daddy is furious with him." I'm not sure why I would mention Mike, who is off at college, last I heard. Bill is watching baseball on television but doesn't seem particularly engrossed. Stewing in his angry juices, I suppose. He pops out of his recliner, mutes the sound, and shakes my hand.

"Mary," Bill says, "get Ollie a beer." He hasn't asked if I want a beer, or would prefer something else, but I don't say no, and Mary is accustomed to obeying her father's commands.

Mary hands me my beer, the Bud Light that Bill drinks and I can't stand, and leads me to the dining room, where Lydia

appears in a red-checked apron bearing a platter of fried chick-
en. A green bean casserole steams in the center of the table
next to a basket of rolls. I feel like I've stepped into an old TV
sitcom.

Bill tells Lydia to bring him another beer, which she does.
Lydia tells Mary to say grace, which she does. I bow my head
with the rest of them. No need to stir up trouble with my dis-
sent from this ritual. A moment of silence won't kill me. Finally,
we lift our heads, smiles all around, ready to dig in.

"How are classes going, Ollie?" asks Lydia while moving an
enormous chicken breast from the platter to my plate. Mary, I
notice, has taken a leg and has used her knife and fork to slice
off a tiny bite.

"What are you teaching?" asks Bill, poised to chomp on the
thigh he holds in his fingers.

"Oh, Bill, you know. Mary told us."

"Let the boy speak, Lydia," Bill says, his mouth full of chick-
en. "He's got a tongue, don't he?"

"Dad. Mom." Mary looks at me and shrugs, takes another
minuscule bite.

I'm sensing tension in the Berger household. Is something
going on here that Mary hasn't told me about? Something to
do with Mike?

Bill opens another beer while Mary and Lydia—they're both
drinking iced tea—talk and talk and talk. These people see each
other every day, eat dinner together most nights, and still haven't exhausted what they have to talk about. My mother and
I would have given up after the first five minutes. Not these
women, although I get the sense that the topic of conversation
is for my benefit, part of a conspiracy. Mary's sorority sister is
getting married in Detroit and has asked her to be a bridesmaid.
Lydia's niece, Mary's cousin Juliana, has just announced her engagement. Dreama, a friend from high school, is having a baby
shower. I think I see where this is going.

I weigh my options. I could excuse myself to find the bathroom, and while I'm up I could slip out the front door and move

back to Indiana. Or I could divulge that I've been sleeping with this gorgeous sex kitten I met in the park. Or I could tell Mary about the piece of fried onion ring that's dangling from her chin. Or I could get up and grab a beer from the refrigerator. One for me and one for Bill.

Instead, I say, "So, how's Mike doing?"

❧

Oliver enlists in the Army Air Corps the day after the Japanese attack Pearl Harbor. With his father's connections in Washington, he trains as a pilot and is among the first...

He's among the first ashore during the invasion of Normandy...

During the Battle of Chosin Reservoir he is wounded as the UN forces break through the Chinese lines.

As the Battle of Khe Sanh drags on...

No, it was Oliver's older brother, Declan, who was destined to carry on the family tradition of military service. Through his father's Harvard roommate, a Congressman, an appointment to West Point, and then a commission in Field Artillery, promotion, a Master of Arts in National Security Studies from the Army War College, postings to the Pentagon, Europe, Asia.

Shortly after the death of their mother from a heart attack at the age of sixty-six, Major Declan Michaels would succumb to wounds received when an improvised explosive device detonated under his Humvee near Ramallah, Iraq.

He was thirty-six.

❧

Mary had told me not to mention Mike, but I couldn't help myself. At the sound of his name, Bill's face turns red and I imagine smoke coming out of his ears. Instead of exploding, yelling at me or at Lydia or Mary, he pushes back from the table and retreats to the living room. Mary and Lydia look down at their plates. I'm not sure Mary is speaking to me.

"What?" I ask.

Lydia stands and begins clearing the table, dinner obviously over, and Mary helps her. They both ignore me.

"What?" I ask again, but the women have disappeared into the kitchen.

Am I supposed to wait there? Or go home? Neither seems to be the right thing to do, so I take my beer out to the porch, sit on the swing, and contemplate my fate.

Mary eventually joins me. She sits next to me, gazing into the night sky, at the taillights of a passing car, at a black cat dashing through the yard.

I figure she's going to lay into me for bringing up Mike when she'd instructed me not to, and I do regret what I'd said, which was purely about pushing her father's buttons. I didn't know he'd have a stroke or whatever. But I really wonder what the deal with Mike is.

"Tell me one thing, Ollie."

"What do you mean?"

"I don't know you, do I? I mean, I know your parents are divorced and you're the baby of the family, but that's about the extent of it. Tell me something I don't know. One thing."

One thing. What is she really asking? Is she asking why I brought up Mike at dinner? Is she asking—again—why I watch him when he's around? Or maybe it has nothing to do with Mike. Maybe she's just curious.

"I have an uncle," I say. "Uncle Scotty."

"Really? You never mentioned him before."

"There's not much to say. He—"

I stop, because I don't know what comes next. He's dead? He's gone? He raped me? But I don't know what's true, and so I say nothing.

Each meditation session with Professor Russell—Clark, I mean—was the same. He and the dog would greet me at the door, the dog would get shut into the kitchen, and Clark and I would settle onto cushions in the den. He'd tap the chime and begin, guiding me through the process in a deep, soft voice that sounded like it was coming from somewhere else, someone else.

Near the end of our semester together, I arrived one night a little before nine and we began right away. I closed my eyes, heard the chime sound three times, and then his soft, disembodied voice.

"Settle into the cushion, take your seat, paying attention to your posture. Make adjustments if you need to." There was a pause then, and I considered if I was comfortable, if there was any part of my body that would distract me. "Now," he continued, "I want you to fill yourself with awareness. Imagine you are a bowl. Lift a pot of green tea and pour. Fill the bowl to the brim." I pictured the bowl, the teapot; I poured.

"If your attention strays, never mind. Fill the bowl with awareness again. See the awareness fill your bowl."

He went on like that, talking about awareness, and being aware of the breath, so that my thoughts were only focused on my breath. Until they weren't. I tried to fill myself with awareness again, then tried counting my breaths, but all I could see, all I could think of was that face in my dream. And Professor Russell. It was no longer the face touching me, it was Clark. They were the same.

"I can't," I said and struggled to my feet.

"Ollie, what's wrong?" He grabbed my arm. "Are you okay, Ollie? What's wrong?"

"I have to go," I said. "Please let go."

At the door I picked up my shoes and ran outside into the dark.

15

I make reservations at The Bakery, our town's nicest restaurant, and by "nicest" I mean most expensive. It's a pre-Christmas celebration, the end of my first semester teaching, and also—Mary's surprised I remember this, but it's the one relationship skill I'm good at—our six-month anniversary.

As I walk from the Impala to Mary's door, I pat my pocket to make sure the small box hasn't somehow disappeared between the jewelry store and Chestnut drive. I know she'll like the gift.

There's no sign of snow, although in the last day or two the temperature has dived below freezing and there are low, gray clouds hovering that may bring flurries, if not more. I ring the bell and watch my breath billow before my face.

Lydia greets me. Her apron is Christmas-tree green, with a pattern of dancing reindeer, including one sporting a red nose that actually lights up. She holds out a plate of cookies. These, too, are in festive colors and shapes: holly leaves with green sprinkles, snowflakes with white frosting, yellow stars.

"Merry Christmas, Ollie," Lydia says. "Mary will be right down."

I take a snowflake from the plate, nibble on the edge, and nod. "Same to you, Mrs. B."

"Ho, Ho, Ho." It's Bill, emerging from the living room with a beer in his hand, Barney at his heels. A bell rings in the kitchen and Lydia hurries off, handing me the plate.

"Cookie, Mr. B.?" I ask.

"What the hell," he says, grabbing a holly leaf and a star. "It's Christmas, after all." The dog looks up hopefully.

Mike is in the living room, eyes glued to the television. I'm surprised to see him. I didn't think he'd be home so soon.

Bill follows my gaze. "Got home last night," he growls. "Hasn't moved from the TV since." Bill gulps from his beer, obviously not pleased with his son, the college dropout, heading for the army instead, which is the reason I wasn't supposed to mention him. I want to tell Bill that Mike never wanted to go to school, that no one listened to him. But it's not my family, so I keep my mouth shut.

Mary chatters on the way to the restaurant. She wants to get tickets for the tour of homes that the local historical society is hosting. The owners of these big fancy houses go all out with their Christmas decorations, she says, and visitors strolling from door to door end up singing, as if the whole point of the event were the carols. She moves on to another topic but I'm thinking about Mike. I've told myself a million times that Mike is just a nice kid, my girlfriend's little brother, and that's why I think about him.

"Okay?" Mary asks.

I'm driving, but I look at her and say nothing. I look back at the road.

"You weren't listening," she says.

"Sure I was," I say. "Tour of homes. Christmas carols."

"That was *ages* ago," she says, and now she turns to look out her window. I see the reflection of her pout in the dark glass.

"I'm sorry, sweetie. I was just thinking about the restaurant, how much fun tonight will be."

She turns back to me. She wipes at her eye, although I see no evidence of tears. She smiles. "It will be fun, won't it?"

"You bet," I say.

At The Bakery, a few tables are occupied, but the restaurant isn't as crowded as I thought it would be. The recession is to blame, I assume. Who can afford to eat out these days, especially at these prices? The hostess seats us at the table I asked for, the one in the front window. The Bakery is actually an old bakery that thrived for years, I'm told, on the town's main street. The windows once displayed towering cakes and trays of cookies and pastries, and downtown shoppers would stop, gaze, and come in the shop to buy desserts and treats for special occasions. Now, the baked-goods business having succumbed to competition from grocery stores and mass production, it's us in the window instead.

I hold the chair for Mary while she sits, and I take the other chair. The waiter pours ice water, and Mary looks around at the other diners, gives a little chest-high wave to someone she recognizes.

Now that our coats are off and we're seated, I get a good look at Mary. She's wearing a red sweater with a Christmas-wreath pin, and her nails, which are on display as she studies the menu, match her sweater. "You got a haircut," I say. "It looks nice."

She looks at me over the menu, her eyes bright and happy. "I didn't think you'd notice."

"I notice things," I say. "Sometimes."

And we both laugh.

Dinner is a long, drawn-out affair of ordering, waiting, plates being cleared, more waiting, and new courses arriving. As usual, Mary's taking her tiny bites, prolonging the main course while she carves her way through a bloody steak. Between mouthfuls, we talk about one of the teachers from the college who may or may not have been fired for inappropriate physical contact with a student, but neither of us has real facts so the subject subsides as soon as it arises. A picture of Sasha, the handsome Russian kid in my class, flashes through my mind, but I change the subject to make it go away. There's a rumor of an increase in class size for next semester, but that's all we know.

"Can you imagine?" she says. "Increasing the load without increasing the pay?"

I nod. We both know that's exactly what will happen. It's happening everywhere, and adjuncts have no choice but to take it and be happy they have jobs.

During the interminable delay before the dessert arrives—we're planning to share a piece of flourless chocolate cake, the chef's specialty—we run out of things to talk about. I'm about to ask Mary about Mike's plans, although I've resisted through the entire meal, when the cake materializes. And just then I remember the box in my pocket.

I let my hand drop below the table and feel the shape of the box through the coarse fabric of the blazer. Candlelight pops, like flashbulbs, in the facets of Mary's broach, the little wreath I've never seen before, that she probably digs out every Christmas.

The cake, a chocolate brick dripping with fudge sauce, absorbs our attention. We are drawn to it, like a black hole of cosmic density, and I leave the box where it throbs in my pocket. We pick up our forks and attack, Mary boldly, as if it is her role in our pack to make the kill, and she does, mercilessly. I take a smaller bite and let the chocolate sit on my fork, weighing it, before moving it to my mouth. Mary is on to her next bite before I've swallowed my first.

I can barely taste it. Is it bitter? Burned? And suddenly the box feels heavy in my pocket, so I return my fork to the table, reach into my blazer, and pull out the tiny black sarcophagus, adorned with a tiny red bow.

"An early Christmas present," I say, although I choke on the words as if the chocolate binds my gullet. I sip the last of my wine, clear my throat, and repeat myself: "Christmas present."

"If it's present, how can it be early?" Mary asks, suppressing a giggle, her eyes wide and bright with anticipation. I laugh at her little joke.

I slide the box toward her across the expanse of bright tablecloth. Mary pushes our cake aside.

"If you don't like it, we can return it for something else." I'm looking at that wreath on her breast.

"I'm sure I'll love it, Ollie." She reaches for the box, takes a deep breath, and opens it. The light vanishes from her eyes. In fact, her whole face has turned dark.

It's hard to read Mary's expression, which is part surprise— the effect I was going for—and part horror—not what I had in mind at all.

"I know how much you like brooches," I say, although by this time I've realized my mistake. She hasn't moved. I take the box from her hands and remove the new pin, this one in the shape of a Christmas tree, with little red stones for ornaments.

I hold it next to the candle. "See how the stones catch the flame?"

Mary pushes back from the table, drops her napkin on the chair, and rushes toward the rear of the restaurant. Everyone else in the room watches her go and then turns to look at me. I'm a cad. They've suspected as much all along.

I return the brooch to the box and put it back in my pocket. I thought she'd like it. Women like jewelry, don't they? And I'd shopped at the nicest store in town, spending more than I could really afford. Her parents paid for her college, but I'll be weighed down by student loans until I'm fifty. It was thoughtful, but frugal. The clerk was sure Mary would love it. I don't know why I bothered.

The check comes and I pay it, choking again, this time on the size of the bill. I sip water, since the wine is now gone, and I wait. Two nearby tables empty. A couple along the side wall leaves. I begin to wonder what I did wrong. And where's Mary? I'm about to go looking for her, wondering if she might have slipped out the back door, when she emerges from the bathroom. She walks slowly toward me, retrieves her napkin from the chair, and sits. She takes a drink of her water.

"You don't like it," I say.

"I like it fine, Ollie."

"What's the matter, then? Are you sick? Or is it that time...?"

"Honestly, when I saw the box," she says, and then stops. She drinks more water. "When I saw the box, I thought it was something else."

Uh-oh. What a dolt I am. I get it now.

"But what else were you expecting?" If I admit that I know what she was expecting, doesn't that make my misstep worse?

"Honestly," she says again.

The waiter returns, asking if there's a problem. We both shake our heads.

"Honestly what?"

After a moment she says, "A ring."

"A ring," I say.

"Yes. And why not? We've been dating for six months, it's

our anniversary, which you were so sweet to remember, and it's Christmas. My favorite time of year. This is such a romantic spot and the meal was superb. A perfect night to propose. Or so I thought."

"Oh."

The restaurant is empty now. The waiters are standing in the back, arms folded across their chests.

"I'm sorry," I say.

"I'm sorry, too, Ollie."

So we go, and I feel the box in my pocket, a lead weight.

When I get home after dinner at The Bakery, an expensive fiasco, I pour myself a drink from my mother's liquor stash, which she now keeps in a kitchen cabinet. I'm not sure who she thinks she's fooling.

I long for someone to talk to, someone to give me advice. Not just about Mary, although God knows I need help there, but about everything. Teaching, which I don't love. My writing, such as it is. My future. Life in general. But there is no one to talk to. I've tried talking to Q, my big brother, who used to be my go-to guy for this kind of thing, but his one-word answers to my questions are less than helpful. My father is a financial whiz—I guess you have to be to keep track of sales and accounts payable and all that—but he's never been good at dealing with personal matters, and since Mom escaped his clutches he's been beyond useless. I couldn't talk to Silly even if she'd hold still for five minutes. I have buddies from college, but we're not close, and we've already lost touch.

I'm tempted to pick up the phone to call Clark. Professor Russell. But I can't. After that last meditation session, when I thought I was making progress in the exploration of my consciousness, when I began thinking of him differently, I knew I could never talk to him again.

It was the voice. Sensuous, probing, reaching inside me, touching something deep within. The face.

16

I've been writing in my notebook and have accumulated dozens of pages about Oliver and his travels, but don't know who to show the work to or what to do next. I've never written anything before. Is it any good? Is it publishable? I've read plenty, of course, and Oliver seems as intriguing a character as anyone in contemporary fiction, with the added benefit, that, in a way, he isn't fiction. He lives inside my head. He knows me. I've always known him. He's thinking my thoughts.

I've got plenty of time to write, too, because Mary isn't speaking to me. Again. Without distractions, Oliver's story flows.

At school, between classes, I'm in my cubicle. I know where Mary's office is, and I avoid her, moving between classes along a parallel corridor. I even use a restroom that is out of my way in order to minimize the chance of bumping into her. At my desk, I push aside the textbook we're using, unable to read for the umpteenth time about the Misfit and the Grandmother, which in any case is beyond my mystified students' comprehension. I love Flannery O'Connor, but "A Good Man is Hard to Find" will fly right over their heads. Instead, I pull the morning's newspaper from my book bag. I'm not really reading it. I'm turning the pages. I'm browsing headlines. But something catches my eye in the community calendar: a talk and book signing by a local author, a novelist and short story writer, to be held at that coffee shop I like. And it strikes me that's exactly what I need. A writer—a real writer—who can look at my work and tell me how to get it published.

So after my classes are over, I go. It's cold. The roads are slick, but at least there's plenty of parking. As I walk from the Impala to the coffee shop, icy rain peppers my face. My book bag is bouncing on my hip and my hands are dug deep in my pockets. I'm miserable, but it's a momentous occasion. My heart races as I think about what the future holds once I've made this connection. I turn the corner, the shop now in sight, and slip on a patch of invisible sidewalk ice. My feet launch into space, and I land on my ass.

It's mostly my ego that's bruised by the fall, but my butt is going to feel the collision for some time. I look around, embarrassed, and am relieved that the street is empty. I struggle to my feet and step carefully around the ice.

The coffee shop is warm but nearly empty. There's an older guy in a tweed sport coat leaning on the counter, as if he's waiting for something, and I peg him as the writer. A couple of teenagers, who look as if they could be my students or Mary's, are at a table along the wall, but I doubt they're here for the reading. I'm not sure what to do, having never attended anything like this before, so I take a seat, and then I feel conspicuous because I don't have a coffee or anything in front of me on the table. The older guy is looking around, seems as uncomfortable as I am, but he's the one who's going to be reading just to hear his own voice. I wonder if now is the time to approach him with a copy of my story about Oliver.

Just as I open my bag to pull out the binder, a couple comes in. They claim a table next to mine, drape their black leather coats on the chair, and go up to the register to order.

Then another couple enters. The place isn't empty, but it's still not exactly a crowd, and I wonder if they'll call the whole thing off. I bet the weather has kept folks away. Will this writer want to read to only a handful of people? Isn't that embarrassing? Demeaning?

But I see him signal to the woman behind the counter— pretty, pale complexion, dark hair in a bun, with a pencil tucked behind her ear—that he's ready. And so she abandons her station, comes out into the room, and addresses the patrons.

"Okay," she says, wiping her hands on a streaked canvas apron, "I guess we should get started."

It wasn't exactly noisy in the shop before, but now all con-versations have stopped, and eyes turn toward the woman. I realize I haven't seen her before, although I've been coming to this place for months.

"Thank you all for coming."

I look around the room and count five, including myself but not counting the teens who have packed up their gear and are heading toward the door.

"I'd like to introduce Bruce Owens"—she turns toward the guy in the sport coat and indicates him with both hands, as if displaying a used car—"who's written a novel—"

"Short stories," he says.

"—a collection of short stories. I haven't had a chance to read it, but I'm sure it's terrific. Okay, then. Bruce?" She claps her hands together lightly and we, the audience, follow her lead with our own polite applause.

She steps back to allow Owens to move in front of the three occupied tables. As he does this, I notice that one of the cou-ples is looking at each other questioningly, each offering a shrug in response, as if they have found themselves in this audience entirely by accident, have considered leaving, but are now re-signed to stay to see what happens.

Bruce Owens clears his throat. He opens a book that looks as if he might have let it sit out in the rain overnight, its cover faded and splattered, and begins to read.

Instantly, my mind is on Oliver and the pages I plan to show this writer. I imagine them one day being part of a short story or a novel, in an actual printed book. But am I being presump-tuous? Is there some rule about imposing your work on other people, especially when the other person is a published writer and you're nobody? But if what I propose to do is not done, how can I ever break in? How can I be like this Bruce Owens, a book in his hands, reading his own words to an audience? An audience that has now shrunk to three, because the couple who was there by mistake have slipped away. But still.

I should listen. What if I speak to him afterward and he asks if I liked the reading? Wouldn't I ask, if I were in his place? You there, the fellow clutching those pages as if they hold the last secrets of the universe, what did you think about the climax of that story?

But now he's finished already, having read for only a few minutes, and the couple at the next table, the only other people in the shop, are applauding. I applaud with them, although I haven't taken in a single word the man said. The couple stands, so I also stand. I see now that they have a copy of Owens's book, one that is just as shabby as his own, and they step forward, holding the book out to him. As proof they know who he is? Or a gift—look what we found and present to you?

The writer pats his pockets and extracts a pen. He laughs and smiles and he writes at length in the couple's book, which I now understand they have offered to him to inscribe. I suppose I've heard of autographed copies of books, but I never thought about how the autographs came to be there. He returns the book to the couple. They nod cheerfully and retreat, clutching their cherished treasure.

Which leaves me. I will hand him my pages, explain that I am also a writer, and wonder if he would give me his opinion—his honest opinion, of course. He will confirm for me that the work is brilliant, maybe not brilliant but noteworthy, that I should be the one standing up in front of people reading stories, and he's surprised that he hasn't heard of me. What books have I published?

But he's already slipping into his topcoat. He's pulled a cigarette out of the pack in his shirt pocket and settled a fedora on his head. As he passes me, his sleeve brushes against the pages in my hand, and I am unable to move or speak. He raises his collar and seems to brace himself for the cold, his lighter poised before the cigarette that is now held tightly between his lips. He opens the door, I hear the ignition, and before the door has closed behind him the smoke of his cigarette has entered the coffee shop as if to fill the void. He turns, marches briskly past the shop's window, and hurries up the street.

The pages are still in my hand.

❧

I'm standing at the coffee shop window looking out at the cold street and Bruce Owens's retreating figure.

"Can I get you something?" says a voice behind me.

Having lost sight of the author, I turn away from the window to see the woman with the pencil behind her ear who has come out from behind the counter again. She's bent over, wiping a table with a cloth, and now she stands up straight before me.

"Coffee? Tea? Anything?"

"I—"

"What did you think of that guy?" she asks

"The writer?"

"Yeah."

"I'm not sure what to think." If I'd listened, maybe.

"Because I loved it. He really captured that experience, you know?"

"You read a lot?"

She blushes and looks away. "Mostly junk," she says. "It's an escape. A place I can go to get away from this." Her sweeping gesture takes in the coffee shop, and maybe the whole downtown, the city, her life, as if it is the source of some deep, dark oppression. "You know?"

"I think I do."

"But his stuff. It was heavy. Makes you think. I loved it."

"Yeah. Makes you think."

"My name's Jennifer," she says.

"Jennifer. It's nice to meet you." I should buy a coffee, have a reason to stay. Jennifer is young and attractive, maybe a student, with clear, smooth skin and bright eyes. If Mary and I are done, it wouldn't hurt to meet someone new, would it? I look out to the street again, then back to the shop and the crazy paintings on the wall.

"And you?"

"Me? My name is Ollie."

"Hello, Ollie."

I order a coffee. "I'm a writer too."

17

The semester is over and the holiday break looms. I'm looking forward to the time to write, but I also know I'm going to be bored out of my mind. No Mary to see bad movies with. No Mary to get me out of my mother's house. I'm actually thinking of calling her to apologize for whatever it was that I did—or didn't do—when my cell phone rings. It's her.

"I'm sorry for the way I behaved, Ollie," Mary says. "The holidays make me a little crazy."

"I'm sorry, too," I say, although I don't think my non-proposal was exactly a crime against humanity.

"It's just that Lydia is putting a lot of pressure on me these days, you know? She wants a wedding and grandchildren, and it got to me. I cracked. I'm afraid I took it out on you."

Grandchildren? We're getting way ahead of ourselves here, I think.

"Anyway," Mary says, "let's not let it spoil our Christmas, okay?"

"Okay," I say. "Sounds good."

What I don't say is that I've got a date with coffee-shop Jennifer, hoping to at least partially fill the void. Discretion is the better part of valor, said someone, I have no idea who.

And just like that, the empty holiday break gets refilled. Mary rattles off a list of engagements—brunches and parties and Christmas dinner and New Year's Eve—and my head is spinning.

⁊

It's Christmas morning. Mary calls first thing, while her family is sitting around their tree opening presents and eating Lydia's special coffee cake with almonds and raisins. She's calling to make sure I'm coming to dinner that afternoon. My mother is invited, too, although I'm not at all sure that's a good idea.

At our house, it's just me and Mom. Silly is in Indiana with her husband and their boys, and I gather that my father has invited them all to his house for dinner, along with Q. I have to give my sister credit for accepting that invitation.

My mother has opted not to have a tree this year, although we did decorate the hanging philodendron with lights and little silver balls. Festive enough. When I enter the kitchen after speaking to Mary, Mom is beating eggs for an omelet, bacon is sizzling in a skillet, the toaster glowing on the counter, and I could swear I smell cinnamon rolls baking in the oven. Mom hardly ever cooks anymore, so this is something of a surprise. I pour coffee and sit at the kitchen table to await an explanation.

"Are you seeing Mary later?" she asks.

"We both are, Mom. We're going to the Bergers' house for dinner, remember?"

"I don't think I can, Ollie. I'm not feeling well."

"And yet you're out of bed, looking chipper, cooking up a storm."

"I didn't say I was sick. Just…not well."

She serves the runny eggs and undercooked bacon. The toast is burned, two black shingles staring back at us from our plates; we both ignore it. I must have been imagining the cinnamon rolls. No Christmas miracle after all.

"I'm not thrilled about dinner over there either," I say. "You know I don't even like gatherings of our own family, never mind someone else's. But I have to go. No choice. If you come, at least I'll have someone to talk to."

She smiles. She likes the conspiracy angle. I've said the right thing.

"Shall we open our presents?" she asks. She's already standing, abandoning the barely touched food on her plate.

"Sure," I say. "Let's."

There's a small pile of wrapped packages in the living room. It's a far cry from the excesses of my childhood, when mounds of gifts threatened to overwhelm the tree, mostly for Silly, Q, and me, from various grandparents and aunts and uncles we barely knew. But we'd mailed our presents to Silly and Q weeks ago, and Silly's gift for me is an Amazon.com voucher that arrived by email. I had a rare text message from Q, something about "keeping it loose."

"You start," Mom says.

We're on the sofa and the presents are on the coffee table. I take the littlest one first. It's a CD, obviously, and I can see through the thin wrapping paper that it's a Greatest Hits album by New Kids on the Block, a band I haven't thought about in years, much less listened to, in a format that's as outdated as the band. But Mom remembers that I couldn't get enough of them when I was in middle school, listening to the same album over and over, and I'm sure she's proud of herself for this choice. I pull the paper off and give her a kiss on the cheek.

"It's great, Mom. Thanks. You next."

There's only one for her and it's a big box with wrapping that I obviously had nothing to do with; the gift department at Belk does a great job with ribbon and paper.

"You shouldn't have," Mom says perfunctorily, impressed, I suppose, with the size of the box and struggles with that ribbon.

"Let me get scissors," I say.

"Don't you dare," she says, because she'll save the ribbon and bow for another present, or for a decoration she intends to make but won't actually get around to.

Finally she wrangles the bow off the box, unfolds the tissue inside, and pulls out a blue terrycloth robe. She normally wears a thin flannel thing that she's had forever, and she seems happy with this replacement, although after taking it out and modeling it for me, she refolds the gift and puts it back in the box. I predict she'll never wear it.

There's one more package, and it's for me. My mother has wrapped this herself, with what appears to be an entire roll of tape. Finally I'm able to break through the tape and the paper to find an atlas. Not just any atlas, but a 1923 atlas, leather-bound, published by the Rand MacNally Company. An atlas?

"You said you wanted to travel, Ollie," my mother says. "I thought…"

It's such an odd present, I hardly know what to say. Odd and oddly appropriate.

"It's great, Mom, thanks."

I flip the pages, landing on India, a possession of the United Kingdom, and notice how the borders have changed. No Bangladesh, no Pakistan. I think of Oliver's travels to these places, places that don't exist in the world as it used to be. A simpler time? Less dangerous?

We arrive for dinner at the Bergers' at three o'clock, the appointed hour, just as flurries have begun. Even though I smell nothing on her breath, I can see in my mother's glazed eyes that she's been drinking. I don't know how she managed this without me noticing earlier, because we have been together the entire day. While I occupied the living room, studying my new-old atlas, she baked in the kitchen, within sight, not twenty feet from where I sat on the sofa. She bears the result of that effort now, a soupy pumpkin pie, and I imagine—this makes me chuckle, but I'm sure my mother doesn't notice—that the pie is as soused as she is. It's not funny, though, and I mentally rebuke myself.

I press the doorbell, but no one answers. I hear Christmas music and laughter inside, so, with a shrug to my mother, I push open the door.

We are greeted by the smell of the roast goose and something else, something with garlic I think, but also with a holiday cacophony that our family once exuded but has now lost. Besides the music—it's a brass group, brassily playing carols—the television is on in the living room, laughter bounces in stereo from the dining room and kitchen both, and I swear I also hear angry shouts coming from upstairs. Barney appears, tail wagging. I close the door and aim my mother toward the kitchen.

"Hellooo," I call, doubting I can be heard over the din. But when we enter the kitchen, there's Mary and an older woman who looks a lot like Lydia but isn't. At the sight of us, the not-Lydia woman puts down her glass of wine and wipes her hands on a dishtowel.

Mary kisses my cheek and manages to grab the pie from my mother's hands just as it's about to dive toward the floor. I can't help thinking it might have been better for all of us if she'd let it fall. But with the pie safely stowed on the kitchen table along with the other pies—far more successful pies, from the looks of them—Mary takes my mother's hand.

"Welcome, Mrs. Tucker. Merry Christmas! We're so glad you could come." Now the other woman steps forward, her hand on Mary's elbow. "And this," Mary says, "is my aunt Helen."

"Drink?" asks the elderly aunt, as she hands my mother a glass of wine before I can intercept it.

I'm hopeful that dinner will happen soon, before too much damage is done, but by the state of the kitchen I estimate that we're still a good two hours away from sitting down to eat, by which time my mother will have killed a bottle of Chardonnay. At least.

I can't bear to watch what I'm powerless to stop, so I move into the living room. It's empty, despite the blaring television and the stereo, as if each is trying to be heard over the other.

But now I see Lydia coming down the stairs, her face a solemn mask. I'm sensing the Berger house is not all sleigh bells and Santa Claus on this Christmas Day. She spins into the hallway toward the kitchen without acknowledging my presence, pastes on a smile, and greets my mother. I move into the dining room, but I can hear the kitchen chatter of the four women.

What would happen if I left? What if I opened the front door, went out to my car, and drove away? We're not far from I-81. I could head north, pick up I-70 and be in Indiana before midnight. Or south. South would be better, through the Valley, following the Blue Ridge, away from family, looking for Oliver, wherever he is. Looking for salvation. Civilization. Comfort. Looking for a sign.

The door opens, as if my prayer has been answered. And there's Mike, in his hoodie and sweatpants, back from a frigid run.

"Hey," Mike says.

"Hey," I say as Mike bounds up the stairs. It's all I can do not to follow.

&

After Mike has gotten himself cleaned up, Aunt Helen opens a second bottle of wine, and Bill finally emerges from wherever it is he's been sequestered. We are called in to dinner, and Mary and her mother deliver platters of food to the table, removing the pine-scented Yule log centerpiece to accommodate it all. We sit where Mrs. Berger directs: my mother and Aunt Helen on one side, Mary on the other between Mike and me, and Bill at the foot, as far away from Lydia as she can manage without banishing him to the patio.

Before anyone can begin, Lydia pops up, switches off the overhead fixture, and lights three tall candles on the table that cast ghoulish shadows on us all.

"Oh, hell, I can't even see the damn food," Bill says, but it's a feeble protest. As Bill reaches for the mashed potatoes, Lydia says, "Mary, will you say grace?" and Bill sits back in his chair. Mercifully, Mary's blessing is short, and Bill is freed to begin.

"Mary," Lydia says, "will you please ask your father to pass the potatoes?"

Ah. I remember that kind of tension at the dinner table: booze flowing freely; Mom and Dad not speaking to each other; the kids forced to act as go-betweens. Maybe the Berger version of this story will have a different outcome, but I doubt it.

"Such a handsome boy," my mother says in Mike's direc-tion. "Are you in school?" I'm sure I warned my mother not to mention Mike and school, but the truth is I don't think she can make the atmosphere much darker than it already is, so I don't try to change the subject. Mike, who wasn't paying attention, apparently, realizes that we're all staring at him, waiting for his answer. He looks up, grunts a reply—whether he means yes or no is anyone's guess but it seems to satisfy my mother—and stuffs a forkful of goose into his mouth. Bill scowls.

The second bottle of wine is now empty and Aunt Helen

and my mother have switched to drinking spiked eggnog that Helen serves out of a massive crystal bowl on the side table. Neither woman is eating.

"I was telling Barack the other day how glad I am he was reelected," Helen says. She sips her punch.

"You spoke with Barack Obama?" I ask. "That's amazing." I feel Mary's hand gripping my leg, her fingers digging into my thigh. That's a clear signal, even for me. I shut up.

"Of course. He and Michelle come to see me all the time. Delightful people, for coloreds."

"Don't listen to this loony-bird," Bill says. "She's gotten it into her head that the orderly who cleans her bed pan at the nursing home is President of the United States and the nurse's aide is First Lady. And that's just the start of it."

Lydia stands, and I wonder if she's going to start yelling at Bill for insulting her aunt, who doesn't seem to be the least bit offended. Instead, Lydia retreats to the kitchen and returns with a pie that she drops in front of her husband before removing her apron, flinging it on the dining room floor, and running up the stairs. Stunned into silence, even Helen and my mother, we all watch her go. Upstairs, a door slams.

It's among the deadliest holiday dinners I've ever attended, and I've been to some Tucker family doozies.

Bill now turns his attention back to the table and says, "Who wants pie?"

While Bill mangles the pumpkin pie—not the one we brought—and loads up the dessert plates, my mother rises to help herself to an eggnog refill. For a moment she gazes into the empty punch bowl, frozen with disappointment.

"I'll just make another batch," is what I think she says. Her face contorts with a mix of resignation and determination as she wraps her arms around the bowl and heads into the kitchen.

Bill smothers his mound of pie with whipped cream and has inhaled most of it when we hear a monstrous crash. Mary and I jump from the table and rush into the kitchen to find the tile floor awash with eggnog and shards of crystal. My mother, who looks puzzled, stands in the middle of it all, surveying the disaster.

☙

I've driven my mother home, put her to bed, and returned to the Bergers' house. Mary is waiting for me, with her coat on and her gloves in her lap, and before I have a chance to sit down she takes my hand and leads me back out to the Impala.

"Let's take a drive," she says.

"It's cold," I say.

She glares at me, shakes her head, and gets in.

I get in. "Well, it is," I say.

The sky is thick and black. It may be those little bacteria swimming in my eyes, but I see flurries at the edges of my vision, a flake to the left, two to the right. No one is on the road. The town is quiet and dark; sensible people are at home sitting by the fire.

We pull away from the house.

"I'm sorry about my mother," I say.

"What?"

"I should have told you." It's not something you go around telling people, though, even your girlfriend. Hi, my name's Ollie, and my mother's a lush.

Mary raises her hand from her lap and lets it fall, dismissing my apology, or my mother, I'm not sure which.

"She'll buy Lydia a new tureen." I can't stop apologizing. Out of necessity, it's something of a Christmas tradition in my family. "It was an accident you know." At least I think it was an accident.

Although my eyes are on the road, I know Mary has now turned to look at me. I steal a glance at her.

"I don't give a damn about the stupid tureen," she says.

If it's not the tureen and it's not my mother, what then?

I've turned into the old part of town, where some of the historic homes have been dressed elaborately for the holidays, with garlands of evergreen, giant red bows, and hundreds of white lights. I drive slowly so we can take in the beauty, so there will be no need to talk.

"I'd like to live in a house like this one day," Mary says, pointing to a massive brick colonial set back from the street and guarded by two towering oaks.

"Must be hell to rake the leaves," I say, and I feel Mary's glare again. I'm apparently missing the point.

"Of course I'd have to be *married* to live in a house like this."

So that's it. Again. That's the subject we're meant to be discussing. Not the horror show of a dinner. Not my mother. Not the broken bowl. Not the Christmas decorations.

I open my mouth to speak, but nothing comes out. There's nothing I can say that won't further upset Mary. Even a proposal, which is out of the question, is likely to set her off. It's too late for that. My best course of action, now and almost always, is to keep quiet. I close my mouth.

As I drive—there's a stop sign just ahead that I'm slowing for—I think of Oliver and what he might do in this situation. Of course Oliver would be in Beijing, or Jakarta, or Paris, and the woman sitting next to him would be exotic, a Eurasian woman, perhaps, with roots in China and France, royalty maybe, but she'd demand a commitment, because that's what women want.

Not that I blame them, but I'm not ready.

After we drive around for an hour or so, Mary has cooled down some. She even makes a crack about my mother and her aunt Helen being soul mates. She instantly apologizes for saying it, but I laugh because I'd been thinking the same thing. My mother's not quite as crazy as her aunt, but she seemed to enjoy having a drinking buddy for the evening.

When we get back to her house, she invites me in, but I think I've had enough of the Berger family for one day, so at the front door I wrap my arms around her, pull her close, and give her the deepest, longest kiss I can manage.

"Merry Christmas," I say, when I disengage. I get back into the Impala with Mary watching me from the porch, a little breathless, I think. She waves as I drive away. The snow has begun in earnest.

After Christmas, I resume my search for Uncle Scotty, but I'm stymied. I'm no private investigator, and while I did a fair amount of research in college, back then I was looking for things like alternative translations of Heraclitus and journal articles on the origins of phenomenology, not the whereabouts, which could be anywhere on the planet, of a particular human being, who may or may not be alive.

Still, having reached a dead-end on the internet, I make phone calls: to the Marion County Clerk of Court in Indiana to find out if they have any record of Scott Tucker—birth, death, or otherwise—but I run into the same problem there I had online—too many hits. I call the local newspaper, the *Indianapolis Star*, but I can't even get anyone there to talk to me. I call the Indiana University on the off chance Scotty had been enrolled there, but the registrar won't give me any information about anybody.

He could be anywhere. How will I ever find him?

Although we cannot be said to know something about which we admit even a molecule of doubt, we can know other facts intuitively. And yet, our intuition is not infallible. Put another way, my intuition that Uncle Scotty is alive does not make the fact true.

What I sense, what I perceive, could very well be wrong. It may be little better than a guess.

Professor Russell had once asked our class, "Does knowledge come from within? Or is it external to the knower?"

At first I was puzzled by the question. Isn't it circular?

Tentatively, I raised my hand, and Russell nodded in my direction.

"The answer, it seems to me, is unknowable," I said. "Kind of like the proverbial tree falling in the forest. We *assume* it makes a sound, but we can't be certain."

"So knowledge depends on both the known and the knower?"

"Yes."

"How, then, can we consider anything to be true?"

I pondered his question.

"We can't," I said, sinking into a pool of undergraduate despair.

If there's nothing we can know, what's the point?

Fortunately, Mary hasn't programmed all of my time while we're on Christmas break, so I'm still able to contemplate where this Oliver story is going. I head into the coffee shop to see Jennifer and write, occasionally taking a break to talk to her. She's a student, as it turns out. She'd like to study literature—I am delighted when I hear this—but is leaning toward nursing or something practical. My father would be pleased, but I'm disappointed.

I drink coffee and focus on Oliver. What does he know? What's he thinking? What's he doing with his life?

18

A few days after Christmas, Mary and I are visiting the only bookstore in our town. She picks up a thick paperback, the latest saga by Erin Mallory, and I say, "Her work is the epitome of schlock. It's so schlocky I haven't even read it yet and already I've forgotten it."

Mary says, "How can you say that? It's exciting to read. It tells a story. I love her work."

And I say, "Stories are for children. I don't want a story. I want to be transported." I'm not sure I really believe this. It sounds like something a serious writer, someone like Bruce Owens, might say. It's what I'm trying to do with the Oliver stories, telling tales that are important, not just entertaining.

"I don't understand you sometimes, Ollie. When I enter the world she's created I'm totally transported. She excels at transporting the reader."

"That's just escapism, honey. I'm not talking about time travel or whatever it is. Fantasy worlds with wizards and dragons. Corporate sado-masochism. I want to go to a higher plane. I want to read something that makes me think." Mary must have forgotten that we've seen all the Harry Potter movies together, and that I told her I'd read all the books, because she doesn't call me on this blatant untruth. I'm actually fine with wizards and dragons, so I'm not sure why I'm arguing with her.

"That's just it, Ollie. I have to think enough at work. When I read for pleasure, I really don't want to think."

I don't say, *Yes, that's it exactly.*

I pick up a copy of a Somerset Maugham book I read in college and show it to her. "This, for example," I say. "This guy transports me. To India, Southeast Asia. He's dealing with important issues, too—class conflict, oppression. It's exactly what great art should be."

"I bet it's deadly dull," Mary says.

"Just the opposite."

"Of course that's the sort of thing you'd like," she says. "Why am I not surprised?"

❧

It's New Year's Eve, and Mary and I have been invited to a party at the home of one of her high school friends. It's a celebration I've never enjoyed, although this year, at least, I am attached— if that's the right word for it—and will not be spending the evening with my mother, getting drunk and waiting for the ball to drop on TV.

Still, I struggle, as I always do, with expectations. The perfect frame of mind. The perfect kiss at midnight. The perfect predictions for the year ahead. Will I find Uncle Scotty? Will I finally propose? Will I call the whole thing off?

Will I meet someone else?

We are in a corner of the kitchen. The fluorescent ceiling lights here are bright, painfully so, and I see Mary's pores, an oily strand of hair. Is that a scar on her chin? How have I not noticed that before? Do I really want to spend the rest of my life with this woman? When the light shines on me, does she see my flaws? Those ears I've always hated, my crooked front teeth. And let's not forget my missing toes, which she has yet to notice.

I drink deeply from the mug of too-sweet red wine, then reach for the bottle at my elbow for a refill. It is unbearably hot in the kitchen, and someone opens a window. I feel a welcome draft of cold air and catch a whiff of marijuana. It feels like I'm back in college, the cheap wine, the weed. Now all I can think about is finding my coat—did we leave our jackets in the upstairs bedroom?—and going outside to join the pot smokers. I take a step in that direction and Mary grabs my arm.

"Ollie," she says, "this is Johanna."

I shake Johanna's hand. She's almost as tall as I am and has a broad, square face, brown hair that dangles in a braid down her back. I have no idea who this person is.

"You know, my friend from Sweet Briar. I've told you about her. She and Somchai might be moving here, too. Isn't that wonderful?"

I nod and smile. Who the fuck is Somchai?

As if summoned by my unspoken question, a guy materializes at Johanna's side, and we are all shaking hands and laughing. This Somchai is the color of creamy peanut butter and I can't help feeling that I've seen him before. He towers over Johanna and I'm looking up into his bright, handsome smile.

And now I remember. I haven't seen him, but I've written about him.

Oliver, on a visit to rural Thailand, strolls through the placid grounds of a Buddhist temple. He is troubled by his relationship with Maria, but in this place his worries evaporate. He listens to the chant of monks in the temple hall, breathes the smoke of burning incense.

As he walks, he catches sight of a young monk watching him. A novice surely. He is so young, a teenager, with a close-cropped shadow of black hair that frames his handsome face, wide brown eyes that distinguish it.

As the monk approaches, Oliver sees that he is taller than the others. His one-shouldered robe reveals a solid build, muscled arms that suggest a life more active than contemplative. A boy from the fields, honed by toil, his face is smooth and brown. The monk bows toward Oliver as he walks, his hands pressed together in greeting.

The monk's crooked grin appears. "Hello," he says.

But that seems the limit of his English, because he continues in Thai, which Oliver does not understand. The monk points to himself and says, Somboon. Oliver says his own name and holds out a hand. Somboon raises his and limply lets Oliver grasp it. Somboon motions to a bench and they sit. But there is nothing they can say to each other, so there are smiles and gestures. Somboon points to the temple and Oliver says it is very beautiful; Somboon nods, says something in response, and

Oliver believes they are in agreement. The temple certainly is beautiful.

Who is this boy, this beautiful young monk?

❧

At the New Year's Eve party, standing next to Mary, I say, "It's a pleasure to meet you, Somchai."

"You, too, Ollie."

"I'm sure Mary and I will be seeing more of you two."

"You bet."

"You look familiar. Have we met before?"

"I don't think so," he says.

And then it hits me. This is Mike's friend, the guy he was with at the coffee shop in the mall. I'm sure of it.

"Guess I'm mistaken," I say, but I know I'm not. How well does Mike know him? How well does Johanna know him?

I whisper to Mary that I need fresh air.

"Are you out of your mind? It's freezing out there."

Somchai and Johanna exchange a glance, no doubt wondering what's gotten into Mary's crazy boyfriend.

"I'll be right back," I say, and wave, a silly gesture that I stop halfway. Instead of finding my coat, I go immediately to the door and I'm shivering before I can close it behind me. But it's too late; I can't change course now. I have to get away, from Mary, from Somchai.

The smokers are gone. I'm by myself outside, staring at the frozen sky.

❧

The next day, the first day of the New Year, Mary is furious with me because at midnight I was nowhere to be found. She exchanged kisses with Johanna and Somchai, making excuses for my inexcusable behavior.

I've apologized. I explained that the door locked behind me. She was right about it being ridiculously cold outside, so I ran around to the front and...

She raises her hand. "Don't even," she says. "I don't want to hear it."

"But, Mary—"

"Don't," she says again.

So this is what the future holds.

&

"Some things we just know," said a guy named Tom in my epistemology seminar with Professor Russell.

"Are you talking about intuition?" asked Russell. "Intuition is sensing without a rational process, often based on experience. That is, without thinking. Is that what you mean?"

"Okay. Maybe that's the word. I mean, you just know some things without having any proof."

"Like what? Give us an example."

Tom thought about it. "Like the sky. I know the sky is blue. I can see that it's blue."

"What would you say if I told you that the sky is *not* blue?" The class laughed.

"No offense, Professor, but I'd say you were nuts." The class laughed again.

"What color is the sky at night, Tom?"

"Black. But that's different. That's due to the absence of light."

"So during the day the sky looks blue because of the presence of light?"

"Correct." We could hear a moment's hesitation in Tom's voice as he began to sense the trap.

"Then maybe it's the light that's blue, and not the sky?"

Tom was stumped, and then tried again. "But everyone just knows. Sky blue. Blue sky."

"Except when it's black, or red or yellow and occasionally green."

"Um, right," Tom said. "I mean, no."

Trap sprung.

"How is your knowledge in this case different from belief?"

"Belief isn't based on anything. It's just faith."

"Like belief in God?"

"Yes."

"Why do you believe in God?"

"Because He exists."

"And you know that how?"

"It's just something I feel. I've always known it."

"So it's an *a priori* belief, right? Something you know without proof."

"Exactly."

"Is it something you can prove, Tom?"

"You don't need to prove it, Professor. Because you just *know*."

"Like knowing the sky is blue, Tom? Is that it?"

Despite my failure to propose and despite my disappearance on New Year's Eve, Mary has decided, apparently, that I'm better than nothing or, at least, the best she can do for now. Despite my recent dalliance with Katrina, which I don't disclose to Mary, discretion, valor, etc. Despite my frequent visits to Jennifer at the coffee shop, which have not progressed any further than pour-overs and literary chitchat and are unlikely to do so now that I've learned she's a single mother. Not that I have anything against single mothers, or children, for that matter, but life is already pretty complicated and I'm just not ready to go there. No offense, Jennifer.

So Mary and I keep going to movies and eating ice cream afterward even though the nights now are frigid, but the subject of marriage no longer comes up. She, presumably, is biding her time, waiting for someone better to come along. Or for that Brian guy to come to his senses.

And what am I doing here?

Knowing that she's given up on me, having concluded, possibly after a long discussion with her mother and a gaggle of her sorority sisters, that I'm hopeless, I come to my own conclusion: now is the perfect time to pop the question. I'm fond of Mary and hopeful that I will grow to love her in time. I could do far worse. Marriage, settling down, will make everyone happy. Mary, of course. My mom. Bill and Lydia. Mike. Maybe not Mike, but everyone else for sure.

A romantic setting, another dinner at The Bakery, with candlelight and champagne, would give it all away. She'd suspect something was up.

I consider other options. Surprises.

19

I t's Q," Silly says when she reaches me on my cell phone. "He's done it."

She doesn't need to say what it is he's done. Unbelievably, we haven't discussed it in the family—that's how we've always dealt with worrying issues—but I'm sure we've all been thinking about it. Whatever he did in the war, whatever he saw, whatever happened to him, it has affected him to his core. Every day there's another horror story, another gruesome statistic, and so it's not really a surprise to Silly or to me when Q kills himself.

Except, of course, it's a total surprise.

I don't know what to say to my sister. I start to cry, although I never cry. Q. Unspeakable. So I say, barely getting the words out, "He was deeply troubled."

"No shit," says Silly.

Could I have done anything? Could anyone have done anything?

I imagine Oliver faced with someone like Q, a brother, a friend, a classmate, someone with whom he'd once had a connection.

Would he have realized there was trouble? Would he have known the time had come to intervene? Would he have rushed to his brother's side, taken the gun from his hand, forced him to tell him what he needed?

What could Oliver have done?

Fuck. Why didn't Q call me? Why didn't he talk to me? I could have helped him. Why didn't I know. Why didn't I call him?

❧

Silly leaves it to me to tell Mom about Q. Of all the tasks I have had to perform in my life, this seems the hardest. Nearly impossible. Beyond impossible.

Never on very solid ground herself—crying over nothing when she's sober, raging against invisible demons when she's not—she will be devastated. There will be fierce sobs, thrown dishes, more ebullition than I can handle. I consider calling Silly back. She's the big sister, the eldest. She was closer to Q at the end. She should be the one. I can't. I really can't.

"Mother," I practice, working out the sobs, "there's been…"

"Mom," I try again, "Q…"

She comes in the door after work, kicking off her heels immediately, heading straight for the liquor cabinet. I'll wait, I tell myself, until she's numb, and then I'll tell her. Better for both of us that way.

We make spaghetti and garlic bread, a salad. She doesn't ask why I'm home for dinner, she doesn't ask about Mary, or my classes, or why I'm so quiet. Our topic is the weather, the latest political scandal, an outrageous neighbor whose dog is allowed to roam free, crapping on our lawn. And then the phone rings.

"Get that will you, Ollie?" she says. "I'm too tired to get up."

"Mom, there's something I have to tell you," I say. The phone keeps ringing.

"Ollie, the phone."

I push back from the table, go to the phone, and lift the receiver. I hang up.

"Ollie, what did you just do?"

"Mom—"

The phone rings again. I lift the receiver and hang up again. I'm sure it's one of her friends from Indiana, someone who knows, someone calling to offer condolences for a loss she doesn't yet know she's suffered. I have to tell her now. Right now.

And so I say, "Q's dead."

Silence.

And then she says, "There's been some mistake."

"No mistake Mom."

"Someone else. That happens all the time. You misunderstood."

"No, Mom."

Her lips tremble. She looks at the floor as if studying the whorls in the tired carpeting. I expect her to cry, to explode, but whatever storm has been unleashed is raging inside her.

"How?" she asks.

I tell her the truth. PTSD. Afghanistan. Mission creep. Senseless. IEDs. No one to trust. Buddies dead. For some a holy war. For others a patriotic call. For Q, the last bad option. And how can any of us pretend to understand. We didn't know him. We couldn't know. We didn't see what he saw. My father's pistol, a .38. In his brain.

I imagine how I might write the scene in a book. There is no pretty way to paint that picture.

The spaghetti sits on our plates, growing cold, the marinara sauce taunting us. Our chianti glasses mock us, untouched. She pulls a piece of bread apart but leaves both halves on her plate.

Q is fifteen and I'm ten. Our parents argued about something that morning, something new or something old, it's all the same, and we're outside, pretending we didn't hear the shouting. But we did hear.

He is showing me basketball moves he learned from the JV coach at his school. There's the proper dribbling technique, the two-handed shovel pass, the hook shot. I like the hook because it allows me to shoot the ball over taller players, which is just about everyone. We play HORSE. Q doesn't let me win, but he does let me come close.

Next, we play war in the backyard. This has always been Q's favorite game and invariably he is the U.S. Army battling the enemy in World War II. Sometimes I am the Germans, sometimes the Japanese, but today he says we are both on the same side, storming the beaches at Normandy. We run down the hill behind our house and hide behind bushes. With our superior weaponry and marksmanship we manage to wipe out the enemy in a matter of minutes, seizing control of the battlefield. Victory is ours!

When we hear our father's car pull out of the garage and leave, we declare peace and go home.

What is death? Silly says she's comforted by the belief that we leave this life to join Jesus in a better one. Mary is less specific but believes there is a heaven, somewhere in the clouds, that takes us all in.

It's a pretty fantasy, and I know it gives them comfort, but I don't buy it. How do they know? Where's the proof?

When you die, you're dead. Buried in the ground or ashes scattered to the wind. Dust to dust. Dead. I believe Q is at peace (i.e. the absence of strife), but I have no expectation that we'll be reunited.

"Death," Professor Russell once said, "is the ultimate unknowable." The course was one on existentialism, but Russell on that day was sidetracked from our examination of Sartre and de Beauvoir. News had come that morning that a student at the college, a classmate of ours named Lacy, had been killed in an automobile accident while driving back to campus from Indianapolis.

I looked at the seat she usually took, now empty. Lacy. I was having a hard time picturing her. We'd gone to different high schools in Indy, we lived in different dorms. I'd spoken with her maybe twice. And when she talked in class I didn't look at her. I looked at my own notes, or thought about what I might say. Was she pretty? I couldn't remember. She had vanished.

"We can speculate about death," said Professor Russell, slumped in a stiff chair at the front of the lecture room. "We can believe that it has its own energy, a force that survives beyond life. Or we can posit that it is simply the opposite of life—a void, the absence of energy. Unconsciousness as opposed to consciousness. But the fact is that we cannot know. Despite religious superstition, despite claims by charlatans of paranormal activity, encounters with God or bright lights, no one has ever returned from the dead. No one has ever communicated with the dead. And no one knows, with certainty what the hell death really is."

I meet Mary for coffee. It's a struggle, and I no sooner begin when I have to stop to regain my composure. But I tell her.

"He's in a better place now," she says.

"No," I say. "He's not."

"He—"

I hold up my hand and she stops.

Q's dead. It's not better. It's just fucking nothing.

At first, Mom refuses to go to Indiana for the funeral.

"What's the point?" she asks.

"For Q," I say. "For Silly. For me."

She can't leave work, she protests. She doesn't want to see my father. She can't bear to look at the casket.

"I failed him," she says.

Not in a million years would I have said so, but I believe she's right. Didn't we all fail him? By being distant, by not asking questions, by not reaching out to hold him when we knew he needed us, by not even trying to feel his pain, didn't we make the pain worse? Isn't that the hard, cold truth?

"No," I say. "Mom, there was nothing you could have done. Nothing anyone could have done."

Mary offers to come with us, but I tell her I don't think it's customary to bring a date to a funeral. In any case, it's too intimate, and a step I'm not ready to take.

"You didn't know him," I say, puzzled that she would even suggest such a thing.

"For you," she says. "I'd be going to comfort you."

But I don't want to be comforted. This is Q we're talking about. My brother. I want to grieve. It's supposed to hurt. I want it to hurt.

And so my mother and I climb into her Audi. I'm behind the wheel, her tears finally come, and she cries all the way to Indiana.

20

I had wanted to spend the drive dwelling in my good memories of Q, how he protected me, taught me things, how he was the best big brother ever, but instead my mother demands my attention. She is a quivering sack of bones in the passenger seat, alternately moaning and clutching my arm. It's a miracle I don't slam into a bridge abutment on I-70.

Just when I think I can't stand to be in the car with my mother for another minute, we arrive at Silly's. The house is chaotic, as I knew it would be. The twins run from dining room to living room to kitchen and then make the circuit again, their shrieks meant to extract as much attention from the visitors as possible. Silly seems not to notice, a serenely pregnant Buddha ensconced on the sofa. I shake Jacob's hand—he also seems oblivious, and I wonder if this is a natural condition of parenthood or if he and my sister have made an effort to achieve this sort of grace. Meditation, maybe. But then I take a closer look at his eyes, and I understand. My brother-in-law the undertaker is stoned.

I unload Mom's suitcase from the car. She, at least, seems overwhelmed by the raucous boys, momentarily stops crying, and gratefully accepts Jacob's offer of a bourbon. I remain standing near the front door, anxious to leave this chaos, but reluctant to move to my destination: I'll be staying at my father's, in the house where I grew up, in the house where Q shot himself in the head.

As I finally withdraw from the turmoil and return to the Audi, I wonder if there isn't another option. A motel? An old friend? Or maybe I could just sleep in the car, blame the long drive for my insuperable exhaustion.

All of which will only postpone the inevitable, and so I take my leave from my sister's house and head across town to the home of Quentin Tucker, my father.

This used to be my home. Is it still? I stand on the front stoop and I wonder. Should I ring the bell? Should I use my key?

Before I can make my choice, the door opens. There stands a shrunken little man, my father, unwashed hair combed over his balding head, dandruff liberally sprinkled on the dark shoulders of his sweater, the same maroon cardigan he's worn for at least twenty years. A haze of cigarette smoke swirls in the living room behind him, and I'm already finding it difficult to breathe.

My father looks at me, his eyes open wide as if he might have seen the ghost of Q. I'm told I resemble my brother: same height, our hair the same dirty blond, our ears on the large side, same for our noses, all cut from the same Tucker cloth.

"How are you, Pop?" I say. Then, recognition.

"Ollie," he says. Disappointment clouds his voice.

I don't blame him. I'm disappointed too.

We're seated in the living room. I'm in the recliner that has always been his domain, he's on the sofa where my mother used to fall asleep each evening, reluctant, I always assumed, to join my father in bed.

"Why did he do it, Ollie?" my father asks. He's smoking again. I thought he'd quit years ago when his doctor said it was either that or die strapped to an oxygen tank. Q smoked too, a habit he picked up in Afghanistan. It's something they shared then, a way to hold on to his namesake. Or maybe Dad has started recently, after Q's death, no longer concerned about the consequences. That seems likely and understandable. A slow death he would probably welcome.

"I don't know, Pop. I really don't."

"You must have talked. He said you two talked sometimes."

It's true. He was my older brother and sometimes I called to say hi, or he did, and I had called to ask what he knew about Scotty. But there's talking, and then there's talking, and we hadn't really communicated for years. I didn't know him anymore.

"He never said anything about what was bugging him. Or not much, anyway. He wouldn't talk about the war."

"The fucking war," he says.

"Yeah," I say. "The fucking war."

Other than Silly, no one in my family is religious, and I'm relieved that Q's service is held in the funeral home and not a church.

I'm surprised by how many people turn up, though—my parents' friends mostly, older couples who look vaguely familiar. But there are younger people too—men who look like they might have gone to high school with Q, some clearly veterans of Iraq or Afghanistan, a good many in uniform. I suppose I should feel sorry for them, wonder who's next to succumb to the epidemic, victims like my brother. But I don't give a damn about them. Why couldn't they help Q? Why didn't they stop him? How dare they come here, when it was their war that killed my brother?

A woman who arrives alone is, I'm reasonably sure, Q's old girlfriend, Natalie. They broke up shortly before Q joined the service, and that may have been part of the reason he went. She's crying, clutching a handful of tissues. Maybe she blames herself for what he's done? Join the club, Nat.

The casket is closed, of course. Silly never said, but Jacob has confided that Q was barely recognizable. He'd blown his brains out and taken half his face along with them. Nothing there for the mortician to reconstruct. Jacob wasn't involved, as the funeral home has a policy forbidding its people to work on their own family members. On the one hand, I'm glad I don't have to see him. I don't think I could stand it. On the other, I'd like to put my hand on my brother's body, to touch him one last time, to say goodbye.

The planned service is abbreviated. No one from the family will say anything, as if we're still in shock. There is no eulogy for a life so short, no greeting to his friends, no words of comfort. The music is over and the funeral director looks as though he's about to herd the mourners out of the building. Really? That's it?

"Wait," I say, surprising even myself. Did I say that out loud?

"Ollie, what are you doing?" my mother asks, more of a hiss than a whisper.

I stand, push past Silly and Jacob, and stumble toward the front. There's the casket, surrounded by flowers, the white roses my mother selected. I gaze upon it, picture Q at rest within, and turn to face the crowd.

"That's all he gets?" I ask. "Recorded organ music and a prayer to a god he didn't believe in? Where are the stories? His high school exploits? The cute shit he did as a boy? You, in the back, you Marines or whatever you are, haven't you got stories about Q in Afghanistan?" My voice has grown stronger, louder, and I can see on their faces—on the face of the old girlfriend, on the faces of his buddies, on the faces of my parents and my sister—that they are horrified.

What am I doing, indeed. This isn't like me. I don't have outbursts. I sit quietly and obediently while the world goes on around me. I don't take my abuse seriously. I don't tell anyone. I don't do anything to find the uncle who abused me. I don't go off on the adventure I tell myself I want. I don't tell my girlfriend how I feel about her. I don't admit to myself how I feel about her brother, for Christ's sake. And I sure as hell don't make a scene at my brother's funeral.

My fury spent, I take a step toward my seat, sensing the relief of all present that my rant is over. Then I spin back in front and face them again.

"Really, people. I want to know. Can anyone tell me? Why the fuck did he do this? What could we have done to stop it? What could you have done?" I'm pointing at them all. "What could you have done? And you? And you?" I clutch my chest. "What could *I* have done?"

&

After my rather public paroxysm, my mother and sister both hug me and ask if I'm okay, and my father grips my arm, which is as demonstrative as he ever gets. Jacob, accustomed to the histrionics of the grief-stricken, puts his arm around me and hustles me through the back door of the mortuary, where, out of the sight of the other mourners, he produces a doobie the size of his index finger, like a magician conjuring a rabbit from a hat. I don't decline. I'm soon my mellow, oblivious self and am able to rejoin the family in time to trail the hearse to the cemetery to say our final goodbyes to Q.

Following the burial, which, even under the influence of Jacob's dope, is as cold and lifeless as the funeral had been, a few people stop by Dad's house to express condolences. It's a struggle to keep our parents apart, but somehow they're never in the same room at the same time, another minor miracle for which I am grateful. Along with the people, who are all a blur to me, come flowers and casseroles aplenty. Also booze, but not enough, and soon the house empties. When the guests have gone and Silly and Jacob have taken my mother home with them, it's just Dad and me.

Being in this house brings back memories. Oliver isn't my first foray into the world of fiction. As a kid, I created a secret identity: Revilo. Revilo was a dynamic point guard on the basketball court, a dazzling tight end on the football field, gifted at anything he attempted. Need a star for the school musical? Revilo's your man. Hoping to find a leader to breathe life into the student council? Look no further, Revilo's here.

"Are you all right?" my father asks.

He sounds genuinely concerned, but he's the one who looks as if he might be swallowed by the couch.

"Yeah, I guess," I say. He's afraid, I suppose, that I'll be the next to crack, that Q's death will somehow show me the way. Another fragile son lost. Maybe that's because he knows, has known all along, what Scotty did to me.

"We'll get by," he says.

"Sure," I say. The thing is, though, I'm not so sure.

My father lights a cigarette, and I open the last beer. As we sit there, the silence weighing on us, I think we're going to talk about Q, but the moment passes. Q will slip away from us, forgotten. We'll never speak of him again. What could I have done?

"Do you remember Revilo?" I ask.

"Who?"

"Never mind," I say.

It's time for me to get back to Virginia. The Audi is out in front of Dad's house. It's loaded up with my stuff, and I'm leaving in a minute to collect Mom from Silly's before hitting the road. While I'm waiting for Dad to get out of the bathroom so I can say goodbye, I pull the photo album out from under the coffee table.

The picture of Uncle Scotty is gone.

Mom's still upstairs packing when I arrive to pick her up. Silly is beached on the sofa again. The twins are as frenetic as ever, racing up and down the stairs; I see a diagnosis of ADHD in their future. This would be a good time for a private chat with my sister, maybe one more reminiscence of our Q, maybe a bit of worry about our father, maybe my own burdens, as inchoate as they are.

So I begin, telling her about my memories of Uncle Scotty, what I think he did, but Silly raises her hand to stop me. She shakes her head.

"I'm telling you, Ollie, you're wrong. Dead wrong."

"I don't think so, Silly. I've been having these memories. Dreams too. The more I think about it, the more it comes back to me."

She narrows her eyes, like she's seeing me for the first time. "What's this really about, Ollie?"

"I—" I start, but I don't know how to say it. Professor Russell. Mike. Uncle Scotty. "I think, well maybe, in some sort of ambiguous way, I mean, when I think about men, that is, certain men, I guess what I'm saying is, I'm confused. And I think it has something to do with Scotty."

There's a shriek from upstairs and a thud right above our

heads. What mayhem have the twins gotten into? Silly doesn't flinch, but she does shake her head. Because of the twins? Or because of what I've told her? Did she even hear me?

"Do you think Scotty knows about Q?" I ask.

"Doubtful."

"Maybe he was there. One of the people we didn't know? He'd come back for his nephew's funeral, wouldn't he?"

"Ollie. Stop. You're off the deep end now. Way off. Let it go."

Another crash erupts upstairs.

Why do I always feel uncomfortable in this house? If Silly is in one of her fastidious moods, I don't feel as if I'm allowed to touch anything. If the place is a mess, as it is today, there's nothing I'd want to touch.

I need to try one more time. "I'm telling you—again—I think that's what Uncle Scotty did. It explains a lot."

"And I'm telling you—again—it's impossible."

"What happened to him, then? Where did he go? And why?"

"A million things could have happened. Dad told us he was dead, so maybe he is. And even if he's not, he obviously doesn't want to have anything to do with us. Why can't you leave it at that?"

"I'm not lying, Silly."

"I didn't say you were. You're just wrong."

"Maybe I am. But I have to find out."

"Waste. Of. Time."

She sounds so certain. Does she know something she's not telling me?

"Why don't you believe me, Silly? Q didn't believe me, either. Why doesn't anyone believe me?"

At last, Silly reaches out a hand for my help and rises from the couch to check on her hooligans upstairs. Mom still hasn't come down, so I'm left alone in the living room.

Detecting a sweet odor emanating from the basement, I follow my nose and find Jacob in his man cave, eyes fixed on the wide-screen TV that displays what I think at first is a cartoon but soon realize is a video game. I played my share of video games in college, although nothing like a kid on my floor in the dorm—we all called him Tommy, but I don't think that was his real name—who practically lived in front of the set and still managed to graduate cum laude. I've never seen a setup like Jacob's though. The TV is enormous and there are massive speakers on either side, aimed right at the leather chair where Jacob sits entranced.

When he notices me, he waves his arm in the air, trying to clear the smoke, I guess, and points me to another chair, where there is a second game controller waiting, as if he's been expecting me. The twins are too young for this stuff, and I wonder if this is how Silly and Jacob entertain themselves. It seems like not such a bad way to escape the frenzied reality of their lives upstairs. No, not Silly. It would be totally out of character for her. She's never liked games.

I sit. I don't notice Jacob doing anything, but the action commences on the screen as soon as I pick up the controller. It's a game I've heard of but never played called Puppetmaster, which is essentially a game within a game where two rival puppeteers race to assemble marionettes that then do their bidding to build and dominate a world that resembles the backstage of a theater, with its complicated system of pulleys and curtains. It doesn't take long for Jacob to sever the strings of my puppet and send my puppetmaster tumbling to his death from the catwalk above the stage—head, limbs, and appendages scattering into the shadows. Game over.

Jacob lights a joint and passes it to me. I've always wondered what Silly saw in her husband, but until the funeral I've not spent much time with him. He's a good-looking guy, in a nerdy sort of way: tall, sturdy, dark, but with horn-rimmed glasses. He's a computer science geek who also happens to do triathlons, but couldn't manage to escape his family's mortuary business. No wonder he's a pothead.

"Ollie, I'm ready," my mother calls down the stairs.

If she smells anything, if she recognizes what she smells, she says nothing. I take a last hit on Jacob's joint, pass it back, and then head up to begin the long drive home.

❧

On the drive home, my mother is mostly silent, staring out the window. When we cross the border into Ohio she remarks on the welcome sign in the shape of the state, which vaguely resembles a human heart.

"It's an ugly state," she says. "I've always hated Ohio."

She also hates Indiana, as I recall. I don't feel compelled to talk, and she doesn't speak again until we hit West Virginia. At least she's stopped crying.

Traffic just then is heavy. There are trucks merging from the right and we are being passed on the left by a string of motorcyclists a mile long, with their unmuffled bikes, gray ponytails flapping in the wind behind them that make me think of Professor Russell. It takes all my concentration. But then the trucks and bikers are gone, fading in the distance ahead, and I can relax again.

And then she says, "I knew he was going to do it."

"Who was going to do what?" I ask.

"Q," she says. "I knew he was going to kill himself."

"I think on some level we all knew," I say.

"No. I mean I *knew*. That day, I had a feeling. A vision."

"A vision?"

"Don't sound surprised. It happens all the time, Ollie. It happens all the time."

"No, Mom, it really doesn't."

"Suit yourself. But I can see the future."

21

Silly's baby is born: Suzanne Quentin Reynolds, to be known as Suzy Q. Silly emails pictures. Mom *oohs* and *aahs* and bugs me to drive her back to Indiana for a quick visit. So here we are, just weeks after Q's funeral.

Mom's upstairs with the baby and the twins, who are quiet for a change. Jacob is at work, I suppose. With nothing better to do, I head over to Dad's because Silly says he's having a hard time dealing with Q's death. She thinks it will do him good to be reminded that he has another son.

I phoned from Silly's, so I know he's expecting me. I let myself in.

"Pop?" I call.

He's sitting in his recliner, eyes open, staring straight ahead. No mistaking me for Q's ghost, at least, but he doesn't seem to recognize me at all.

"Are you okay, Pop?"

Now he looks at me, lifts just his fingers in a sort of wave. I sit and we stare at each other for a minute, then I get up and go to the kitchen.

"You want something?" I ask. There's beer in the fridge so I grab one for each of us. I open the cans, stall, then head back into the living room.

We sip our beers. I know he's still suffering over Q's death. I am too. But drinking beer and keeping my father company is not the real reason I'm here. No time like the present, so I take a deep breath and start.

"Pop, why won't anyone talk about Uncle Scotty?" I pull that old album out from under the coffee table and turn to the page where his picture used to be. I point to the blank spot. "Not Mom, not Silly, not you. What's the deal?"

"Dead," he says.

"So you said. But I don't believe you. If it were that simple, I'd know about it. You've all erased him from memory, and I want to know why."

"No."

"Tell me about him."

"My little brother. You were named after him."

"My real name is Scott?"

"His real name was Oliver. Oliver Scott Tucker." My father's eyes close, and he appears to have fallen asleep.

"Dad?"

He begins to snore, and the interrogation is over.

I had his name wrong all this time. No wonder I couldn't find him.

With everything that's been going on in my life—teaching and Mary and especially Q's death, trips back and forth to Indiana—my writing has fallen by the wayside. I've missed it, missed escaping into Oliver's world.

What's he been up to?

We're back in Virginia now, and I pull out the notebook.

Oliver has long suspected that the reason his Uncle Sandy disappeared is that he was involved with drugs, using or selling. But no one in his family talks about him, and so he can't be sure. What else could it be?

Oliver wonders, what happened to Uncle Sandy?

Coffee-shop Jennifer comes up with the bright idea that the cafe should host an open mic night for local writers, and she urges me to sign up.

I don't know what to expect, having never done anything like this before. I'm hoping there are one or two familiar faces in the audience, although I can't imagine who that might be. In fact, when I show up, the shop is packed, but I recognize no one. Jennifer has set up an actual microphone, which seems unnecessary in such a small venue, but it does provide a semblance of professionalism to a production that is otherwise strictly amateur.

I'm scheduled for the middle of the program, which means I'm unable to focus on the early readers. They look mostly very young, like high schoolers. I think they're reading poetry, although it's hard to tell. One girl recites her stuff without once looking at the paper in her hands, which is impressive. Another girl speaks so softly no one can hear her, even with the mic, but we applaud anyway. A scruffy guy wearing grease-stained jeans strums an out-of-tune guitar and mumbles something about being homeless. If that was an act, it certainly was convincing.

Then it's my turn. I've chosen not to read from *Oliver's Travels*, stories that I've come to realize are about me, and maybe not sufficiently disguised to preserve the facade of fiction. Not sure I've made the right choice, though.

I rise, step to the microphone, shuffle the clipped pages of my story. For a moment I imagine myself as Bruce Owens, reading from my very own book before an audience. A dream. I clear my throat, a deep, amplified rumble that rolls across the café, now much larger than I realized. Not like the classroom to which I've become accustomed, this is cavernous, an arena, a stadium. Spotlights bore into my eyes. I sweat. My thirst is unquenched by the glass of water I find in my hand, in which swim bits of man-shaped ice. I clear my throat. Again. Rumble.

"Quentin," I read, "is drowning: in muck to his knees, in air thick as blood. The platoon is on the move before dawn. He's alert. His rifle, a faithful M-16, is poised. His buddy Zack stumbles, and only then does Quentin hear the crack. Then another. Anderson falls, then Joyner. He braces, dives deeper into the mud, he—" and at this point my voice sputters and stops.

"He..." I begin again, but don't—can't— go on. I step back from the microphone, sip the water, horrified now by the swarm of icy cadavers. And then the steamy rain begins, pouring down on Quentin, on Zack, on Anderson. I wipe my eyes with the back of my hand, but I'm not crying. Crying would be normal.

Jennifer comes to my aid, grips my shoulder and takes the

pages. I step back, bury my face in my hands while the rain falls in torrents, and Jennifer reads to the end. The end of Quentin. The end.

I've been trying to think of a fresh angle on this whole proposal thing—maybe at the top of the Washington Monument, or on a hike in the Shenandoah National Park, or during the previews at one of those romantic comedies Mary drags me to every week. But in the end my imagination fails me and I realize that she'll prefer something conventional, something right out of her girlhood fantasy of the fairytale engagement. So, conventional it is, and we're back at The Bakery. Fancy dinner, ring, the works.

"Mary Berger, will you marry me?" I ask over dessert.

The stunned look on Mary's face is priceless. She'd given up on me, I'm sure of it, and now there's an engagement ring sitting in front of her. Chef Ian leads the restaurant's staff in applause, in which other diners join. A cork pops and now there's a waiter filling two glasses of champagne. I feel pats on my back, hear shouts of "Congratulations!" I'd been full of doubts, my hand shaking when I put the box on the table and asked the question, but now my smile is so wide it hurts.

When the hubbub has subsided and the well-wishers have left the table, back to the kitchen or wherever, Mary says, her voice soft and barely audible, "I can't marry you, Ollie."

I'd lifted a champagne glass ready to toast our engagement, but now I put it back on the table. Carefully.

"Can't marry me?"

She nods solemnly, eyes riveted to the table.

"I thought that's what you wanted. What you've wanted since we started dating."

My voice may have been a little too loud, because Ian is back.

"Is there something wrong?" he asks.

While Mary chugs her Veuve Clicquot, I say, "No, no, everything is just dandy."

Mary stands and writhes into her coat. She pushes her chair in, picks up her purse, and hurries toward the exit.

I have my wallet out, I'm standing, I'm looking at the check, I'm trying to figure out what the hell just happened here, and Mary is already out the door and into the cold.

"Mary, wait," I say, but it's too late.

ॐ

I have no idea what to do about Mary. I need a distraction.

Bruce Owens is giving a reading at the big book festival a couple of towns over, and I make plans to go. Since our last meeting, if you can call it that, I've managed to find a copy of his book at the used bookstore, a tiny, dusty shop hidden in an alley behind the courthouse. The book's already signed, and I wonder how anyone could part with such a valuable book.

It's an amazing book. Brilliant. The stories are all really long and not much happens in them, but the language is mesmerizing. They seem to be about men who treat their wives badly, cheat on them, think they can get away with it, and in the end mostly do. Amazing stuff. I've never read anything like it, although I suspect Owens doesn't have a big following among readers of the female persuasion.

The attendance at this event is a bit better than the first time I saw him, but it turns out there are three short story writers on a panel and the venue is a big chain bookstore in a mall. I sit near the front on a cold metal folding chair and nod at Owens when he takes his seat behind the speakers' table. He smiles. Does he recognize me from the coffee shop? I was hoping he would, but I can't tell.

A woman with a red face and long white hair fiddles with the microphone—"Is this on? Can you hear me in the back?"—and begins with a few announcements, cell phone reminders, thanks to sponsors, etc. Then she introduces herself as the moderator of the panel and reads from a page with the short biographies of each of the panelists, which, I notice, are printed right in the program that we're all clutching in our hands and could easily read for ourselves.

The writers speak in alphabetical order, which means that Owens will go last. The first reader is a young graduate of a prestigious MFA program in the Midwest. When she mentions in her introductory remarks the name of her mentor, to whom she will be eternally grateful for the help he gave her on the stories in the book, several people in the audience utter an *ooh* of recognition, although the name is not one I know. Apparently I should, so I jot it down in my notebook. The woman reads the beginning of a story about a college student who is strung out on booze and pills and is struggling in an abusive relationship. She ends just at the point where the protagonist is about to pass out at a fraternity party in the company of a roomful of horny boys. The room erupts in enthusiastic applause, but I can't help feeling that I've read the story before, more than once, and it just doesn't seem interesting to me—even though I'm not too far removed from that milieu myself.

The second author is a young man, and his story is shockingly similar except that his protagonist is a gay poet who has recently come out to his parents. He also gets drunk at a party, and I wonder if the author collaborated with the first writer on the scenes they would read. He snaps his book shut to signal that he's done. More wild applause.

Finally, Bruce Owens takes his place at the microphone. He clears his throat. He takes a sip of water. He adjusts the microphone so that it's right in front of his mouth. I'm remembering the disaster of the recent open mic where I tried to read my story about Q, but Owens is a pro. Nothing like that would ever happen to him. He clears his throat again.

"This is all bullshit," Owens says. His voice booms through the store, and more than one gasp erupts behind me. "Literature has been dying a slow death for a long time, but these two poseurs have just pounded the nails in the coffin. And you people actually applauded that crap? I don't know what possessed me to agree to do this. There's nothing creative about creative writers these days and in my considered opinion the so-called MFA programs are to blame. We'd all be better off at home, watching reruns of *The West Wing*." And with that, he picks up his satchel, salutes the moderator, and disappears between the shelves of the bookstore.

A shocked silence settles on the audience. The faces of the two young readers are frozen in horror. I get up to follow Owens.

I exit the bookstore in time to see Owens ducking into an Irish pub two doors down and hurry to catch up, slipping in behind him, nearly colliding with him when he stops abruptly. Second-guessing his decision? Regretting what he said in the store? In any case, he moves on, deeper into the dark pub, and settles onto a stool at the bar. I'm surprised by my uncharacteristic boldness, but I take the stool next to him.

He orders Jameson, I order a Guinness. While we're waiting for our drinks to arrive, I pull his book out of my bag and set it on the bar.

Owens looks at the book, then at me, then down at the bar. "Jesus," he mutters and slides off his stool.

"I agreed with what you said in there," I say quickly, gesturing in the direction of the bookstore. *Please don't leave*, I beg silently. "Those stories were awful. Juvenile. Derivative."

He looks at me now with interest, scratches his white beard, and resumes his seat. "You forgot one-dimensional, but, yes, that's it exactly," he says. "I'm sure I'll hear from my publicist about it, but I just couldn't stand it another minute."

I nod, knowingly, I hope, and thrust out my hand. What's gotten into me?

"I'm Ollie Tucker."

He looks at my hand, as if the gesture is alien to him, and then shakes.

"Bruce Owens," he says. "Don't tell me. You're a writer too."

Begrudgingly, I'm sure, Owens allows me to stay, or at least tolerates my presence, when I confess that I don't have an MFA. He regales me with stories about writers he's known, benders he's been on, lousy reviews he's received. He starts to tell me about a woman, a former student, but stops himself.

During his monologue, urged on by my questions, he has three whiskeys to my one stout. When it's over, he agrees to look at one of my stories.

"I can tell you're perceptive," he says. "Not like those morons. Those teat-sucking, cliché-spewing, lucre-worshiping fakes."

Owens seems a little drunk, but his compliments make me giddy.

"It's like their stories were filled with nothing but air," I say. "But your book, that had real meat to it. Meat and meaning. Something you could sink your teeth into." I'm not sure I remember the specifics of any of his stories, much less titles, so I hope he doesn't ask which was my favorite.

"That's exactly it, my boy. Meat. It's all about the meat. Very perceptive indeed."

Driving home, I can barely steer the car, partly because of the Guinness, but mostly because I can't believe I'm going to get help from this famous author. Semi-famous. Published, at least. I actually had the story with me, but after listening to those other two writers read their work, I realize it's crap, just as empty and pointless as theirs, and so I have to make revisions before I show it to Owens. I dare to imagine that he'll be the mentor I've dreamed of, someone who will teach me as much as Professor Russell did. This time, I won't fuck it up.

I'm supposed to call Mary as soon as I get home, but I don't. Instead, I sit down at the computer and open a new file, anxious to rewrite. My hands are shaking. I can barely breathe.

22

I'm rewriting my story to show it to Bruce Owens, working at the kitchen table, but it's so bad I'm distracted by the slightest thing—passing clouds that change the light in the room, a sound outside that might be a car pulling into the driveway, a distant ringing, possibly my cell phone that I left upstairs. And then the big distraction: the internet.

It's amazing what you can learn on the internet if you're searching for the right thing. For example, I found my brother's obituary, published in the *Indianapolis Star* three days after his death. The piece lists his date of birth, the high school he graduated from (North Central, same one I went to) and the sports he played there, his unit in the army, and his service in Operation Enduring Freedom, including two deployments to Afghanistan. Survivors include his parents, siblings, and nephews. No mention of an uncle, so that's no help. It also leaves out that he suffered from PTSD and shot himself in the head.

While I'm searching, now that I know Uncle Scotty's full name—Oliver Scott Tucker—I also plug that into Google.

There are over half a million hits. I scroll through a dozen pages and none of the links, as far as I can tell, has anything to do with my uncle.

I need more information. I'm just not sure where I'm going to get it.

❧

My mother tells me I'm going to be famous. She's certain of it. She claims she foresaw Q's suicide, so maybe there's something to it. I wonder if she reads minds too. How does that work? I wonder.

If I know what you're thinking, *how* do I know ? If I know that something will happen before it actually happens, *how* do I know?

Are visions of the future in some way related to memory? Does precognition exist independent of consciousness? If we have a vision of the future, can we be said to know that this future will exist? Can we be certain? Does our certainty in some way affect our future's outcome?

I've had a new dream, one in which I come face-to-face with Uncle Scotty. I'm walking in a fine mist, a mangy dog trotting in and out of my path. Is it just wishful thinking? Or is it a vision of the future?

"In some ways," Professor Russell once said, "there is no present." We'd been reading Heidegger's *Being and Time*, and really struggling to understand the concept. "Every present moment is instantly past, and until then it is the future. Isn't it conceivable then, that the future is already determined, simply a memory of an event that has not yet occurred, a future memory?"

So maybe my mother did have a vision of Q's suicide. Maybe she's seen my future too. If so, what else has she seen? Scotty's future? Where's Scotty?

≈

I wish I could see the future, at least what the future holds for Mary and me. Every time I think we're done for good, she calls, or I call, and we're back together. Or if not exactly together, we're at least not apart.

We're both being cautious, tiptoeing around subjects that might cause an argument. I don't voice my disagreement with her views on movies or books or religion or...anything, and she doesn't mention commitment, hers or mine. Our last conversation on that subject, my failed proposal, is too painful to recall.

One night, at her house—her father is out somewhere and her mother, after a brief attempt to engage me in conversation is occupying herself in the kitchen—we're watching a movie in the living room. It's a historical drama that neither of us objects to, with enough romance to satisfy Mary and almost enough substance for me. Still, my mind wanders to Bruce Owens and the work I sent him to read. I'm worried that it's awful, that I have no talent, that I'm wasting his time *and* mine.

"Ollie?"

I look at Mary and realize the movie is over, or a commercial is on and she's muted the sound.

"What were you thinking about?"

What will piss her off least? I decide to go with honesty.

"Bruce Owens."

She rolls her eyes.

"I know you don't think much of him," I say. "But right now, he's all I've got."

Her eyes narrow.

"In the literary world, I mean."

"I've read one of his stories, Ollie. It's obvious what kind of man he is."

"You're saying you know this from reading his fiction? Stories he *made up*? Isn't that like judging a book by its cover?"

"Not at all. The cover isn't the book, but the author is. I'm pretty sure I don't like this author and it worries me that you're so enamored of his work."

Seriously, do I have a future with this woman?

And, I wonder, does Oliver have a future with Maria?

"You will meet a dark stranger," the fortune-teller says to Oliver, her unblinking eyes fixed on his palm, and already he knows this much is true. Isn't her skin umber, her hair black as the Hanoi night? A village near Hanoi is the site of one of the community building projects he's involved with and his hosts have brought him to this alley in the old part of the city.

"Tell me more," he says.

"She will be young and beautiful; she will bear a child."

A child? Could the old woman mean Maria? Is Maria expecting?

Here, in this land of so much turmoil, the fortune-teller unsettles Oliver. Because, against all evidence, he believes. It is something he will not admit to his friends, but since a teenage parlor game—past life regression with a hypnotic quack—he has treasured these glimpses back and forth. A medieval monk, a plague-wracked publican, a silversmith in the American colonies. His long life has been foretold in tea leaves, the death of his mother in snake blood. But no seer yet has conjured offspring.

He withdraws his hand. The old woman's lips flare; her teeth, shadowy with rot, protrude. Her vision swirls around him, the dark stranger and the child, and in his mouth he tastes decay, old blood of past lives. Lives passed.

Oliver does not believe in destiny. And yet, what does the fortune teller see if not that which has been predestined. A dark woman. A baby.

He longs for Maria and, perhaps, their unborn child.

Bruce Owens is already seated at the table when I arrive at the bar, our designated meeting spot where he will deliver the bad news about my story. On the drive over here, Mary's complaints about my preoccupation with Owens running through my head, I steeled myself for the abuse that I knew was coming my way. I'm no writer. I have no idea what I'm doing. I know it. And now Bruce Owens, the only published author I've ever met, knows it too.

I don't approach immediately. I watch him sip his drink, riffle through the pages of the story, squeeze another note—there appear to be lots of notes—into the margin. I think I might throw up. But I can't back out now. I step toward the table.

"Hi," I say, dropping into the chair opposite him. "You got the story, I see."

A waitress comes by and Owens raises an eyebrow when I order a Coke, as if to say that real writers don't drink Coke. I'm pretty sure real writers don't vomit when they're having their work torn to shreds, either.

"Well," he says.

"I know it's crap," I say, and I push back from the table, ready to flee, preempting his judgment. This whole thing was a pipe dream of epic proportions and it's time for me to be realistic. Who am I kidding?

He puts his hand on my arm. *Shut up*, his expression is telling me. I do. I nod and move back toward the table.

"Yes, it's crap," he says, "but it's crap with potential."

Did he say, *potential?*

He begins then: "What are you afraid of? What's the story really about? Why have you left so much unexamined? Oliver is intriguing, in a sketchy sort of way, but what's he hiding? Why is he doing what he's doing? What's his motivation? What does he want? What's he running away from? More importantly, Ollie, what are *you* hiding? This stuff is all on the surface. Dig! Think like Morrison. O'Brien. McCann. Get real. Touch some live wires."

We go through the story line by line. He points out where I'm being dishonest, where my sentences are ambiguous, where I could show the reader the real experience, let the reader share the sensations and the emotions, instead of just telling the reader how to feel and what I want him to understand. Let the reader do some of the work, he insists.

When we're done, I'm breathless.

"Above all else," Bruce Owens concludes, "when you are writing a story like this, something this personal, because I can tell it's personal, you must tell the truth." He downs the rest of his drink. "You must be…brave."

Mike is gone. After his short-lived attempt at college, he has joined the Army, as he had intended all along. Mary was surprised, as were Bill and Lydia, who are furious, but hadn't he confessed his plans to me? Despite Q's experience, and the demons it summoned that he could not handle, I didn't try to talk Mike out of it.

He was dashing in his uniform.

"Better," says Bruce Owens at our second meeting. "Oliver is feeling threatened. I like that. The stakes are raised, the tension mounting. You've mentioned relationships, and that's very good, although we need to know more."

We're back in the bar, going over the revision to my story. Owens has his Jameson, I've got a light beer, which is not much better than a Coke in his view. No real writer would… etc.

"Oliver has a secret, doesn't he?" Owens downs the whiskey and orders another. "I can feel it, somewhere under the words. Lurking. Keep digging. Very nice."

Bruce Owens has a secret too. I still haven't been able to find out anything about Uncle Scotty with my internet searches, but there's plenty of information about Bruce Owens out there in cyberspace. For example, I learned how he got drunk one night and confessed to his wife of twenty-five years, now ex-wife, that he was cheating on her, had been cheating for years. Thirteen years.

The wife, a novelist I've heard of but not read, published a memoir in which she recounted her shock at learning of this transgression, and then revealed Owens's many perversions, including a taste for bondage and sadomasochism.

Had she not read the man's stories? How could any of this have been a surprise? (Mary was right.)

❧

We're at the Ice Dream and Mary says, "Do you still have that ring, Ollie?"

"The engagement ring?" What other ring is there, you fool. But I'm stalling. "Um, yes. Why?"

"Oh, no reason," she says.

❧

Here's what happened with Professor Russell and the real reason I had to leave Indiana and can't call him for advice.

I'd been going to his house twice a week for our meditation practice. The sessions got longer and longer and I felt I was making real progress. Not that I'd found enlightenment, or even begun to explore my consciousness in a serious way, but none of that mattered. It was the journey I looked forward to each week, closing my eyes and listening to Clark's soft voice as he guided me through the darkness.

Afterward we stretched our legs and talked quietly in his dim
study. He offered the LSD again, but when I said I wasn't ready,
he produced a joint instead. More my speed.

By the time I was a senior, this was a semi-regular thing. On
the last night, shortly before graduation, after we'd meditated
and gotten high, I was sure he was hitting on me. He extended
his leg and his foot brushed mine. Maybe that was an accident,
but when he passed me the joint with his right hand he held my
hand steady with his left. And then there were those eyes, those
piercing dark eyes. What was I supposed to think? Or do?

I admitted this to myself: I was a little in love with Professor
Russell and was going to miss him terribly when I left school.
He knew so much about the world and really understood me.
And he was beautiful, with the long hair and lean body. More
truth: I wanted him to touch me.

So when I passed the joint back to him I grabbed his arm
and wouldn't let go. I tried to pull him closer.

"Jesus, Ollie, what are you doing?"

"I thought—"

"What the fuck?"

And suddenly that yippy dog of his jumped between us and
growled at me. Professor Russell stood up, stumbling toward
the door.

"Wait," I said, "you don't understand."

"You better leave, Ollie."

"You don't understand."

But he did understand. I was the one who didn't understand.
And that's what really happened with Professor Russell.

I'm up earlier than usual and Mom is still in the kitchen drinking coffee, reading the paper. It's the point in the morning when
she's at her best—awake and no longer grumpy, but not yet
rushing off to work and feeling stressed. It's a short window.
Best to jump through while it's open.

"So, Mom," I say while pouring my coffee, "I was wondering."

She's humming a show tune of some kind, one I remember she and Dad listened to on the stereo often in the old days, but she doesn't take her eyes off the paper. "About what, Ollie?"

"About my name. If Uncle Scotty is so persona non grata for reasons that no one in this family is willing to talk about, why did you name me after him?"

I feel the window closing. She folds the paper, takes a last sip of her coffee.

"We didn't, dear. You're named after your father's father, the first Oliver Wendell Tucker."

"But still, it's Uncle Scotty's name, too, right?"

"Yes and no. When Scotty was born, he was named Oliver, after your grandfather, everybody called him Scotty to distinguish him from Grandpa Oliver. You were born shortly after your grandfather's death, and your father wanted to honor him by passing along the name to a new generation, since…"

"Since what?"

"Nothing, dear. I have to run or I'll be late for work."

There's just one little problem with the ring I told Mary I still had.

It's gone.

When Mary turned me down, I was embarrassed. I should have returned the ring to the jewelry store, of course. It hadn't yet been sized and, in any case, the store had a wise policy of allowing exchanges, knowing that fiancées usually like to pick out their own rings, and usually those rings are more expensive than the one chosen by the man. It's good business for them in the long run. But a return? That's less common. "She said no, did she, son?" Yes, that's exactly what it means, asshole. I couldn't bear to see the expression on the jeweler's face.

But I didn't want to keep the ring, either. It's not that I was heartbroken. I was more than a little relieved, to be honest. I mean, *completely* honest. Mary is sweet, and I think I love her. Or sort of love her. But I'm not sure I should be married to anyone just now, given my…doubts. And there are so many ways in which we're incompatible—our taste in books and movies, for example, and then there's religion. We haven't talked about politics, but I think she voted for Romney.

Still, what to do about the ring?

I had been thinking about Oliver, and what a do-gooder he is, always working on projects to help the poor, even starting a charity to support orphans in Vietnam and victims of sex-trafficking in Thailand. Bruce Owens says that Oliver is both a reflection of who I am and who I want to be. Of course I knew that, on some level, but I hadn't actually thought about it, and I hadn't thought about emulating Oliver, who is, after all, made up. It would be like trying to act like Superman. I loved the idea of helping people, but doing something about it, actually getting off my ass and doing good deeds, is another thing altogether. More and more, though, Oliver inspires me.

So I went into one of those homeless shelters on the west side of town and handed the ring to the first person I saw, a grizzled old guy with gray stubble and no teeth. Just dropped it in his hand, turned, and fled. I hope that was okay to do. I bet he was surprised.

But now, Mary seems to have changed her mind about not marrying me. There's just that one little problem.

"This story about the girl in Vietnam is quite moving—real emotions, life and death, secrets," says Bruce Owens. "Have you been? To Vietnam?"

"No," I confess. "I didn't know Americans could go there. I mean I've read a lot about it. The war. And, um, after." He seems to like the story, in which Oliver rescues an orphan in Hanoi. I know it's crap. At least I thought it was crap.

"Ah, yes, the war. That fucking war. For some of us, pro and con, it will never be over."

"You were in the Army?"

"Briefly," Owens says. He sips from his drink, stares into the

amber. I wish I knew what he's thinking, what he's not saying.
How is one in the Army only briefly? What happened? Was he
wounded? I'm not sure how to ask.

"Were you—"

"What if you went there?" My question forestalled.

"Went where?"

"Vietnam."

"Me?"

"Sure. Or somewhere else. You're sending this Oliver fellow all over the place in these stories. Thailand, Switzerland,
Mexico, Vietnam. Why should *he* have all the fun. Why not go
yourself? Nothing stopping you, is there? Travel! See the world,
and *then* write about it. Think of the stories you'll be able to tell!
Why not?"

"There's work, for one thing."

"Teaching? Nonsense. There's always more work, another
teaching gig, or something even more rewarding than grading
essays by kids who don't know a semicolon from a smiley face.
Travel will improve your résumé, not to mention your writing."

Travel is the key to the locked door of consciousness, Professor Russell had said. But it's not possible.

"And there's Mary. That's my girlfriend. Fiancée." Not really
my fiancée, but that now seems inevitable.

"She'll wait, won't she? They do wait, sometimes."

"Do you really think I should?"

"Absolutely, my young friend. Travel deepens the soul.
You're young. Now is the time for you. Join the Peace Corps or
something. Build a hospital in Africa, dig wells in Nicaragua. Or
just take off on your own. Be a beachcomber. See the world."

"The world," I say.

"That's right. And whatever you're looking for, whatever
you're writing about in these stories, you'll find it out there."

Out there. Whatever I'm looking for. Uncle Scotty is out
there.

Part II

23

Mom's been going to AA meetings. I wonder if Silly had something to do with that, but Mom doesn't say and I don't ask. I'm proud of her for making a stab at getting her drinking under control, though, and I want to help.

I seem to remember reading that part of AA was owning up to your past mistakes, so I wonder if this isn't a good time to finally get a straight answer from her about Uncle Scotty. Even though my life is in a good place right now, he still pops up in my dreams occasionally—I've convinced myself that's his face looming over me—and I'd like to know what it's all about.

"Mom," I say when I find her in the living room one evening.

She sticks her finger in the book she's reading—*Moby Dick*, if you can imagine it—and takes advantage of the interruption to sip from her glass of iced tea. She looks up at me. I wonder briefly if there's something other than tea in her glass, but dismiss the thought. Her eyes are clear and bright. She looks sober. She probably *is* sober.

"Don't you think it's odd that no one will talk about Uncle Scotty? Is he in jail? Did he kill someone? Was he a drug dealer? Arms merchant? Terrorist?"

"None of the above, Ollie."

"Glad to hear it," I say, "but then where the heck is he?"

"Singapore," she says, and goes back to reading her book as if nothing remarkable has just happened.

Did I hear that right?

"Wait. Just like that? You're telling me where he is, after I've been asking for, like, a million years?"

"I don't think you ever asked me where he was before. You've asked about his name. You've asked what happened to him. You've asked why he left. Never where he was. For anything else you want to know, you have to ask your father. But the last I heard, he was in Singapore."

"Singapore?"

"Singapore."

ॐ

That night, I can't sleep. Isn't it odd that I've sent Oliver to Singapore in his travels? Did I already know on some level that Scotty had gone there?

On top of that, I'm convinced that my life lacks spontaneity. Other than my disastrous flirtation with Professor Russell, what have I ever done in my entire life that I haven't analyzed endlessly, looking for the perfect solution, the right thing to do. Overthinking. Bruce Owens told me to see the world, didn't he? That's given me an idea. So I hop in the Impala and drive over to Mary's house. I know it's early, but the Bergers are early risers, even on their days off.

Mike answers the door—home on leave already, something of a surprise to the family, I gather, because Mary hasn't mentioned he'd be visiting. He returns my smile and greeting, I praise his buzzed haircut, we shake hands, his now rough and calloused, and he leads me to the back of the house. Has he gotten taller? Bigger? The whole clan is in the kitchen—Lydia poking at sausage and eggs frying on the stove, Bill at the kitchen table drinking coffee, muttering over the *Washington Post*, and Mary, listening to her iPod through the tiny earphones that have become a near-permanent attachment—an audio book, probably. I'd be willing to wager it's *Pride and Prejudice*, or something else by Austen. Either that or *Twilight*. Barney is under the table gnawing on a rawhide bone and doesn't register my arrival.

"Hey there, big guy," says Bill. "You're up and about early. To what do we owe the honor?"

"So nice to see you, Ollie," says Lydia, flipping the sizzling sausages with a spatula.

"Ollie!" says Mary. "What are you doing here?" She shuts off her iPod and stands, although the earbuds are still in place. She's wearing jeans and a ratty University of Virginia T-shirt, no makeup, and maybe it's the excitement of what I'm about to do, but in this moment I think she's never looked more beautiful.

"I have a proposal to make," I say, and then, realizing my poor choice of words given our lousy history on that score, I add, "I mean, I've got an idea I want to run past you."

"Dude, you couldn't do that on the phone?" asks Mike.

"You'll stay for breakfast, won't you, Ollie?" asks Lydia.

"You're not running off to elope, are you, fella?" asks Bill.

"So what's the idea?" asks Mary.

"Let's drive up to DC for the day," I say. "Visit a museum or two, have a nice lunch, browse in that big bookstore you like.

"Right now?" she asks. "DC?"

"Right now. DC."

She giggles and looks at Lydia first, then Bill, and says, "Give me five minutes to get ready."

"What about breakfast?" Lydia asks.

I decline Lydia's offer of breakfast—I'm too excited to eat—but take a cup of coffee to the porch to wait for Mary while she's upstairs getting ready. I think about the story I worked on last night: Oliver in Singapore. Oliver being spontaneous.

On a Thursday evening, Oliver meets Maria for drinks at Buckthorn in Duxton Hill, one of their favorite out-of-the way spots in Singapore. It's been a hectic week. He's been in Hong Kong, she in Kuala Lumpur, and they've only seen each other in passing. He's waiting at the bar and stands when she enters, a smile blooming as she spots him. He kisses her, a long, hungry kiss on the lips, and guides her to a table.

"You look stunning," he says. Indeed, she's wearing a sleek black cocktail dress that he's complimented her on before and a flowered silk scarf, lush and tropical.

"You look pretty nice yourself, handsome," she says. It's common in Singapore to wear a tie without a jacket, because of the heat, but he's just come from the more formal business environment of Hong Kong, so he's wearing a suit—one, in fact, that Maria had picked out for him—with a sapphire blue tie.

Buckthorn is one of the many sophisticated wine bars that have sprung up in recent years. It's expensive, but it has the largest wine selection on the island, many served by the glass. Maria orders a glass of Sauvignon Blanc from New Zealand and Oliver gets a high-end Australian Shiraz. They sip, talk about their respective travels. Oliver strokes Maria's hand.

"I have an idea," he says.

"I have an idea also," she says, and winks at him.

"Yes, well, that too, and very soon, but I was thinking of something else. Something we haven't done before."

"We've never had sex in a public bathroom before."

"I like how you think, you sexy Mexican, but what I meant was, let's go away tomorrow. Let's go to Jogja to see Borobudur, or Siem Riep to see Angkor Wat, or someplace. We can fuck anywhere, but let's do it someplace exciting."

"But we can't just go. What about flights and a hotel? What about work?"

"They won't even notice we're gone, or they'll think we've gone back to KL and Hong Kong. Say the word, and I'll call the travel agent right now."

She sips her wine and looks around the room as if there might be someone there who would stop them. Her father. Her mother. She takes another sip.

"Why not?" she says. "Let's go."

Professor Russell entered the classroom, more disheveled than usual, tie loose at the neck. He stacked his books on the lectern, adjusted his glasses, looked up and, taking stock of the class waiting expectantly, asked: "How can you be certain?"

No one answered. Certain of what?

"Is there anything of which you can be certain?" Russell asked.

Again, no one answered.

"Let me ask a different question, since that one's got you stumped," he said. "Is certainty necessary? Must we be certain of anything?"

I raised my hand, and Russell nodded at me. Reluctantly, I thought, given what had recently transpired between us.

"If we can't be certain, then we can't really know anything," I said. "Truth depends on certainty." I was only parroting what he'd told us in previous discussions and wasn't sure I understood what I was saying.

"Then I come back to my first question: of what can you be certain?"

"We can be certain of things we can prove," I said. "Like math."

Someone else said, "We can also be certain of things we can see and touch."

"Example," said Russell, his standard command to provide detail, to bolster our arguments.

The student slapped his desk. "I am certain of this desk because I can feel it. I am experiencing this desk. If it were not real, I'd be sitting on the floor."

That got a laugh from the class, but not even a smile from Professor Russell.

"So, some of you are certain of what you can see and touch, and others—" he looked at me, "are certain of what you can prove, like math."

There was a murmur of agreement.

"But," said Russell, "what if you are deceived?"

Traffic is light on the highway—we're still well outside the DC beltway—and I'm tapping my fingers on the steering wheel to Radiohead, a CD I listen to over and over. And over. Even Mary, who usually lobbies for a change to something more melodic, is bobbing her head, trying to hum along to music that isn't really hummable.

"What's gotten into you today," Mary asks over the music. "So spontaneous. It's not like you."

"It's not?" Is it still spontaneous if I've been up all night making plans?

"Not really, no." She laughs. "It's nice for a change."

"I know, right?"

We listen to the music awhile and then I say, "So, what do you think about the Peace Corps?"

This was the whole objective of our little trip, spontaneity aside, and here I am springing it on her in the first half hour. Too soon, probably. But now the subject is on the table.

"The what?"

"Peace Corps. You know, 'Toughest job you'll ever love,' President Kennedy's big idea and all that. The Peace Corps. What do you think?"

"I don't know. I guess I haven't thought about it much. Is it still around?"

"Yes! And they're doing amazing work all over. Africa, Asia, everywhere." I was on the internet much of the night checking it out. I had no idea.

"Oh. Well. I'm sure—"

"I was thinking about joining."

"You were what? You want to go to Africa? With all those diseases? And snakes? Are you out of your mind?"

"It's just—"

"And what about me?"

"Hear me out, sweetie. They take couples, see, and we could go to, like, Thailand or somewhere like that and we could both teach school. We're teachers, right? So we teach. And it will look great on our résumés, don't you think? It'll be awesome."

"Isn't China threatening to invade them?"

"I think that's Taiwan."

"Still."

"Okay, maybe not Thailand. There are lots of other places they could send us. It would be a hoot. An adventure. Bruce Owens says—"

"You've been talking to that old drunk again?"

"He's a great writer."

"Who cheats on his wife and drinks like a whale."

"I'm not sure whales—"

"So what does the old lech say?" She shuts the music off.

I can feel her eyes on me, but I watch the road. I-66 can be treacherous.

"He thinks it would be good for me. For us, I mean. An adventure, while we're young. See the world before we're settled. Expand the mind."

That's not exactly what he said, of course, but more or less, with a little Professor Russell thrown in.

Traffic is heavier now as we approach the beltway and navigate the vehicles entering the ramps and coming off the ramps and the rest of them, like us, heading into our nation's capital.

"So what do you say? You'll think about it?"

"An adventure? That's what you want?"

"Right. An adventure. For both of us. What do you think?"

"I think you've lost your fucking mind."

ॐ

I'm in the National Gallery staring at a Gaugin with bare-breasted native women and wondering if the Peace Corps has volunteers in Tahiti.

I see Mary across the gallery, in silhouette, with a bright window behind her. She looks angelic, admiring a Mary Cassatt portrait, thoughtful, intelligent, blissful. I approach and stand next to her, admiring the picture, one I recognize from my single art history course, of the girl in the blue armchair. I see a little dog in the other chair, and I don't remember that detail. I'm looking at the dog and almost forget that Mary is there until she takes my hand.

"I'm so glad we came to the museum," she says.

"Has that dog always been there?" I ask.

"I'm sure it has, Ollie. It's an old painting."

"I guess you're right. But you'd think I'd remember something like that."

We move on, through room after room of paintings, everything old is now new. I'm thinking of Oliver, his sudden visit to Borobudur with Maria. He'd visited years earlier, during his backpacking days, but now sees the temple in a different light. It towers, mountain-like, above the surrounding countryside, row after row, layer upon layer of Buddha statues and stupas. First they circle the temple at ground level and then begin the climb. The exertion silences them, but it becomes a meditation, each new beatific statue only deepening Oliver's calm, his certitude. Later, at the hotel, Oliver and Maria lie down to rest and Maria is asleep instantly. Oliver, though, rises and sits nearby, watching her sleep. The calm that he felt at the temple, the certainty, is still with him. He recalls the hag in Hanoi, the child she foretold. Oliver can't predict the future, but for the first time in a very long time, after all his travels, he knows what he wants right now.

Before long, Maria stirs. She looks at Oliver, who is still looking at her.

"What?" she says.

"You're beautiful," he says.

"Very funny," she says.

"No, I mean it. I've been watching you."

"Well, stop. At least until I've washed my face." She gets up and starts toward the bathroom.

"Wait," he says, and goes to her.

"What?"

"Marry me," he says.

"No," she says, and pulls away from him.

"No?"

"No. I mean, yes. Yes, I love you and of course I will marry you, but no, you can't ask me this way."

"I can't?"

"No."

She's laughing now, so Oliver is laughing with her, but he's not sure if she's accepted his proposal. Why are they laughing?

"This will sound crazy, but you can't ask me directly. You have to go to Mexico and ask my father."

"Go to Mexico? I can't just call him?"

"No, Oliver. We have to go."

They're still laughing.

"Okay," Oliver says, "if that's what we have to do, we're off to Mexico."

Certainty is elusive. I thought I knew what to do, just as Oliver is sure about Maria. But the dog in the Cassatt painting, I don't remember it. Can I be certain? Am I doing the right thing?

&

"I love this museum," Mary says over lunch in the National Gallery's cafeteria. She has a fancy salad with cold shrimp and I've got an even fancier sandwich, and we're being really spontaneous by splitting a small bottle of white wine.

"Me too," I say. "Amazing art from all over the world."

"Right here in our own backyard," she says. "Who needs to travel, when we've got this."

"Marry me," I say.

She nearly chokes on her salad and has to take a big gulp of the wine to clear her throat.

"I'm serious," I say while she recovers. "You wanted to do it before and I was a jerk, and then I wanted to and the timing wasn't right for you or whatever. But now it's perfect. We both want it. Don't we? We're in love. Let's get married."

At least I think we're in love.

She takes my hand and looks into my eyes, as if she's searching for the truth. Do I really mean it? Can she trust me this time? Will I disappoint her again?

Her hesitation is beginning to trouble me, and I worry that I scared her off with all that talk of the Peace Corps and adventure. Or maybe that guy Brian is still in the picture. Or she's adding up all the ways in which we're basically incompatible, because if we start down that path the whole enterprise is doomed. Or, maybe, in her conservative world I'm supposed to be asking her father's permission first? But then she squeezes my hand.

"Yes," she says.

"Really?" I'm just as stunned now as when she turned me down. This is huge. This changes everything. "You mean it?"

"Yes, Ollie. I mean it. Let's get married."

&

Although we're now officially engaged—I maxed out a credit card to buy a replacement ring and I'm never, ever going to tell anyone what happened to the original—I'm sensing from Mary that the Peace Corps idea has not gained much traction. Or any traction. Since we came back from our DC day trip, I suspect she's conjured images of thatched roofs and privies, bugs and snakes, tropical diseases, cold-water showers, and spear-carrying natives, and has concluded that it's not for her.

To tell the truth, I'm relieved. Bruce Owens said, "Be brave," but I don't think I can be quite that brave. It's not in my nature, and as a writer I have to stay true to that, right? So the Peace Corps is probably out. I look for alternatives.

It's nearly midnight a few days later when I find the answer, but I call Mary anyway. This won't wait.

"International schools," I tell her when she picks up. On the phone, late at night, I tend to whisper so as not to disturb my mother. But tonight I'm practically shouting.

"Ollie?"

Apparently I woke Mary up.

"We can have our teaching adventure, sweetie," I say. "But we can do it someplace civilized, like Paris. Or even London. No thatched roofs."

"Thatched what?" She's not quite awake yet.

I don't tell her posts in places like that are almost impossible for new teachers in the system to get right off the bat, and that we're more likely to be offered an assignment in Tashkent or Timbuktu, but one step at a time. Or, if we're lucky, Singapore, because what I'm really excited about is the vacancies I found in the American School there.

She's warming to the idea, I can tell.

"Paris?" she asks.

24

It's not exactly Paris," I say. I had to look Singapore up on a map myself, in that antique atlas Mom gave me for Christmas, and it's about as far away from Paris as you can get. An Asian island near the equator, a former British colony. Really? Oliver's travels notwithstanding, I had no idea.

"No," she says. "It's not Paris."

"But it's modern. And super clean. And they speak English. Sort of. And there are openings in the American school."

"But it's not Paris."

"No," I say. "It's not Paris."

"Ollie, this is insane."

"It's better than Paris, sweetie. It's exotic. It's warm. It's tropical. They have beaches." I made that part up, but they must have beaches, right? It's an island.

"Ollie, you said we could go to Paris."

I'm not sure what changed Mary's mind, but it might have been the accelerated date for our wedding that the move would require. That, and the dozens of internet links I emailed to her, proving beyond doubt that Singapore wasn't just *not Paris*, it's way better than Paris—cleaner, friendlier, warmer, safer, more modern, green, seaside. Did I mention warm? What sealed the deal, though, were the job offers we received within weeks of submitting our applications and being interviewed on Skype. It didn't seem real, at first, it all happened so fast, but now that our expedited passports have arrived, it does.

"I can't believe we're doing this," she says. "Talk about spontaneity."

"I know!" I say. I consider telling her about Scotty, but I'm not sure how. I don't want to rock the boat just yet.

The wedding is in two weeks. We leave in a month. I hope

this isn't a huge mistake, but I keep remembering Bruce Owens's words: "Be brave!"

❧

We're sitting on the porch at Mary's, Barney snoozing at our feet.

"What do you mean, we can't take Barney?" Mary asks. Her entire face is twisted in horror.

"It's not that we can't, sweetie, but think of what's best for him."

"What's best for him is to be with me," she says.

"Yes, of course. But we've been through this. Singapore has a strict pet quarantine and he'd be locked up all by himself for weeks, maybe months, before he could join us in our place. That would be awfully hard on the old boy, don't you think? Not to mention the plane ride. Think about it. Twenty-four hours in a jumbo jet cargo hold? We can't put him through that."

"No Barney?"

The dog opens his eyes and looks at her without lifting his head. For a minute, I think the deal is off. Will she be able to leave him behind?

"He'll be fine here with your folks," I say, because that's what she needs to hear. "This is the only home he's ever known."

"I guess you're right," she says, clearly unconvinced.

❧

"What's the rush?" my mother asks when I tell her about the impending wedding. "That girl's not pregnant, is she? Because that's no reason to get married nowadays. When your father and I…Well, let's just say things were different when I was younger."

"Wait. What?"

"I'm just saying, you don't need to get married. You can wait for the right one to come along."

"No, Mom, Mary's not pregnant. And she *is* the right one."

"Oh. Well, then. That's nice, dear."

❧

"Are you out of your fucking mind?" my sister says when I tell her I'm getting married. "Not that married life isn't heaven-ly"—I can't tell here if she's laughing or coughing—"but you're so young!"

"Did you know Mom was pregnant with you when they got married?"

"Wait. What?"

"That's what I said."

"She's not, though, is she?"

"Why does everyone keep asking me that? No, she's not pregnant. We've been going out for a year and we're ready to get married."

"You're being defensive, Ollie. No need to shout."

"That's what people do when they're attacked, Silly. It's a perfectly rational response."

"Yes, but still. And anyway, I thought you were confused. What about all that stuff with Uncle Scotty?"

In a moment of weakness, I'd confessed to my sister that I might be—sometimes, but certainly not all the time, and not in any definitive way—attracted to men. I guess she was paying attention after all.

"Maybe I was confused. A little. For a while. But I'm not now. Mary's the one."

&

"Good for you," says Bruce Owens, when I tell him about moving to Singapore. I leave out the part about getting married, because he hasn't met Mary, and I suspect he doesn't currently hold a high opinion of the institution.

"I have you to thank," I say.

"Me? What did I do?"

"You encouraged me to be brave, to have an adventure."

"Oh, right. That. Sure, I guess babysitting for a horde of overprivileged American high school brats in the Disneyland of Asia will be an adventure. Not sure how much serious writing you can do about that *kind* of adventure, but be sure to let me know how it turns out."

"That's it? That's all you've got to say?" He's not very good at this mentoring thing. He's supposed to be encouraging, give me reading suggestions, travel tips, that sort of thing. I miss Professor Russell.

"There *is* something else," he says.

"What's that?" I'm eager for his last pearls of wisdom.

"Bon voyage."

I imagine Oliver and Maria's wedding in Mexico. He's sought her father's permission to marry her and now the extended family is gathered in the village for the ceremony in the old cathedral. Maria and her mother have spent weeks planning—the dress, the flowers, the reception. Oliver will be a mere appendage, but he recognizes his role and accepts it.

Maria has told him she doesn't think her brother Miguel will be able to get there from New York in time, but on the Thursday before the wedding, Miguel appears. There is much celebrating his arrival, not least because he completes the wedding party puzzle: he is to be Oliver's best man. But also, Oliver is coming to realize, unlike his own family, these people are actually fond of each other. After greeting his parents and his sister with kisses, Miguel comes to Oliver and takes him in his arms. This warmth, this *love*, fills Oliver with hope.

Because of the short notice, Silly and Jacob can't come to the wedding. I understand. They've got the twins and Suzy Q, and it's a long trip, and expensive, and…No, really, I understand.

Dad's not coming either. I know it's not long after Q's death, but I still thought he'd come. Marriage is a big step. You'd think he'd want to be present at the moment I defy his expectations. Also, I want to tell him about Singapore, that I'm going there to find Uncle Scotty. I figured he still wouldn't explain himself, but at least I'd be able to see his reaction, get a sense of what I'm dealing with.

Mike can't get leave and isn't going to be there either, perhaps the greatest disappointment. But probably for the best.

I thought of inviting Bruce Owens, but after our last

meeting, which felt like a brush-off, I've changed my mind. I'm pretty sure Professor Russell wouldn't come.

None of Mary's friends can come, which both hurts and disappoints her. I, apparently, don't have any friends.

It will be a small wedding.

It's not as if I needed a big bachelor party, with a stripper and a lot of booze. But something would have been nice. Dinner, drinks, anything. Pathetic.

Instead, I fantasize about the celebration Oliver's experiencing while Maria is sequestered on the night before the wedding. Miguel would be taking Oliver to the cantina in the village with a dozen assorted cousins. There are no women here, scantily clad or otherwise, as it isn't the custom, but there is loud music. The first bottle of tequila materializes, toasts are made. Three shots in succession—he must keep up with the cousins, Miguel insists, or his manhood will be questioned—and Oliver knows he is doomed. If he survives the night, he will be comatose in the morning.

He pulls Miguel aside. "Please help me," he says. Miguel holds Oliver's head in his hands, and kisses him on the lips. Then his mouth is on Oliver's ear. "I will protect you, my brother," he says, and pours another shot for them both.

Small wedding, small reception. It's just Mom and the Bergers and us at a restaurant. No music, no dancing. But there is champagne, and Mom falls off the wagon for the occasion. Big time. I was hoping Mike would surprise us at the last minute, but Mary says he's gotten into a bit of trouble at the base and can't get away. His last surprise visit home was, as she puts it, unauthorized. She doesn't elaborate, but it doesn't sound good.

I keep thinking Mike will show up anyway, that the story of trouble is just a setup to enhance the eventual surprise. I glance at the door occasionally, certain he'll appear at any minute.

It seems like a good time to tell my mother we're moving.

Not a good time, maybe, but the best of all available bad times.

"Mom, I've got something to tell you."

"She's pregnant!"

"Would you stop with that? She's not pregnant. It's nothing like that. But it is big."

She looks at me expectantly, swigging her champagne. I glance at the door. Still no Mike. I take a deep breath.

"We've accepted jobs at the American School in Singapore. We leave next week. We'll be gone for at least a year. I'm sorry I didn't tell you sooner, but everything happened so fast. Please don't be upset."

The champagne flute tumbles from my mother's hand and shatters on the restaurant's dark wood floor. She jumps up and runs in the direction of the restrooms, or possibly out the door to her car.

Mary says, "You hadn't told her? When we're practically getting on the plane? My God, what were you thinking?" And she runs after my mother.

Not my best moment.

"Way to go, fella," says Bill.

25

Given that we're leaving for Singapore in a week, we don't really have time or money for a honeymoon, so we spend our first night as husband and wife in a Holiday Inn. It's actually the first time we've slept together. We've had sex, of course, furtively, in my bedroom or hers and, once, in the Impala, but we've both been living with our parents, so sleepovers have been out of the question until now.

The consummation of the marriage is perfunctory, I have to admit. Anti-climactic. So to speak. With the disappointment of the small wedding, the absence of relatives and friends, with the worry over our impending move, and then my mother's reaction to the big news, neither of us is in a particularly passionate mood. But we do it. And then we sleep.

Or, at any rate, Mary sleeps. I'm awake, thinking what a terrible mistake I've just made.

Despite my newlywed postcoital worries, I have apparently fallen asleep. I'm aware of waking gradually, of daylight in the room, of Mary lying next to me in the bed. It's a beautiful new day, the wedding no longer feels like a mistake, I'm excited about the adventure we're beginning, and I turn to look at my bride. And she's looking back at me! It reminds me of the day we met, the shy glances we exchanged in the coffee shop. I smile. She smiles back. I kiss her. She kisses me back. She reaches for me, and that's all the encouragement I need. We're off to the races, doubts or no doubts.

In the afterglow, I wonder if it's time for a little honesty. I should tell her what Uncle Scotty did to me. And, more to the point, I should tell her what I'm looking for in Singapore.

But, no. I can't ruin the moment. I can't tell her yet.

৵

We're still in bed. My phone rings.

Mom apologizes profusely both for calling me on the morning of the first day of my married life and also for her behavior at the reception. She wants to talk.

So, after we've had our champagne brunch in bed—a gift from the Bergers—Mary and I pack up our things and head home. Or rather, to her home. For the one week we have left here, we're staying with her parents. As soon as we arrive at the house, I explain that I have to go see my mother. Bill and Lydia seem as relieved to be rid of me as I am to leave, and besides, they understand I have to clean up the mess I've made.

I'm not sure what to expect at home. Mom said it was important.

The smell of baking greets me when I open the door, a hopeful sign. Mom is in the kitchen, stirring something on the counter.

Her hands and forearms are covered in flour, but she comes to me, holds her arms out like wings, and kisses me on the cheek.

"Thanks for coming, Ollie. I'm sorry again about calling you. I remember my own first morning, and...Well. Coffee?"

"Sure, Mom. What's cooking?"

"A cake. Trying to keep busy. Idle hands, you know."

"Smells great."

She pours coffee for us both and we sit at the kitchen table.

"So," she says, "how's married life?"

"Mom, it's been less than twenty-four hours. A little early to tell."

"I suppose."

We sip our coffee. A bell chimes in the oven and she rushes to take the cake out and set it on a rack to cool, relieved, it seems to me, to be distracted. She comes back to the table.

"So. About this Singapore business."

"I'm really sorry I didn't tell you about the move sooner. It all happened so fast, and—"

"Ollie, I have a confession to make."

I put down my cup. My mind races to all the possible stories she's about to tell me.

"You know how I told you your uncle Scotty was in Singapore?"

I nod. She's nodding along with me, but then her nod morphs into a shake.

She hands me a postcard. It's a picture of some weird lion-headed mermaid spitting water into the ocean, a symbol that for some reason the Singaporeans are proud of. I know that much from my internet searches and the links the school sent us.

"I received this in 1997. What I'm saying is that Scotty isn't in Singapore and probably never was. Or maybe just long enough to buy this postcard."

The postmark says Hong Kong. On the back, scrawled in big letters, just like the note he left for me: *Sorry. XOXOX Scotty.* The guy's a serial apologizer.

"I'm sorry if I misled you, Ollie. I never thought you'd pick up and move to the other side of the planet to look for him. I feel terrible. I guess that's why I panicked last night."

A little honesty for a change. And how do I feel about this revelation? Yes, I picked Singapore because I'm looking for Scotty and that was my best—my only—clue as to where he might be. That and the spooky coincidence that it's where I sent Oliver and Maria in my story. I don't know what I'll do if I ever do find him, though. I haven't gotten that far in my thinking. Honestly, the more I've thought about it, the move isn't *just* about Scotty. It really isn't. This is the adventure I need to give my life meaning, to give me something to write about. I can't just sit here forever dreaming about someone else's life. Okay, so it's not Bruce Owens's idea of an adventure, and it's not Oliver's, either, but this is me being brave.

I look at the postcard again. It's in perfect condition, as if she'd just bought it off the rack herself. No wear and tear. Other than the postmark, no sign of it being mailed halfway around the world or, for that matter, sitting in some drawer for the last decade and a half.

"I'm really sorry, Ollie." There's something else in her voice, though. It's not just about Singapore, it occurs to me.

"Sorry for what, Mom?"

I'm pacing in the Bergers' living room, increasingly certain that we're going to miss our flight. I look at my watch, pace, look at my watch again, sit briefly on the edge of the couch, then pace. Mary can barely escape Lydia's clutches, for one thing, and for another, Mary's farewell to Barney is a serious sobfest that drags on and on. Bill and I finally get her and our mounds of luggage into his car, and we pull away from the house with no time to spare, off to Washington's Dulles International Airport. I have a sinking feeling, though. We're going to be late.

But Mary has forgotten something, vitamins or a magazine or something else she says she can't live without or replace, and we have to go back. She grabs whatever it is, hugs Barney and then Lydia again, and when we're at last on the way for real, Bill says, "Not to worry, I know a shortcut."

He doesn't say anything for a few minutes after that, white-knuckling the steering wheel, eyes focused on the road and the street signs, and it seems to me that we're lost. I'm practically holding my breath because I'm now certain we're going to miss the flight, which probably wouldn't upset Mary a bit but would put a major crimp in my carefully arranged itinerary.

Finally, Bill loosens his grip on the wheel, a smile appears on his face, and the airport entrance is in sight. I breathe again. We pull up at the terminal, unload everything, Bill hugs Mary, shakes my hand, and, having performed his duty, zooms off.

Given how the morning has gone so far, I fully expect a trip-killing wait at check-in, or security, or on the shuttle to the gate. But none of that happens. And then I expect dirty looks from the other passengers as we rush to get on the plane and stow our carry-ons, but we aren't even the last to board the massive jumbo jet, not by a long shot, and no one pays us any attention. We find our seats, I stash our stuff overhead, and as we buckle ourselves in for takeoff we both, comically, sigh.

It's good to see Mary laugh. I take her hand.

"This is going to be great," she says.

"Definitely great," I say, and kiss her.

Now that we're on our way, now that it's too late for her to change her mind, I mean, I consider telling Mary about Scotty. Telling her everything. How I'm convinced Scotty abused me when I was a kid, how he was banished from the family because of it, how that's all connected to my apparent attraction to Mike, and the reason we're going to Singapore—part of the reason anyway—is that I thought I would find him there and finally confront him about what he did. But she's grinning like a lunatic and flipping through pages in a glossy fashion magazine, looking up now and then at me or out the window at the endless sky, and although I know I should tell her all those things, I just can't.

26

Mom's revelation has convinced me that Scotty is probably no longer in Singapore, if he ever was. Still, he has to be somewhere, and as Mary and I navigate halfway around the world, through Dulles and O'Hare and Narita and on to Singapore's Changi Airport, I keep an eye out for him, as irrational as that may seem. That man in the tweed jacket over there by the departures monitor. Is that Scotty? Or the guy sitting at the bar with a bottle of beer in front of him while he watches soccer on TV? The soldier in dress fatigues coming out of the restroom?

At first, Mary and I talk about our great adventure and how excited we are, but the hours and the layovers and the bad food and the engine roar and stale air and the smell of the bathrooms right behind us, cast a pall, and the excitement turns to boredom. We watch the bad movies, we read, we eat the food deposited on our tray tables by indifferent flight attendants, we doze.

The man snoring three rows ahead of us? The pilot? The guy in the suit in the noodle shop at Narita?

At long last, blurry with fatigue, barely able to keep my eyes open, I take Mary's hand again just as we land in Singapore.

There's some required reading for every new American expat in Singapore, a book called *Culture Shock*, about all the things newcomers encounter that will take getting used to, and almost nothing about life in our new home doesn't qualify: the heat; the humidity; the rain; the geckos—try convincing your squeamish wife that having lizards inside the house is a good thing; the language, known as Singlish, which is almost, but not quite, English; the traffic—although we couldn't possibly own a car here, they're too expensive because of taxes, but I already miss my Impala; the food, tasty, but oh-so-strange; the people; the religion; the students; the other teachers; the trees and lush greenery; the insects; the smells; the parts of the city that are like separate countries, Little India, little this, little that. It never ends. I find it exciting, but Mary is having some trouble adapting.

"Be brave," I tell her. She looks at me like I've lost my mind.

The superintendent of the school assures us we will get used to everything.

"It just takes time," he says. "Fortunately, soon you'll be so busy with work you won't even have time to notice where you are." He laughs, and we laugh along with him, uncomfortably. We've made possibly the second biggest mistake of our lives. That's what I'm thinking, and I'd bet a large amount of money, if I had it, that Mary is thinking exactly the same thing.

But the superintendent is right. Between lesson planning and the actual teaching, which Mary, especially, throws herself into, not to mention all the faculty meetings and sessions with parents—mothers, mostly, who have accompanied their working husbands on their exotic expat assignments—and paperwork and furnishing the small flat the school found for us, we've barely had time to feel, much less articulate, the regrets I know we both harbor: the hasty move, the even hastier marriage.

But there are contracts to be fulfilled. Vows.

No way out.

On our first Sunday, we wake up early because the air-conditioning in our flat died during the night and the air grew hot and stuffy as soon as the sun hit our windows. We call the landlord, but it's Sunday, and so there are no promises about when the problem will be fixed. We had both planned to work—there's still so much to do at this point in the semester—but it's unbearable inside. By noon we're ready to get out, to go somewhere, anywhere.

We've been told that the quintessential Singapore dining experience can be found in a hawker center, which resembles a shopping mall food court, except that it's outside and nowhere near a shopping mall. Mary is unconvinced, but we can't stay in the apartment, so we head toward Newton Circus, one of the oldest hawker centers in the city.

"Walking is a great way to get to know our new home," I say as we embark, full of optimism. I point out a flowering tree and lush greenery along the roadside and I wish I knew the names of these plants. They don't call it the "Garden City" for nothing.

"It's awfully hot, though, isn't it?" she asks. "Is this normal?"

We've looked at the map in my antique atlas countless times. She knows we're just a little north of the equator, and so, yes, it's normal. How often do I have to explain it? "Endless summer," I say, aiming for a positive spin on our discomfort.

Positive spin aside, it *is* bloody hot. Sweat is dripping from my forehead before we've walked five minutes. Mary was smart to wear a hat.

Because of the heat, we're not doing much talking. She gazes at an unusual flower, I point to a weird building. Mostly we're concentrating on moving forward and squinting against the bright sun.

After twenty minutes or so, Mary says, "Ollie, I think we've made a mistake."

Here it comes. She's realized this whole plan was flawed from the start. Our marriage, Singapore.

"Mary—" I begin, although I don't feel like arguing. I didn't get enough sleep and I'm choking in this heat.

"Don't you think we should have taken a taxi?"

"What?"

"A taxi. I think maybe we read the map wrong."

"A taxi. Yes, you're absolutely right, sweetie. A taxi."

What I thought would be a pleasant half-hour walk has already taken us well over an hour and we're not there yet. I'm so drenched I might as well be swimming. But just as we're about to surrender and flag down a cab, we see a sign that indicates Newton Circus is straight ahead. With some relief, despite our exhaustion, we pick up the pace.

A circus, we discover, has nothing to do with clowns and trapeze artists, but is instead a traffic roundabout, this one absorbing and disgorging vehicles from five different roads, not to mention the elevated highway that soars overhead. To get to the hawker center, we have to cross the busiest of the roads on a pedestrian bridge, and with that final exertion we are both fully depleted when we arrive.

We examine the offerings of the food vendors, a couple dozen of which are scattered around the complex. I'm game for anything, but at the first place, after we watch a cook assemble an oyster omelet, Mary shakes her head. I'm not really an oyster fan either. At the next stall they're dishing up steaming bowls of fishhead curry, and Mary doesn't even stop to look. I like the smell of the fried noodles at the next place, but Mary points to the bits of octopus in the dish and shakes her head again.

"Come on, Mary, it's just like calamari."

"It looks horrible, Ollie. I can't eat it."

"Suit yourself," I say, my patience spent, "but I'm starving." I step up and order a plate of the noodles, which look amazing to me. I hear a faint squeal behind me, like a mouse caught in a trap, but I don't turn to look at her. Hey, I'm hot and tired, too, okay? When I have my noodles and turn around, she's vanished. I get a cold bottle of Tiger beer, find a table in the shade, and dig in. I'm determined not to look for her. I'm also determined to love the noodles, which are greasy and bland and harder to eat with chopsticks than I thought they'd be. The bits of octopus are rubbery and awful, but I keep eating.

Eventually, she returns and sits at my table. She has a cup of some frothy juice, which looks wonderful and refreshing.

"How are the noodles?" she asks.

"Delicious," I say.

"Really?"

Her eyes go to the little pile of octopus bits I've been building on the side of the plate, so it's hard to keep up the pretense. "No," I admit. "It kind of sucks."

She laughs, then stops, cautious. But then I laugh too, and we're both laughing.

"Hawker centers may take some getting used to," I say. She nods.

Now that we're past that rough patch, I can look around. There are several families who look like they're probably locals: Chinese mother and father with a couple of unruly kids. But there are a few foreigners too. One couple with a map laid out on their table are obviously tourists, but another couple, a little older than us, with a toddler in a stroller, may be expats. And there's a man by himself at a distant table. He's got brown hair and a mustache and I realize it's him: Uncle Scotty.

My face must have gone white, because Mary says, "What's the matter, Ollie, what's wrong?"

The man stands and he comes our way. I can't breathe. After all this time, what am I going to say? He's wearing jeans and a T-shirt that says something in French, and now that I'm getting a better look at him I see that he's not Scotty. Not even close. This man is much younger, closer to my age. I begin breathing again.

"Ollie?" Mary asks. "Are you all right?"

I still haven't told her about Scotty. I haven't told her anything.

"Just tired. And hot."

"Me too. Can we take a taxi home?"

I nod.

કે

Finally, after six weeks or so, our lives have settled into a routine. We still barely have time to catch our breath, but that may be a blessing: we don't notice how miserable we are. It's funny that Oliver loves it in Singapore and I'm struggling, but then his Singapore and mine are very different. For one thing, his air-conditioning never fails.

At first, Mary and I spent all our time together except while in our separate classrooms, and everything was new and exciting, if somewhat intimidating and strange. But now, having found our footing, more or less, we move more independently, which is surely good for our relationship and sanity. Mary has joined a book club with other teachers from the school. Given our disparate literary tastes, I don't even ask what they're reading. I play basketball a couple of nights a week in the school gym, which makes me think of the time I spent with Q, shooting baskets in our driveway. Other than jogging and a little baseball in high school, I'm not much of an athlete, but most of the guys I play with aren't either, and I relish the time to myself—or at any rate, away from Mary.

One night we get to the gym and find it locked. No sign, no explanation, no alternative. I'm discovering that stuff like this happens in Singapore all the time. People just shrug and go about their business. Some of the guys head home, back to their wives, but the single guys go to a pub. As I'm already at the school, I seize the opportunity to do some work on the internet that I've been reluctant to do in Mary's company. The longer I keep Uncle Scotty a secret, the harder it's going to be to tell her, but I'm just not ready.

I discover that the Government of Singapore's archives are nothing if not thorough, and much of the information is now available online, so I begin there first. These people keep track of *everything*. If Oliver Scott Tucker left any mark in this country, it will show up here. I try several variations of the name: Oliver S. Tucker, O. Scott Tucker, O.S. Tucker. Over the years, there have been a good many Tuckers, but most are on the books as British civil servants during the colonial era, decades before Scotty's time. No mention of my uncle that I can find.

If he was, indeed, just passing through the country, no more than a tourist, then my search is futile. And that's what Mom's postcard might suggest. He was here for a short visit, and then on to Hong Kong, and who knows where after that. If so, I'll never find him.

But it's also possible he was here longer, so I keep looking.

I ask myself: What would he have done here that might be traceable? What do most Americans do here? They join the American Club, if they can afford it, which teachers like us generally can't. They join the American Business Council to connect with other business-minded expats. I can investigate their membership records, if they'll let me. Not likely.

He might have taught right here in this school. If I'm qualified to do it, he certainly would have been. It's a long shot, but worth checking.

I browse the school's website, external and internal, and see no listing of former teachers. But something else catches my eye: yearbooks. There are digital versions of every yearbook produced by the school over the last twenty years or so. I click on 1997, the year Scotty's postcard was sent, scroll through to find pictures of the faculty—no Tucker. Could he have used a different name? I go through all the pictures and none of the men match. A few are the right age, but I've got a reasonable idea of what he looked like from that photo of him and Dad I found in the album, and he's not there.

Where are you Scotty? What brought you to Singapore?

On basketball nights, I usually get a ride home with one of the other guys who has a car, but since we didn't play tonight and we all went our separate ways, that's not an option. Now I'm wishing I'd gone to the pub after all. It would have been a fun distraction and I'd probably have gotten a lift home. I wait for the bus that will take me to the apartment block where we live—I try not to think of it as a housing project like the low-income developments I remember seeing downtown in Indianapolis, although that's what it is—but it doesn't come and it doesn't come. The apartment is only about a mile from the school, though, so I set off on foot. Even at night, the humidity here gets to me, and I'm a sopping mess by the time I arrive.

"Where have you been?" Mary demands.

"The game—"

"Don't give me that. I know the game was canceled. Andy's wife is in the book club, remember? He called."

"That's what I was trying to tell you. The game was canceled, so I went to my office to do some work."

"What work?"

"Research. For a story I'm writing."

"What kind of—"

"What's with the interrogation?" I ask. "I don't think I like it."

She's been pacing the tiled floor of our tiny living room and now she stops.

"You're right. I'm sorry. It's just that—"

"What?"

"Don't ever lie to me."

I have no idea where that came from.

"I won't," I say. "I promise."

෧

"So," Professor Russell said, "there are some things about which we can be certain."

I immediately sensed a trap after all the blind alleys he'd sent us down that semester, but we'd had this conversation before and most of the other students were nodding, so I did too.

"We may know something because it is accepted *a priori*. Or we may accept as true, and therefore known, something we experience for ourselves. Or we may know something because it is proven, beyond doubt, to be true."

More nodding. So far the argument was familiar.

"But what if," said the professor, an impish grin flashing briefly on his face, "we are mistaken?"

If there is doubt about a truth, then it cannot be said to be known. I remember this much from our earlier discussion. We can only know what is certain. If there is the possibility that we're mistaken, then we cannot know. We'd heard all this.

"What if," Russell continued, "we have been deceived?"

27

The day after the canceled basketball game, it occurs to me that I'd been too limited in my yearbook search for Uncle Scotty. The postcard had been mailed in 1997, but of course I should have checked other years. The school library has hard copies of the yearbooks, so I pull a few off the shelf and start looking. 1998—nothing, although there's a woman on the faculty who looks exactly like my eleventh-grade English teacher. Weird. I've already seen 1997, but I page through it just in case I missed something. Nope.

The library is standard-issue: kid-sized tables and plastic chairs, lots of plastic-covered books on low shelves, giving a clear field for supervision of any trouble-making students who might wander in. No place to hide.

The librarian is watching me and comes over to the table where I've spread out the books. I must look suspicious.

"Is there something I can help you with?" he asks.

"Just curious about what the place was like in the old days," I say. "I don't suppose you were working here in the '90s, were you?"

"No, not me. I only started here last year. Most people move on after a few years. I was in Korea before this. Wanderlust, you know."

I smile and nod, thinking it will be a miracle if Mary and I last even that long. The librarian returns to his desk, and I grab 1996. I think it was about that year, when I was six, that Uncle Scotty disappeared, maybe '95. I page through the faculty section, looking at every name and every photo. There is no one named Oliver Tucker.

There is, however, one very familiar looking face, and under that picture is the name Tucker Scott.

I'll be damned. I found him.

Emails from home:

> Dear Ollie, so proud of you for striking off on your own like this, even though it's for the wrong reason. I'm sorry (again) for the little part I may have played in that. I only wish you were closer so I could visit. Isn't Singapore that place where they executed a kid for chewing gum? Love, Mom.

> Dear Mom, I think that was Indiana. LOL. Love, Ollie

> Dear Ollie, Mom is so disappointed in you. She calls and cries and cries. How could you just up and leave like that? Especially so soon after Q. She's a complete wreck and hitting it pretty hard. And then there's Dad. Don't get me started. He's driving me nuts. Thank God I have the twins and the baby to keep me sane. Hah hah. But seriously, I could use some help with the old man. The burden shouldn't fall on me just because I'm nearby. First Q deserts me and then you. Love, Sally-Ann.

> Dear Silly, really sorry Dad is being a pain, but this is something I had to do. Love, Ollie.

And this one I found on the computer screen one day when Mary forgot to log out:

> Dear Mary, your father is a lying, cheating bastard, and I'm leaving him. Love, Mom.

According to the helpful librarian who has done some checking for me, the only current employee at the American School who was here back in 1996 is a Singaporean woman, a secretary. Mrs. Liew is her name, and I go to see her. She's petite, with tightly permed black hair and eyeglasses dangling on a chain around her neck. She's got the tidiest workspace ever. No loose papers. A row of sharpened pencils on her desk—how did she get them all to be exactly the same length?—is the only clutter.

"My name is Ollie Tucker—"

"I know who you are. Who do you think processes all the personnel files around here?"

"Of course. I'm sorry. I was wondering—"

"You were wondering about one Tucker Scott, a former teacher at this school, whose picture, not to mention name, bears a striking resemblance to yours."

"Are you clairvoyant, Mrs. Liew?"

"No such thing. I just have a damn good memory, especially for handsome young men like Mr. Scott. You're related, I take it?" Mrs. Liew winks, and I wonder if it's possible that this relic is coming on to me.

"I'm not sure, to be honest. I was browsing through old yearbooks here at the school and came across his picture. We do look a little alike, I suppose."

"A coincidence then? A rather striking coincidence, isn't it?"

"The world is full of mystery, don't you think, Mrs. Liew?"

Mrs. Liew goes to a massive file cabinet and pulls out a manila folder. She returns to her pristine desk and consults a typed form she's extracted from the folder.

"It's even more of a coincidence, Mr. Tucker, that both you and Mr. Scott list Indianapolis, State of Indiana, as your place of birth. Isn't that peculiar, Mr. Tucker?"

"Indeed, Mrs. Liew."

Indeed.

"Is there anything else I can help you with?"

"I was wondering if you know what became of Mr. Scott. I understand teachers frequently move to other international schools, and maybe Mr. Scott did that?"

"I wouldn't know, Mr. Tucker. But I do have a forwarding address here. Confidential information, as I'm sure you understand. I'm not supposed to give it out to anyone. Of course this was 1996, so that was a long time ago, and who knows if the address is still good. I don't think there's any harm in passing this along to you now." She takes one of her sharpened pencils, writes the address on an index card, and hands it to me.

It's in Tokyo.

ৡ

I can't help but envy Oliver, whose life is so different from mine. If I were Oliver, if I were rich and ran my own company like he does, I'd leave for Tokyo immediately to find Scotty. And I wouldn't be afraid of my feelings toward Mike. I'd do something about that too. But no, probably not.

Still, as the semester grinds on, I'm feeling content here, and I think the same goes for Mary. Or, if not quite content, then settled, at least. Singapore is without doubt the hottest place either of us has ever been, but it's also fantastically beautiful and lush. One day, just outside our apartment building, a crew was cutting off the limbs of a gorgeous tree, a rain tree, as I learned later. At home, I might have asked them to stop, insisting that they were hurting the tree and damaging the environment. But I didn't do that, and it was just a matter of weeks before the tree had regenerated, more luxuriant and beautiful than before. Now I realize that given half a chance the jungle would reclaim the entire city.

Mornings are always a rush during the week, but on weekends we start the day on our tiny balcony, sipping coffee and reading the paper, the *Straits Times*, which isn't half bad for a government-controlled rag. Until the heat builds, forcing us into our air-conditioned refuge (when it works, we're in heaven).

We're doing just that, when Oliver and Miguel come into my head, followed by Mike.

"Say," I say, "something just occurred to me."

Mary looks up from the paper.

"I bet your brother would like it here. He should visit. Wouldn't that be fun?"

ৡ

Dear Mary, Are you out of your fucking mind? I have zero interest in visiting you and whatshisname in that fascist police state. But thanks for asking. Love, Mike

Dear Ollie, Jacob says it was you who gave him the pot. You really shouldn't encourage him. It's Un-Christian. Yours in Christ, Sally-Ann

Dear Silly, Un-Christian? Since when? Love, Ollie

Dear Ollie, Since I was born again. It's the only way to cope with the little bastards. Yours in Christ, Sally-Ann

Dear Bruce, I was thinking of writing a story based on my sister who's turned into an evangelical nut job because her husband is a pot-smoking, video-gaming undertaker. Promising idea? Yours, Ollie

Dear Ollie, Families don't understand fiction. All life is fiction and all fiction is life. You're fucked if you do and you're fucked if you don't. Go for it. Bruce

Dear Silly, Thanks a lot. Now I'm probably on the watch list of Singapore's anti-drug SWAT team or something. By the way, anything you say or do can and will be used in a work of fiction. Just so you know. Love, Ollie. P.S. Your husband's a liar.

Dear Ollie, I'm so sorry for falsely accusing you. Jacob has confessed it was his brother who gave him the pot. He has promised to come to church with me this week to atone for his fib. Yours in Christ, Sally-Ann

Dear Silly, Are you sure Jacob even has a brother? If I were you I'd check his text messages from someone named brn2bbad, who may or may not be a kid who hangs out on a street corner in Broad Ripple. You didn't hear that from me. Love, Ollie

Dear Bruce, Thanks for the advice. Are you saying that your last book was based on your family? That was some steamy stuff. Yours, Ollie

Dear Ollie, Your family will see themselves in your work no matter what you do, so you might as well make it entertaining. Be brave! Bruce

❧

I've thought of writing an essay about my family, about the abuse I believe I suffered as a child, and about my search for Uncle Scotty. My brother's suicide. My crazy father. My crazy sister and her crazy husband. My crazy mother. Me, probably crazy.

But, however vivid a portrait I might be able to create, the nature of nonfiction is such that these people, these characters, would be pale imitations of themselves. They would not be real. I could never do them justice. My efforts to create realistic characters on the page, paradoxically, would reduce them to two dimensions. They would be mere representations and not the actual beings.

Whereas, in a work of fiction, the characters on the page are the originals. They are real, not shadows, and have the potential to be multi-dimensional. In that way, fiction is more real than reality.

That's what Bruce Owens says, anyway. He says that family, or other real live human beings, provide only models. The writer can't know what they're really thinking, for example, or how they really feel. But the characters we create, we know them. Their thoughts are our thoughts. Their feelings are our feelings.

The more I write about Oliver, the more real he becomes.

28

Mary and I can't afford to go home for Christmas, and my idea of having Mike visit went nowhere, obviously, so we plan a beach getaway at a resort in Malaysia. Because of her parents' problems, Mary has been especially homesick lately, so I let her plan the whole thing, and I'm happy to see the enthusiasm with which she tackles the project. It's not going to get me any closer to finding Uncle Scotty, but it will be a welcome diversion.

She books us into a hotel, gets us onto a flight during one of the region's busiest travel periods, and makes a list of all the things we're going to do when we get there: go snorkeling, explore caves, take in a show in the resort's nightclub, shop in the local crafts market, visit a traditional village, and learn about tea ceremony.

"I thought tea ceremony was Japanese," I say.

"Malaysians drink tea, too, apparently," she says.

This is the first time we've left Singapore since our arrival, and we are struck by the vastness of the airport, something we didn't notice the night we landed here, flight-weary as we were. It's a marvel, and we're a little proud of ourselves that we live in such a modern, clean city. At least, I am.

"Don't you think this place is awfully phony?" Mary asks.

"Who are you all of a sudden, Holden Caulfield?"

"Ho, ho, ho," she says.

Briefly, I think she's in the holiday spirit, but then she sticks her tongue out at me.

"It's just so goddamn clean," she says, and, before I can make another *Catcher in the Rye* crack, continues, "like some kind of alternate universe Disneyland."

Whoa. Has she been talking to Bruce Owens?

"It's clean, I grant you," I say, "but since when is that a bad thing?"

"You don't get it, do you?"

"Every time we go to DC you complain about trash on the street, beggars, dogshit on the sidewalk. Here? None of that."

"Because they hide the poor people and throw you in jail for littering. It's just not real."

"You want real? You want litter? You want poverty? So, naturally, we're going to an exclusive resort where the natives are kept safely outside locked gates, except when they're asked to perform like trained seals."

"Not the same."

"Let's drop it. We're not going to agree on this."

"Fine," she says.

"Fine," I say.

We board the flight, but we're not speaking. We sit next to each other, but I'm reading a Robert Stone novel I picked up in the airport and she's reading the airline's in-flight magazine. About an hour into the flight, I hear her groan.

"What's the matter?" I say.

"I think I've made a terrible mistake," she says. Here it comes, I think. For real this time. I'm finally going to hear all about her regrets—marrying me, letting me talk her into coming to Singapore. I knew this day would come.

"It was just a little argument, sweetie," I say. "I'm sorry. You were right, really. Singapore is pretty phony."

"No, no, not that."

"What, then?"

"I booked us on this flight to Phuket."

"Yeah, it's sweet. Free wine, snacks. You did great."

"Uh-huh. Very nice. The thing is, the hotel room I reserved is in Langkawi. Which is in Malaysia. Not Phuket. Which is in Thailand. For some reason I thought they were the same place, but I'm looking at this map and they're not. They're hundreds of miles apart."

If we weren't in a pressurized cabin 25,000 feet above the

planet among a few hundred other passengers, it's safe to say
I would explode. Even for Mary, this is a colossal fuck-up. But
then the truth dawns on me. And I relax, take a sip of wine,
reopen my book.

"Ha ha, very funny," I say. "You had me going there for a
minute. Good one. Hilarious. This is going to be so much fun.
We're going to have a blast."

"Ollie, don't kill me. But I'm not kidding." She shows me the
printout of our hotel reservation in Langkawi, a resort along
the Malaysian coast that we're probably passing over right now,
five miles down.

We'll be landing in Phuket, in Thailand, in another hour or
so. Wrong time. Wrong place.

The minute we disembark, Mary is in line at the customer service counter in the airport terminal. Everyone else from our
flight—Singaporeans, Americans, Brits, a dozen other nation-
alities, all dressed in resort attire for their seaside holiday—is
heading toward customs and immigration.

She explains the mix-up to the ticket agent, vaguely placing
the blame on the airline for delivering us to the wrong destination. The agent is, understandably, confused.

"You wanted to go to Langkawi, but instead you fly to
Phuket?"

"Yes, that's correct."

"Your travel agent made a mistake?"

"Something like that, yes," says Mary, still polite, still deflecting responsibility, although I can see the panic building. Despite
the months in the tropics, her skin is quite pale, and the anxiety
is manifesting itself in bright red splotches on her cheeks and
arms.

"Let's see what we can do," says the agent, cheerfully,
politely, masking, I'm sure, her utter disdain for these stupid
Americans who have arrived in the wrong country. She types
on her keyboard, studies the computer monitor. Mary is leaning
forward on the counter as if trying to see the screen, where lies

possible absolution for her idiocy. I believe I can almost hear her silent prayers.

"So. Unfortunately, there are no direct flights from Phuket to Langkawi. There is a flight leaving here in one hour for Kuala Lumpur. From there you could connect to another flight to Langkawi." She types some more.

"Thank God," says Mary. Her prayers are answered. Hallelujah.

"Unfortunately," says the agent, peering at her screen, "the flight to KL is overbooked, so I can't even put you on standby." More typing. "In two hours there is a flight to Singapore—"

"We just came from there!" says Mary, annoyance finally creeping into her voice.

"But there are no seats available, anyway. Unfortunately." More typing.

"Please help us," Mary pleads. "We have to get to Langkawi. My husband's life depends on it."

The agent looks up from her computer, first at Mary, then at me, a robust picture of health, then back at Mary.

"Okay, not really," Mary says. "My life, though, is in jeopardy if we don't get there, because my husband will most likely kill me." She laughs, a very nervous laugh, to let the agent know she's joking. The agent doesn't crack a smile. She looks back at the screen.

"I can get you two first class seats on the flight to Bangkok that leaves tonight, connecting to a flight to KL, and I can put you on standby for the first flight to Langkawi from KL in the morning. That's the best I can do. Shall I book that for you?"

A line has begun to form behind us, people with real problems that they probably didn't create for themselves. Mary's eyes are about to overflow with tears and she can't even speak to the agent. I step forward, gather our boarding passes and tickets, and take Mary by the arm.

"Thank you for your help," I say. "But we'll just stay here in Phuket."

We step up to the Thai immigration counter. The agent there is staring at us with not-unwarranted suspicion. The arrival forms ask us to specify our address on the island, but the hotel where we have reservations is in a different country, so there is puzzlement on the face of the official. He looks at me, and I shrug. The other passengers from our flight have already cleared immigration, and now tears are streaming down Mary's face. I'm wondering if those tears might not somehow be to our benefit if it looks like they'll refuse to let us in, and sure enough he is soon stamping our passports and pointing us in the direction of baggage claim and customs.

While we wait for our luggage to tumble onto the carousel, I put my arm around Mary and kiss her forehead. Now is not the time for blame. Now is the time for comfort and generosity of spirit. "Someday," I say, "we'll both find this terribly amusing."

She twists away from me and scowls. "If you ever, and I mean *ever*, tell anyone about this, I will cut off your balls and stuff them down your throat. Do you hear me?"

"Loud and clear, sweetie."

Loud and clear.

Once we're in the arrivals hall, we are confronted with a dozen taxi drivers clamoring for our attention, but we push past them. I spot an information counter that appears to have brochures about hotels and resorts, and I aim in that direction. Mary is trailing behind me, wishing, I'm certain, that she were dead. Or I was, one of the two. I stop, and she bumps into me, which should be funny, but isn't.

"What now?" she asks. There's exasperation in her voice, as if one more snafu, no matter how minor, will push her over the edge.

"There's the solution to our problem, sweetie." I point to the counter. "Cheer up. It's not the end of the world. Go over to that desk right there and find us a nice place to stay here in Phuket. I'm sure we'll have a lovely time." I nudge her toward the counter, but stay close behind for moral support.

She starts to cry again. "But it's a holiday, Ollie. Everything's been booked solid for weeks. It's hopeless."

"Just give it a try. It won't hurt to ask, will it?"

Off she goes, shuffling across the tiled floor like a little girl who has been sent to bed without her supper.

While she's engaged in discussion with the smiling man behind the desk, I marvel that this place is even standing. It wasn't so long ago that Phuket was devastated by a tsunami. Tens of thousands of people were swept to sea and their bodies never recovered. Whole villages wiped out. It makes me kind of glad we're here. We're helping them heal and get on their feet.

Mary turns back to me, smiling now, no sign of her recent tears. She waves me forward and I join her at the counter.

"It's not on the beach," she says, excitement and relief in her voice. "Most places are full, of course, but this *pension* had a cancellation this morning. Pool, café, short walk to the ocean. It actually sounds nice. Very nice, considering." Her confidence is restored. She's beaming. I kiss her again, and this time she doesn't pull away.

A shuttle bus takes us from the airport to the *pension*. The Phuket sky is cloudless. I think of the money we've lost by paying for two hotels—the one where we'll stay and the one in Langkawi—but when the victims of the tsunami come to mind again, I don't mind. I take Mary's hand and don't let go until we get to the hotel.

Professor Russell continued his discussion about deception. We had come to the conclusion that there are some things that can be known with certainty, unless, of course, we're wrong.

Descartes, he told the class, posited the existence of a malignant demon who has persuaded us of the certainty of ideas that are not actually true. If the demon exists and has deceived us, of what, then, can we be certain?

Blank expressions all around the room.

"I think," Professor Russell said, "therefore I am."

That sounds familiar, but we were still puzzled.

"The demon cannot deceive us about thinking," he went on, patiently. How many times had he explained this paradox over the years, to each new crop of clueless undergraduates?

"Because even if we are deceived about the subject of our thought, we are still thinking. If we doubt that we are thinking, we are *still* thinking. Therefore, Descartes would have it, this is the ultimate proof of existence, the one thing of which we can be absolutely certain. *Cogito ergo sum.*"

I think.

It's Christmas morning. We're on the little lanai off our room, from which the ocean can be glimpsed if one's neck is craned at just the right angle, drinking jasmine tea and eating a breakfast of bananas and papaya. The day promises to be another hot one, but right now there's a breeze and the temperature is still pleasant. Later we'll lie on the beach, maybe rent some snorkel gear and paddle offshore.

"Open yours first," Mary says. The trip itself was our big treat—we needed to get away from Singapore and the school more than we realized—but we've also brought small gifts for each other to open.

As I tear the wrapping off, she says, "I didn't know what to get you."

Inside the small box is a tiny silver antelope on a leather strap. It's beautiful. It really is. I'm speechless. She's seen the T-shirt I sometimes wear, and the poster in my room at Mom's house, but I'm sure I haven't told her that the antelope is my spirit animal, the creature that most embodies the characteristics I would wish for myself.

"I know you don't wear jewelry, but I thought you'd like this, not to wear maybe but just to have?"

"It's beautiful, Mary. It really is. Thank you." I kiss her and slip the strap over my head. I touch the antelope, a talisman that will bring me strength. "You next."

My track record with Mary and gifts is not good, but I put a lot of thought into this one. She opens it and her eyes actually twinkle. I'm sure that's a good thing.

"A Japanese language computer program?"

I think she was expecting something else. Just about anything other than this, from the look on her face.

"You know how we get that long break over the Chinese New Year? We haven't seen anything in the region outside of Singapore. Wouldn't it be great to visit Tokyo? It's one of the world's great cities and we're so close. And I know you're interested in foreign languages." Not that we can really afford to go, especially after paying for two hotels on this trip, but we'll borrow from our folks or something. I need to get to Japan.

"You're joking, right?" That's not just disappointment in her voice. More like anger. Fury, even. She's standing now. "Is this your idea of a joke?"

"I thought you'd love the idea, sweetie. It could be like a real honeymoon for us."

"Ollie. You don't know anything about me, do you? If you did, you'd know that the only place I want to go right now is home. And by home, I do *not* mean Singapore. If you want to go to Japan, be my guest. But I sure as fucking hell am not going with you."

She yanks open the door into our room and leaves me alone on the narrow lanai.

Back in Singapore, things are a bit tense around our apartment. Mary is pouring herself into work, either because she loves teaching that much or because she needs the distraction from me. And I've decided that she's being totally unreasonable about Japan, so I dig in my heels. If she doesn't want to go to Tokyo, I'll go without her. If she doesn't want to study Japanese on the CDs I bought, then screw it. I'll learn the language myself just to spite her.

"*Ohayo gozaimasu*," I say to her each morning, knowing it will piss her off. It does.

But I persist with my studies, memorizing dialogues that I hope will be useful. I haven't yet made reservations, because I keep hoping Mary will change her mind and agree to come with me, but also because I know there is something cataclysmic about my going alone. It's a break that I don't think we can survive. I suspect that I can bring it all to a head by telling her about Scotty, but at this point, having waited so long, that's a considerable gamble. Either she'll forgive me and we'll move on, or she won't and we'll be done.

One night toward the end of January—I keep thinking it should be cold, but the Singapore heat and humidity are just as oppressive as always—she joins me on our apartment's tiny balcony where I am marking papers from my tenth graders, every one of them a rehash of the trite themes of *Ethan Frome*. I'm grateful for the distraction, so I set the essays aside and look at her expectantly. It looks like she's got something important to say. I prepare for the worst.

"Ollie, I've been thinking. I've been a bitch about this Tokyo thing, and I apologize."

That's certainly not what I was expecting. I sit up, on the edge of the chair.

"So you'll come?" I ask.

"No," she says. I'm confused, and I'm sure that's obvious from my expression. "I'm not going with you," she says, "but it's fine with me if you go alone."

I sense a trap, just like in those tricky college philosophy discussions Professor Russell conducted.

"Really?"

"Really. We've spent nearly every minute together since we got married. It won't kill us to be apart for a few days. I think maybe the problem with my parents' marriage is that they never developed any kind of identity of their own as individuals. It's always been 'Bill and Lydia,' never just 'Bill' or 'Lydia.' I'm happy being 'Ollie and Mary,' but I want to be 'Mary,' too. Does that make sense."

It does, remarkably. I nod.

"I'll stay here and relax, get some reading done, sit by the pool. It'll be good for me. Restorative. So you go to Tokyo, have your adventure, enjoy the Forbidden City."

"I think that's in China, sweetie."

29

The new semester at the Singapore American School is barely underway when we break for the Chinese New Year. I pack my bags while Mary reads on the couch. I can't believe I'm doing this, actually going without her. I call a cab, Mary says, "Have a good trip, Ollie," as if I'm the neighbor or some stranger, and all the way to the airport I ponder what has just happened.

As I'm boarding the flight to Tokyo, I almost get out of the queue and head back to the apartment. What is she up to? Is there another man? Is Brian back in the picture? That's unlikely given where we live at the moment, but leaving Mary now seems monumental. A fissure in our marriage that can't be mended, even though she gave me permission and sounded totally sincere about it. On the one hand, it's huge. On the other, she told me to go. Gigantic. But with consent. What to do?

I have to go. That's where Uncle Scotty is. Or might be. If I don't pursue this lead, I'll never find him and I will regret it as long as I live. I don't know what purpose finding him will serve, ultimately. I don't know what I'm going to learn. I just know I have to do it. Maybe when I get back I'll explain it to Mary. That will be hard, but if we're going to get past this bump in our relationship—it's more than a bump, I get it—I suppose she needs to understand why I had to go.

I board the plane and take my seat. It's a seven-hour flight, so there's lots of time to think about what I'll say to Scotty when I find him. In the end it boils down to one question: What happened?

❧

The flight from Singapore to Tokyo was expensive enough, but there's no way I can afford to stay in a hotel without rocketing the credit cards over their limits, especially since I'm still paying

off the charges for two engagement rings and two tropical resorts. So maybe it's just as well that Mary didn't come. This way,
I can travel on the cheap. I don't feel like a "youth" anymore,
but apparently anyone can stay in a youth hostel.

The place I've booked is in Central Tokyo and *should* be easy
to find. It isn't. And I had no idea Japan would be this cold.

I've taken the bus from the airport, which is far away from
the city, and it dumps me at a train station somewhere, I'm not
sure where. I've done exactly as my guidebook instructed, and
still I have no idea where I am. I've always hated to ask for
directions, but I can see that's my only option here. That, or
sleep in the frigid subway station.

But when I take a closer look at my surroundings, I realize
that most of the signs are in Japanese and English, or at least in
Romanized Japanese, so I can make out the street names. More
importantly, I see a trio of young foreigners with backpacks
getting off a bus just like the one that delivered me here. They
seem to know where they're going, so I follow them, and sure
enough we soon arrive at the hostel, which has a big sign out
front: two hands clasped in friendship.

This was so hard, how the hell will I ever find Scotty?

The people at the hostel speak great English. Heavily accented, but the words are recognizable and mostly in the right
order. "*Arigato gozaimasu*," I say, over and over again, right now
the only phrase I remember from my studies: "Thank you!"
They give me a map of the vicinity, directions to the subway,
and help me figure out the money I've obtained from the foreign exchange counter at the airport.

After the long flight, I'm tired and hungry—there's a West-
ern-style coffee shop in the hostel that I've got my eye on—but
I decide to check out the neighborhood first to get my bearings.
Tomorrow I'll find the address I've been given for Scotty.

Tomorrow's the big day.

Roppongi? I can barely say it, never mind find it. But the guy
who works the hostel's front desk offers to help.

"Roppongi here," he says, jabbing his finger at a gray spot on my map. "Take Nanboku line here." Now he's pointing on the map to the station I noticed as I walked around the area to orient myself. "Go to Roppongi." He smiles.

I think I've got it.

I find the station. So far so good. I watch other people use the vending machine to buy tickets, so I follow their lead. I stick some coins into the machine, press the green button, and am rewarded with a ticket and coins tumbling into the change box, which I retrieve. Then I follow the crowd and am confronted with choices of platforms, but no signs for the Nanboku line.

I see a policeman in a black uniform—at least I think that's a policeman—and I approach him. "Roppongi?" I ask.

He points toward an escalator. I nod, mumble, "*arigato go-zaimasu*," and head down the moving stairs.

I'm in the middle of a crush of passengers, and I no longer care if I'm going in the right direction. I just want to get on the train and see where it takes me, watch and learn, and hope for the best.

But, miraculously, I seem to have done the right thing. There are broadcast announcements of train stops and also a lighted sign that displays where we're headed next. The map above my head gives me assurance that, in fact, I'm on my way to Roppongi. Inordinately pleased with myself, I get off, find the exit, and emerge into daylight. I feel like I might deserve a prize, although I know I'm going to face the same anxiety as I stumble my way back to the hostel. But that's later. First, I'm going to find Scotty.

Except, now I'm on another busy street with cars and buses zooming past, and I really have no idea how to find the address I'm looking for, despite the map I hold in my hands. I wander down the street, trying not to look lost, and in about a hundred yards I spot a familiar logo. Starbucks! I'm cold and hungry and tired and a tall coffee is just what I need to recover my wits.

I remember the word for coffee from my Japanese studies—*cohi*—but it seems ridiculous to pretend I speak the language when I'm in an American chain store, so I just ask for a tall coffee. The clerk doesn't miss a beat, even tells me in English what I owe, and with a smile picks the coins out of my hand when it's clear I'm struggling. I take a seat and pull out my map. I'm a tourist, all right? I'm not trying to fool anyone.

"You are looking for a place?" It's the woman at the next table speaking, and I'm struck with the memory of how I met Mary, not yet two years ago, at the coffee shop back home. This woman, though, is Japanese, with long black hair and a baggy sweater that droops off one shoulder.

"Yes, an address here in Roppongi," I say, and point uselessly to the map. I show her the address, still written on the card Mrs. Liew from school gave me.

"It is not far," the woman says. "Walk maybe five minutes from here." She moves to my table and leans over the map, finding the exact location. "Here," she says.

In gratitude, I smile. Not only am I that much closer to finding Uncle Scotty, but I no longer feel quite so lost. I have mastered the subway, I have purchased delicious coffee and a pastry, and I know where I am on the map. The anxiety that has threatened to overwhelm me all morning has, for the moment, subsided.

"Thank you so much," I say. "My name is Ollie." I stick out my hand to shake, instantly realizing that's probably the wrong thing to do in Japan.

"Ali?" she asks. "Like boxer?" She jabs the air with her left and then her right hand, leaving mine adrift in space. I withdraw.

"No," I say, laughing, and then spell it for her. She follows along by drawing the letters on her palm.

Now she laughs, too. "Ollie," she says. "My name is Mariko."

Mariko agrees to show me the way. We bundle up, leave the coffee shop, and she leads me to a crossing where we wait for the walk signal along with what seems like a thousand other obedient pedestrians. When the signal finally comes, it is a familiar green light with a stick figure, accompanied by music that sounds like it's coming from a kazoo.

We all cross together, but Mariko is drifting right while I'm being pulled to the left by the crowd. She disappears from my sight and my anxiety resurfaces, my heart racing, when I feel a hand grab mine. It's Mariko, and she pulls me with her, free of the crush.

Now we walk, hand in hand, to a quieter street, up a slight hill. For a moment, I worry that I've made a mistake placing my trust in this woman. Where is she taking me? Has she lured me onto this side street where an accomplice awaits, ready to bash in my head and steal my valuables?

But no. Mariko's shy grin is transparent. This woman doesn't have a sinister fiber in her. She's helping me, that's all. Altruism is not dead.

Tiny cars are crammed into parking spaces on both sides of the street, which is a canyon of high-rise apartment buildings. On the ground floor of most of the buildings are shops—convenience stores, laundries, noodle stalls—and we have to dodge customers coming and going.

"Show the paper, please," Mariko says. I hand her the slip of paper with Scotty's address. She studies it, nods, and returns it to me. We continue up the hill.

She stops in front of an electronics store. Dozens of cell phones and tiny radios and music players and tablets and watches and televisions fill the shop window. Next to the window are two doors, one leading into the shop and the other into a hallway. We enter the hall, which opens onto a tiny lobby for the apartment building above the shop.

Mariko checks the building directory next to the elevator.

"Many foreigners live here," she says. We look at the directory together, but I see no sign of Scotty's name, either his real name or the inverted form he was using in Singapore.

When the elevator doors open, we go up to the sixth floor and find Scotty's apartment number. If I were alone, I would not have come this far, I suspect, but Mariko presses the doorbell. We wait. I am tempted to press the bell again, but Mariko is patient and I keep waiting. When I hear shuffling feet inside, I step back. I am about to see Scotty for the first time in years. I need to confront him, but of course I am also terrified to learn the truth. I want to run, but I cannot run now. It's too late.

The door opens to reveal a petite blonde woman.

Even though Mariko had said many foreigners live here, I am inexplicably surprised to see a non-Japanese face and at the same time disappointed that the face isn't Scotty's.

"Hello," I say. "Is Tucker Scott here?"

The woman appears puzzled by the question, turns to Mariko, and says something in Japanese. Now *I'm* confused, disoriented. Why is this foreigner speaking Japanese? Mariko responds to the woman and then says to me, "She is from Russia and does not speak English."

And then Mariko speaks to her in Japanese again, a question that I assume is about Scotty. There is an exchange. Mariko nods to me and the Russian woman looks me over. She shakes her head, says in halting English, "I am sorry," and closes the door.

"She does not know your friend," Mariko says, gravely, sorry to be the bearer of bad news. "She has lived in this apartment with her husband for five years. The apartment was vacant when they came here, but she understands that the previous tenant—an American—died."

Died? So Scotty's dead after all? Dad's right? I mean, assuming Scotty was the American who lived here last. Maybe he'd already moved on by then? Maybe this Russian woman is wrong? I'm feeling a jumble of emotions. Relief that I can't confront him but also frustration, and anger, too, because of what I think he did to me. I won't let myself cry.

"Ollie?"

That's it then. I've probably destroyed my marriage by insisting on this wild uncle chase. I've spent a fortune in airfare and the hostel which, even though it's cheap, costs more than I should be spending. And what have I got? Scotty's dead after all.

At least now I can get on with my life.

❧

It's my second morning in Tokyo. I wonder, briefly, how Mary is getting along without me, and if she's done anything to celebrate the Chinese New Year. It's surprising that there is so little fuss made of the holiday here in Japan. I've seen a few red signs that say "Happy New Year" on them, but I wonder if they're not left over from January 1.

In any case, I don't feel much like celebrating myself. I'll never be able to exorcise the ghost of Uncle Scotty now, because he really is a ghost. I'm not enjoying the work at the school in Singapore, and Mary and I are barely speaking to each other. I miss Q more than ever. The rest of the family is a mess, too, based on the emails I get from Silly and Mom, and so what is there to celebrate? Prospects for the new year are not good.

I sit in the coffee shop in the hostel, drinking weak coffee and gnawing on dry toast. I'll go back to Singapore tomorrow and look for a way out, or at least a way forward. Maybe I'll convince Mary to move to Indiana so I can help Silly with Dad. What's a little more suffering when you're already miserable?

When I look up, I see a familiar face.

"Good morning, Ollie," says Mariko.

I'm shocked to see her, a little suspicious, but also happy. Mariko might be the closest thing I've got to a friend right now. As I swallow a last bite of toast, I point to a chair.

She sits down across from me. "I have news for you. Last night I am thinking about the apartment and realize that the Russian people must rent it from the owner. And probably your friend also rented from the owner. So, the solution to your problem is to find the owner. Simple."

"But my uncle—my friend, I mean—is dead. The Russian woman told us."

Mariko shakes her head. "She told us the previous tenant died. I am thinking maybe this is some other foreigner."

There's still hope! "Mariko, that's brilliant! So how do we find the owner?"

"I already did! I am a good detective! No?"

"Yes, you are an excellent detective. What did you find out, Miss Excellent Detective?"

She giggles and slides a piece of paper across the table.

I can't bear to look at it. "He's alive?" I ask.

"Alive! Yes. Look."

Now I look at the paper. In neat script is the name Tucker Scott and an address. In Paris.

"Paris?" I ask.

"Paris, France," she says. "Since five years."

"I can't believe it."

Mariko frowns.

"No, no, I believe you, it's just something Americans say when we're surprised." I'd been so sure I would find him here in Tokyo, so excited to finally confront him, and then in despair to discover he was dead. But now! Here he is again, resurrected, and there's still hope. But Paris?

I look at the address and then up at Mariko, struggling not to cry. "Thank you," I say.

She's grinning at me, and I'm probably grinning back and crying at the same time. This is turning into a day to celebrate after all. Instead of empty hours stretching before me, the day is suddenly filled with possibility. I fold the paper with Scotty's Paris address into my pocket.

"You will go to Paris now?" Mariko asks.

I laugh at the absurdity of the idea, but wonder if that isn't exactly what I ought to do. Why am I going back to Singapore? I should exchange the return ticket for a flight to Paris. Why not?

Mary is why not.

"No, not now. Too far. Probably I'll just write a letter."

"Then you have time? Today? I will show you my favorite place in Tokyo."

"As a matter of fact, I do have time." Nothing but time.

Mariko stands and moves toward the door and it's all I can do to keep up with her. We rush to the subway station, board the train, transfer to another line, and reemerge. Again, very briefly, I worry about what kind of setup this might be. But Mariko takes my hand and smiles at me, and the worry goes away.

Have I told her about Mary? No, I don't think I have. I don't think I will.

We walk for a few minutes and stop before a gleaming building of metal and glass.

"This is my favorite place," Mariko says. "You are a writer, so I think you will like it also."

It's the biggest bookstore I have ever seen. We dive in, swimming through an ocean of books. Most of what I see are Japanese books, but Mariko leads me to the foreign language department, a whole floor as it turns out, filled with books that are mostly in English. I've never seen anything like it. I imagine that they must have every book ever written. But I look for Bruce Owens's book and can't find it. Not every book, then, but still it is impressive. Mary would love it.

We take a break in the coffee shop in the ground floor—another Starbucks. We drink coffee and Mariko tells me about her dreams of travel. She would like to go to Australia and New Zealand. America, too, she assures me, but she is an opera buff and would love to see an opera in Sydney at the famous Opera House.

"What else would you like to see in Tokyo?" she asks. I think of the famous places—the Imperial Palace, the fish market—but now that I have Scotty's address, I don't really need to see anything else.

I shrug. At this moment, I am content to sip coffee in the world's largest bookstore with a beautiful Japanese woman. I think I should tell her about Mary. Has she noticed that I wear a wedding ring?

And then Mariko's face beams. She stands, and I understand that I am expected to follow. We are back on the subway. We change trains again. I wish I had a map because after so many changes, twists, and turns, I am thoroughly disoriented. If I am separated from Mariko now I will be lost forever in Tokyo, prisoner of these polite, orderly people. But finally we emerge in sight of an enormous temple.

We stroll through the grounds, always in a crowd. Mariko looks for my reaction and I am apparently suitably impressed because she claps her hands together with pleasure. She guides me to a small shrine in the back of the complex where we light incense. She shows me how to bow and pray.

"What are we praying for?" I ask.

"We pray that you will find your friend, of course," she says.

And I think, that might just be worth a prayer.

As we're leaving the temple grounds, I realize I know next to nothing about Mariko. She graduated from a Japanese university, an English major, and lives at home with her parents and a younger brother. She wants to travel and likes opera. I don't believe in a god, so for me prayer is a waste of breath, and yet at the temple I was praying that I would find Uncle Scotty. But I have no idea what Mariko might have been praying for. What does she want?

She takes my hand and we stroll toward the subway station.

"Thank you for everything," I say. "For helping me find my friend's address. And for showing me the bookstore and the temple."

"You are welcome, Ollie."

By the time we get back to the hostel it's getting dark. It's been a good day, and I don't want it to end. And I don't want to say goodbye to Mariko just yet. I haven't forgotten that I'm married, but I'd like to thank her properly.

"Are you hungry, Mariko?" I ask.

She nods, and there's a childlike excitement in her eyes. She, too, wants to delay our separation.

We find a sushi bar. It's small and loud, with patrons and staff alike shouting to be heard over the din. We sit at the counter, and as plates of sushi and sashimi parade by on a conveyor belt, Mariko snatches the ones she wants.

"This one is eel," she says. "This one is salmon eggs. This one is sea urchin. I think maybe you not like that. But it is very good."

She shows me the correct technique for mixing wasabi in soy sauce, dipping the fish, savoring the texture and flavors on the tongue before chewing and swallowing, taking a bite of pickled ginger to cleanse the palate, and then beginning again. We drink beer. The noise in the shop escalates.

When we've eaten our fill and finished our beer, I say, "Shall we take a walk?"

"I should go home," she says. "My parents will worry."

But we do walk, just the short distance to the subway station. Tokyo at night is transformed. There are no stars, but the office towers and shops, the restaurants and bars, are ablaze. The sidewalks are crowded, the streets bustle with traffic. Horns blare, music floats all around us, a fusion of sounds. I'm falling in love with Tokyo.

"Thank you again for everything," I say. "Tomorrow I leave." I no longer worry that she means me any harm, but I wonder if there isn't something else she wants from me. Does she want money? Does she want to stay with me? Is she hoping to snag an American boyfriend? Is that what this has been about?

From her purse, Mariko pulls a blue cloth with characters on it and presents it to me with both hands.

"It is nothing," she says. "A hand towel or a headband, called a *tenugui*. It is traditional in Japan. This one says 'you learn love by crossing swords together.' It was very nice to meet you, Ollie. I hope you find your friend."

I am gazing at the cloth in my hands, wishing I had something to give to her, wishing I could ask her to stay, but all I can do is utter another "Thank you," and when I look up she has disappeared into the station.

30

In the morning, I half expect to see Mariko waiting for me when I come downstairs to get breakfast. But she does not appear, and I eat alone.

I make the long trek to the airport, wait for my flight, board the plane, and head home. It occurs to me that there's a story here that I could write, the kind of adventure Bruce Owens encouraged me to find. Lost in Japan? Death in Japan? Love in Japan? On the plane I fall asleep thinking of Mariko and our tour of Tokyo.

It's late when the plane lands in Singapore. I consider splurging on a taxi, but the trip has already been so expensive—my sushi dinner with Mariko alone cost over a hundred dollars—that I feel the need to pinch pennies, so I take a bus. It's after midnight when I slip my key in the lock of our apartment door. I'm met with silence, although Mary had my itinerary and knew exactly when I was coming home.

No, of course she wouldn't wait up for me. Why should she?

The apartment is hot, the air-conditioning, which we usually leave running all night so we can sleep, is off.

Then it hits me. She's gone. I go to Tokyo by myself, even though she told me I could go, and while I'm gone she leaves me, running off to be with Brian, or just home to Lydia and her dog. I should have realized that's what was happening. That's why she urged me to go. She had it all planned, just like my mother when she walked out on my father.

Fine, if that's the way she wants it. But I'm not going to fall apart the way my father did.

I could have stayed with Mariko. I could have gone to Paris. Did she at least leave a note?

From the bedroom comes a cough. Then feet padding on the tile. And then Mary appears in the doorway.

"Ollie?"

"You were expecting someone else?" I'm feeling foolish for jumping to conclusions.

"It's so late."

"I'm sorry to wake you."

"No, it's okay." She comes to me and wraps her arms around me. "I missed you."

"I missed you too."

"How was Tokyo?"

"Nothing special," I say. "I'll tell you about it tomorrow."

"Ollie?"

"Yes?"

"Don't leave me again, okay?"

"Okay."

"Promise?"

"I promise."

&

It turns out that our air-conditioning is broken again and Mary didn't want to leave windows open at night for fear of flying bugs or bats or burglars, even though the apartment turns stifling almost immediately. In the morning, we open windows, and that gives us a bit of breeze, we've learned, but as the day warms it will only make the problem inside worse. We've got a fan, and that at least will blow the hot air around.

I'm eating breakfast in our tiny kitchen when Mary calls from the bedroom.

"Ollie? What's this?" She comes into the kitchen carrying the *tenugui* Mariko gave me.

"A souvenir. It's a headband, I guess, or a dish towel."

She lifts it to her nose. "Why does it smell of perfume?"

"Does it?"

I know it does. When I carried it up to my room in the hostel I could smell it in the elevator. It's Mariko's scent.

"Can't you smell it?"

"That's just how they sell them, I guess."

"Ollie, are you lying to me? Did you go to Tokyo to see a woman?"

I stand and go to her, take her in my arms, and say, "No, I'm not lying, Mary. It's just a souvenir."

She sniffs, holding back tears, I assume, or anger. The crisis has not yet passed.

"Say," I say, "I've been thinking."

I pour coffee for both of us while I think of what it is that I've supposedly been thinking about.

She's looking at me, waiting.

I've got it.

"The school year will be winding down soon, and I was thinking we should travel a bit on our way home for the summer." Or forever, because I seriously doubt we'll be coming back to Singapore next year, although we haven't discussed it.

"Ollie, I don't want to go to Japan. I told you that."

"Not Japan, sweetie. France. We should go to Paris."

We can't afford to go to Paris.

"Paris?"

"Paris. Definitely."

The plan to visit Paris has mollified Mary, and for now we're doing well. She throws herself into the teaching, and I begin to think she might want to stay here another year. I don't mind it so much, either. The people at the school are nice, although the kids are just as spoiled as Bruce Owens predicted. And because the calendar says it's spring, even though the weather is no different, the sky seems brighter, bluer. Plus, what do we have waiting for us at home?

One day after work we take the subway down to Marina Bay and stroll along the water among a crowd—there's always a crowd in this city—of tourists and locals. Mary takes my hand, smiles at me shyly, and for a moment I forget everything else: the arguments, the mistrust, the wide gulf between us. I smile back.

Panhandlers are rare in Singapore, but as we stroll I spot one ahead of us, sitting on the ground, a hat in front of him, head bowed. Mary sees him, too, and digs in her purse. I remember the argument we had about charity months ago. We both know how futile a gesture it is, but maybe, for this one day, for this one poor soul, we can do some good. Mary drops a bill in the man's hat, and I put my arm around her shoulder.

A few minutes later we stop and gaze at the city's skyline, the peaks of modern high-rises soaring above the squat colonial buildings further inland.

"It's amazing, isn't it, Ollie?" Mary says. "When you told me how modern Singapore was, I don't think I believed you."

"Seeing is believing," I say. "I was just telling you what I saw on the internet, but this is truly incredible."

Part of me wants, in this tender moment, to come clean about why we've come here. It wasn't the adventure. It wasn't the teaching job. It certainly wasn't résumé-building. It was Scotty. And now that I know where he is, or where he might be, I need to go to him. But I can't say this to her. I can't disappoint her again.

I pull her to me and we kiss.

We had planned to get dinner in town, but instead we rush home. I open a bottle of wine and pour glasses for us both, but they're untouched when we move to the bedroom.

When we first came here I thought it was too hot and humid to run, but I discovered it's almost pleasant outside in the early morning, so most days I slip on my running gear and head out. The streets are nearly empty, almost quiet. I run along Mandai Road to Seletar Reservoir, past the zoo, and lose myself on the paths through the jungle.

This morning it's hard to leave Mary. Last night was nearly perfect, but it might as well have been a dream. We haven't solved anything, and I don't think we can, so is there any point in postponing the inevitable? Should we end it now? Forget Paris and just go home?

I go downstairs to stretch in the dim early light and warm up with slow, easy strides. It must have rained in the night because the pavement is wet, a smell of damp earth in the air.

If I'm not satisfied with Mary, who is sweet and gentle, who is passionate about teaching and music and faith, what the hell am I looking for? Is it Mike I want? I may be in denial, I may not understand what it is that Scotty did to me, but I don't think that's it. Professor Russell? No. That's not it either.

I pick up the pace now, remembering those exciting runs with Katrina, how she pushed me in more ways than one. If it's Katrina I'm looking for, why did I let her get away?

I'm momentarily distracted by a troop of squirrel monkeys in the jungle canopy, racing along with me, their urgent squeaks keeping my stride. It's cool here, and dark, and I could run forever.

And then my thoughts turn to the day ahead, the classes I'll teach, the arguments I'll settle, the parents I'll coddle and lie to. The notes I'll scribble about Oliver's travels. The excuses I'll make to Mary, the excuses I'll make to myself.

The path emerges from the jungle and I leave the monkeys behind. There's more traffic on Mandai Road at this hour and I have to dodge a bus to cross the street, one of those red and white double-decker behemoths. I'm slower now, part warm-down, part reluctance to go back up to the apartment.

I hear Mary's sobs even before I push the door open. She's sitting in our tiny kitchen, staring at an email on her laptop screen.

"Mary?" More Lydia and Bill nonsense, I think, and Mary hasn't yet gotten over the shock of her father's infidelity. Or has something happened to Mike? The fucking war.

She turns to me. "You bastard," she says. "You made me come here. I didn't want to move to this godforsaken place and you made me come. I hate you!" She stands, and for an instant I think she's going to attack me with her fists, but she runs into the bedroom and slams the door.

I look at the computer. The email is from Lydia, all right, but it's not what I thought: Dear Mary, I'm so sorry to tell you that Barney is gone. I'm sure he would have wanted to wait for you to get home, but he just couldn't. He was an old dog, Mary, and he had a great life. Love and kisses, Mom.

෨

On the one hand, the year in Singapore has been a huge mistake. It was no adventure and there was neither time nor income to explore the region or even the city the way I thought we might. It wasn't at all what Bruce Owens said I needed.

I had also hoped that love would deepen between Mary and me after our rushed wedding, and plainly that has not happened. We got along most of the time—we *did* eventually laugh together about her Phuket blunder, as it turned out, for which I was grateful—but we also encountered long spells of resentment, anger, or not feeling anything at all. I recognize the signs of a troubled marriage, and given what's happening with her parents back home she knows what to look for too. My little trip to Japan didn't help, although she didn't ask again about the perfume on the *tenugui* and I didn't tell her about Mariko. After all, nothing happened. Still, being objective here, I'd have to say our prospects are not good. And to top it all off, I didn't exactly find Uncle Scotty.

On the other hand...there's not much on the other hand. Letters from home have grown increasingly frantic, both from Mom, who struggles with sobriety, and Silly, who thinks our father might need to be committed to a mental hospital, lest he do himself harm. Mary's folks briefly reconciled but now seem headed for divorce; Bill is living in an apartment with the mistress he's been seeing for years, news to us all. Little has been heard from Mike, but no one thinks that's a good thing. In fact, we assume it means trouble. And Barney's death is the final straw. Mary blames me that she wasn't with him at the end.

The most I can say about the year was that I now know that Uncle Scotty, a.k.a. Oliver Scott Tucker, a.k.a. Tucker Scott, left Singapore for Tokyo in the mid-1990s and then, five years ago, moved on to Paris.

So now we're off to France, looking for a needle in Monet's haystacks.

31

"I want to see everything, Ollie," Mary says. We're on the bus from de Gaulle airport, headed toward the little hotel we've booked in the Marais District. I replaced the Japanese language program I'd stupidly given her for Christmas with a French course, and Mary has been studying that nearly every day since I returned from Tokyo. She even engaged the French teacher at school in conversation practice. She sounds good to me, but what do I know? I took Spanish in college and barely passed. The Japanese CDs didn't do me much good in Tokyo, and certainly won't help in Paris.

"You're the one with the lingo," I say. "Lead the way. *Madame.*"

"*Mais oui!*" she says.

The bus lets us off at Montparnasse and we study our map to see where we are in relation to our hotel. For some reason, Paris is far less confusing to me than Tokyo. It's a short walk, during which we get our first taste of the City of Lights. We stop at a café and savor a genuine, dark French espresso—I can't bring myself to add sugar, but I notice that Mary drops in two lumps—listening to the sounds of the language swirling around us, the smell of the city, which is a mix of fresh-baked bread and bus fumes. Intoxicating.

We are greeted—"Bonjour!"—as we enter the hotel. Mary takes a deep breath and launches into the dialogue she has rehearsed: "Good Morning. We have a reservation at this hotel for one room. May we please have the key?" It's as if the hotel clerk has learned the exact same dialogue, and it all goes according to script, until he asks to see our passports. This trips Mary up, but the clerk switches to impeccable English and the matter is quickly resolved. Who said Parisians weren't friendly?

The room is tiny and wonderful, just as I've imagined it.

"You did great, sweetie," I say. "Fluent."

"The clerk is probably down there laughing at me now. And his English is perfect. I feel like a fool."

"Nonsense. You made the effort. Lots of people don't." I'm capable of being insincere, especially to smooth Mary's frequently ruffled feathers, but I really mean it. She did great.

"I know you're exhausted," she says, "but let's not waste a single minute of daylight."

"It's like you read my mind," I say. "Let's go."

For the next two days, we're on the run, nonstop. The Louvre, the Musee d'Orsay, the Pompidou Center, the cemeteries, the gardens, Notre Dame. You name it, we see it. Most of that is on foot, which is exhausting, but Mary has learned a dialogue for buying Metro passes, so we also spend a lot of time on the subway. Singapore's underground is cleaner and more efficient, and Tokyo's is more extensive, but the Paris Metro is historic and otherworldly. I could ride forever.

On our third day in Paris, I realize I've done nothing to find Uncle Scotty, the real purpose for our trip, although Mary still doesn't know that, and time is slipping away. Our whirlwind pace has caught up with Mary and she's developed a scratchy throat and sniffles, so she's resting in our room, reluctantly but prudently, while I go out on my own. I promise to stay close by and we plan to meet for lunch at a café near the hotel.

I have the address Mariko procured for me and, in fact, I chose our hotel because of its proximity. So in just a moment I'm standing before an apartment block where my Uncle Scotty lives. Or once lived. Or where, at least, his mail was delivered at some point in the recent past. Either way, I'm one step closer to finding him.

There is a column of buzzers at the door along with a list of names. Several of the names are faded and nearly illegible. Near the bottom of the list I see the one I'm looking for: Tucker Scott. Got 'im. I think I might be whistling.

I can't believe it's been this easy. Easy, that is, if you ignore the year in Singapore and the crazy trip to Japan.

My finger hesitates over the bell. What the hell am I doing here? What do I hope to find? What's Scotty going to say when I confront him? I'd started asking those questions in Tokyo, but I still have no answers. "Yes, I did terrible things to you, Ollie. I hope you can forgive me." Doubtful. He'll deny everything, accuse me of lying. Will I at least learn why he and my father are estranged? Was my father just protecting me from the horrible truth? Maybe. But I've gone against my father's wishes to find out, and I wonder if it will have been worth the price.

But: I've come all this way, and I'll always regret it if I don't see this through.

I press the button. Somewhere, far away, a buzzer sounds. I watch the traffic on the street. I listen for any kind of reaction to the bell. I place my hand on the door handle, ready to pull the moment it is unlocked. I try again, hear the distant buzz, and wait.

He could be out, of course. At work. Or shopping. Or anything. Although I am deflated, I resolve to try again later. All is not lost.

It's too early to meet Mary for lunch, so I stroll. Parisians and tourists alike rush past me, all with somewhere they are supposed to be—a job, an exhibit, a performance. A train to catch, a flight. In a few days, Mary and I will return to Virginia and, I suspect, our marriage will implode. Or it will crumble, gradually, like our parents' marriages, leaving us both permanently scarred. I will have failed to find my uncle. I will have deceived my wife and family. I will have no job and no prospects. I will have soured my relationships with Professor Russell *and* Bruce Owens, and I'll have absolutely nothing to show for my efforts.

I come to a bridge over the Seine and I gaze into the roiling waters as if I expect to find answers in their murky wake.

❧

In one of our last sessions together before I left for Singapore, Bruce Owens offered yet another pearl of writerly wisdom.

"Ollie," he said while waiting for the bartender to pour another Jameson, "all good stories are mystery stories."

"Mysteries?" I asked. "You mean like whodunits? Agatha Christy?"

"Christ, no," he said. "Those kinds of books are fine, as far as they go, don't get me wrong. Mindless for the most part, demanding no real effort on the reader's part, but fine as entertainment."

I wasn't sure what he was getting at, but I figured he'd make his point eventually. His drink arrived, he took a swallow, then turned to me.

"I'm talking about bigger mysteries. Not, 'whodunit,' but how does a man—or a woman—respond to a challenge? When the wife dumps the guy, how does he react? Does he kill her lover? Does he take a lover or two himself, assuming his lover wasn't the reason for the dumping in the first place? And what happens as a result? What does he do next, and why? Plot is all about causation, my friend. Something happens and then something else happens as a result. Got it?"

"Got it. Plot. Causation."

"But the real mystery is even bigger than that." He finished his second drink. I was still on my first beer.

"Bigger," I said. I was jotting this stuff down, afraid I wouldn't remember it later.

"Right. Bigger. Why does your character go on at all? I mean, it would be easier to just throw himself off a bridge, right? But he wants something. He's got a goal. And until he reaches that goal, or finds that it's out of his reach, the story's not over. So that's the real mystery. Why does the guy even get out of bed in the morning? What floats his boat?"

I thought of what Oliver wants, and I realized it *is* a mystery. He just wants to know what happened and why. Like me.

∾

As I gaze into the dark Seine, lost in my thoughts about life after Mary, I become aware of another person on the bridge. He's young, a teenager, wearing a thin T-shirt and jeans. I'm not sure why, but he doesn't look French to me. Maybe it's the scruffy Nikes.

Here's someone who needs help, a great way to get my mind off my own troubles. What would Oliver do?

"You need some help, friend?" I ask.

The guy looks up at me. "A Yank. Blimey, that's all I need."

"You're from England? You just look like you could use some help, is all."

"You're not a perv, are you? Because I'm not into anything like that." I shake my head. "Because if you're not a perv, I sure could use a couple of quid if you could spare 'em."

"Hungry?"

"Christ, does it matter what I need the dosh for?"

People are rushing past us on the bridge and I edge closer to the kid to give them room.

"I can't give you cash," I say, "but come with me to a café and I'll buy your lunch." It sounds like Oliver speaking, but I think it's the right thing to do.

"You're joking, right? You can't be serious."

"Perfectly serious. The café's not far from here. Let's go."

"Well, why the fuck not. I could stomach some fish and chips."

We walk, and in a few minutes I spot Mary at our favorite street-side table. She waves, then sees my companion and her arm drops. A puzzled expression creeps across her face.

"I'm Nigel," the guy says.

"I'm Ollie," I say, "and this is my wife, Mary."

"Ollie?" Mary asks.

"I just met Nigel here," I say, clasping him on the shoulder. "He's going to join us for lunch."

"What he means is he saw me on the Pont Neuf and thought I was going to toss myself into the Seine. Isn't that right, Ollie?"

"Something like that, yes. Was I wrong?"

"No, Ollie, you were not wrong. You were definitely not wrong."

I tell Nigel to order whatever he wants. In perfect French,

he orders a steak and fries and a bottle of beer. Mary laughs nervously and says, "*Moi aussi*," and then I hold up three fingers and say, "*Trois*," or something close to that.

Nigel regales Mary and me with tales of being a penniless Brit in Paris, and by the time our crème brûlée arrives, I'm feeling less sorry for Nigel. He may be penniless, but he's got charms, and I'm also beginning to suspect his despairing act on the bridge was just that—an act. He's been entertaining, though. I have to say that for him.

"Thank you, Yanks," Nigel says. "Feeling much better about life now, I am. Restored my faith in humanity, and all that. I'll be off." He stands, as if to depart.

"It was nice to meet you, Nigel," Mary says.

"And you, dear Mary. Ollie, might I have a word with you in private?"

I follow him around the corner. It's a quiet side street, no one in sight.

With one hand he pulls my head to his and smashes our mouths together in a deep, hungry kiss; with the other hand he grabs my crotch and squeezes. I'm taken by surprise, to say the least, but when I realize what he's doing I push myself free of his grip.

"Now give me your wallet," he says, all traces of the English accent gone. He's American, just like us. And a thief.

"No, Jesus, Nigel, what are you doing?"

"It's like this, Ollie. If you don't give me your wallet right now, I scream bloody murder, shout in my impeccable French how you're a pervert and you're trying to feel me up, the police come, toss you in the pokey, and by the time you get things straightened out your little Parisian holiday will be ruined. Got it?"

"You—"

"Yeah, yeah, you'll think of all kinds of rotten things to call me later. No time for that now. Give me your fucking wallet."

❧

When I get back to the table, I'm shaking all over, whether from rage, or fear, or embarrassment, I'm not sure. All three.

"Ollie, what's wrong? You're white as a sheet. What did Nigel want to talk to you about?"

"Nigel, or whatever his name is, stole my wallet."

"No!"

"I was just trying to help a kid down on his luck."

"And this is how he repays you. That's terrible."

"You don't get it, Mary. It was all a lie. A scam. It was what he planned all along. He saw me on the bridge, he pretended to be desperate, he played on my charity. An act!"

The waiter has brought the bill, which is enormous, and now Mary has to pay because my wallet is gone. She busies herself with the check, figures out what tip to leave even though the tip is included, as I've explained frequently, and excuses herself to find the restroom, leaving me alone with my darkest thoughts.

Across the street I see "Nigel," complete with quotation marks as I've come to think of him. He waves, and I slink further into my seat.

Although Mary had rallied for lunch, her cold is tiring her out now, so she goes back to the hotel to rest. While I plot my revenge against "Nigel," I return to the address I have for Uncle Scotty. This time there's no hesitation. My anger has fueled my determination. I press the button, hear the faraway sound of the annoying buzzer, and then press again. Nothing happens. So I press all the other buttons. It works and the security door clicks open. I enter the building and climb the stairs looking for apartment 3A.

The stairs are circular and dark, only dim light filtering from above. I stop on what I think is the third floor, but the numbers here are 2A and 2B, so I climb higher. I knock on 3A.

Nothing.

I knock again, louder.

If he's there, I'll say, "Scotty, I know what you did." I'll say, "How could you do that to me?"

The door across the hallway opens and a plump woman, her hair in a tight bun, asks, "Who are you looking for?" At least I think that's what she says, because she's speaking in rapid-fire French and my Japanese crash-course is doing me no good at all.

I say, "Does Mr. Tucker Scott live here?"

She says, in heavily accented English, "Monsieur Scott? Oui. Long time live here. But no more." She backs into her apartment and the door closes.

Wait. That's it? Dead end? I'm about to knock on the old woman's door to ask her some questions, when it swings open again.

"You are related, perhaps? There is a, how do you say, *ressemblance*." And she hands me a piece of paper. "Monsieur Scott, very quiet man, no loud music, very quiet."

I look at the paper. It's an address in Mexico, in a town I've never heard of.

"He moved to Mexico?"

"*Oui*," says the woman. "*Il y a un an*. One year ago. Very quiet man."

I give up.

When I leave the building, I check to see if I can spot "Nigel," and then I hurry back to the hotel.

We still have our passports. Maybe we can go home early.

We don't go home early, but Mary's cold is bad enough that she wants me to find a pharmacy and buy medicine, which I do in my nonexistent French. Whatever I bought knocks her out, though, so she's been sleeping around the clock.

Meanwhile, I sit in a café, fantasize about Hemingway and Fitzgerald, and scribble in my notebook. It's more about Oliver and how he deals with his own petty thief, but this time something about me, too. "Nigel" makes an appearance. As I'm writing it I realize it makes a funny story, and I'm looking forward to showing it to Bruce Owens when we get home, if he's still willing to work with me. "It just came to me one day in

Paris," I'll say. "Stories come from everywhere, you never know when the muse will show up, do you?" As if I know what the hell I'm talking about.

I stroll through Luxembourg Gardens, imagining Uncle Scotty doing the same thing, not that long ago. What must it have been like for him to live all that time outside the United States, first in Singapore and Tokyo, and then Paris, now Mexico. What happened that was so bad that he won't come home? Or can't come home?

Finally, the day has come. We board the flight at de Gaulle, Mary still sick but dopey from the medicine, and we're bound for Washington Dulles. There are no delays, the ride is smooth, the customs and immigration people don't hassle us—no heightened suspense for us, apparently we've had enough—and we emerge to see not Lydia, whom we're expecting to meet us at the airport, but Mike.

"Bon voyage," he calls.

"Mike, that's what you say when someone's leaving," Mary says groggily.

"Whatever," says Mike, and hugs his sister.

He hugs me too.

32

Dear Uncle Scotty,
It's a long story, but an old woman in Paris gave me your address in Mexico. Small world, huh? Ha ha.

I don't know what happened between you and Dad, but he's been telling people you're dead. Guess you're not, though. Say, there's something I wanted to talk to you about, and I wonder if you'd be agreeable to that? It's not really anything I want to discuss on the phone, so if we could meet, that would be best.

Do you ever come to the States? I guess I could come there, now that I'm a world traveler, although I don't even know where *there* is. I hope to hear from you.

Ollie

It's a stupid letter and I crumple it the minute I sign it. Then I uncrumple it and tear it to shreds so no one can read it. Then I take the shreds and empty them directly into the garbage can in the garage so no one will see them. Then I take the can to the street, even though trash day isn't until Wednesday.

For now, I have no plans to go to Mexico. Silly was right when she told me to drop it, that I can't blame other people for my problems, especially when I'm not sure what my problems are.

❧

One day at a time, I'm getting on with my life. Which, right now, mostly sucks, although, for the moment, Mary and I are hanging in there. On the flight home from Paris I realized that a lot of the tension between us was caused by my need to find Scotty. If I forget about Scotty and leave whatever happened to me in the past, maybe we've got a chance to make it. Not a great chance, but if it was a mistake to rush into marriage, it might be just as big a mistake to rush out.

We're staying with Lydia until we line up jobs and can commit to an apartment. It looks good for Mary to get her teaching job back at the community college and they'll probably hire me as an adjunct again, with more options for classes now that I've got some decent experience. ("See," I tell Mary, "I was right about that, at least.")

Lydia is a wreck. Bill keeps calling, begging her to take him back because his girlfriend dumped him, or he dumped her, and either way he's sorry for what he did, he says, and wants to come home. Lydia, meanwhile, sits in her kitchen and sobs. She's begun to see a psychiatrist, but that doesn't seem to help, and may be making things worse. He's got her examining her whole life, which is beginning to look like one horrific mistake after another, and that's got her more depressed than ever. The drugs don't help, but she's taking them anyway.

Mary isn't sure we should see her father, clearly the bad guy in the whole mess. She won't talk to him, but he somehow got my cell phone number and he's been calling me. "Fella, you've got to help me out," he says. "Can you put in a good word for me with Lydia? Tell Mary I love her." Every day. Usually twice.

Mike is the voice of reason around here. He's living with a girl down in Harrisonburg and thinking about giving college a try again. I asked him what happened in the army, how it is that he's out already, and all he'll say is that his personal philosophy does not allow him to be caged. I can't disagree with that, it's a perfectly reasonably personal philosophy, but it doesn't answer the question.

Mary has dropped hints about getting a puppy, but she hasn't quite forgiven me for taking her away from Barney, and she weeps if she so much as looks at the handsome wooden box containing his ashes.

I spend as little time as possible at Mom's house. When I *am* there, Mom makes a show of drinking from her coffee cup, but she's fooling no one, least of all herself. I haven't said a word to her about Scotty, how I traced him from Singapore to Tokyo to Paris and now Mexico.

I phone my Dad every day, and usually get his answering

machine's cryptic message. When he does pick up, which is almost never, he's practically incoherent: "Your mother's roast is in the oven. Shh! It might fall."

Silly is apparently mad at me because I moved to the other side of the planet and left her to deal with all the drama. Now that I'm back, and can see how nuts they both are, I realize she's got a point.

"Please come to Indiana and help me with him," she begs. "If something doesn't change soon, he's going to be in the loony bin and I'll be in there with him."

"At least you'll be together," I say.

"Not funny, Ollie."

I can tell she's serious about wanting me to come. "It's a tough time for me right now," I say, "but I'll come as soon as I can."

❧

Our room at the Bergers' house is cramped. We sleep in Mary's double bed, which leaves just enough room for her dresser, a single nightstand, Barney's old cushion that Mary refuses to part with, and an armchair that's been squeezed between the bed and the window.

I find it hard to sleep in that bed. This morning I woke before dawn and climbed out as quietly as I could, settling into the chair. I'd hoped I could doze there, but sleep doesn't come and I find myself gazing out the window as light begins to appear through the trees. Dawn's early light. A new day.

Is it the light? The lack of sleep? Or have I just come to my senses? I know what I have to do. It's better to face our mistake now and deal with it before there are consequences. We're both young. We'll move on and it will be as if this never happened. It's going to be painful this fall at school when we see each other in the hallway every day, but it's probably temporary. I don't think I'm really cut out for teaching. I need to be looking for something else to support myself. For now, I'll stay at Mom's and soon I'll look for a place of my own. Or maybe it's time to move on.

I'm already living out of a suitcase—there was no room in the dresser or the closet for my clothes—so it doesn't take long to pack. I try not to wake Mary—am I really going to leave without saying anything?—but when I look back at her, she's watching. So I turn around.

"I have to tell you something," I say. I sit on the edge of the bed and the story spills out. I tell her the whole thing. How I believe I was sexually abused as a child. How my Uncle Scotty disappeared after it happened. How I learned he might be in Singapore. How I rushed us into marriage because I thought I loved her but also because I was in denial about my attraction to men, including her brother, Mike. How I traced Scotty to Tokyo and then Paris and deceived her about my reasons for going to those places. How I don't think I can be with anyone, really *be* with them until I find Scotty and learn what happened. I don't know if she's heard me. Did I say all that out loud? She hasn't said a word.

"I'm sorry," I say and stand. "I have to go."

She nods. I think she nods. I see no tears. She knew it was coming.

Mom saw it coming, too, apparently, or at least she's not surprised when I show up with my stuff. I move back into the guest room. My posters—the scales of justice and the leaping antelope—are still there.

I don't really have anyone I can ask for advice, but I need to talk. Not to Mom, of course. Or Dad. Or Silly. I can't call Professor Russell, although I want to. He'd understand, I think, and would know what I should do. But that's out of the question.

So I call Bruce Owens.

Bruce Owens is in his usual spot at the bar, as if he never left, and maybe he hasn't. I sit next to him.

"What'll you have?" asks the bartender.

"I'll have what he's having," I say.

"Our little boy's grown up," says Owens. "Welcome to the real world."

"I need advice," I say. "My life's a mess."

"Stop right there, Ollie." He puts his glass down hard and some of his drink sloshes onto the bar.

I can't remember a time when he's used my name.

"I can give you writing advice. I can give you publishing advice. I can even give you drinking advice. But if it's life advice you want, you've come to the wrong oracle."

"My wife—"

"Now, see, that's the first problem. Especially if you've got woman troubles, see a shrink. Or a priest. But leave me out of it. You want my advice? Don't *talk* about your problems, Ollie. Write! Less talking, more writing. And more drinking. Barkeep, I'll have another."

"Barkeep," I say, "I'll have another."

I'm hungover after my evening with Bruce Owens and try to sleep it off, but light is streaming through the curtains I failed to close in my drunken stupor. I hear a phone ringing somewhere in the clouds. For a minute I think I'm back in Paris, buzzing Uncle Scotty's apartment, but eventually the insistent ringing bores into my consciousness.

I hear my mother answer, a garbled half of a conversation. When she stops talking, I wonder if I'll be hearing her footsteps on the stairs, then a knock at my door, her telling me I have a phone call. I wait for the footsteps, and wait and wait. Who would be calling? Bruce Owens wouldn't call, although I gather I have him to thank for getting me home last night. Mary wouldn't call. She's still too sad or angry about my leaving or shocked by what I told her and, in any case, would call my cell. My father might call in a delirious state, but my mother wouldn't have spoken to him for as long she spoke to whoever this is. And I'm pretty sure Silly has given up on Mom, so she wouldn't have called the house phone. Briefly I think it might be Uncle Scotty calling in response to my letter, but I remember now I didn't send the letter. I shredded it, didn't I?

When I do eventually make my way downstairs, there's no sign of my mother, but there *is* a pot of coffee, and a note: "Mike called. He wants you to meet him at the coffee shop at noon."

Mike. Of all the possible callers, he's the least likely and definitely the least objectionable. I'm curious, naturally, about what he might want. I remember that he's living with a girl now, planning to give college another try. But maybe I wasn't imagining the chemistry between us. Maybe Mike is looking to test the waters, now that I'm no longer with his sister. What did Mary tell him? What did I tell Mary?

My hangover throbs with questions: Go? Don't Go?

I write about Oliver and Maria's breakup. She wants more. She's seeing another man. She suspects him of seeing another woman. He's buried himself in his work. His charity work.

Or: He's at his office one morning when he takes a call. "Oliver, my brother, it is Miguel. You will come to see me, yes?" It's what Oliver's wanted all along.

I get the sense that Bruce Owens is reluctant to continue helping me, afraid I'll ask again for relationship advice, but he agrees to meet anyway. I have got questions and no one else to talk to. I think he likes having a disciple.

There's this dream I have. I don't remember much of it, but Uncle Scotty is in it, at least I think it's Uncle Scotty. He's holding me, hurting me, and I'm afraid. As much as I've tried to forget Scotty, I just can't.

I know that dreams are supposed to be an expression of the dreamer's wishes, fears, concerns, etc., but that doesn't mean they're easy to interpret. I took a whole semester psychology class in college where we talked about reading dreams, and what I gleaned is that interpreting dreams is about as reliable as fortune-telling.

I meet Bruce Owens at the bar. I don't tell him about my dream, because he's not interested in my life. He only cares about the lives of my characters. Instead, I say, "I'm thinking of starting this story with a dream my protagonist has. It's the inciting incident." I've learned to use words like "protagonist" and "inciting incident" from my talks with Owens.

"Bullshit," says Owens.

"Excuse me?" I say.

"Look. I grant you that real people have dreams, and I further concede that dreams may offer a glimpse into a person's psyche or some goddamn thing. But we, that is, real people, have no control over what we dream. The stuff just happens and it means something or it doesn't. It's like the movies they play on airplanes. Unless you're in First Class, you don't get to choose what you watch. You with me?"

"I think so."

"The whole point of good fiction—we've talked about this—is to get at the truth. But when a writer writes a dream into a story, a reader would be justified in throwing the book across the room. It's not the character's psyche pulling up the images, it's the writer, manipulating the reader, announcing, if you will, 'here are some symbols that are important, dear reader, so please pay attention,' and that's just bullshit."

I write down "Bullshit," in my notebook and ask, "Bullshit?"

"Bullshit," he says.

I go to the coffee shop to meet Mike. I'd have preferred to meet elsewhere, given that Jennifer will probably be there and I basically blew her off when I married Mary and moved to Singapore. I don't know what Mike wants to talk about—I've imagined it when I pictured Miguel with Oliver, of course, although I didn't let myself go too far with the fantasy—and I'd rather not do it so publicly. But Mike didn't give me a choice.

I arrive early and, in fact, Jennifer is on duty. She smiles at me, raises her hand to her chest and waves.

"How've you been?" I ask.

"Good," she says. "I guess you've been away?"

Yes, I guess I have.

She pours my coffee and I sit at the table in the window, then think better of it and move to a dark corner.

Mike comes in. His hair is buzzed short, as if he were still in the army. He's wearing a T-shirt and it looks like he's bulked up since the last time I saw him. I stand and hold out my hand.

"What's up, brother?" I say. He ignores my hand and wraps his arms around me.

He says, "I think this is what I wanted all along."

No, that's not what happens. There is no warm embrace in a dark corner of the coffee shop, no confession of long repressed desire.

When he bursts into the shop, I stand and step toward him, my hand out. He ignores my hand.

"What the fuck did you do to my sister?" he says. His voice is loud and everyone in the shop is staring at us.

"Mike, I don't know what you're talking about."

With both hands against my chest he pushes me backward, and I tumble over a chair, landing hard on the wood floor.

"Stop!" Jennifer shouts.

I scramble to my feet and Mike pushes me again, this time climbing on top of me. He presses his face close to mine. I can smell him, the sweat and anger. "I should kill you," he says, a hiss, a low growl.

"Stop!" Jennifer shouts again.

I push Mike off and get to my feet. "It's between Mary and me, Mike."

Then he backs away. "If you don't treat her right I *will* fucking kill you," he says, and then he's gone, the shop door closing slowly behind him.

I slink back into my seat. I ignore Jennifer. I ignore the stares.

Bruce Owens, after a couple of drinks: "Is Holden Caulfield

telling the truth? Is Nick Carraway? For that matter, can we really believe what that little shit Ishmael is saying? The great irony of fiction is that it gives us access to deeper truths than even the truest non-fiction, but it is, at the same time, a lie. It's made up. It's fake. It's fiction, for crying out loud. The opposite of true. And, furthermore, most narrators are goddamn liars. Why should we believe them?"

33

Even while Mike was threatening to kill me, I couldn't stop thinking about him. Moving to the other side of the planet didn't shake the hold he has on me. It's connected to Scotty, somehow, right?

Scotty did this to me. It's all because of Scotty. I have to go to Mexico. I have to see Scotty or there'll be no peace. He's got the answers.

But first, I'm going to visit my father again. I'll give him one more chance to tell me what happened.

I stop at Silly's house before I go to Dad's, just to say hi and to hear the latest.

"I swear I'm close to having him committed," she says, "and I hope you'll cooperate with me on that."

"That's a big step," I say.

"You don't know what it's been like," she says. "Ask Jacob."

I'm about to do just that, when she barrels on. "He's not bathing, for one thing. He claimed he was going deaf, until I took a peek and saw that his ears were blocked with these enormous globs of wax. He's eating nothing but Cheetos, which is more than a little disgusting. He doesn't change his clothes. The house is a pigsty, including your old room, so if you don't want to stay there, I don't blame you, although Q's room is probably okay, if you can handle the blood stains. I'm pretty sure Dad doesn't go in there."

Q's room? I don't think so.

"What is it you want me to do?" It's not like I'm going to force him into the bathtub, or make him eat better.

"Convince him that he needs to get a grip. Tell him that his only son—his only surviving son—needs him. You do, by the way, you're kind of fucked up yourself with this whole Mary thing, you just don't know it."

"Gee, thanks, sis."

"You're welcome."

Silly is right. When I walk in the house, I am nearly overcome with the stench, a combination of mold, piss, shit, and...I think the last ingredient would be rotten eggs. There's also a low-pitched sound coming from somewhere. At first I think it's the water heater humming and I'm afraid it might explode, but then I trace the sound down the hallway to my father's bedroom and discover him lying naked on top of his bedspread, moaning.

"Dad, what's the matter? Are you in pain?"

"Q? Is that you?"

"No, Dad. It's Ollie." Silly didn't mention he'd been having Q fantasies. I wonder what other hallucinations we can expect. And I wonder if there's a way to take advantage of his condition, to get him to talk about Scotty. Is that wrong?

"Ollie?"

"That's right, Dad. Your other son. Ollie."

"Ollie's dead."

Oh, great. Now I'm dead. Do you suppose that's "dead," as in he thinks I'm the one who killed himself instead of Q? Or dead as in just like Scotty he refuses to acknowledge my existence?

"I don't think so, Dad. Alive and kicking, I'm afraid."

Don't ask me how, but I manage to get Dad into the bathroom, run the shower, and thankfully some kind of bathing instinct takes over because I don't care what Silly says I am *not* giving the guy a bath. He comes out, more or less clean, and wraps himself in a towel. So far, so good. I help him shave—this I don't mind doing—and we go in search of fresh clothes.

That turns out to be a challenge. His dresser drawers are empty. There are piles of clothes on the floor, but I take these to be dirty. I could run out and *buy* him some underwear, but that would involve leaving him alone, and I'm pretty sure that's a bad idea, so laundry seems like the best bet. In the meantime, I find his robe and set him up in the living room to watch television, a documentary about the breeding habits of giraffes, which looks pretty interesting, but I don't have time right now to sit down with him. I get the laundry started—there's a full unopened box of detergent in the laundry room, compliments of Silly, I'd guess—and then return to Dad. He's not sleeping, but he doesn't appear to be watching the giraffes, either. His eyes are open, but he's catatonic.

"Are you hungry, Dad? Want me to make you something to eat?"

He doesn't say anything, which I take for a yes.

The kitchen is Old Mother Hubbard city, other than a giant bag of Cheetos, although I do locate one can of soup. It's past its sell-by date, but I figure Dad won't care. I ignore the pile of dirty dishes in the sink and find a relatively clean pan, into which I pour the soup. When it's ready, I wash one bowl and one spoon, pour a glass of water, serve up the soup, and go check on Dad.

The living room is empty. And Dad's robe is lying on the floor.

"Dad?" Praying that he's still in the house, I call down the hall. "Dad?" There's no answer. I run to his room and right back again because I already know that he must be wandering around the neighborhood, stark naked. I rush outside and spot him on the sidewalk, strolling toward the intersection where the school bus stops. I grab his robe and give chase.

"Dad!"

It's not hard to catch him, and the look on his face tells me he's puzzled. What am I doing here? Who am I?

"Q?" he asks.

I shake my head, help him into his robe, and maneuver him back to the house.

"Q?" he asks again.

"No, Dad. We've been through this. I'm Ollie."

If this were a novel or a movie, the door would be locked

and my keys would be inside the house.

I know my sister has a key to the house, so the situation isn't dire. We head to the back patio where we'll sit and try to make conversation until Silly comes to our rescue. I'll convince Dad that I'm not Q, that I'm Ollie and I'm not dead, either literally or figuratively, and by the time it's all over we'll have made progress in bringing him to his senses.

I call my sister, but there's no answer. Not even voicemail, which seems odd. Unless she's blocked my phone, which doesn't seem odd at all. Now that I'm here, she's probably taking a break from the family.

Dad and I, we're on our own.

I try the back door and all the windows to see if I can find a point of entry, turning every few seconds to make sure he hasn't budged from the patio table. He's catatonic again, and I'm grateful for that. I take a risk and go around front to make sure there isn't a spare key stashed under the mat or in a planter, but when I find nothing I rush to the back again.

There seems to be no choice now but to break in. I dislodge a brick from the patio—it's been crumbling for as long as we've lived in this house—and smash it into one of the little panes of glass in the back door. It's obviously not my day, though, because, in the process, I slice open the back of my hand. It doesn't hurt, which surprises me, but now blood is streaming down my fingers as I reach inside to open the door. And Dad is right behind me, walking over the broken glass in his bare feet, although he doesn't seem to notice. As I ponder what I should do about my hand, I hear from the laundry room a noise that sounds like a jet engine revving for takeoff, and I don't think the washing machine is supposed to sound like that. The laundry room seems as good a place as any to find something to wrap around my hand, so I follow the noise and discover that the washer has marched across the room. It's now pulled the water hose tight from its wall connection and tiny geysers are spraying from the faucet. Before I can reach the machine to turn it off, the hose comes uncoupled, and now the geysers might as well be Old Faithful. The tile floor is instantly a slippery puddle; I slide toward the wall to find the water shut off, and just as I manage to stop the rising flood, I hear a crash from the kitchen.

I'm afraid to look. Imagine me peering around the corner into the kitchen. I see: the dirty dishes that had been in the sink scattered—some in many pieces—on the floor; all four burners on the stove ablaze; the refrigerator door open; my father sitting at the table eating his cold soup. Is this madness an everyday occurrence? Or has my presence somehow created a flux in the universe, veritable butterfly wings, that results in chaos?

I turn off the stove, close the refrigerator door, and sit at the table with my father. My hand is throbbing. I see blood spatters all over the kitchen floor, probably from Dad's feet.

"Want me to heat that up for you, Dad?" I ask.

My phone rings. It's Silly.

"Help me," I croak.

At Urgent Care, my hand receives twelve stitches—not as many as I expected and I'm a bit disappointed—and a dozen or so pieces of glass are removed from Dad's feet. Silly can barely contain her laughter as I recount the story—cupboard bare, naked Dad on street, locked door, broken window, gushing blood, laundry room flood, kitchen avalanche—but instead of being angry, even I can see the humor in it all and begin to laugh with her. Dad's laughing, too, but I'm pretty sure he doesn't know why.

Dad's in his room, asleep, sedated. Silly and I are in the living room, in the dark, drinking wine that we picked up on the way home from Urgent Care, and I for one am enjoying the quiet.

"We've got a problem here," Silly says, nearly in a whisper.

"No shit," I say.

"I've been trying to tell you."

"Alzheimer's?" I ask. He still thinks I'm Q, and he called Silly by our mother's name, Tinker.

"I think so. I've never seen him so bad, but it's been heading in this direction for a while."

We get the ball rolling the next day: psych evaluations, blood work, etc. While he's in the hospital, I find a plumber to deal with the mess in the laundry room, and, with Silly's money, hire a service to clean the house. We haven't discussed it, but it's likely we'll have to sell the place to pay for the care Dad is going to need because his insurance isn't going to cover it. I have no sentimental attachment to the house; I doubt Silly does either. Fond memories are far outweighed by the bad.

We bring him home. His stay in the hospital has calmed him, I think, or depressed him, because he's quiet, but in a thoughtful, somber way. There's food in the house now, so I offer to fix him something to eat.

"No thanks, Ollie," he says.

"Ollie? You know who I am?"

"Of course I know who you are. Don't talk crazy."

And so we enjoy a few lucid hours, watching TV, chatting calmly about inconsequential things: the Colts, the weather, Silly's twins and the baby. It's almost pleasant. As much as I want to raise with him my questions about Scotty, I can't bring myself to upset this moment of tranquility. I hope his mind will still be clear in the morning; my questions will wait until then.

I get up early, relieved to see that Dad is still sleeping and that gremlins haven't destroyed the house in the night. I make coffee. I strategize.

I wonder what Oliver would do, but Oliver's relationship with his father isn't any better than mine.

Dad comes out, dressed. He's missed a few spots shaving and his shirt is wrinkled from yesterday's laundry fiasco, but still it's an encouraging sign. He pours coffee for himself and sits with me at the table.

We have to talk about what happened yesterday and his need for treatment, but for that I need Silly, and we should probably do it in the presence of the doctor so he can fill in the details

that are beyond us. But there are other things we need to talk
about, just the two of us.

"Dad—"

"Ollie, what's past is past."

Has my subject been foreclosed before I've even raised it?

"But—"

"Q is dead. I know that."

"He—"

"How's that wife of yours? Mable? Minny?"

"Mary. But we—"

"I'm sorry I missed the wedding."

"It's just as well," I say.

"Sally-Ann was there?"

"No."

"Q?"

"No, Dad."

We sip our coffee. The refrigerator hums and the coffee pot
hisses occasionally.

"Dad, I have to get back to Virginia soon and I wanted to
ask you a question." He seems lost in thought, maybe slipping
back into that tunnel of confusion, and I wonder if I've missed
my chance. "What happened between you and Uncle Scotty?"
Obviously, I haven't succeeded in putting the subject behind
me.

"I always wanted a brother," he says.

"That makes no sense," I say. "What the hell happened?"

But that's all I can get him to say before he slips away again.

34

I'm on the road back to Virginia when Mary calls.
"I'm pregnant," she says, and hangs up.

I nearly drive off the highway. I'm guessing this explains my little get together with Mike last week. When I call back, I get her voicemail.

Home now, Mary won't return my phone calls, and Bill, who has succeeded in gaining admittance to his home, bars the door when I try to see her. Which makes my decision that much easier.

It's not the best time—when will it ever be?—but I find a cheap flight to Mexico City. I don't tell anyone I'm leaving. Mom is so out of it, she thinks I'm still in Indiana, "visiting my nephews," as if my father didn't require constant attention or deserve a visit from his son.

Off I go. One final chance to close this loop.

It's not as long a flight as I would have thought, and after navigating the gigantic airports in Singapore, Tokyo, and Paris, Mexico City is a breeze. Also, despite that D in Spanish years ago, enough of the language comes back to me that I manage with no problems. I've booked a small hotel in the historic center of the city, and my plan is to figure out how to get to Scotty's village from there. It feels good to be away from the ruins of my life back home, and I wonder if this is how Scotty felt when he made his own escape. Maybe, after he left, it was just easier to stay gone. To that, at least, I can relate.

My hotel is cheap and adequate, there's a cantina across the street that serves great Mexican food, and I can get a Negra

Modelo for less than a buck at the bar on the square. All with-out having to think about my troubles.

I sit on one of the benches in the Zocalo in the bright sun-light of the city they call DF, for *Distrito Federal*, and watch the people go by, chicas in short skirts, the chicos who follow them. I pick up more Spanish than I did in two years of high school and college study. I visit Frida Kahlo's Blue House, Diego Ri-vera's studio, the great museums of anthropology and folk art. I master the subway, wary of the pickpockets I've heard about. On one excursion I think I see "Nigel," but it must have been my imagination. Nowhere do I spot anyone who reminds me of Mike.

There's a Starbucks just across the park, but I prefer the local coffee shop that serves sweet Mexican coffee with cinna-mon. The barista there is a gap-toothed kid with stringy hair, a perpetual smile. After I've been in a few times he asks my name—his is Alejandro—and from then on greets me when I enter. I pull out my notebook and write. I'm still writing about Oliver, but I'm beginning to think I might want to write about Ollie. Ollie in Singapore. Ollie in Paris. Does Ollie finally have something of his own to say?

I know I'm stalling, putting off the thing I most want and fear, but I can't help it.

ॐ

"This above all, to thine own self be true," Bruce Owens said.

We were at the bar, and I had asked which of the great con-temporary writers I should try to imitate. Franzen? DeLillo? Atwood? And instead of answering the question, he quoted from Hamlet.

"Polonius gave writing advice too?" I asked.

"No, but like a lot of Shakespeare, it has universal applicabil-ity. You can't be somebody else, kid. You can't try to write like somebody else, either. You've got a story to tell, and only you can tell it. Fuck Franzen."

"Easy for you to say," I said.

"Let me tell you." Owens finished his drink and nodded to

the bartender for a refill. "I spent the first year of my writing life imitating Hemingway. And I don't mean just on the page. Then I gave Fitzgerald a try, Faulkner. I even wrote a whole novel in the style of Thornton Wilder, if you can believe it. Garbage, all of it. It wasn't until I found my *own* voice, my own vocabulary, that it started to make sense."

"How will I know when I've found it?"

"You'll know," he said. "You'll know."

While I'm sitting in the coffee shop in Mexico City, tuning out the ever-cheerful Alejandro as he greets his customers, I start to write a story about Ollie and Mary and their ill-fated trip to Langkawi/Phuket. I call them Oscar and Mimi. It's pretty funny. Mary will kill me if she ever sees it, but she might kill me anyway, so there's probably no marginal risk. I'm beginning to see what Bruce Owens meant about finding my own voice.

Speaking of Mary, I make a daily visit to an internet cafe where I write and discard and rewrite long missives to her, sentiments that are too complex to tap out on my phone. I apologize, I plead, I explain, I promise to visit when I get back and will do all I can to help with the baby. She doesn't reply.

Eventually, having stalled long enough, I'm ready for the final leg of my trip to Scotty's village. I check out of the hotel, strap on my backpack—at the last minute I pull out the antelope medallion Mary gave me and put it around my neck—and make my way to the bus station. I buy my ticket for the village, drink a Coke while I wait, and time suddenly is a bullet—I board, find my seat, sleep, and wake to find that we've stopped.

I've arrived, ready to face Scotty.

35

The bus drops me at the village square. Under welcoming trees, old men and women sit in restful conversation. Adjoining the square is an imposing cathedral and next to that is a bustling market. I spot a cantina, a coffee shop that boasts free Wi-Fi, a bookstore. It all looks very livable. It's not Paris, but I can imagine this place as a comfortable refuge, a fine place to hide from one's demons.

In the guidebook I picked up in Mexico City I've read about a B&B near the village square. I didn't book a room in advance, so it's a gamble, but I head there now, following the book's directions. On a path rising toward the range of mountains that shelter the village, I spot the sign: El Colibri, The Hummingbird. I enter the courtyard and find a quiet retreat, complete with burbling fountain, birds flitting in the trees, and a mongrel dog sleeping in the sun.

"Hello," I call. "Is anyone here?"

A toddler appears, braided black hair, barefoot, dirty cheeks, followed by an older girl, a young woman really, with thick blonde hair, a golden tan.

"*Hola*," she says, "*bienvenidos*." But her accent doesn't sound quite right. She's a foreigner, I guess, and so I answer with,

"Hello. Do you have any rooms?"

"I am a guest here also," she says, grinning, and now I detect a Scandinavian lilt. She turns behind her and calls, "Gabriela?"

A darker woman emerges from the shadow, the toddler's mother, I guess, and the proprietress of the B&B. With the Swedish girl's help—her name is Inge—my room is secured at a rate to my liking. Inge, it turns out, is in this village because it boasts a famous language school, and she hopes to improve her Spanish through immersion.

"If you like," she says, "I can show you around, the cafés, the shops."

So, after my backpack is stowed in my room, which is small but spotless, I go for a stroll with Inge, who is eighteen, not so much younger than I. I fantasize that we're a couple visiting this town, and that all the men are jealous of me because of the beautiful young woman by my side. But then I remember why I'm here, and instead I imagine spotting another gringo, my uncle Scotty, and what I will say to him when we finally meet.

We sit in the café and order espressos. I hear about Inge's education in Uppsala, her travels around Europe and North America, her desire to visit Southeast Asia, and she listens to my stories about living in Singapore and visiting Tokyo. Her skin has a lovely toastiness, with a smattering of freckles across her nose and cheeks, blisteringly white teeth, as even as piano keys. She sees a friend, an Asian girl—Korean, I think—and they speak quickly in Spanish.

"That's one of the rules of our institute," Inge says to me. "When we see each other in the town we are supposed to speak only Spanish. It is such a relief to be speaking English with you!"

"But maybe it's not good for your studies?" It's a tentative hypothesis, and I am relieved when she shakes her head.

"No, no, I think it's good. My brain needs a little vacation and then it will be ready to learn more Spanish." She laughs, and there are those amazing teeth again.

So far, I'm finding Mexico very much to my liking.

The weather in this mountain town is perfect and dry, and so the café doors and windows are wide open. A man comes in, his hand on the shoulder of a petite Mexican woman. He's wearing a hat with a wide brim and so I can't see his face, but already I know it's Uncle Scotty. Despite my mother's psychic claims, I don't believe in the paranormal, or a sixth sense, or anything like that, but my skin tingles and I just know. This is why I've come here, for this moment. My hand rises to the medallion at my neck.

Spirit animal notwithstanding, I'm not ready. I consider getting up now, leaving before the man turns and sees me.

"What's wrong?" Inge asks. "You look like you've seen a ghost."

"Exactly," I say.

She is so charming, and I do not want to leave her, so I turn my face to the wall instead and wait for the man and woman to get their coffees and go.

"There was something about that man," Inge says when they've gone. "Wasn't there? You were hiding from him?"

Perception is an excellent indicator of intelligence.

"Ridiculous," I say.

I don't mean for it to happen, and I certainly don't expect it, but Inge and I sleep together. It seems perfectly natural. There is no seduction involved, on my part or hers. At the end of the night, after a lovely evening of strolling and sitting in cafés and sipping beer in the cantina, we simply go to my room and make love. I do not give a thought to revealing my deformed toes. I do not think of Mike, or Scotty, or Oliver. I do think of Mary, briefly and guiltily, and our unborn baby, but they don't cause me to change course.

She is still with me in the morning, even more beautiful. She kisses me lightly, returns to her own room to bathe and dress, and then we meet in the courtyard for breakfast, which is simple, coffee and a bit of bread with jam and fruit, exactly how I am feeling—light, fresh, uncomplicated. Relieved. Optimistic.

A gardenia has fallen and I pick it up, place it behind Inge's ear. She laughs.

"How do I look?" she asks.

"You are a goddess," I say.

She laughs again and we are consumed by our breakfast, by the cool morning breeze, by the lovely garden, by the towering mountains. There is music in the air, Bach, I think, coming from everywhere, nowhere, in front, behind, and when I look for the source I see tiny speakers hidden in the garden. I am spreading jam on my bread in time to the music.

"That man," Inge says, "in the coffee shop."

"Yes." I'd almost, but not quite, forgotten.

"I know him."

I stop, as if the music had ceased, and put my knife and the bread on my plate.

"Oh?" I ask.

"Not like that," she says with her beautiful laugh, that luscious smile, deflecting the jealousy she assumes is behind my reaction. "I don't even know his name. But I've seen him around the village, always with that woman."

"Ah," I say, relieved that she thinks she knows what I am thinking, and pleased with the answer she has given.

"Is he American?" she asks.

"I don't know," I say. "I've never seen him before."

"In your eyes, the way they have darkened, I see you are not telling me the truth. You do not have to tell me, Ollie, but I think you know this man."

Suddenly, there is no rush. I am here, with Inge. Scotty is here. When I am ready, I will speak with him. For now, this is enough.

In the afternoon, I write. Oliver, still in Singapore, has met Ming, the niece of a shipping magnate. She's quick-witted and exotic, with skin like silk and deep, penetrating eyes. They talk easily about books and music, they have sweet, prolonged sex, and he begins to forget about Maria.

Inge comes to me some nights and not others. We breakfast together some mornings and not others. I haven't discerned a pattern, but it is always her choice. She is busy with her studies, she says. I haven't seen her with other men, so I am content.

I explore on my own. There is the ruin of an Aztec temple on the side of the mountain that stands to the north of the village. Visitors to the town climb the steep path to the temple, one of the only tourist attractions in the area, but locals frequently make the pilgrimage as well, because the spot is considered, if not quite holy, a source of spiritual energy. It makes me think of Professor Russell and his quest for enlightenment.

As I approach the shrine I am greeted by vendors who wish to sell me postcards and cold drinks, but also by coatimundi, curious creatures that resemble a cross between a raccoon and a possum. They beg, and some of the visitors want to feed them, for which purpose the vendors will gladly sell a bag of food. It only encourages them, the little thieves, and I think of "Nigel," the pretty boy in Paris who accepted my generosity and then stole my wallet.

I sit on a stone bench and gaze out over the plateau. Although it is not visible from here, I know the volcano is behind me, looming on the other side of this mountain. I close my eyes and begin to count my breaths. I feel the breeze and hear the sound of rustling leaves, the laughter of visitors encountering the furry little beggars.

Then those sensations vanish and I am alone in the darkness without thought. Untroubled, my mind is a blank canvas, and when thought returns, it's Mary I see. She's carrying my baby, and it horrifies me that I've abandoned her. But she wouldn't speak to me. What was I supposed to do? And yet, there is the baby. My future is there.

Back in the village, I visit the shops, some selling local artwork, some selling the new age trinkets for which the town, I'm informed by Inge, has become known: crystals, incense, healing oils. The juxtaposition of the temple ruins and these modern quacks strikes me as odd, even funny. But then again, maybe not. It was the energy of this place that attracted the temple builders in the shadow of the volcano. Today's spiritual practitioners are drawn by a similar force, I suppose. Perhaps it is the same thing that has drawn Scotty here, and Inge, and, ultimately, me.

On Saturday I visit the weekly *mercado* that spills over from the market hall into the square. Farmers display their abundance: almonds and pecans, oranges and tangerines, apples and bananas, greens and carrots and tomatoes. And then there are dry-goods merchants selling underwear and toys and tools and spools of wire and small appliances. But there is another market for the tourists who come down from Mexico City, and here I see the crafts that the village is also known for: colorful woven scarves and sweaters, carved statues and furniture, ceramics, paintings.

I've come to the craft market by myself, but up ahead I spot the unmistakable blonde tresses of Inge, whom I haven't seen since Thursday.

She's talking to the man in the wide-brimmed hat.

That night she comes to me. I resist the urge to tell her I saw her with the man, because there is a stronger urge and I do not want to be distracted. We make love, her youthful vigor overpowering my innate reticence, and we end in a sweaty tangle of sheets and pillows.

After we have rested, after the glow has faded and we have untied the knot of our bodies and bedclothes, she says, "His name is Oliver."

Which, of course, I knew.

❧

On Sunday, Inge says she has a treat for me, so when we leave the inn I willingly follow. The building I have thought of as a cathedral is, in fact, a former convent, referred to by everyone in town as the ex-convento. It is now something of a community center and museum, displaying artifacts from both the indigenous peoples of the region and the area's colonial past. Inge explains that the signs on the exhibits are in both Spanish and Nahuatl, the language of the local people.

As we enter the building, I realize I've seen it before, the site of Oliver and Maria's wedding. It's exactly as I pictured it.

We have come to hear a concert in one of the magnificent vaulted rooms in which the acoustics are nearly perfect. No amplification is necessary and a word spoken at one end of the hall can be heard easily at the other.

Metal folding chairs are arranged in semicircular rows, about ten deep, around a raised platform on which, when we enter, four musicians are tuning their instruments—a cello, a viola, and two violins. Because of the acoustics it doesn't matter where we sit, and Inge leads us toward the back row. From here we watch as others enter and take their seats.

Scotty and the woman, with whom he is holding hands, enter and sit in the front row.

I look at Inge, questioning.

"Yes," she says. "He told me he would be here. I sense that you two are meant to meet, and that is why we have come." She doesn't apologize for not telling me sooner.

"Are you some kind of witch, my beautiful Swede?"

In this space, the music is magical. It seems to come from above and behind and in front of us all at once, but this time there are no hidden speakers. The musicians are young, but skilled. The first violinist, especially, is masterful, but all of them, two boys and two girls, have an intense concentration. The audience is rapt, no movement, no rustling of programs, no fidgeting, or perhaps I simply don't notice because I am myself entranced.

During the intermission my eyes are drawn to Scotty and the woman. The concert resumes. I close my eyes and lose myself in the music.

"What are you afraid of, Ollie?" asked Bruce Owens. Professor Russell asked the same question as we began our exploration of consciousness.

I didn't answer the question. I can't.

"Look. I don't believe that writing is the equivalent of therapy. Not exactly. But doesn't it make sense that we can confront on the page issues that we may not be able to handle in real life?"

I suppose I nodded my agreement.

"Work it out on the page, if you have to. Pour your soul into it. Be brave."

The audience greets the final chord with enthusiastic applause, which in this space is almost deafening. A few people stand, a few more follow, and then we are all on our feet to salute the young quartet. The proud musicians take their bows, the ovation subsides, and people begin to exit the room. I look for Scotty, but he has vanished. Am I relieved? Disappointed?

We are the last to leave the room, but eventually we emerge into the sunlight, and there they are, Scotty and the woman. Oliver and Maria. Now that I'm face to face with him, I think maybe it isn't my own life I've been writing, it's his.

He drops the woman's hand and rushes toward me, wrapping his arms around me, nearly tackling me in the process.

"Ollie," he says. "Is that really you? It's so good to see you. My God, you're all grown up!"

I'm crying, I think. After all this time, the dreams, the memories, my parents' lies, I can't believe it's him. Alive. I loved him once. I don't know what I feel about him now. Hate? I'm definitely crying, and yet I manage to reply, "It's great to see you too."

The look on Inge's face is one of amusement and triumph. "I knew you knew him. I just knew it. And now that I see you together, it's so obvious. You're related. How wonderful!"

He releases me and I introduce Inge. Scotty introduces Marisol.

"Oliver," Marisol says, "we have to go."

She called him Oliver. Inge had also called him Oliver. Of course. That's his name: Oliver Scott Tucker.

"You must have a lot to talk about," Inge says, stepping away as if she will leave us now.

"Yes," Scotty says. "But not now, not here. Meet me at the cantina at nine. We'll talk then."

"But—" Why not now, I want to say. Don't run from me again. Don't disappear.

"It's so good to see you, Ollie."

I choke back the tears as Scotty and Marisol go off. I've searched for him so long, I'm reluctant to let him let him out of my sight. What if he runs? He knows I'll confront him about what he did, the terrible things he did. I've let him get away. He's gone forever and now I'll never know.

"What a nice man," Inge says.

36

I leave The Hummingbird and walk toward the zocalo in the dark. A fine mist hovers in the air. One of the stray village dogs appears at my side, crosses my path, drops back, nose to the dirt road, then crosses again.

The cantina does not appear to have been dressed up to appeal to tourists, as some of the other shops and restaurants have, and when I enter I see only locals in the dim light. Locals and Scotty. He stands as I approach his table. He hugs me again, a tight embrace. It surprises me that I welcome his touch, given what I remember. Or think I remember.

I'm barely able to speak and my voice trembles, but I say, "I thought you were dead."

And he says, "Until I met Marisol, I was."

He releases me. We sit.

He has two glasses in front of him, one is a shot of tequila, I guess, this being Mexico, and the other a shot of something red, like tomato juice.

"It's sangrita, 'little blood,'" he says. "A specialty of this place. It makes the tequila go down easy. Too easy, maybe." He calls to the bartender and orders one for me.

"But maybe Tinker wouldn't like to have me corrupting her son with drink," he says.

"My mother is not in a position to judge," I say. Scotty raises a brow, but doesn't ask what I mean.

My drink comes, we clink glasses, sip from the tequila, and I copy him by sipping the sangrita. We finish without speaking, and he orders another round.

"So," he says at last, "what brings you to Mexico?"

I don't know where to begin, what to ask, what to tell.

"Fate," I say. "I think I was destined to meet Inge."

We laugh. How can I joke with this man, this monster?

"She's a beauty, all right," he says. "But seriously. Why are you here?"

"Seriously?" I drink the tequila. "I'm here because of you, of course."

"Me? You knew I was here?"

"Yes, eventually."

"Is everything okay at home? I haven't heard anything in a long time. Your mother used to send me news, but it's been awhile. I guess she's the one who told you?"

"No. Wait. She knew where you were? She knows you're here?"

"Yes."

"She lied about that."

"I expect she did, yes. That was our agreement."

Agreement. Collusion. They've all been hiding the truth.

"So. The news." I finish off the tequila and call for another. Bruce Owens would be proud. "She and my dad got divorced, but I guess you know that. She moved to Virginia and when I graduated from college I joined her there because I couldn't stay in Indiana—too many ghosts. I started teaching in a community college, but I'm not really cut out for it. I met a girl and we got married, a little hastily as it turns out. Oh, and Q committed suicide, Mom's a drunk, Dad has lost his mind, Sally-Ann, as she now insists we call her, has found Jesus, I split from my wife who is pregnant and fantasize about having sex with her brother, and now I'm here. I guess that brings us up to date. What about you?"

"Christ, Ollie."

We drink.

"I don't know what to say. That's...quite a story. I'm so sorry about everything. Q? Shit. Your mom told me he was messed up after the war. I didn't know it was that bad."

"I miss him, Scotty."

"I'm sure you do. Christ, I'm sorry."

We drink another round, to Q.

"You better slow down with those things. They can really sneak up on you."

"I don't think so," I say. "I can see 'em coming."

He laughs. I don't.

"So. You came to this little village in the middle of Mexico, and what a coincidence, you run into me. Small world."

"Not exactly."

"I didn't think so. If your mother didn't tell you where I was, how did you find me?"

Another long story, and I tell him about Singapore, leaving out Phuket, about Tokyo, leaving out Mariko, and about Paris, leaving out "Nigel."

"Nice detective work, Sherlock. So you came here to find me. The question is: why?"

"A very good question, Watson." A very good question indeed.

അ

Can I really do this? The truth is all, Professor Russell said. Be brave, Bruce Owens said. I don't think this is what they meant. I touch the talisman at my neck.

"Is that an antelope?" Scotty asks.

I nod.

"Do you remember that poster I gave you? I'd taken you kids to the Indianapolis Zoo and for some reason you loved the antelope herd. So I found a poster and we put it up in your room."

"You gave me that?"

"You remember?"

I nod again. I remember the zoo, watching the antelopes jump, like they were flying.

"When I was a kid," I begin.

"You were a very cute kid," Scotty says. "God, I loved you guys."

Scotty, you're not helping.

"When I was a kid, you and I spent some time together. Didn't we?"

"We did. I was, what, seventeen, eighteen when you were born? When I was finishing up college in Bloomington, I was at loose ends. Your mom worked, and I helped out some, babysat, that kind of thing."

"Okay, so I remember this one time—"

"You were no trouble at all. Q was a handful, getting into stuff he wasn't supposed to and always wanting to play games. And Sally-Ann, my word she was impossible."

"All of us? You watched all of us?"

"Sure. From the beginning your sister insisted she didn't need a babysitter, but she changed her tune when she nearly burned the house down trying to cook something. I can't remember what it was. Popcorn maybe?"

"But I remember one time when it was just you and me. We were riding in your car and we were going downhill. You took your hands off the wheel. It was just us."

"I remember that day. I couldn't think of anything to entertain you guys, so we went for a drive. Q and Sally-Ann were in the backseat and all three of you were wild. We'd gone out for ice cream so maybe it was the sugar. Whatever it was, you were jumping up and down in the front seat and I was scared to death if something happened on the road you'd go flying."

"I don't remember Silly and Q being there."

"They were there. All three of you were always together. What's this all about anyway? What does it matter?"

"You touched me."

"Well, sure. I pushed you into your seat to keep you from going through the windshield."

"No. You touched me. Inappropriately. And it wasn't the only time."

"What? Oh, God, you don't think—"

"And that time in the bushes when you picked me up and put me to bed."

"Ollie, I was scared to death. I thought you'd been kidnapped or something. I couldn't find you."

"You touched me. And there were other times."

"Jesus, Ollie, no, I would never—"

"And you came into my room at night sometimes."

"Ollie, no. You're wrong."

"It's what I remember, Scotty! But it's all I remember. I've been so confused all these years, with mixed-up feelings, and I thought, wait a minute, there's an explanation, a reason for how I feel. Scotty touched me and I just don't remember the rest. I've repressed it, what really happened. But deep down I remember."

"Ollie, listen to me. You don't remember details because nothing else happened. I would never do that, not in a million years, not to anyone, but especially not to my own brother."

Brother?

"Brother?" I ask.

"Shit. I swore I'd never tell you. Never. Your mother didn't want me to."

"Did you say *brother*?"

"I have to make you understand that I'd never hurt you, Ollie. God. Never."

I drink a shot, and Scotty orders another for us both, although I'm already having trouble focusing.

"How? I don't understand."

"I don't suppose it matters now. I guess it never really mattered, but it was what your parents wanted. Here it is, the God's honest truth: your father, Quentin Tucker, is also my father. He knocked up a girl he knew in school. That would be my mother, Lisa Scott, hence the nickname by which your family has always known me. My mother refused to get an abortion and Quentin wouldn't marry her, so the plan was to give me up for adoption. Except Mom changed her mind when I was born, named me Oliver Tucker Scott, after my grandfather—also your grandfather—and raised me on her own. It was tough for her, being a single mother, especially back then when that wasn't so common, and she struggled. Quentin helped out with money sometimes, but mostly she was on her own. By the time I was a teenager, your dad was married to your mom and they'd started their own family. I've got to give him some credit, because he didn't hide me from Tinker. Told her about me from the start and let me come around and be part of a family, which I was not getting much of at home. But for public consumption, and for you kids, they had a cover story: I was Scotty Tucker, Quentin's much younger little brother, and nobody knew the difference."

"Did Q know? Does Sally-Ann?"

"I don't think so, no."

I'm having a hard time taking this all in. Is he telling the truth? Not only was I not abused by Scotty, but it turns out he's my brother? If that's true, then what *did* happen? What is it I'm remembering? What memory am I blocking?

"I don't get it," I say. "Okay, Dad was a schmuck originally, which I totally believe, but he did right by you later? You and your mom?"

"That's what I thought too. Until just before my mom died. She was in the hospital, a mental hospital, which shouldn't be too surprising after all she'd been through, and it wasn't long after that day you remember in the car that I went to visit her. And that's when she told me the truth. That she'd been seeing Quentin all along, that he'd been sleeping with her the whole time he was married to Tinker. And worst of all he was an absolute prick to her. Violent. Physically abusive. But she felt she had no choice. She couldn't go to the police. She needed him. She needed his money."

"That part I find hard to believe."

"Ask your mother, Ollie. She knows all about his temper. He's a violent man."

"Mom? He hit her?"

"You were just a kid, but that part Q knew. Sally-Ann knew. The divorce was a long time coming. But it's never been easy for a woman to fight a man like that."

"So what did you do?"

"I went ballistic. When Mom told me what he'd done to her, I went to his office and threatened to tell the world what a monster he was. I threatened to tell Tinker about the affair. I threatened to tell you kids the truth about dear old Dad. But he knew he had me over a barrel. He was paying her bills. He was supporting her and me both, and anything I did to expose him would be the end of that. Basically, I had to choose between my mother and the truth."

"I don't believe you."

"Ollie—"

"I don't believe any of it. He wouldn't do those things."

"It's all true, Ollie. I swear."

"So why did you disappear, Scotty? Why did he suddenly pretend you didn't exist? His own son?"

"You really don't remember?"

"I thought, or I don't know what I thought, anymore, but I *guessed* that he found out about you…and what you'd done to me, and he banished you to protect me. Made you go away or he'd do something to you. He told us you were dead."

"Jesus."

"And I have these memories I can't explain."

"No, Ollie, that's not what happened."

"So what *did* happen?"

The cantina has grown quiet. We're the last customers, and Scotty lowers his voice.

"My mother died. She was in the hospital and she was supposed to be watched constantly, but somehow she tied sheets together and hanged herself." Scotty stops, downs another shot, and looks out toward the square. "It's terrible to think of it this way, but her death set me free. I was grown, I could support myself, so I didn't need him anymore. He had nothing over me and I could have carried out my threats. I could have exposed him."

"Why didn't you? Jesus, if what you're saying is true, then he deserved it all. And then some."

"Yeah, but it didn't matter anymore. It would only have destroyed more lives—your mother's, yours. My mother was dead, and it was easier to leave, to make my own way, give up the charade, use my own name. And so I left."

The tequila's gone, the cantina closing.

"God, I'm so sorry, Scotty."

"Yeah, me too," he says. "But there's more."

"What else?"

"Maybe this is what you remember. When I came over to your house to tell him my mother was dead, he was in the middle of a fight with your mother."

"Mom?"

"Yes. You were there, too, Ollie. You and Sally-Ann and Q were in the living room and your folks were in the kitchen, yelling and screaming. Your mom finally found out he'd been cheating on her for years, with my mother and other women. You three were all on the couch. I think you had your hands over your ears and Q's face was red and serious. Anyway, I tried to stop the fight, to tell them they shouldn't do that in front of you guys. I stepped between them and Quentin slugged me good, sent me sprawling. And then he hit Tinker. Over and over again. I couldn't let him do that, not again, so I grabbed a knife off the counter and told him I'd kill him if he didn't stop."

"Jesus," I say.

"And just then, you came into the kitchen. Not Q or Sally-Ann, but you, the littlest one. You were so brave! I don't remember what you said, but they both turned to look at you, saw the sad expression on your face. Not crying, but just terribly sad and afraid. I still had the knife in my hand and I swear I was going to use it, to kill him and put an end to it. But he grabbed you, Ollie. He picked you up and used you like a shield. You were looking right at me and shrieking, as if I were trying to kill you and not your father."

"Oh, Christ. I remember."

"I dropped the knife. You were so terrified."

"Shit, I remember."

"He turned to me and told me to get the hell out of his house, out of his life, and never come back."

"I remember."

"Do you, Ollie? Do you remember?"

"I do. That's what I remember."

∾

I stumble back to The Hummingbird, focusing on where I'm going and actual walking, not what I've just learned from Scotty, or Oliver. Inge's not in my room, which is just as well, because I'm drunk, drunker than I've ever been in my life. I puke in the bathroom, try to lie down, and get up to puke again.

Light through the window wakes me, so apparently I'd fallen asleep. My head hurts, but I only have myself to blame for that. I drink water, I shower, I head to the garden for breakfast. There's no sign of Inge. While I'm drinking my coffee, beginning to feel human, the landlady, Gabriela, brings me a note.

"Dear Ollie, it has been delightful these past days with you. I wanted to tell you yesterday that I was leaving this morning, but there was already much drama in your life, so I decided to spare you this. I'm traveling for a while, but will return to Stockholm in a few months. Here is my address if you want to look me up. I wouldn't mind at all. Love, Inge." Her card with her address falls on the table.

So that's that. Scotty mystery solved. The good witch of the north is gone. Nothing keeping me in Mexico. But can I face what's waiting for me at home? I could keep running, like Scotty.

But where else can I go?

37

Scotty has invited me to visit him at home, so before I leave the village I go to the house on the hill that he shares with Marisol. They both welcome me with hugs, then lead me to a courtyard filled with hibiscus and bougainvillea, an oasis in an already idyllic setting. Marisol serves us fragrant cinnamon coffee, and we drink in silence, because everything we need to talk about seems too weighty. I see now that Scotty is not Oliver, or at least he isn't the Oliver I've imagined. He isn't sophisticated and worldly, not in the same way Oliver is. He isn't a superhero. And Marisol is no Maria, not volatile, not selfish. She's gentle and kind, more like Mary than Oliver's Maria.

Eventually, Marisol rises, kisses me on the cheek, speaks words to me in Spanish I do not understand, and leaves us. Scotty pours more coffee and tells me his story. He and Marisol met in Paris where he was teaching at the American school and she was a student at the Sorbonne. He'd grown disenchanted with roaming, with the life he was living, with life generally. But Marisol gave him something to live for. When she finished her studies and her visa expired, they decided to go to Mexico. He had no particular reason to stay in France and had grown tired of teaching. Like me, it was simply something he'd fallen into. Marisol had family in nearby Cuernavaca; this village in the shadow of the volcano was peaceful, and life was good. He thought he might never leave.

We drink more coffee. We listen to neighborhood dogs bark in the street. A breeze carries a sweet fragrance, like honeysuckle.

"You haven't asked any more about the family," I say.

He shakes his head. "I need you to understand something, Ollie. I loved being with you and Q and Silly. I'm heartbroken about Q and wish I could have done something to help him. And your mother was kinder to me than I deserved. I wish her well. But I hope our father goes straight to hell. After what he did to my mother, and then what he did to you that day, I vowed never to look back. To move on and become the man I was destined to be. And I mean no offense by this, Ollie. I'm happy to see you and sorry you've had some troubles, but I have no intention of coming back, ever. I'd just as soon you forget you found me. You said Quentin told you I was dead. It felt that way for a long time. Maybe it would be for the best if you accepted that version of the story."

What of Oliver? I can't go on with Oliver's story. He is content with Ming, I suppose, and they stay together in Singapore, united by their good works. Or, when Oliver's father dies, as he inevitably does, Oliver returns to New York and takes over management of the firm. Or, when he learns that his Uncle Sandy was forced to take the blame for his father's misdeeds, he leaves the firm and begins a new life, without the burdens of the old. That's Oliver's story. Not Ollie's.

My return trip is a blur: bus to Mexico City, taxi to airport, flight to Washington Dulles via Atlanta. There's barely time to process what I've learned from Scotty, never mind make plans to deal with what lies ahead.

I open the door to my mother's house with no idea of what to expect. What calamity has occurred in my absence? Is she in a drunken stupor? Is she even alive? I should have called from Mexico.

The house is quiet. The living room appears orderly. I stand in the foyer and survey: pillows placed symmetrically on the sofa; chairs in proper diagonals; tracks of the vacuum cleaner still visible in the carpet; curtains drawn; lampshades, wall hangings, photographs, all straight and aligned as they should be, but in recent memory never have been.

"Mom?"

I pass through the living room into the kitchen. There are

no dishes in the sink, no clutter on the counters or table. The floor gleams.

"Mom?"

My mother's room is similarly neat and tidy, the bed made. Even the air smells fresh, lemony.

In my room, where I drop my backpack, I find a note on the pillow.

> Dear Ollie,
>
> Welcome home. I hope you found what you were looking for. I apologize for my part in keeping the truth from you. I thought it was for the best, but maybe I was wrong. It hasn't been easy to take this step, but I've checked myself into a program. I'm going to kick this thing. Apparently I can't do it on my own. Don't come visit, not just yet. I'll call you when I'm ready.
>
> Love, Mom.

As much as I want to talk to her about what I learned in Mexico, I'm proud of her for what she's doing.

❧

Lydia answers when I call Mary.

"May I speak to her please?" I say, not a question.

"Do you think that's wise, Ollie?"

"Yes, Lydia, I do." I don't think I've ever stood up to Lydia before, but she has no business screening Mary's calls.

Mary comes to the phone. She doesn't want to talk with Bill and Lydia listening, which I totally understand, so we agree to meet. Her parents may be mad at me, but Mary knows that our decision to split was, ultimately, mutual, and our marriage as much her mistake as mine.

I have nothing else to do, so I get to the coffee shop early and am relieved to discover that Jennifer isn't working. Instead, it's Simon, a tall skinny kid who never seems to remember me from one visit to the next. Which is fine with me. I don't have to wait long before Mary comes through the door. She doesn't look pregnant, but it's early days yet. I stand, kiss her on the cheek, hold the chair for her.

"You're being very gentlemanly, Ollie."

"I'm trying."

"Where have you been? I haven't heard from you in a while."

"It's a very long story, Mary."

"You don't want to tell me?"

"Not really, no." When I left, I tried to tell her about Scotty and what I thought I remembered. Now that I know the truth about my father, it's even harder to explain.

We order coffees, take test sips.

"How are Bill and Lydia?" I ask.

I sense energy building in Mary, warming to a subject she can grasp, a problem that is hers, but is external to her at the same time and has nothing to do with us.

"Oh, they're just awful, Ollie! Living with them is like living with a couple of caged gryphons. They circle around each other, give each other dirty looks, occasionally snarling. And sometimes I feel like red meat that's been tossed into the cage. They fight over who loves me best, who can take care of me. I hate it. I'm desperate to get out of there."

I think this is the moment I'm supposed to offer reconciliation. It's not as though I haven't thought about it, even before I went to Mexico. There's the baby to consider, for one thing. But I can't be married to Mary. I don't love her. I just don't. So if she's hinting at getting back together, I don't bite.

"How are you feeling? The baby?"

For the first time, she smiles. "Actually, I feel great. The doctor says everything is fine. I didn't want to go by myself, so Mike came up and took me. He's going to be a terrific uncle."

"How's he doing?" I wasn't going to ask about him. I don't think Mary knows he threatened me.

"He's enrolled in some classes. He thinks he'll marry Teresa. She's been good for him. I'm not too worried about him, honestly. He'll be fine. You should call him some time."

"I'm glad for him."

"Do you want to know about the baby? The sex, I mean?"

"Sure. But whichever is great, you know? Either way."

"It's a boy."

A boy. Wow. Somehow knowing the sex—boy or girl—makes the whole thing seem real. I'm going to be a father. Life is going to get really complicated for all of us.

"You know I won't let you down, right? I'll help. I'll be here for you and the baby."

"I know you're not going anywhere, Ollie. You're a good man."

38

For the moment, all is calm with the Virginia side of my family, at least until the arrival of the baby, whom I've come to think of as Little Oliver. Now I'm off to Indiana to see if the same can be said for the Midwestern side.

When I arrive, though, the twins and their little brother are all screaming about something. Silly is watching television, balancing a bowl of ice cream on her belly—is she pregnant again?—and Jacob is nowhere to be found, probably in the basement getting high and playing video games. I need to have a talk with Silly, but I don't think I can do it here in the midst of her chaos.

I pull her out to the back patio and close the sliding glass doors. I can still hear the kids, but they're muffled.

"I found Uncle Scotty," I tell her.

"In Mexico?"

"You knew?"

"Mom told me while you were gone. Before, you know, rehab."

"She was drunk?"

"Quite."

"What else did she say?

"Not much. She launched into an anti-Dad tirade and wouldn't let it go."

"Can't say I blame her, based on what Scotty told me. And, by the way, we can stop calling him Uncle Scotty."

I fill her in on everything Scotty told me. "Did you know that Dad hit Mom? Often?" A particularly loud scream emanates from the house and we both turn to look, but all three kids seem to be alive and kicking, literally, so there's no reason to take action.

"I suspected," she says, her voice nearly a whisper. "I was the oldest. I should have done something."

"You were just a kid, Silly. There was nothing you could do."

"I know. Still, did you figure out that repressed memory of Scotty?"

"You were right. I was looking for excuses for my own confusion, barking up the wrong part of the family tree. Scotty said you and Q were in the car that day, the day I thought he touched me. I'd forgotten that, but now I remember both of you laughing and shrieking in the back seat. Scotty did nothing wrong. If anything, he was my guardian angel. What I saw, the memory I've hidden all this time, was Mom and Dad fighting, a knockdown drag-out argument and Dad threatening Scotty. My own terror at being in the middle of it all."

"And you're okay? Comfortable with who you are?"

"Yeah. Comfortable. Still a little confused, but okay with that. Not looking for any more excuses."

"Nothing's easy, Ollie."

No, nothing's easy.

"Speaking of which, what do we do about Dad? I want to go see him, tell him that I know the family secret, finally, no thanks to him."

"He's too far gone. I appreciate your coming, but honestly he won't know you. What good would it do?"

"I don't know, but it will make me feel better. Maybe it's for Scotty. And Mom."

❦

So I go to my father's treatment center. I don't use the word "visit" because that implies something pleasant and conciliatory, both of which are as far from my mind as they can be. I plan to confront. I plan to aggress. There will be no conciliation. Ever.

I show ID, sign in, and am taken to where my father sits by himself in a sunny room that reminds me of my high school cafeteria. He's unshaven, his gray stubble makes him look grizzled and rough, and yet his shoulders are slumped. He appears folded in on himself, trying to hide in a place where there can be no hiding. I feel a twinge of pity, but it doesn't last long.

I sit next to him. He gives no indication that he even notices my presence, much less recognizes who I am. That doesn't matter to me. I will say what I have to say, and if he understands, if somewhere deep in his consciousness he gleans that his secret has been exposed at long last, that's great. But I will never know if I've hit the mark, and that's okay too. This is for me, not him. For Scotty, and Mom, and me.

"Dad," I begin. No sign that he's heard. "I know you're in there, somewhere. At least I think you are. And I've come to let you know that I know everything now. I know what you did to Mom and Scotty and his mother. And me. You thought you could hide the truth from us forever, but you've failed. In fact, you've failed at everything, your whole life. If there's a hell, that's where you're headed.

"But that's not what I came to say. I'm here to tell you that I know that Scotty is your son, my half-brother, not my uncle. I know your life has been a lie. I know that you abused his mother for years, and drove her to suicide. You forced Scotty into silence and then banished him, lying to all of us about him. I know that you also abused Mom, and for that alone I hate you and will never forgive you. And I know what you did to me. You're a vile old man and I have no pity for you."

Except, maybe I do pity him. I will never return to this place and I doubt that Silly will either. He will die here, a forgotten wreck, alone. It's what he deserves, but it does make me sad.

"Have you heard any of that, old man? Does it have any effect on you at all? Is there even a shred of remorse in there somewhere?"

I stand, and I think I see his eyes move. If he has finally registered my presence, maybe he did hear what I said. I hope so.

I have to make one more stop before I head back to Virginia.

I aim the Impala south of Indianapolis, then head west to Cambridge, the college town that was my first safe harbor when

I left home. It feels odd to be back, like I've traveled through time to get here. The campus looks exactly the same.

I pull into the visitors' parking lot near the student center and turn the engine off. I watch the college kids—they look so young!—rushing to class or meals or coffee dates or intramural games or whatever, and I wish I could return, have this life again.

No, I don't. Not really. I understand a lot more now than I did then, and I can't go back.

I leave the parking lot and steer off campus, to a familiar tree-lined street, and stop in front of Professor Russell's house.

I'd thought about calling first, but I wasn't sure he'd agree to see me, so here I am. I walk up to the porch and ring the bell. I hear the familiar bark of that little dog, just one burst and then quiet. The door opens.

"May I help you?" The woman who has answered the door is young and pretty and reminds me of Inge. Her blonde hair is pulled into a ponytail and she's wearing running shoes and shorts.

"I'd like to speak with Professor Russell—Clark—if he's home," I say.

And then he appears behind her, hands on her shoulders. "Ollie! What a nice surprise."

Clark introduces Kristin, a graduate school classmate, to whom he's been married just a few months, and then shows me to his study. The two of us sit on cushions and Kristin heads out on a run.

"It's good to see you, Ollie. I've thought of you often and wondered what you were up to. What brings you back to school? Is there a reunion or something?"

"No, nothing like that. I'm here to see you. I want to apologize for the way I behaved on my last visit."

"Ollie, do you know what 'transference' is? It's a concept we have from Kant, but it's now used in psychoanalysis to refer to the shifting of emotion, usually affection or desire, from one person, usually a parent or another loved one, to someone else, often the psychiatrist. I think what happened, and I don't mean this to minimize what you were feeling, was something like that. It's common enough in the academic setting, honestly, and in our case I was acting in some way as a spiritual guide, not unlike a therapist."

"That makes total sense to me," I say. "I'm so sorry."

"But I'm saying, don't be sorry. I was flattered. Startled, maybe, by the abruptness of it all, and I didn't react as thoughtfully as I should have, but one of the joys of teaching is being able to connect with a student on a deeper level, and I felt we had done that. I truly enjoyed our time together."

I'm relieved beyond words. I've spent the last couple of years feeling embarrassed about what I'd done and how I'd felt, but I'd also missed Professor Russell terribly. Now that's one less burden for me to carry.

Clark tells me a little about his current classes and says he's not surprised to learn that I'm teaching.

"You should consider graduate school, Ollie. There's not a booming job market for philosophers, but I always thought you understood what we were doing in our explorations better than most."

"That's probably out of the question, at least for now." I fill him in on my marriage, my travels over the past year, and, most importantly, the impending arrival of Little Oliver.

"Tell me if this is too much of an imposition," I say, "but do you have time for a short meditation session?"

Clark grins, eager, apparently, to reclaim what we lost. He lights the incense, taps the bell, and we're off on our search for enlightenment.

When I get home from Indiana, a letter from Mom is waiting for me. The plain white envelope is addressed in a familiar, but steady, hand. I turn it over and over and finally slip my finger under the flap to open it.

Dear Ollie: Are you home? I'm still not ready for visitors, but if you wanted to write me a letter, that would be nice.

I'm doing much better, taking everything one day at a time. I apologize for the mess I've been, especially these last few years.

Love, Mom.

I don't know if it will help her to know that I've learned the whole story—about Scotty and his mother, how Dad mistreated all of them, all of us. And I don't know if it will help for her to know that Dad has nowhere left to hide. Or, rather, that the only place he can hide is some dark, fetid hole deep within himself.

So I write her a letter in which I say none of these things, only that I'm well and making plans for the future. That should give her comfort, I think. It has the benefit of being true. With a baby on the way—which I've not yet mentioned to anyone other than Scotty and Professor Russell—I'm looking into better jobs, something that will pay enough to support two households. I want a career where I can use my creativity. I don't think I want to return to the classroom, which in any case wouldn't pay enough, but marketing and communications might suit me. And I'll continue to write fiction on the side. Oliver's travels are over, but Ollie's got a few stories of his own. We'll see how that goes.

☙

Shortly after I mail my letter to Mom, Mike calls. I brace myself for more threats and I realize his hold over me is gone.

"Mary's sick," he says. "She wants to see you."

"Is it the baby?" I ask.

"Just get over there," he says. I can't tell anything from his voice, which has lost its anger.

When I get to the house, Mary is sitting in the living room hugging a pillow to her stomach. Lydia is there too, arms crossed, and I'm expecting some kind of lecture about responsibility and fatherhood, and what a cad I am to disappear the way I had while her daughter is suffering, but instead I get a sympathetic look and a pat on the arm.

"I'll leave you two alone," she says, gives Mary a stern look, and then disappears into the kitchen.

"What's wrong, Mary? What happened? Are you okay?" She looks fine, actually, not sick at all. Unhappy, maybe, but fine.

"I lost the baby, Ollie. He's gone." There are tears in her eyes and she clutches a handful of tissues. I sit next to her and take her hand. Little Oliver is gone?

"Mary!" Lydia shouts from the kitchen.

"I'm so sorry, Mary. So, so sorry."

The baby's gone? A miscarriage? It's such a cliché to say that your heart sinks, but that's what happens. It falls from your chest right into the pit of your stomach and it takes your breath with it. I can't believe the baby's gone.

"Mary!" Lydia shouts again. "Tell him, or I will."

"What's going on?" I ask. "Tell me what?"

Mary lets go of my hand. She stands, looks out the window, and then turns to me.

"There's no baby, Ollie. There never was a baby."

"I don't understand."

"Remember that movie we saw? The one where Jennifer Anniston pretends to be pregnant to hold on to the boyfriend who was threatening to leave her?"

"Not really, no," I say. And now, when comprehension dawns, I stand too. "Wait. You made the whole thing up? It's all been a lie?"

39

There are almost no empty seats on my flight to Beijing. I'm by a window near the back, content to enjoy the ride, begin to learn a little Mandarin, and read the book I've brought with me—Bruce Owens has published a memoir in which he tells his side of the breakup with his wife, and so far it's brilliant and gripping.

I'm looking forward to China, where I'll be teaching English for the next few months. Singapore had some Chinese flavors to it, but it was above all else a post-colonial artifact that had remade itself into something new and different, exciting but artificial. China, despite its own transformation, is real, by all accounts, and I can't wait to explore. After this teaching assignment, I might find more work in the Middle Kingdom, or maybe I'll move on. I might like to work for an aid organization in India, or maybe Africa. It occurs to me that this is the kind of adventure Bruce Owens was talking about. This is me being brave, at last.

When Mary confessed the truth about faking her pregnancy, I was at first deeply disappointed. I'd convinced myself that having a baby would be great, and that I'd be a terrific father, despite my own neuroses. But then I was furious. How could she deceive me like that? What did she think she was going to accomplish? And how long did she think she could keep up the charade? But my fury faded, maybe because it offered me a way out. She understood my anger, seemed to welcome it, and was puzzled by my forgiveness.

"Why aren't you mad, Ollie? It was a terrible thing to do. And stupid. I mean, even I know we're not living in a romantic comedy. What was I thinking?"

"I'm not mad because I deserved it. I lied to you long before you lied to me. It was all built on a lie. Singapore. Tokyo. Paris."

At the mention of Paris, she said, "Remember Nigel?"

She laughed and I laughed and I felt my face get hot.

"I'll *always* remember Nigel."

Although Mary was full of apologies for her lie, she put part of the blame on her mother.

"Lydia is driving me bonkers, and I just can't stay here another minute. If you thought I was pregnant, I figured, we might stay together, if only for a little while, but long enough for me to get out from under her craziness. But the plan wasn't working and she just got worse and...Ollie, I'm so sorry."

It wasn't really an excuse for such a huge lie, but it did make sense. I understand difficult mothers, and that gave me an idea. So we moved Mary into our house, just until my Mom gets out of rehab. I helped Mary line up her own apartment, and together we worked on her lesson plans for the coming school year. I think Mary will be okay.

After I accepted the job in Beijing, I wrote to Inge and invited her to visit me there. Bold move, I know. Her reply was almost instantaneous: Yes!

Or, she wrote, in the meantime, why don't I come to Stockholm?

All I needed was an excuse to keep traveling.